The one-eyed man's Story.

The Phantom Lady.

The Phantom Abductors.

A CHRISTMAS CAROL

AND OTHER
HAUNTING TALES

The New York Public Library Collector's Editions are illustrated with original art and handwritten letters, diaries, and manuscripts from the collections of the Library. They are designed to evoke the world of the writer and the book, and to enhance the pleasure of reading the great works of literature.

THE NEW YORK PUBLIC LIBRARY

*Collector's
Edition*

A CHRISTMAS CAROL

AND OTHER

HAUNTING TALES

CHARLES DICKENS

DOUBLEDAY

*New York   London   Toronto
Sydney   Auckland*

FRONTISPIECE: *Portrait of Charles Dickens, engraved by Edward Stodart after the 1837 drawing by Samuel Laurence.*
ENDPAPERS: *Two color plates by Alfred Crowquill from* Pictures Picked from the Pickwick Papers *(1837).* LEFT: *characters from "The Story of the Bagman's Uncle."* RIGHT: *characters from "The Trial from* Pickwick."

PUBLISHED BY DOUBLEDAY
a division of Bantam Doubleday Dell Publishing Group, Inc.
1540 Broadway, New York, New York 10036

D O U B L E D A Y and the portrayal of an anchor with a dolphin
are trademarks of Doubleday, a division of
Bantam Doubleday Dell Publishing Group, Inc.

The New York Public Library is a registered trademark and the property of The New York Public Library, Astor, Lenox and Tilden Foundations.

"Trial from Pickwick," "Sikes and Nancy," and "Mrs. Gamp," from *Charles Dickens: The Public Readings*, edited by Philip Collins, copyright © 1975 by Oxford University Press. Reprinted by permission of Oxford University Press.

Book design by Marysarah Quinn

Library of Congress Cataloging-in-Publication Data
Dickens, Charles, 1812–1870.
A Christmas carol, and other haunting tales / Charles Dickens. —
1st New York Public Library collector's ed.
p.   cm. — (The New York Public Library collector's edition)
Includes bibliographical references.
1. Christmas stories, English.   2. Ghost stories, English.
I. Title.   II. Series.
PR4557.A1   1998
823'.8—dc21   98-8687
CIP

ISBN 0-385-48725-8
About Charles Dickens, About This Edition, Suggestions for Further Reading, captions, and illustrations copyright © 1998 by The New York Public Library, Astor, Lenox and Tilden Foundations.

1   3   5   7   9   10   8   6   4   2

ACKNOWLEDGMENTS

This volume was created with the participation of many people throughout The New York Public Library. For their help in developing this edition of *A Christmas Carol and Other Haunting Tales*, we are grateful for the contributions of the curators and staffs of the Henry W. and Albert A. Berg Collection of English and American Literature, the Miriam and Ira D. Wallach Division of Art, Prints and Photographs, the Rare Books Division, and the General Research Division. Special recognition and thanks go to researcher and writer Kenneth Benson; Anne Skillion, Series Editor; and Karen Van Westering, Manager of Publications.

The New York Public Library wishes to extend thanks to its trustees Catherine Marron and Marshall Rose, as well as to Morton Janklow, for their early support and help in initiating this project.

Paul LeClerc, President

Michael Zavelle, Senior Vice President

CONTENTS

Charles Dickens reading to his daughters, Mamie and Katey, on the lawn at Gad's Hill Place, ca. 1865.

ABOUT CHARLES DICKENS

When Charles Dickens was a small boy, perhaps eight or nine years old, he got lost in the City of London, the teeming financial and commercial center of the great metropolis. A friend of the family had taken him to look at the outside of St. Giles's Church with the hope of quenching a fantastical notion that had taken hold of him, for young Dickens was convinced that on Sundays the beggars of London, having cast off their weekday pretenses to blindness, lameness, and other physical maladies, and freshly attired in their holiday best, were to be seen marching into the temple of their patron saint, where they would then partake of divine service. St. Giles's was viewed "with sentiments of satisfaction" and, one infers, edification all round; but shortly afterward, in the Strand, Dickens somehow became separated from his companion. At first, he was horrified, but he soon rallied and determined to set off to seek his fortune. "Thus I wandered about the City, like a child in a dream," he reminisced in "Gone Astray," an elegiac essay written more than thirty years later, "staring at the British merchants, and inspired by a mighty faith in the marvellousness of everything."

Looking back to his childhood, Dickens saw "a very small and not over-particularly-taken-care-of boy." That very boy grew into the man who, through the sheer fertility of his creative genius and an astonishing amount of hard work, transformed himself into the most famous writer of his age. In April 1856, Dickens wrote to his friend and future biographer John Forster of how clear it was to him that "one is driven by irresistible might until the journey is worked out!" His own mighty journey began in the English seaport of Portsmouth, on Friday, February 7, 1812. On that day, the second child and eldest son of Elizabeth and John Dickens was born, and was named Charles John Huffam Dickens.

A clerk in the Naval Pay Office, John Dickens was a kind-hearted, loquacious, generous, and amiable man who seems to have been constitutionally unable to live within his means. Much given to both the grand gesture and grandiloquent locutions, he would be immortalized by his son as the endearing Mr. Micawber in *David Copperfield*, a character who, in the midst of a crisis, likens himself to "a shattered fragment of the Temple once called Man." Like the genial Mr. Micawber, John Dickens was able to forge his affection for the rhetorical flourish and his own improvidence into a kind of art. Contemplating a long-lived relative, and presumably a little short in the pocket, he once said this: "And I must express my tendency to believe that his longevity is (to say the least of it) extremely problematical." Forster records Dickens's delight in this "celebrated sentence" of his well-intentioned but often exasperating father, whose industry, the son maintained with affectionate loyalty, was always "untiring." Dickens's feelings about his mother were much more ambivalent.

A woman gifted with "an extraordinary sense of the ludicrous," Elizabeth Dickens is said to have gone to a ball on the evening before she brought the future novelist into the world. Like the hapless Mrs. Micawber, she would try to shore up the family's finances with a scheme to open a school, which of course failed. She would inspire her son to draw one of his most amusing portraits, the absurd Mrs. Nickleby in *Nicholas Nickleby* (1838–39), who prattles on with sublime inconsequentiality and to great comic effect. Dickens found it very droll that his mother asked him whether he "really believed there ever was such a woman!"

The Dickens family was both large and almost always hard-pressed. In the profoundly autobiographical *David Copperfield* (with *Great Expectations,* one of only two Dickens novels written in the first person), Mr. Micawber gives David some advice, which could be said to sum up the difference between comedy and tragedy: "Annual income twenty pounds, annual expenditure nineteen nineteen six, result happiness. Annual income twenty pounds, annual expenditure twenty pounds ought and six, result misery." For Dickens, the happiest years of his childhood (1817–22) were spent in Chatham, a bustling port on England's southeast coast. He was sent to school, and began to read voraciously. Rambling about the beautiful countryside one day, young Dickens and his father came upon a handsome country house, Gad's Hill Place. This "wonderful mansion," which basked in a glorious Shakespearean glow (it is the very spot where Falstaff, in *Henry IV, Part I,* relieves the travelers of their treasure), became a sort of childhood dream for Dickens. His father told him, "If you were to be very persevering, and were to work hard, you might some day come to live in it." For once, John Dickens proved prescient. In 1856, Charles Dickens was to purchase the "stupendous property" that had so enchanted him as a child; and four years later, the ever wandering novelist, whom one observer described as the "veriest vagabond," settled there permanently.

The Chatham idyll ended abruptly in 1822, when John Dickens was transferred to London, a move that in no way inspired him to remedy the ill-management of his affairs, which continued to bring terrible strains upon the household and creditors to the door. By early 1824, the house of cards was about to collapse. In early Febru-

An original photograph of Harry Burnett, the boy who is said to be the original of Tiny Tim. The son of Dickens's eldest sister, Fanny Burnett, he died in January 1849, only a few months after his mother. "Harry was a singular child," Fanny's pastor recalled, "meditative and quaint in a remarkable degree."

ary, only a few days after his twelfth birthday, young Charles was sent to work pasting labels on bottles in a tumble-down, rat-overrun shoe polish factory on the Thames. Pay was six shillings a week, hours 8 A.M. to 8 P.M. "It is wonderful to me," he would later write of this catastrophe, "how I could have been so easily cast away at such an age." On February 20, John Dickens was arrested for debt, and soon after, the entire family (except for Charles and his older sister, Fanny, who was studying at the Royal Academy of Music) joined him in the Marshalsea debtor's prison. Declared insolvent in late May, John Dickens was released from prison; and eventually he re-moved his son from the blacking factory and placed him again in school. But Elizabeth Dickens could not comprehend why he should be removed from a situation of gainful employment—and for her son, this was a bitter betrayal. "I never afterwards forgot," Dickens would write years later, in an autobiographical fragment that was not published until after his death, "I never can forget, that my mother was warm for sending me back." By all accounts, Dickens was a remarkably sensitive child, and this awful period of "humiliation and neglect" marked him indelibly. Even at the height of his fame, he would forget himself in his dreams and, as he said, "wander deso-lately back to that time of my life."

His formal education complete at fifteen, Dickens found a posi-tion as a clerk at the office of Ellis and Blackmore, solicitors at Holborn Court, Gray's Inn. Finding the law "a very little world, and a very dull one," Dickens studied shorthand with singular application and was soon free-lancing as a court reporter. Then for *The Mirror of Parliament* and later the *True Sun*, he took on the House of Com-mons, which he described, soberly, as a pantomime that was "strong on clowns." His colleagues in the dingy gallery to which the press was consigned were astonished by the speed and accuracy of his transcriptions. "There never *was* such a shorthand writer," marveled one reporter. It was this "wholesome training of severe newspaper work" (as Dickens joked late in life) that launched his career.

In his early twenties, Dickens began to publish amusing sketches and stories that, when they were collected as *Sketches by Boz* in 1836, were hailed by one reviewer as "a perfect picture of the morals, manners and habits of a great portion of English Society." It was also noted that the young author possessed, not unlike his mother, "a strong sense of the ridiculous." The success of the *Sketches* led to a commission from Chapman and Hall to write the accompanying story for a series of etchings of sporting life by Robert Seymour, which were to be published in monthly parts. This became *The Posthumous Papers of the Pickwick Club*, which was to make Dickens's name. The first of its twenty numbers (the last a double issue) was published on March 31, 1836; and the original intention had been that Dickens's text was to be written to the order of Seymour's drawings. But soon it was the incomparable gallery of originals, with Samuel Pickwick as cynosure, whose "perambulations, perils, travels, adventures and sporting transactions" Dickens narrated with such exhilarating humor and dash, that all England was talking about.

Only a few days after the first number of *Pickwick* was issued, Dickens and Catherine Hogarth were married. The daughter of a prominent editor and man of letters whom Dickens knew from *The Morning Chronicle*, the gentle and diffident Kate was sketched by a woman who knew her about this time as ". . . a pretty little woman, plump and fresh-coloured . . . the forehead good, mouth small, round and red-lipped with a genial smiling expression of countenance, notwithstanding the sleepy look of the slow-moving eyes." She would bear Dickens ten children; but her languorous temperament was poorly suited to her husband's restless and high-spirited nature. It was, as V. S. Pritchett nicely put it, "as if she had been tied to the tail of a comet." The marriage would last for more than twenty years before coming apart very publicly in 1858, a sad spectacle in which Dickens came off none too attractively.

Strangely, it was Kate's younger sisters—Mary and Georgina— who were two of the most powerful presences in Dickens's life. The completely unexpected death of Mary, only seventeen, was a blow that left Dickens reeling. She had come to live with him and Kate after their marriage, and she was, he said, "the grace and life of our home." Late one evening, when the three returned from the theater, Mary collapsed, and the next day she sank away into a "calm and gentle sleep" in Dickens's arms. He wore her ring for the rest of his life. Georgina Hogarth was subsequently to become an indispensable member of the household, gradually assuming all of her sister Kate's responsibilities—and, in the process, taking a position as trusted confidante and companion for Dickens.

The exceptional triumph of *Pickwick* was followed by *Oliver Twist* (1837–39), in which Dickens issued the first of his vigorous assaults on social injustice. This dark tale may have startled readers expecting more of the amiable satire and frolicsome good humor that Dickens had lavished on the adventures of Samuel Pickwick and his friends (see "Sikes and Nancy"—the harrowing reading drawn by Dickens late in life from *Oliver*'s most sensational scenes—included in this collection). But with it he scored yet another success, and it has remained one of his most widely popular novels, what Angus Wilson has called a "pop masterpiece." Perhaps what is most extraordinary is that for a good period Dickens worked at *Pickwick* and *Oliver Twist* simultaneously; and that before he had finished *Oliver*, he had already begun *Nicholas Nickleby* (1838–39), which too would win great acclaim. Years later, an American friend, dazzled by Dickens's conversation, simply threw up her hands, saying that his "variety is so inexhaustible that one can only listen in wonder." With the huge and varied accomplishment of his first three novels, the world began to listen to Dickens in wonder. He became truly famous.

In 1842, Dickens and his wife traveled in America, a nation, we are told, that had been stricken, almost to a man, when the news of the pathetic death of Little Nell in *The Old Curiosity Shop* (1840–41) had at last reached its shores. In Boston, New York, Washington, Cincinnati, St. Louis, Richmond, and many other oases, savory and not, in between, Dickens was lionized, petted, mobbed, swooned over, gaped at, and practically banqueted to death. And in New York on February 14, 1842, at the spectacular "Boz Ball" held in his honor at the Park Theatre, Dickens escorted the Mayoress in the Grand March, which opened the evening; danced quadrilles until he thought he would drop; and, like the other three thousand (!) people in attendance, was able to relish a series of twelve tableaux vivants of scenes from his novels, including the always wonderful "Mrs. Bardell faints in Mr. Pickwick's arms." It was, said a witty man, "the greatest affair in modern times, the fullest libation ever poured upon the altar of the muses, the tallest compliment ever paid to a little man."

Dickens had arrived in America with the greatest enthusiasm and hopes for the young republic, but his journey ended in disillusionment. He was often shocked by the rude manners, flabby rhetoric, and ludicrously excessive boastfulness of Americans, and he found the incessant public spitting (spittoon or no spittoon) loathsome. But more seriously, when Dickens dared to raise the issue of international copyright during his travels, he was savagely attacked by much of the press (numerous American newspapers and booksellers, of course, did a flourishing business pirating his writings, often "adjusting" them to suit their purposes). Dickens did form warm friendships with a number of distinguished Americans during his visit, including Longfellow and Cornelius Felton, a convivial professor of classics at Harvard. With the latter, Dickens got along so famously that one bemused witness reported of the pair that ". . . they have walked, laughed, talked, eaten Oysters and drunk Champagne together until they have almost grown together—in fact nothing but the interference of Madame D prevented their being attached to each other like the Siamese Twins, *a volume of Pickwick serving as connecting membrane.*"

By the end of June, Dickens was back in England. His lively and not exactly reverential *American Notes for General Circulation* appeared on October 19. The *New York Herald* may have urged its readers, "Don't burst, keep cool—be quiet!"—but the book caused an uproar in America nonetheless. And soon enough the *Herald* itself joined the fray (after having printed unauthorized excerpts of the offending work, of course): "[O]f all the travelers," it said of Dickens, "that have ever visited this land he appears to have been the most flimsy—the most childish—the most trashy—the most contemptible. He has neither common grammar, sense, arrangement, or generalisation . . . he seems to be the essence of balderdash, reduced to the last drop of silliness and inanity." This entertaining brouhaha had no lasting effect on Dickens's popularity with his American public. However, readers on both sides of the Atlantic did react coolly to his next serial, *Martin Chuzzlewit* (1843–44), a novel that boasts some excellently stinging satire (of America) as well as two of his most unforgettable characters, Mr. Pecksniff and Mrs. Gamp.

In the midst of his labors over *Martin Chuzzlewit*, Dickens found time to write the little tale that is probably his most beloved work, *A Christmas Carol*. Published on December 19, 1843, this tender fable, the first of his five Christmas Books, received a rapturous welcome, which continues to this day. Of *A Christmas Carol*, Thackeray said, famously, "Who can listen to objections regarding such a book? It seems to me a national benefit, and to every man or woman who reads it a personal kindness."

Dickens had an immediate and unerring sense of his public, and by publishing his novels in inexpensive monthly parts (with hardbound editions to follow), he kept his enormous readership hooked to whatever had just flowed from his pen. As *Every Saturday* commenced the American serialization of *The Mystery of Edwin Drood* on May 7, 1870, it observed that, since the appearance of the first green cover in which the world had first beheld Mr. Pickwick, "numberless happy circles of listeners have been held in thrall by a reader" of Dickens's latest story. It is difficult now to recapture the excitement with which "the new Dickens" was awaited by readers around the world. As a writer for the *Daily Telegraph* said in

1872, looking back on Dickens's meteoric career, "[H]is current story was really a topic of the day; it seemed something almost akin to politics and news—as if it belonged not so much to literature but to events."

With *Dombey and Son* (1846–48), Dickens began the procession of more deeply considered and carefully structured novels upon which his reputation rests today. *Dombey* was followed by *David Copperfield* (1849–50), Dickens's own "favourite child," which was greeted with near universal admiration. Then came the magnificent tapestry of *Bleak House* (1852–53); the hard-hitting analysis of the modern industrial order in *Hard Times* (1854); and the forceful social critique of *Little Dorrit* (1855–57), which Shaw maintained was "a more seditious book than *Das Kapital.*"

In 1850, Dickens founded *Household Words*, a weekly that mixed literature, social commentary, and reportage; and in 1859, after a fight with his publisher, he began a new magazine, *All the Year Round*, which, like its predecessor, served as a forum for Dickens the reformer and Dickens the liberal moralist, and which he would edit until his death in 1870. As the "Conductor" of both journals, Dickens oversaw each and every article, as well as contributing many essays and stories of his own, some of the most interesting of which were collected in *The Uncommercial Traveller* (1861). His contemporaries were understandably amazed and daunted by Dickens's drive and fecundity.

Dickens's novels brought him wealth and worldwide fame, and for anyone else this would have been achievement (and labor) enough. But his energy was seemingly boundless. Always mad for the stage, he poured his great gifts as actor, director, and producer into numerous amateur theatricals. Dickens loved to tramp about London and the countryside, often for miles and miles at a stretch ("If I couldn't walk fast and far I should just explode and perish"); and his zest for life and his curiosity were illimitable. In the words of one amazed observer, he was to be seen everywhere: in "all lodging-houses, station-houses, cottages, hovels, Cheap Jacks' caravans, work-houses, prisons, school-rooms, chandlers' shops, back attics, barbers' shops, areas, back-yards, dark entries, public-houses, rag-shops, police-courts, markets in poor neighbourhoods."

In 1853, Dickens gave the first of his public readings, turning professional five years later. He toured incessantly, some said compulsively, for the last fifteen years of his life. In late 1857, as the tense situation of his private life was working toward the separation from Kate that would take place the next spring, Dickens told Forster, who always opposed the readings as beneath a great writer's dignity, "I can see no better thing to do that is half so hopeful in itself, or half so suited to my restless state." Dickens's reading tour of America in late 1867/early 1868 was an unprecedented triumph.

Dickens separated from his wife, Catherine, in 1858. To Forster, he had written, "It is not only that she makes me uneasy and unhappy, but that I make her so too—and much more so. She is exactly what you know, in the way of being amiable and complying; but we are strangely ill-assorted for the bond there is between us." The year before the separation, Dickens had directed and acted in a series of benefit performances of *The Frozen Deep*, a melodramatic extravaganza by Wilkie Collins that left performers and audiences alike sobbing and absolutely "convulsed with grief." Ellen Ternan, a beautiful eighteen-year-old actress, was engaged for the Manchester performances. Dickens was very taken with her, and she eventually became his mistress. The liaison raised not a few Victorian eyebrows, leading Dickens to take the extraordinary step of blasting the inevitable scandalmongering as "abominably false" on the front page of *Household Words*. Secrecy was, of course, paramount. Ternan was essentially erased from Forster's monumental *Life of Charles Dickens* (1872–74), except for the fact that hers was the first legacy mentioned in the great man's will.

During the late 1850s and 1860s Dickens published *Great Expectations* (1860–61) and *Our Mutual Friend* (1864–65), both of which sledge-hammers; some ran with torches to and fro, to seek them. "I promise Fifty Pounds," cried Mr Brown Low from the nearest bridge, "to the man who takes that murderer alive!"

He set his foot against the stack of chimnies, fastened one end of the rope firmly round it, and with the other made a strong running noose by the aid of his hands and teeth. He could let himself down to within a less distance of the ground than his own height, and had his knife ready in his hand to cut the cord, and drop.

At the instant that he brought the loop over his head before slipping it beneath his arm pits, looking behind him on the roof he threw up his arms, and yelled "The eyes again!" Staggering as if struck by lightning, he lost his balance and tumbled over the parapet. The noose was at his neck; it ran up with his weight, tight as a bowstring, and swift as the arrow it speeds. He fell five and thirty feet, and hung with his open knife clenched in his stiffening hand.

The dog which had lain concealed 'till now, ran backwards and forwards on the parapet with a dismal howl, and, collecting himself for a spring, jumped for the dead man's shoulders. Missing his aim, he fell into the ditch, turning over as he went, and, striking his head against a stone, dashed out his brains.

The End of the Reading

MR. CHARLES DICKENS'S LAST READING.

The revised conclusion of "Sikes and Nancy" (opposite), written out by Dickens on a blank page at the end of the prompt-copy from which he gave his public readings; and the portrait that accompanied an article on "Mr. Chas. Dickens's Last Reading" in the March 19, 1870, number of the Illustrated London News.

show him working with undiminished imaginative force and, if anything, even greater subtlety and artistry. Dickens returned to
England from his tremendously draining American tour in May
1868 with plans for a new series of readings already in the works. It
was now that he shaped the reading from *Oliver Twist*, the coup de
théâtre that shocked his audiences and sent his pulse skyrocketing.

His health failing steadily, Dickens no longer was able to endure
the rigors of touring or public performance. He presented a final
series of twelve readings in London early in 1870. On March 15, in
St. James's Hall, Dickens read for the last time. The program was
comprised of *A Christmas Carol* and "The Trial from *Pickwick.*" As
the *Illustrated London News* reported, Dickens brought this "ever-
memorable farewell reading" to a close with a brief and gracious
curtain speech, which closed as follows:

> Ladies and Gentlemen, in but two short weeks from this time
> I hope that you may enter, in your own homes, on a new
> series of readings at which my assistance will be indispens-
> able; but from these garish lights I vanish now for evermore,
> with one heartfelt, grateful, respectful, and affectionate fare-
> well.

With his customary panache, Dickens thus bade farewell to the public that adored him, simultaneously directing its attention to the im-
pending debut of his new serial, *The Mystery of Edwin Drood*. Less
than three months later he was dead, on June 9, 1870. Only six of the
twelve projected numbers of *Edwin Drood* had been completed.

Just a few weeks before that final collapse, Dickens was walking
with a dear friend when he suddenly asked his companion to guess
what had long been one of his own most cherished daydreams. Without waiting for an answer, Dickens said, "To settle down now for the
remainder of my life within easy distance of a great theatre, in the

direction of which I should hold supreme authority. It should be a house, of course, having a skilled and noble company, and one in every way magnificently appointed . . . the players as well as the plays beings absolutely under my command." And then he laughed: "There, *that's* my daydream!"

Bob Cratchit and Tiny Tim—by Sol Eytinge, Jr.

ABOUT THIS EDITION

For Charles Dickens, Christmas meant hearth and home, games, charades, amateur theatricals, feasting, charity and generosity all round . . . and ghost stories. As Dickens tells us in "A Christmas Tree," the tale that opens this collection,

> There is probably a smell of roasted chestnuts and other good comfortable things all the time, for we are telling Winter Stories—Ghost Stories, or more shame for us—round the Christmas fire; and we have never stirred, except to draw a little nearer to it.

As the *New York Times* itself pointed out in its Christmas day 1997 editorial, the supernatural is essential to a Dickensian Christmas. "A good scare was a way to intensify the pleasure of the season," the *Times* reminded us, "making the plenitude that always accompanied Mr. Pickwick, for instance, seem that much more plenteous, making security itself that much more secure."

In this Collector's Edition of *A Christmas Carol and Other Haunting Tales*, Dickens's most captivating stories are gathered together, richly illustrated with autograph manuscripts, rare portraits, and a splendid portfolio of original prints and drawings from the special collections of The New York Public Library. Here, a glorious host of Dickens's incomparable creations has assembled at the fireside for our delectation: the foulest of murderers, and the feistiest of curmudgeons; happy families, spurned women, and pompous lawyers; gloomy professors, *very* bad husbands, and angelic tots; dastardly scoundrels, wild children, and extremely dense judges; ill-tempered goblins and drunken nurses; and—of course—Christmas ghosts.

Overflowing with vitality, good cheer, merriment, wit, thoroughly enjoyable terror, satire, and even, but only when necessary, what Dickens termed the "sharp anatomization of humbug," the stories in this collection demonstrate, and in abundance, that with a great writer it is indeed possible to travel anywhere.

CHARLES DICKENS AND CHRISTMAS

It has been more than 150 years since Tiny Tim first uttered those famous words: "God bless us every one!"—but to this day no writer is as indelibly associated with the spirit of the Christmas holidays, that season of "hospitality, merriment, and open-heartedness," than Charles Dickens. Between 1843 and 1848 he published five *Christmas Books*, starting off with *A Christmas Carol* and continuing with *The Chimes*, *The Cricket on the Hearth*, *The Battle of Life*, and *The Haunted Man*. After the last of these came numerous stories (seasonal in spirit, if not in setting) for the Christmas issues of his magazines *Household Words* and *All the Year Round*.

This edition opens with the first of Dickens's Christmas stories, "A Christmas Tree," a radiant mediation on the power of the imagination, in which the narrator tells us:

And I *do* come home at Christmas. We all do, or we all should. We all come home, or ought to come home, for a short holiday—the longer, the better—from the great board-ing-school, where we are for ever working at our arithmeti-cal slates, to take and give a rest. As to going a visiting, where can we not go, if we will; where have we not been, when we would; starting our fancy from our Christmas Tree!

This is followed by the darkly powerful but much less familiar *The Haunted Man*, originally published, like *A Christmas Carol*, as a small book. In this tale, Mr. Redlaw is plunged into a nightmarish existence when he makes a foolish wish and it is granted. Dickens finished this "wild and strange" psychological ghost story on No-vember 30, 1848, "having been crying my eyes out over it," he told his publishers, "not painfully but pleasantly as I hope the readers will." No tears will be shed (unless they be tears of joy) over the delectable Tetterby family, who do so much to brighten *The Haunted Man*.

The section "To Be Read at Dusk" gathers together some of Dickens's best seasonal ghost stories. The first, "Nurse's Stories," is more a rumination on the ghastly than it is a straightforward ghost story. John Forster, Dickens's intimate friend and biographer, tells us that Dickens had "something of a hankering" after all such fantastic fare, and one can well imagine him saying, as the Fat Boy does in *The Pickwick Papers*, "I wants to make your flesh creep." The ever-lasting attractiveness of disembodied spirits, goblins, specters, and all their brethren (imaginary or otherwise) is on ample display in this Collector's Edition, which features two of the most famous tales of presentiment ever written, "The Signal-Man" and "To Be Taken with a Grain of Salt." These subtle masterpieces were all first pub-lished in one or another of Dickens's periodicals. "The Story of the Bagman's Uncle" and "The Story of the Goblins Who Stole a Sex-ton" are both taken from *The Pickwick Papers*, the latter narrated by Mr. Wardle of Dingley Dell during the course of a jolly Christmas

Eve celebration which features songs, games of blindman's buff, and "a huge branch of misletoe," and for which he serves as the stout, hearty, and excellent host.

We end with *A Christmas Carol*, that impossibly touching story of a spiritual awakening which has remained Dickens's most loved and enduring success. It is usually read only during the holidays, and that is a pity. For this happy work, which Thackeray said was answerable for a "wonderful outpouring of Christmas good-feeling; of Christmas punch-brewing; an awful slaughter of Christmas turkeys; and roasting and basting of Christmas beef" in the England of his day, has lessons to teach that are not bound by any season.

Writing in 1871, the novelist Margaret Oliphant recalled that this matchless fable of moral renewal "moved us all in those days as if it had been a new gospel." The story's first readers were moved (as we are) not only by the tale's verve and sentiment but by what was so obviously and appealingly the author's own excitement in the telling. In a celebrated letter to his American friend Cornelius Felton, dated the day after New Year's in 1844, Dickens writes with wonderful exuberance and power of the *Carol:*

Now, if instantly upon the receipt of this, you will send a free and independent citizen down to the Cunard wharf at Boston, you will find that Captain Hewett of the Britannia Steam Ship (*my* ship) has a small parcel for Professor Felton of Cambridge; and in that parcel you will find a Christmas Carol in Prose. Being a Ghost Story of Christmas by Charles Dickens. Over which Christmas Carol, Charles Dickens wept, and laughed, and wept again, and excited himself in a most extraordinary manner in the composition; and thinking whereof, he walked about the black streets of London, fifteen and twenty miles, many a night when all the sober folks had gone to bed. He don't like America, I am told, but he has some friends there, as dear to him as any in England; so you may read it safely. Its success is most prodigious. And by every post, all manner of strangers write all manner of letters to him about their homes and hearths, and how this same Carol is read aloud there and kept on a very little shelf by itself. Indeed it is the greatest success as I am told, that this ruffian and rascal has ever achieved.

Forster is out again—and if he don't go in again after the manner in which we have been keeping Christmas, he must be very strong indeed. Such dinings, such dancings, such conjurings, such blindmans buffings, such theatre-goings, such kissings-out of old years and kissings-in of new ones, never took place in these parts before. To keep the Chuzzlewit going, and do this little book, the Carol, in the odd times between two parts of it, was, as you may suppose, pretty tight work. But when it was done, I broke out like a madman. And if you could have seen me at a children's party at Macready's the other night, going down a country dance (something longer than the Library at Cambridge) with Mrs. M. you would have thought I was a country Gentleman of independent property, residing on a tip-top farm, with the wind blowing straight in my face every day.

In *My Father as I Recall Him* (1885), Mamie Dickens, the novelist's second child, looked back to the Christmas holidays of her childhood, a time

. . . which in our home was looked forward to with eagerness and delight, and to my father it was a time dearer than any other part of the year, I think. He loved Christmas for its deep significance as well as for its joys. . . . Our house was always filled with guests, while a cottage in the village was reserved for the use of the bachelor members of the party. My father himself, always deserted work for the week, and that was almost our greatest treat. He was the fun and life of those gatherings, the true Christmas spirit of sweetness and hospi-

Devonshire Terrace London.
Second January 1844.

My very dear Felton.

You are a Prophet, and had best retire from business straightway. Yesterday morning, New Year's day, when I had walked into my little work room after breakfast, and was looking out of window at the snow in the garden – not seeing it particularly well in consequence of some staggering suggestions of last nights' Punch and Turkey, whereof I was host – the Postman came to the door with a knock, for which I damned him from my heart. Seeing your hand upon the cover of a letter which he brought, immediately blessed him – presented him with a glass of whiskey – enquired after his family (they are all well) – and opened the despatch, with a moist and oystery twinkle in my eye. And on the very day from which the new Year dates, I read your new Year congratulations, as punctually as if you lived in the next house. Why don't you!

Now if instantly upon the receipt of this, you will send a free and independent citizen down to the Cunard wharf at Boston. You will find that captain Hewett of the Britannia steam ship (my ship) has a small parcel for Professor Felton of Cambridge; and in that parcel you will find a christmas carol in Prose. Being a Ghost Story of Christmas by Charles Dickens. Over which christmas carol, Charles Dickens wept, and laughed, and wept again, and excited himself in a most extraordinary manner in the composition; and thinking whereof, he walked about the black streets of London, fifteen and twenty miles, many a night when all the sober folks had gone to bed. He don't like america, I am told, but he had some friends there, as dear to him as any in England; so you may read it safely. Its success is most prodigious.

In this famous letter, Dickens, writing on January 2, 1844, informs his American friend Cornelius Felton that a parcel awaits him at the Cunard wharf in Boston, and therein is to be found "a Ghost Story of Christmas by

Charles Dickens. Over which Christmas Carol, Charles Dickens wept, and laughed, and wept again, and excited himself in a most extraordinary manner in the composition." A portion of this wonderful letter is transcribed on pages xxxii–xxxiii.

tality filling his large and generous heart. . . . His conversation, as may be imagined, was often extremely humorous, and I have seen the servants, who were waiting at table, convulsed often with laughter at his droll remarks and stories.

Mamie's sweet and reverential book was written for children, which would have pleased her father. It is he who reminds us in *A Christmas Carol* that "it is good to be children sometimes, and never better than at Christmas, when its mighty Founder was a child himself."

DICKENS ONSTAGE

In 1858, Dickens decided to launch a second career, as a public reader. This was not unprecedented: writers of the day like Thackeray had made a profitable sideline out of delivering as lectures the essays they were later to publish as books; Wilkie Collins, a dear friend and junior novelist, also tried his luck on the stage. When in December 1853, in Birmingham, Dickens gave his first public readings—a series of three for charity—they were rapturously received. "They lost nothing," Dickens reported after a performance of *A Christmas Carol*, "misinterpreted nothing, followed everything closely, laughed and cried . . . and animated me to the extent that I felt as if we were all bodily going up into the clouds together."

Once onstage, "a lithe, energetic man, of medium stature," with a red carnation in his buttonhole, Dickens rarely glanced at the text before him, for through rigorous preparation and rehearsal he had made himself, as he said, "master of the situation." He played variations on the readings, continually adding new material and even "slashing" whole sections on the wing; inspired by the moment and his profound rapport with the audience, he avoided the mechanical repetition of effects and gestures that had scored the night before. Dickens kept each performance a miracle of freshness and invention. He did nothing by rote, he took everything on himself, and the house responded, as one American admirer said, not with applause but with "a passionate outburst of love for the man."

Dickens left traces of his art as a riveting storyteller in the texts he prepared for the stage. These volumes, known as prompt-copies, were special versions of his stories that Dickens prepared for public performance. When he was onstage, they were placed before him on his reading desk. If he forgot a line or lost his place while performing, he could glance down for his "prompt." The only surviving prompt-copy of *A Christmas Carol* is held in the Library's Berg Collection. Two pages from it are reproduced here, showing Dickens's markings for cuts, interpolations, and directions for vocal expression. Dickens's warmth and histrionic flair, as well as an expressiveness that called forth tears, shrieks, laughter, and shouts of "Hear, hear!" from his audiences, must have made for quite a night at the theater.

In the three readings for the stage selected for this Collector's Edition—"Mrs. Gamp," "Sikes and Nancy," and "The Trial from *Pickwick*"—some of the most memorable troopers from Dickens's great repertory company step into the spotlight. The gin-soaked Mrs. Gamp must take pride of place, if only for the sublimity of her wisdom and the extent of her humanitarianism. A nurse and midwife who is also called upon to lay out the dead (". . . If I could afford to lay all my fellow-creeturs out for nothink, I would gladly do it, sich is the love I bears 'em"), Sairey Gamp is blessed with a sibylline streak. Her cock-eyed apothegms and proverbs are—well— Gampian, and Dickens's audiences knew them by heart. It is to her imaginary friend Mrs. Harris that Mrs. Gamp directs her notorious instructions to "leave the bottle on the chimley-piece, and don't ask me to take none, but let me put my lips to it when I am so dispoged . . ."

In *Pen Photographs of Charles Dickens's Readings* (1871), Kate Field gamely attempted to capture Dickens's impersonation of Sairey's voice: "Take a comb, cover it with tissue paper, and attempt to sing through it, and you have an admirable idea of the quality of Mrs. Gamp's vocal organ, providing you make the proper allowance

natured, and not much caring what they laughed
at, so that they laughed at any rate, he encouraged
them in their merriment, and passed the bottle
joyously.

After tea, they had some music. For they were
a musical family, and knew what they were about,
when they sung a Glee or Catch, I can assure you :
especially Topper, who could growl away in the bass
like a good one, and never swell the large veins in
his forehead, or get red in the face over it. Scrooge's
niece played well upon the harp; and played
among other tunes a simple little air (a mere nothing : you might learn to whistle it in two minutes), which had been familiar to the child who
fetched Scrooge from the boarding-school, as he had
been reminded by the Ghost of Christmas Past.
When this strain of music sounded, all the things
that Ghost had shown him, came upon his mind ;
he softened more and more ; and thought that if
he could have listened to it often, years ago, he
might have cultivated the kindnesses of life for
his own happiness with his own hands, without

Toned down to Pathos

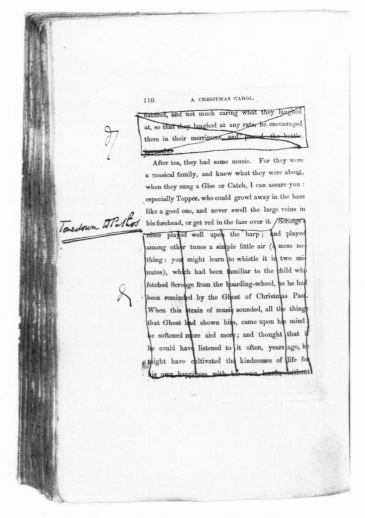

Two pages from the copy of A Christmas Carol *from which Dickens gave his
public readings, showing his cuts and revisions, as well as directions for vocal
expression ("Tone down to Pathos . . . Up to cheerfulness").*

resorting to the sexton's spade that buried Jacob Marley.

But they didn't devote the whole evening to music. After a while they played at forfeits; for it is good to be children sometimes, and never better than at Christmas, when its mighty Founder was a child himself. Stop! There was first a game at blindman's buff. Of course there was. And I no more believe Topper was really blind than I believe he had eyes in his boots. My opinion is, that it was a done thing between him and Scrooge's nephew; and that the Ghost of Christmas Present knew it. The way he went after that plump sister in the lace tucker, was an outrage on the credulity of human nature. Knocking down the fire-irons, tumbling over the chairs, bumping up against the piano, smothering himself among the curtains, wherever she went, there went he. He always knew where the plump sister was. He wouldn't catch anybody else. If you had fallen up against him, as some of them did, and stood there; he would have made a feint of endeavouring to seize

up to cheerfulness

Rough

ed

&

Because the
way in which

for an inordinate amount of snuff." "Mrs. Gamp" went through much reworking before it reached its "final" state, as reprinted in the present volume; and Field, for one, bemoaned the fact that more of Mrs. Gamp's bon mots from *Martin Chuzzlewit* could not be squeezed into "Mrs. Gamp," the reading. But "Mrs. Gamp" was another triumph for Dickens. In America, Sairey's first tender words—"I'm coming"—were met with immediate and enthusiastic applause, in Yankee homage both to Dickens and that "inwallable person," Mrs. Gamp.

Like the immortal Sairey in "Mrs. Gamp," so too was Samuel Weller accorded a "reception" at the first mention of his name whenever Dickens took the stage with his droll and immensely popular reading "The Trial from *Pickwick.*" Even at the first performance, on October 19, 1858, when Serjeant Buzfuz boomed out "Call Samuel Weller," the house "gave a thunder of applause, as if he were really coming in," as Dickens proudly noted. Drawn from Chapter XXXIV of *The Pickwick Papers*, this reading narrates "the great action for breach of promise" brought against Mr. Pickwick by his landlady, Mrs. Bardell. She is in fact entirely mistaken, having construed Mr. Pickwick's innocent request for her counsel (about taking on a servant for himself) as a proposal of marriage. Hence her momentous suit. Second in the affection of Dickens's public only to the *Christmas Carol* reading, "The Trial from *Pickwick*" is a timeless satire of legal buffoonery and of justice gone awry.

The hilarious "Trial" contrasts starkly with the horrific "Sikes and Nancy," the last reading prepared by Dickens and the only one in which he allowed his "murderous instincts" to run riot. First performed privately before a specially invited audience, on November 14, 1868, "Sikes and Nancy" reenacts the harrowing murder scene from *Oliver Twist*, and it originally closed with Sikes slipping out of the room after the terrible deed. But several friends at the trial performance insisted the reading should carry on straight to Sikes's gruesome death. At first, Dickens demurred, but within weeks he was at work, newly fashioning a "fierce and passionate rush for the end."

Written out by Dickens on three manuscript pages, the revised conclusion to "Sikes and Nancy" left audiences gasping. Dickens savored every moment, every horror-stricken face in the house. "It is quite a new sensation," he said, "to be execrated with that unanimity, and I hope it will remain so!"

THE ILLUSTRATORS IN THIS EDITION

From the very beginning of his extraordinary career, Dickens was hailed for the vividly pictorial quality of his writing. One critical seer went so far as to announce his discovery, in 1837, that "the Soul of Hogarth has migrated into the Body of Mr Dickens." No less an authority than Vincent van Gogh proclaimed that there was no writer "who is *so* much a painter and black-and-white artist as Dickens." The public loved the drawings of such notable illustrators as George Cruikshank and Hablot K. Browne ("Phiz") that enlivened the monthly installments of his novels, which, in their familiar green wrappers, were awaited with near breathless excitement by Dickens's vast readership.

Early American editions of Dickens (and many more since then) reproduced the etchings of Cruikshank and Browne, the two English illustrators who for many are the most quintessentially Dickensian in spirit of the almost countless artists who have sojourned in Dickens-Land. But in the 1860s and 70s, American illustrators finally began to have a go at Dickens; and some of them—F. O. C. Darley, Sol Eytinge, Jr., and Edward Austin Abbey, for example—are wonderfully good. Yet they are virtually unknown to today's readers. Eytinge's beautiful and tender illustrations for *A Christmas Carol* have unaccountably been all but forgotten, for it would seem that they have not been reproduced for well over a hundred years, even though Dickens himself had the greatest admiration for this most skillful of his American interpreters.

In this Collector's Edition, a procession of less familiar, but altogether engaging American and English artists, fresh to today's eyes, takes the stage. Some notes on these gifted illustrators are in order.

Sol Eytinge, Jr. (1833–1905), provided more than two hundred illustrations for the fourteen-volume Diamond Edition of Dickens's novels, published in 1867 by the Boston firm of Ticknor & Fields. These very much met with the author's approval. "They are," Dickens said, "remarkable for a delicate perception of beauty, a lively eye for character, a most agreeable absence of exaggeration, and a general modesty and propriety, which I greatly like." In 1868, Eytinge provided the designs for Fields, Osgood, & Co.'s Holiday Edition of *A Christmas Carol*, and it is these fetching pictures (shot from the proofs for the original wood engravings) that are reproduced in this Collector's Edition.

Felix Octavius Carr Darley (1822–88) was a self-taught draughtsman and engraver who enjoyed a long and hugely successful career as America's first "star illustrator." Darley's somber and elegant frontispiece for *A Haunted Man*, executed for the Household Edition's two-volume *Christmas Stories*, is characteristic of his superb level of accomplishment as an illustrator of Dickens. Darley's last completed work, *Sketches from the Works of Charles Dickens*, a large portfolio of photogravure prints after his lustrous wash drawings, was published posthumously in Philadelphia in 1888.

Two of the very finest American illustrators to emerge in the 1870s, Charles Stanley Reinhart (1844–96) and Edward Austin Abbey (1852–1911) are represented in this Collector's Edition by work that they executed for another Household Edition of Dickens. Reinhart's matter-of-factly macabre study for "Nurse's Stories" was one of the thirty-three illustrations he provided for Harper's Household Edition of *The Uncommercial Traveller, Hard Times, and The Mystery of Edwin Drood* (1876). Abbey's expressive drawings for *The Haunted Man*, executed for Harper's Household Edition of the *Christmas Stories* (1876), are characteristic of his caressing but still vivacious touch.

The leading American political cartoonist of his generation, the man who brought down Boss Tweed and his Tammany Hall cronies with the "sledge-hammer force" of his pictorial satire, Thomas Nast (1840–1902) also did a good deal of work in which he was able to give his slashing pen a breather. In his day, he was celebrated for his Yuletide sketches, some of the more delightfully goofy of which are to be found in an 1867 children's book, *Dickens' Christmas Story of the Goblins Who Stole a Sexton*.

The English comic illustrator, caricaturist, and writer Alfred Crowquill (1804–72) was closely associated with both *Punch* and *Bentley's Miscellany*. He issued his own *Pictures Picked from the Pickwick Papers*, a set of forty lithographs after his fluid and funny drawings, in 1837. On two of the most diverting plates, a number of the *dramatis personae* of "The Story of the Bagman's Uncle" and "The Trial from *Pickwick*" are arrayed in all their finery—and it is these happy designs that serve as the endpapers of the present volume.

F. W. Pailthorpe (active ca. 1870–after 1899) was an English illustrator and etcher who produced several sets of illustrations inspired by the novels of Dickens, including *The Pickwick Papers* (1882), *Great Expectations* (1885), and *Oliver Twist* (1886). Issued in limited editions, usually loose in portfolio, and some hand-colored by the artist, these illustrations appealed to the collector, who often had them bound into copies of the novels, which would then be said to be "extra-illustrated." Reproduced in this Collector's Edition is Pailthorpe's original pencil-and-watercolor drawing "A foul deed," which captures the shocking moment when Sikes murders Nancy, a scene enacted by Dickens in his readings with such ferocity that audiences gaped at him with fixed expressions of horror, as if he "had been going to be hanged."

Edward Gurden Dalziel (1849–89) was the eldest son of Edward Dalziel, one of the founders of the London-based Dalziel Brothers, the influential firm of wood engravers, illustrators, printers, and publishers. He was selected as one of the illustrators for Chapman and Hall's Household Edition of the works of Dickens. Sir John Gilbert, in a warm letter of appreciation, told Edward Dalziel that his son's drawings showed "a certain weirdness most telling in some subjects."

This was excellent praise indeed, coming from one of England's most eminent artists, and it could as well be applied to E. G. Dalziel's illustration for "To Be Taken with a Grain of Salt," which took its spooky place in the Household Edition of the *Christmas Stories*.

Dickens's enormous popularity was a continual source of inspiration to artists. They labored diligently to supply a clamoring public with illustrations of their favorite characters and scenes from the novels, usually issuing their work without authorization. An early example was a set of ten etchings by the English painter and illustrator Thomas Sibson (1817–44), issued under the title *Sibson's Racy Sketches of Expeditions, from the Pickwick Club* (London, 1838). An original drawing of his accompanies "The Story of the Bagman's Uncle" in the present volume. It comes from an album of ten pen-and-ink drawings, beneath each of which the artist wrote out a portion of Dickens's ghostly tale. Apparently, these dreamy renderings by Sibson have never been published.

A CHRISTMAS CAROL
AND OTHER
HAUNTING TALES

Of Holidays Past

A CHRISTMAS TREE

I HAVE BEEN looking on, this evening, at a merry company of children assembled round that pretty German toy, a Christmas Tree. The tree was planted in the middle of a great round table, and towered high above their heads. It was brilliantly lighted by a multitude of little tapers; and everywhere sparkled and glittered with bright objects. There were rosy-cheeked dolls, hiding behind the green leaves; there were real watches (with movable hands, at least, and an endless capacity of being wound up) dangling from innumerable twigs; there were French-polished tables, chairs, bedsteads, wardrobes, eight-day clocks, and various other articles of domestic furniture (wonderfully made, in tin, at Wolverhampton), perched among the boughs, as if in preparation for some fairy housekeeping; there were jolly, broad-faced little men, much more agreeable in appearance than many real men—and no wonder, for their heads took off, and showed them to be full of sugar-plums; there were fiddles and drums; there were tambourines, books, work-boxes, paint-boxes, sweetmeat-boxes, peep-show boxes,—all kinds of boxes; there were trinkets for the elder girls, far brighter than any grown-up gold and jewels; there were baskets and pin-cushions in all devices; there were guns, swords, and banners; there were witches standing in enchanted rings of pasteboard, to tell fortunes; there were teetotums, humming-tops, needle-cases, pen-wipers, smelling-bottles, conversation-cards, bouquet-holders; real fruit, made artificially dazzling with gold leaf imitation apples, pears, and walnuts, crammed with surprises; in short, as a pretty child, before me, delightedly whispered to another pretty child, her bosom friend, "There was everything, and more." This motley collection of odd objects clustering on the tree like magic fruit, and flashing back the bright looks directed towards it from every side—some of the diamond-eyes admiring it were hardly on a level with the table, and a few were languishing in timid wonder on the bosoms of pretty mothers, aunts, and nurses—made a lively realisation of the fancies of childhood; and set me thinking how all the trees that grow and all the things that come into existence on the earth have their wild adornments at that well-remembered time.

Being now at home again, and alone, the only person in the house awake, my thoughts are drawn back, by a fascination which I do not care to resist, to my own childhood. I begin to consider, what do we all remember best upon the branches of the Christmas Tree of our own young Christmas days, by which we climbed to real life.

Straight, in the middle of the room, cramped in the freedom of its growth by no encircling walls or soon-reached ceiling, a shadowy tree arises; and looking up into the dreamy brightness of its top—for I observe in this tree the singular property that it appears to grow downward towards the earth—I look into my youngest Christmas recollections!

All toys at first, I find. Up yonder, among the green holly and red berries, is the Tumbler with his hands in his pockets, who wouldn't lie down, but, whenever he was put upon the floor, persisted in rolling his fat body about until he rolled himself still, and brought those lobster eyes of his to bear upon me—when I affected to laugh very much, but in my heart of hearts was extremely doubtful of him. Close beside him is that infernal snuff-box, out of which there sprang a demoniacal Counsellor in a black gown, with an obnoxious head of hair, and a red cloth mouth, wide open, who was not to be endured on any terms, but could not be put away either; for he used suddenly, in a highly magnified state, to fly out of mammoth snuff-boxes in dreams, when least expected. Nor is the frog with cobbler's wax on his tail far off; for there was no knowing where he wouldn't jump; and when he flew over the candle, and came upon one's hand with that spotted back,—red on a green ground,—he was horrible. The card-board lady in a blue-silk skirt, who was stood up against the candlestick to dance, and whom I see on the same branch, was milder, and was beautiful; but I can't say as much for the larger card-board man, who used to be hung against the wall and pulled by a string; there was a sinister expression in that nose of his; and when he got his legs round his neck (which he very often did), he was ghastly, and not a creature to be alone with.

When did that dreadful Mask first look at me? Who put it on, and why was I so frightened that the sight of it is an era in my life? It is not a hideous visage in itself; it is even meant to be droll; why, then, were its stolid features so intolerable? Surely not because it hid the wearer's face. An apron would have done as much; and though I should have preferred even the apron away, it would not have been absolutely insupportable, like the mask? Was it the immovability of the mask? The doll's face was immovable, but I was not afraid of *her*. Perhaps that fixed and set change coming over a real face infused into my quickened heart some remote suggestion and dread of the universal change that is to come on every face, and make it still? Nothing reconciled me to it. No drummers, from whom proceeded a melancholy chirping on the turning of a handle; no regiment of soldiers, with a mute band, taken out of a box, and fitted, one by one, upon a stiff and lazy little set of lazy tongs; no old woman, made of wires and a brown-paper composition, cutting up a pie for two small children, could give me a permanent comfort for a long time. Nor was it any satisfaction to be shown the Mask, and see that it was made of paper, or to have it locked up and be assured that no one wore it. The mere recollection of that fixed face, the mere knowledge of its existence anywhere, was sufficient to awake me in the night, all perspiration and horror, with, "Oh, I know it's coming! Oh, the mask!"

I never wondered what the dear old donkey with the panniers—there he is!—was made of then! His hide was real to the touch, I recollect. And the great black horse with round red spots all over him—the horse that I could even get upon—I never wondered what had brought him to that strange condition, or thought that such a horse was not commonly seen at Newmarket. The four horses of no colour, next to him, that went into the wagon of cheeses, and could be taken out and stabled under the piano, appear to have bits of fur-tippet for their tails, and other bits for their manes, and to stand on pegs instead of legs, but it was not so when they were brought home for a Christmas present. They were all right then; neither was their harness unceremoniously nailed into their chests, as appears to be the case now. The tinkling works of the music-cart, I *did* find out to be made of quill tooth-picks and wire; and I always thought that little tumbler in his shirt-sleeves, perpetually swarming up one side of a wooden frame, and coming down, head foremost, on the other, rather a weak-minded person—though good-natured; but the Jacob's Ladder, next him, made of little squares of red wood, that went flapping and clattering over one another, each developing a different picture, and the whole enlivened by small bells, was a mighty marvel and a great delight.

Ah! The Doll's house!—of which I was not proprietor, but where I visited. I don't admire the Houses of Parliament half so much as that stone-fronted mansion with real glass windows, and door-steps, and a real balcony—greener than I ever see now, except at watering-places; and even they afford but a poor imitation. And though it *did* open all at once, the entire house-front (which was a blow, I admit, as cancelling the fiction of a staircase), it was but to shut it up again, and I could believe. Even open, there were three distinct rooms in it; a sitting-room and bedroom, elegantly furnished, and, best of all, a kitchen, with uncommonly soft fire-irons, a plentiful assortment of diminutive utensils—oh, the warming-pan!—and a tin man-cook in profile, who was always going to fry two fish. What Barmecide justice have I done to the noble feasts wherein the set of wooden platters figured, each with its own peculiar delicacy, as a ham or turkey, glued tight on to it, and garnished with something green, which I recollect as moss! Could all the Temperance Societies of these later days, united, give me such a tea-drinking as I have had through the means of yonder little set of blue crockery, which really would hold liquid (it ran out of the small wooden cask, I recollect, and tasted of matches), and which made tea, nectar. And if the two legs of the ineffectual little sugar-tongs did tumble over one another, and want purpose, like Punch's hands, what does it matter? And if I did once shriek out, as a poisoned child, and strike the fashionable company with consternation, by reason of having drunk a little tea-spoon, inadvertently dissolved in too hot tea, I was never the worse for it, except by a powder!

Upon the next branches of the tree, lower down, hard by the green roller and miniature gardening-tools, how thick the books begin to hang. Thin books, in themselves, at first, but many of them, and with deliciously smooth covers of bright red or green. What fat black letters to begin with! "A was an archer, and shot at a frog." Of course he was. He was an apple-pie also, and there he is! He was a good many things in his time, was A, and so were most of his friends, except X, who had so little versatility that I never knew him to get beyond Xerxes or Xantippe—like Y, who was always confined to a Yacht or a Yew Tree; and Z condemned for ever to be a Zebra or a Zany. But, now, the very tree itself changes, and becomes a bean-stalk—the marvellous bean-stalk up which Jack climbed to the Giant's house! And now those dreadfully interesting, double-headed giants, with their clubs over their shoulders, begin to stride along the boughs in a perfect throng, dragging knights and ladies home for dinner by the hair of their heads. And Jack—how noble, with his sword of sharpness, and his shoes of swiftness! Again those old meditations come upon me as I gaze up at him; and I debate within myself whether there was more than one Jack (which I am loth to believe possible), or only one genuine, original, admirable Jack, who achieved all the recorded exploits.

Good for Christmas time is the ruddy colour of the cloak, in which—the tree making a forest of itself for her to trip through, with her basket—Little Red Riding-Hood comes to me one Christmas Eve to give me information of the cruelty and treachery of that dissembling Wolf who ate her grandmother, without making any impression on his appetite, and then ate her, after making that ferocious joke about his teeth. She was my first love. I felt that if I could have married Little Red Riding-Hood, I should have known perfect bliss. But it was not to be; and there was nothing for it but to look out the Wolf in the Noah's Ark there, and put him late in the procession on the table, as a monster who was to be degraded. O the wonderful Noah's Ark! It was not found seaworthy when put in a washing-tub, and the animals were crammed in at the roof, and needed to have their legs well shaken down before they could be got in, even there— and then ten to one but they began to tumble out at the door, which was but imperfectly fastened with a wire latch—but what was *that* against it! Consider the noble fly, a size or two smaller than the elephant; the lady-bird, the butterfly—all triumphs of art! Consider the goose, whose feet were so small, and whose balance was so indifferent, that he usually tumbled forward, and knocked down all the animal creation. Consider Noah and his family, like idiotic tobacco-stoppers; and how the leopard stuck to warm little fingers; and how the tails of the larger animals used gradually to resolve themselves into frayed bits of string!

Hush! Again a forest, and somebody up in a tree—not Robin Hood, not Valentine, not the Yellow Dwarf (I have passed him and all Mother Bunch's wonders, without mention), but an Eastern King with a glittering scimitar and turban. By Allah! two Eastern Kings, for I see another, looking over his shoulder! Down upon the grass, at the tree's foot, lies the full length of a coal-black Giant, stretched asleep, with his head in a lady's lap; and near them is a glass box, fastened with four locks of shining steel, in which he keeps the lady prisoner when he is awake. I see the four keys at his girdle now. The lady makes signs to the two kings in the tree, who softly descend. It is the setting-in of the bright Arabian Nights.

Oh, now all common things become uncommon and enchanted to me! All lamps are wonderful; all rings are talismans. Common flower-pots are full of treasure, with a little earth scattered on the top; trees are for Ali Baba to hide in; beef-steaks are to throw down into the Valley of Diamonds, that the precious stones may stick to them, and be carried by the eagles to their nests, whence the traders, with loud cries, will scare them. Tarts are made, according to the recipe of the Vizier's son of Bussorah, who turned pastry cook after he was set down in his drawers at the gate of Damascus; cobblers are all Mustaphas, and in the habit of sewing up people cut into four pieces, to whom they are taken blindfold.

Any iron ring let into stone is the entrance to a cave which only waits for the magician, and the little fire, and the necromancy, that will make the earth shake. All the dates imported come from the same tree as that unlucky date, with whose shell the merchant knocked out the eye of the genie's invisible son. All olives are of the stock of that fresh fruit, concerning which the Commander of the Faithful overheard the boy conduct the fictitious trial of the fraudulent olive merchant; all apples are akin to the apple purchased (with two others) from the Sultan's gardener for three sequins, and which the tall black slave stole from the child. All dogs are associated with the dog, really a transformed man, who jumped upon the baker's counter, and put his paw on the piece of bad money. All rice recalls the rice which the awful lady, who was a ghoul, could only peck by grains, because of her nightly feasts in the burial-place. My very rocking-horse—there he is, with his nostrils turned completely inside-out, indicative of Blood!—should have a peg in his neck, by virtue thereof to fly away with me, as the wooden horse did with the Prince of Persia, in the sight of all his father's Court.

Yes, on every object that I recognise among those upper branches of my Christmas Tree, I see this fairy light! When I wake in bed, at daybreak, on the cold dark winter mornings, the white snow dimly beheld, outside, through the frost on the window-pane, I hear Dinarzade. "Sister, sister, if you are yet awake, I pray you finish the history of the Young King of the Black Islands." Scheherazade replies, "If my lord the Sultan will suffer me to live another day, sister, I will not only finish that, but tell you a more wonderful story yet." Then the gracious Sultan goes out, giving no orders for the execution, and we all three breathe again.

At this height of my tree I begin to see, cowering among the leaves,—it may be born of turkey, or of pudding, or mince pie, or of these many fancies, jumbled with Robinson Crusoe on his desert island, Philip Quarll among the monkeys, Sandford and Merton with Mr. Barlow, Mother Bunch, and the Mask,—or it may be the result of indigestion, assisted by imagination and over-doctoring,—a prodigious nightmare. It is so exceedingly indistinct that I don't know why it's frightful—but I know it is. I can only make out that it is an immense array of shapeless things which appear to be planted on a vast exaggeration of the lazy tongs that used to bear the toy soldiers, and to be slowly coming close to my eyes, and receding to an immeasurable distance. When it comes closest, it is worst. In connection with it I decry remembrances of winter nights incredibly long; of being sent early to bed, as a punishment for some small offence, and waking in two hours, with a sensation of having been asleep two nights; of the laden hopelessness of morning ever dawning; and the oppression of a weight of remorse.

And now I see a wonderful row of little lights rise smoothly out of the ground, before a vast green curtain. Now a bell rings—a magic bell, which still sounds in my ears unlike all other bells—and music plays, amidst a buzz of voices, and a fragrant smell of orange-peel and oil. Anon, the magic bell commands the music to cease, and the great green curtain rolls itself up majestically, and The Play begins! The devoted dog of Montargis avenges the death of his master, foully murdered in the Forest of Bondy; and a humorous Peasant with a red nose and a very little hat, whom I take from this hour forth to my bosom as a friend (I think he was a Waiter or an Hostler at a village Inn, but many years have passed since he and I have met), remarks that the sassigassity of that dog is indeed surprising; and evermore this jocular conceit will live in my remembrance fresh and unfading, overtopping all possible jokes, unto the end of time. Or now, I learn with bitter tears how poor Jane Shore, dressed all in white, and with her brown hair hanging down, went starving through the streets; or how George Barnwell killed the worthiest uncle that ever man had, and was afterwards so sorry for it that he ought to have been let off. Comes swift to comfort me, the Pantomime—stupendous Phenomenon!—when Clowns are shot from loaded mortars into the great chandelier, bright constellation that it is; when Harlequins, covered all over with scales of pure gold, twist and sparkle, like amazing fish; when Pantaloon (whom I deem it no irreverence to compare in my own mind to my grandfather) puts red-hot pokers in his pocket, and cries, "Here's somebody coming!" or taxes the Clown with petty larceny, by saying, "Now, I sawed you do it!" when Everything is capable, with the greatest ease, of being changed into Anything; and "Nothing is, but thinking makes it so." Now, too, I preceive my first experience of the dreary sensation—often to return in after-life—of being unable, next day, to get back to the dull, settled world; of wanting to live for ever in the bright atmosphere I have quitted; of doting on the little Fairy, with the wand like a celestial Barber's Pole, and pining for a Fairy immortality along with her. Ah, she comes back, in many shapes, as my eye wanders down the branches of my Christmas Tree, and goes as often, and has never yet stayed by me!

Out of this delight springs the toy-theatre,—there it is, with its familiar proscenium, and ladies in feathers, in the boxes!—and all its attendant occupation with paste and glue, and gum, and water colours, in the getting-up of The Miller and his Men, and Elizabeth, or the Exile of Siberia. In spite of a few besetting accidents and failures (particularly an unreasonable disposition in the respectable Kelmar, and some others, to become faint in the legs, and double up, at exciting points of the drama), a teeming world of fancies, so suggestive and all-embracing, that, far below it on my Christmas Tree, I see dark, dirty, real Theatres in the daytime, adorned with these associations as with the freshest garlands of the rarest flowers, and charming me yet.

But hark! The Waits are playing, and they break my childish sleep! What images do I associate with the Christmas music as I see them set forth on the Christmas Tree? Known before all the others, keeping far apart from all the others, they gather round my little bed. An angel, speaking to a group of shepherds in a field; some travellers, with eyes uplifted, following a star; a baby in a manger; a child in a spacious temple, talking with grave men; a solemn figure, with a mild and beautiful face, raising a dead girl by the hand; again, near a city gate, calling back the son of a widow, on his bier, to life; a crowd of people looking through the opened roof of a chamber where he sits, and letting down a sick person on a bed, with ropes; the same, in a tempest, walking on the water to a ship; again, on a sea-shore, teaching a great multitude; again, with a child upon his knee, and other children round; again, restoring sight to the blind, speech to the dumb, hearing to the deaf, health to the sick, strength to the lame, knowledge to the ignorant; again, dying upon a Cross, watched by armed soldiers, a thick darkness coming on, the earth beginning to shake, and only one voice heard, "Forgive them, for they know not what they do!"

Still, on the lower and maturer branches of the Tree, Christmas associations cluster thick. School-books shut up; Ovid and Virgil silenced; the Rule of Three, with its cool, impertinent inquiries, long disposed of; Terence and Plautus acted no more, in an arena of huddled desks and forms, all chipped, and notched, and inked; cricket-bats, stumps, and balls, left higher up, with the smell of trodden grass and the softened noise of shouts in the evening air; the Tree is still fresh, still gay. If I no more come home at Christmas time, there will be girls and boys (thank Heaven!) while the World lasts; and they do! Yonder they dance and play upon the branches of my Tree, God bless them, merrily, and my heart dances and plays, too!

And I *do* come home at Christmas. We all do, or we all should. We all come home, or ought to come home, for a short holiday—the longer, the better—from the great boarding-school, where we are for ever working at our arithmetical slates, to take and give a rest. As to going a visiting, where can we not go, if we will; where have we not been, when we would; starting our fancy from our Christmas Tree!

Away into the winter prospect. There are many such upon the tree! On, by low-lying, misty grounds, through fens and fogs, up long hills, winding dark as caverns between thick plantations, almost shutting out the sparkling stars; so, out on broad heights, until we stop at last, with sudden silence, at an avenue. The gate bell has a deep, half-awful sound in the frosty air; the gate swings open on its hinges; and as we drive up to a great house, the glancing lights grow larger in the windows, and the opposing rows of trees seem to fall solemnly back on either side, to give us place. At intervals, all day, a frightened hare has shot across this whitened turf; or the distant clatter of a herd of deer trampling the hard frost has, for the minute, crushed the silence, too. Their watchful eyes beneath the fern may be shining now, if we could see them, like the icy dewdrops on the leaves; but they are still, and all is still. And so the lights growing larger, and the trees falling back before us, and closing up again behind us, as if to forbid retreat, we come to the house.

There is probably a smell of roasted chestnuts and other good comfortable things all the time, for we are telling Winter Stories—Ghost Stories, or more shame for us—round the Christmas fire; and we have never stirred, except to draw a little nearer to it. But no matter for that. We came to the house, and it is an old house, full of great chimneys where wood is burnt on ancient dogs upon the hearth, and grim portraits (some of them with grim legends, too) lower distrustfully from the oaken panels of the walls. We are a middle-aged nobleman, and we make a generous supper with our host and hostess and their guests—it being Christmas time, and the old house full of company—and then we go to bed. Our room is a very old room. It is hung with tapestry. We don't like the portrait of a cavalier in green, over the fireplace. There are great black beams in the ceiling, and there is a great black bedstead, supported at the foot by two great black figures, who seem to have come off a couple of tombs in the old baronial church in the park, for our particular accommodation. But we are not a superstitious nobleman, and we don't mind. Well! we dismiss our servant, lock the door, and sit before the fire in our dressing-gown, musing about a great many things. At length we go to bed. Well! we can't sleep. We toss and tumble, and can't sleep. The embers on the hearth burn fitfully and make the room look ghostly. We can't help peeping out over the counterpane, at the two black figures and the cavalier—that wicked-looking cavalier—in green. In the flickering light, they seem to advance and retire; which, though we are not by any means a superstitious nobleman, is not agreeable. Well! we get nervous—more and more nervous. We say, "This is very foolish, but we can't stand this; we'll pretend to be ill, and knock up somebody." Well! we are just going to do it, when the locked door opens, and there comes in a young woman, deadly pale, and with long fair hair, who glides to the fire, and sits down in the chair we have left there, wringing her hands. Then we notice that her clothes are wet. Our tongue cleaves to the roof of our mouth, and we can't speak; but we observe her accurately. Her clothes are wet; her long hair is dabbled with moist mud; she is dressed in the fashion of two hundred years ago; and she has at her girdle a bunch of rusty keys. Well! there she sits, and we can't even faint, we are in such a state about it. Presently she gets up and tries all the locks in the room with the rusty keys, which won't fit one of them; then she fixes her eyes on the portrait of the cavalier in green, and says, in a low, terrible voice, "The stags know it!" After that she wrings her hands again, passes the bedside, and goes out at the door. We hurry on our dressing-gown, seize our pistols (we always travel with pistols), and are following, when we find the door locked. We turn the key, look out into the dark gallery; no one there.

We wander away, and try to find our servant. Can't be done. We pace the gallery till daybreak; then return to our deserted room, fall asleep, and are awakened by our servant (nothing ever haunts *him*) and the shining sun. Well! we make a wretched breakfast, and all the company say we look queer. After breakfast, we go over the house with our host, and then we take him to the portrait of the cavalier in green, and then it all comes out. He was false to a young housekeeper once attached to that family, and famous for her beauty, who drowned herself in a pond, and whose body was discovered, after a long time, because the stags refused to drink of the water. Since which it has been whispered that she traverses the house at midnight (but goes especially to that room where the cavalier in green was wont to sleep), trying the old locks with the rusty keys. Well! we tell our host of what we have seen, and a shade comes over his features, and he begs it may be hushed up; and so it is. But it's all true; and we said so, before we died (we are dead now), to many responsible people.

There is no end to the old houses, with resounding galleries and dismal state bed-chambers, and haunted wings shut up for many years, through which we may ramble, with an agreeable creeping up our back, and encounter any number of ghosts, but (it is worthy of remark, perhaps) reducible to a very few general types and classes; for ghosts have little originality, and "walk" in a beaten track. Thus it comes to pass that a certain room in a certain old hall, where a certain bad lord, baronet, knight, or gentleman shot himself, has certain planks in the floor from which the blood *will not* be taken out. You may scrape and scrape, as the present owner has done, or plane and plane, as his father did, or scrub and scrub, as his grandfather did, or burn and burn with strong acids, as his great-grandfather did, but there the blood will still be—no redder and no paler—no more and no less—always just the same. Thus in such another house there is a haunted door, that never will keep open; or another door that never will keep shut; or a haunted sound of a spinning-wheel, or a hammer, or a footstep, or a cry, or a sigh, or a horse's tramp, or the rattling of a chain. Or else there is a turret-clock, which, at the midnight hour, strikes thirteen when the head of the family is going to die; or a shadowy, immovable black carriage which at such a time is always seen by somebody, waiting near the great gates in the stable-yard. Or thus it came to pass how Lady Mary went to pay a visit at a large wild house in the Scottish Highlands, and, being fatigued with her long journey, retired to bed early, and innocently said, next morning, at the breakfast-table, "How odd, to have so late a party last night, in this remote place, and not to tell me of it, before I went to bed!" Then every one asked Lady Mary what she meant? Then Lady Mary replied, "Why, all night long, the carriages were driving round and round the terrace, underneath my window!" Then the owner of the house turned pale, and so did his Lady, and Charles Macdoodle of Macdoodle signed to Lady Mary to say no more, and every one was silent. After breakfast, Charles Macdoodle told Lady Mary that it was a tradition in the family that those rumbling carriages on the terraces betokened death. And so it proved, for, two months afterwards, the Lady of the mansion died. And Lady Mary, who was a Maid of Honour at Court, often told this story to the old Queen Charlotte; by this token that the old King always said, "Eh, eh? What, what? Ghosts, ghosts? No such thing, no such thing!" And never left off saying so until he went to bed.

Or a friend of somebody's, whom most of us know, when he was a young man at college, had a particular friend, with whom he had made the compact that, if it were possible for the Spirit to return to this earth after its separation from the body, he of the twain who first died should reappear to the other. In course of time this compact was forgotten by our friend; the two young men having progressed in life, and taken diverging paths that were wide asunder. But, one night, many years afterwards, our friend being in the North of England, and staying for the night in an inn, on the Yorkshire Moors, happened to look out of bed; and there, in the moonlight, leaning on a bureau near the window, steadfastly regarding him, saw his old college friend! The appearance being solemnly addressed, replied, in a kind of whisper, but very audibly, "Do not come near me. I am dead. I am here to redeem my promise. I come from another world, but may not disclose its secrets!" Then the whole form, becoming paler, melted, as it were, into the moonlight, and faded away.

Or there was the daughter of the first occupier of the picturesque Elizabethan house, so famous in our neighbourhood. You have heard about her? No! Why, *She* went out one summer evening, at twilight, when she was a beautiful girl, just seventeen years of age, to gather flowers in the garden; and presently came running, terrified, into the hall to her father, saying, "Oh, dear father, I have met myself!" He took her in his arms, and told her it was fancy, but she said, "Oh, no! I met myself in the broad walk, and I was pale, and gathering withered flowers, and I turned my head, and held them up!" And that night she died, and a picture of her story was begun, though never finished, and they say it is somewhere in the house to this day, with its face to the wall.

Or the uncle of my brother's wife was riding home on horseback, one mellow evening at sunset, when, in a green lane close to his own house, he saw a man standing before him, in the very centre of the narrow way. "Why does that man in the cloak stand there!" he thought. "Does he want me to ride over him?" But the figure never moved. He felt a strange sensation at seeing it so still, but slackened his trot and rode forward. When he was so close to it as almost to touch it with his stirrup, his horse shied, and the figure glided up the bank, in a curious, unearthly manner,—backward, and without seeming to use its feet,—and was gone. The uncle of my brother's wife, exclaiming, "Good Heaven! It's my cousin Harry, from Bombay!" put spurs to his horse, which was suddenly in a profuse sweat, and, wondering at such strange behaviour, dashed round to the front of his house. There he saw the same figure, just passing in at the long french window of the drawing-room, opening on the ground. He threw his bridle to a servant, and hastened in after it. His sister was sitting there, alone. "Alice, where's my cousin Harry?" "Your cousin Harry, John?" "Yes. From Bombay. I met him in the lane just now, and saw him enter here, this instant." Not a creature had been seen by any one; and in that hour and minute, as it afterwards appeared, this cousin died in India.

Or it was a certain sensible old maiden lady, who died at ninety-nine, and retained her faculties to the last, who really did see the Orphan Boy; a story which has often been incorrectly told, but of which the real truth is this—because it is, in fact, a story belonging to our family—and she was a connection of our family. When she was about forty years of age, and still an uncommonly fine woman (her lover died young, which was the reason why she never married, though she had many offers), she went to stay at a place in Kent, which her brother, an Indian merchant, had newly bought. There was a story that this place had once been held in trust by the guardian of a young boy, who was himself the next heir, and who killed the young boy by harsh and cruel treatment. She knew nothing of that. It has been said that there was a cage in her bedroom in which the guardian used to put the boy. There was no such thing. There was only a closet. She went to bed, made no alarm whatever in the night, and in the morning said composedly to her maid when she came in, "Who is the pretty, forlorn-looking child who has been peeping out of that closet all night?" The maid replied by giving a loud scream, and instantly decamping. She was surprised; but she was a woman of remarkable strength of mind, and she dressed herself and went down stairs, and closeted herself with her brother. "Now, Walter," she said, "I have been disturbed all night by a pretty, forlorn-looking boy, who has been constantly peeping out of that closet in my room, which I can't open. This is some trick." "I am afraid not, Charlotte," said he, "for it is the legend of the house. It is the Orphan Boy. What did he do?" "He opened the door softly," said she, "and peeped out. Sometimes he came a step or two into the room. Then I called to him, to encourage him, and he shrunk, and shuddered, and crept in again, and shut the door." "The closet has no communication, Charlotte," said her brother, "with any other part of the house, and it's nailed up." This was undeniably true, and it took two carpenters a

whole forenoon to get it open, for examination. Then she was satisfied that she had seen the Orphan Boy. But the wild and terrible part
of the story is that he was also seen by three of her brother's sons, in
succession, who all died young. On the occasion of each child being
taken ill, he came home in a heat, twelve hours before, and said, Oh,
mamma, he had been playing under a particular oak tree, in a certain
meadow, with a strange boy—a pretty, forlorn-looking boy, who
was very timid, and made signs! From fatal experience, the parents
came to know that this was the Orphan Boy, and that the course of
that child whom he chose for his little playmate was surely run.

Legion is the name of the German castles, where we sit up alone
to wait for the Spectre—where we are shown into a room, made
comparatively cheerful for our reception—where we glance round at
the shadows, thrown on the blank walls by the crackling fire—where
we feel very lonely when the village innkeeper and his pretty daughter have retired, after laying down a fresh store of wood upon the
hearth, and setting forth on the small table such supper-cheer as a
cold roast capon, bread, grapes, and a flask of old Rhine wine—
where the reverberating doors close on their retreat, one after another, like so many peals of sullen thunder—and where, about the
small hours of the night, we come into the knowledge of divers
supernatural mysteries. Legion is the name of the haunted German
students, in whose society we draw yet nearer to the fire, while the
schoolboy in the corner opens his eyes wide and round, and flies off
the footstool he has chosen for his seat, when the door accidentally
blows open. Vast is the crop of such fruit, shining on our Christmas
Tree; in blossom, almost at the very top; ripening all down the
boughs!

Among the latter toys and fancies hanging there—as idle often
and less pure—be the images once associated with the sweet old
Waits, the softened music in the night, ever unalterable! Encircled by
the social thoughts of Christmas time, still let the benignant figure of
my childhood stand unchanged! In every cheerful image and suggestion that the season brings, may the bright star that rested above the

poor roof be the star of all the Christian world! A moment's pause, O vanishing tree, of which the lower boughs are dark to me as yet, and let me look once more! I know there are blank spaces on thy branches, where eyes that I have loved have shone and smiled; from which they are departed. But far above I see the raiser of the dead girl, and the Widow's Son; and God is good! If Age be hiding for me in the unseen portion of thy downward growth, oh, may I, with a grey head, turn a child's heart to that figure yet, and a child's trustfulness and confidence!

Now the tree is decorated with bright merriment, and song, and dance, and cheerfulness. And they are welcome. Innocent and welcome be they ever held, beneath the branches of the Christmas Tree, which cast no gloomy shadow! But as it sinks into the ground, I hear a whisper going through the leaves: "This, in commemoration of the law of love and kindness, mercy and compassion. This, in remembrance of Me!"

"Keep My Memory Green":

A Wild and Strange

Christmas Book

As the gloom and shadow thickened behind him, in that place where it had been gathering so darkly, it took, by slow degrees . . . an awful likeness of himself.
—by F. O. C. Darley

THE HAUNTED MAN
and the Ghost's Bargain

CHAPTER I

THE GIFT BESTOWED

E VERYBODY said so.

Far be it from me to assert that what everybody says must be true. Everybody is, often, as likely to be wrong as right. In the general experience, everybody has been wrong so often, and it has taken in most instances such a weary while to find out how wrong, that authority is proved to be fallible. Everybody may sometimes be right; "but *that*'s no rule," as the ghost of Giles Scroggins says in the ballad.

The dread word, GHOST, recalls me.

Everybody said he looked like a haunted man. The extent of my present claim for everybody is that they were so far right. He did.

Who could have seen his hollow cheek, his sunken, brilliant eye; his black-attired figure, indefinably grim, although well knit and well proportioned; his grizzled hair hanging, like tangled sea-weed, about his face,—as if he had been, through his whole life, a lonely mark for the chafing and beating of the great deep of humanity,—but might have said he looked like a haunted man?

Who could have observed his manner, taciturn, thoughtful, gloomy, shadowed by habitual reserve, retiring always and jocund never, with a distraught air of reverting to a bygone place and time, or of listening to some old echoes in his mind, but might have said it was the manner of a haunted man?

Who could have heard his voice, slow-speaking, deep, and grave, with a natural fulness and melody in it which he seemed to set himself against and stop, but might have said it was the voice of a haunted man?

Who that had seen him in his inner chamber, part library and part laboratory,—for he was, as the world knew, far and wide, a learned man in chemistry, and a teacher on whose lips and hands a crowd of aspiring ears and eyes hung daily,—who that had seen him there, upon a winter night, alone, surrounded by his drugs and instruments and books; the shadow of his shaded lamp a monstrous beetle on the wall, motionless among a crowd of spectral shapes raised there by the flickering of the fire upon the quaint objects around him; some of these phantoms (the reflection of glass vessels that held liquids) trembling at heart like things that knew his power to uncombine them, and to give back their component parts to fire and vapour,—who that had seen him then, his work done, and he pondering in his chair before the rusted grate and red flame, moving his thin mouth as if in speech, but silent as the dead, would not have said that the man seemed haunted and the chamber, too.

Who might not, by a very easy flight of fancy, have believed that everything about him took this haunted tone, and that he lived on haunted ground?

His dwelling was so solitary and vault-like—an old, retired part of an ancient endowment for students, once a brave edifice planted in an open place, but now the obsolete whim of forgotten architects; smoke, age, and weather darkened, squeezed on every side by the overgrowing of the great city, and choked, like an old well, with stones and bricks; its small quadrangles, lying down in very pits formed by the streets and buildings, which, in course of time, had been constructed above its heavy chimney stacks; its old trees, insulted by the neighbouring smoke, which deigned to droop so low when it was very feeble and the weather very moody; its grass-plots, struggling with the mildewed earth to be grass or to win any show of compromise; its silent pavement, unaccustomed to the tread of feet, and even to the observation of eyes, except when a stray face looked down from the upper world, wondering what nook it was; its sun-dial in a little bricked-up corner, where no sun had straggled for a hundred years, but where, in compensation for the sun's neglect, the snow would lie for weeks when it lay nowhere else, and the bleak east wind would spin like a huge humming-top, when in all other places it was silent and still.

His dwelling, at its heart and core—within doors—at his fireside—was so lowering and old, so crazy, yet so strong, with its worm-eaten beams of wood in the ceiling and its sturdy floor shelving downward to the great oak chimney-piece; so environed and hemmed in by the pressure of the town, yet so remote in fashion, age, and custom; so quiet, yet so thundering with echoes, when a distant voice was raised or a door was shut,—echoes not confined to the many low passages and empty rooms, but rumbling and grumbling till they were stifled in the heavy air of the forgotten Crypt where the Norman arches were half buried in the earth.

You should have seen him in his dwelling about twilight, in the dead winter-time.

When the wind was blowing, shrill and shrewd, with the going down of the blurred sun. When it was just so dark, as that the forms of things were indistinct and big—but not wholly lost. When sitters by the fire began to see wild faces and figures, mountains and abysses, ambuscades and armies, in the coals. When people in the streets bent down their heads and ran before the weather. When those who were obliged to meet it were stopped at angry corners, stung by wandering snow-flakes alighting on the lashes of their eyes,—which fell too sparingly, and were blown away too quickly, to leave a trace upon the frozen ground. When windows of private houses closed up tight and warm. When lighted gas began to burst forth in the busy and the quiet streets, fast blackening otherwise. When stray pedestrians, shivering along the latter, looked down at the glowing fires in kitchens, and sharpened their sharp appetites by sniffing up the fragrance of whole miles of dinners.

When travellers by land were bitter cold, and looked wearily on gloomy landscapes, rustling and shuddering in the blast. When mariners at sea, outlying upon icy yards, were tossed and swung above the howling ocean dreadfully. When lighthouses, on rocks and headlands, showed solitary and watchful; and benighted sea-birds breasted on against their ponderous lanterns, and fell dead. When little readers of story-books, by the firelight, trembled to think of Cassim Baba cut into quarters, hanging in the Robbers' Cave, or had some small misgivings that the fierce little old woman, with the crutch, who used to start out of the box in the merchant Abudah's bedroom, might, one of these nights, be found upon the stairs, in the long, cold, dusky journey up to bed.

When, in rustic places, the last glimmering of daylight died away from the ends of avenues; and the trees, arching overhead, were sullen and black. When, in parks and woods, the high wet fern and sodden moss and beds of fallen leaves, and trunks of trees, were lost to view, in masses of impenetrable shade. When mists arose from dyke, and fen, and river. When lights in old halls and in cottage windows were a cheerful sight. When the mill stopped, the wheelwright and the blacksmith shut their workshops, the turnpike gate closed, the plough and harrow were left lonely in the fields, the labourer and team went home, and the striking of the church clock had a deeper sound than at noon, and the churchyard wicket would be swung no more that night.

When twilight everywhere released the shadows, prisoned up all day, that now closed in and gathered like mustering swarms of ghosts. When they stood lowering in corners of rooms, and frowned out from behind half-opened doors. When they had full possession of unoccupied apartments. When they danced upon the floors, and walls, and ceilings of inhabited chambers while the fire was low, and withdrew like ebbing waters when it sprung into a blaze. When they fantastically mocked the shapes of household objects, making the nurse an ogress, the rocking-horse a monster, the wondering child, half scared and half amused, a stranger to itself,—the very tongs upon the hearth a straddling giant with his arms akimbo, evidently smelling the blood of Englishmen, and wanting to grind people's bones to make his bread.

When these shadows brought into the minds of older people other thoughts, and showed them different images. When they stole from their retreats, in the likenesses of forms and faces from the past, from the grave, from the deep, deep gulf, where the things that might have been, and never were, are always wandering.

When he sat, as already mentioned, gazing at the fire. When, as it rose and fell, the shadows went and came. When he took no heed of them, with his bodily eyes; but, let them come or let them go, looked fixedly at the fire. You should have seen him, then.

When the sounds that had arisen with the shadows, and come out of their lurking-places at the twilight summons, seemed to make a deeper stillness all about him. When the wind was rumbling in the chimney, and sometimes crooning, sometimes howling, in the house. When the old trees outward were so shaken and beaten, that one querulous old rook, unable to sleep, protested now and then, in a feeble, dozy, high-up "Caw!" When, at intervals, the window trembled, the rusty vane upon the turret-top complained, the clock beneath it recorded that another quarter of an hour was gone, or the fire collapsed and fell in with a rattle.

—When a knock came at his door, in short, as he was sitting so, and roused him.

"Who's that?" said he. "Come in!"

Surely there had been no figure leaning on the back of his chair; no face looking over it. It is certain that no gliding footstep touched the floor, as he lifted up his head with a start, and spoke. And yet there was no mirror in the room on whose surface his own form could have cast its shadow for a moment: and Something had passed darkly and gone!

"I'm humbly fearful, sir," said a fresh-coloured busy man, hold-

ing the door open with his foot for the admission of himself and a
wooden tray he carried, and letting it go again by very gentle and
careful degrees, when he and the tray had got in, lest it should close
noisily, "that it's a good bit past the time to-night. But Mrs. William
has been taken off her legs so often—"

"By the wind? Ay! I have heard it rising."

"—By the wind, sir—that it's a mercy she got home at all. Oh,
dear, yes. Yes. It was by the wind, Mr. Redlaw. By the wind."

He had, by this time, put down the tray for dinner, and was
employed in lighting the lamp, and spreading a cloth on the table.
From this employment he desisted in a hurry, to stir and feed the fire,
and then resumed it; the lamp he had lighted, and the blaze that rose
under his hand, so quickly changing the appearance of the room, that
it seemed as if the mere coming in of his fresh red face and active
manner had made the pleasant alteration.

"Mrs. William is of course subject at any time, sir, to be taken off
her balance by the elements. She is not formed superior to *that*."

"No," returned Mr. Redlaw good-naturedly, though abruptly.

"No, sir. Mrs. William may be taken off her balance by Earth; as,
for example, last Sunday week, when sloppy and greasy, and she
going out to tea with her newest sister-in-law, and having a pride in
herself, and wishing to appear perfectly spotless though pedestrian.
Mrs. William may be taken off her balance by Air; as being once
over-persuaded by a friend to try a swing at Peckham Fair, which
acted on her constitution instantly like a steamboat. Mrs. William
may be taken off her balance by Fire; as on a false alarm of engines at
her mother's, when she went two mile in her nightcap. Mrs. William
may be taken off her balance by Water; as at Battersea, when rowed
into the piers by her young nephew, Charley Swidger, junior, aged
twelve, which had no idea of boats whatever. But these are elements.
Mrs. William must be taken out of elements for the strength of *her*
character to come into play."

As he stopped for a reply, the reply was "Yes," in the same tone
as before.

"Yes, sir. Oh, dear, yes!" said Mr. Swidger, still proceeding with his preparations, and checking them off as he made them. "That's where it is, sir. That's what I always say myself, sir. Such a many of us Swidgers!—Pepper. Why, there's my father, sir, superannuated keeper and custodian of this Institution, eigh-ty-seven year old. He's a Swidger!—Spoon."

"True, William," was the patient and abstracted answer, when he stopped again.

"Yes, sir," said Mr. Swidger. "That's what I always say, sir. You may call him the trunk of the tree!—Bread. Then you come to his successor, my unworthy self—Salt—and Mrs. William, Swidgers both.—Knife and fork. Then you come to all my brothers and their families, Swidgers, man and woman, boy and girl. Why, what with cousins, uncles, aunts, and relationships of this, that, and t'other degree, and what not degree, and marriages, and lyings-in, the Swidgers—Tumbler—might take hold of hands, and make a ring round England!"

Receiving no reply at all here, from the thoughtful man whom he addressed, Mr. William approached him nearer, and made a feint of accidentally knocking the table with a decanter to rouse him. The moment he succeeded, he went on, as if in great alacrity of acquiescence.

"Yes, sir! That's just what I say myself, sir. Mrs. William and me have often said so. 'There's Swidgers enough,' we say, 'without *our* voluntary contributions,'—Butter. In fact, sir, my father is a family in himself—Castors—to take care of; and it happens all for the best that we have no child of our own, though it's made Mrs. William rather quiet-like, too. Quite ready for the fowl and mashed potatoes, sir? Mrs. William said she'd dish in ten minutes when I left the Lodge."

"I am quite ready," said the other, waking as from a dream, and walking slowly to and fro.

"Mrs. William has been at it again, sir!" said the keeper, as he stood warming a plate at the fire, and pleasantly shading his face with it. Mr. Redlaw stopped in his walking, and an expression of interest appeared in him.

"What I always say myself, sir. She *will* do it! There's a motherly feeling in Mrs. William's breast that must and will have went."

"What has she done?"

"Why, sir, not satisfied with being a sort of mother to all the young gentlemen that come up from a wariety of parts, to attend your courses of lectures at this ancient foundation—it's surprising how stone-chaney catches the heat, this frosty weather, to be sure!" Here he turned the plates, and cooled his fingers.

"Well?" said Mr. Redlaw.

"That's just what I say myself, sir," returned Mr. William, speaking over his shoulder, as if in ready and delighted assent. "That's exactly where it is, sir! There ain't one of our students but appears to regard Mrs. William in that light. Every day, right through the course, they put their heads into the Lodge, one after another, and have all got something to tell her, or something to ask her. 'Swidge' is the appellation by which they speak of Mrs. William in general, among themselves, I'm told; but that's what I say, sir. Better be called ever so far out of your name, if it's done in real liking, than have it made ever so much of, and not cared about! What's a name for? To know a person by. If Mrs. William is known by something better than her name—I allude to Mrs. William's qualities and disposition—never mind her name, though it *is* Swidger, by rights. Let 'em call her Swidge, Widge, Bridge—Lord! London Bridge, Black-friars, Chelsea, Putney, Waterloo, or Hammersmith Suspension—if they like!"

The close of this triumphant oration brought him and the plate to the table, upon which he half laid and half dropped it, with a lively sense of its being thoroughly heated, just as the subject of his praises entered the room, bearing another tray and a lantern, and followed by a venerable old man with long grey hair.

Mrs. William, like Mr. William, was a simple, innocent-looking person, in whose smooth cheeks the cheerful red of her husband's official waistcoat was very pleasantly repeated. But whereas Mr. William's light hair stood on end all over his head, and seemed to draw his eyes up with it in an excess of bustling readiness for anything, the dark brown hair of Mrs. William was carefully smoothed down, and waved away under a trim tidy cap, in the most exact and quiet manner imaginable. Whereas Mr. William's very trousers hitched themselves up at the ankles, as if it were not in their iron-grey nature to rest without looking about them, Mrs. William's neatly flowered skirts—red and white, like her own pretty face—were as composed and orderly, as if the very wind that blew so hard out of doors could not disturb one of their folds. Whereas his coat had something of a fly-away and half-off appearance about the collar and breast, her little bodice was so placid and neat, that there should have been protection for her in it, had she needed any, with the roughest people. Who could have had the heart to make so calm a bosom swell with grief, or throb with fear, or flutter with a thought of shame! To whom would its repose and peace have not appealed against disturbance, like the innocent slumber of a child!

"Punctual, of course, Milly," said her husband, relieving her of the tray, "or it wouldn't be you. Here's Mrs. William, sir!—he looks lonelier than ever to-night," whispering to his wife, as he was taking the tray, "and ghostlier altogether."

Without any show of hurry or noise, or any show of herself even, she was so calm and quiet, Milly set the dishes she had brought upon the table,—Mr. William, after much clattering and running about, having only gained possession of a butter-boat of gravy, which he stood ready to serve.

"What is that the old man has in his arms?" asked Mr. Redlaw, as he sat down to his solitary meal.

"Holly, sir," replied the quiet voice of Milly.

"That's what I say myself, sir," interposed Mr. William, striking in with the butter-boat. "Berries is so seasonable to the time of year!—Brown gravy!"

"Another Christmas come, another year gone!" murmured the

"I'm eighty-seven!" —*by E. A. Abbey*

Chemist, with a gloomy sigh. "More figures in the lengthening sum of recollection that we work and work at to our torment, till Death idly jumbles altogether, and rubs all out. So, Philip!" breaking off, and raising his voice as he addressed the old man standing apart, with his glistening burden in his arms, from which the quiet Mrs. William took small branches, which she noiselessly trimmed with her scissors, and decorated the room with, while her aged father-in-law looked on much interested in the ceremony.

"My duty to you, sir," returned the old man. "Should have spoke before, sir, but know your ways, Mr. Redlaw—proud to say—and wait till spoke to! Merry Christmas, sir, and Happy New Year, and many of 'em. Have had a pretty many of 'em myself—ha, ha!—and may take the liberty of wishing 'em. I'm eighty-seven!"

"Have you had so many that were merry and happy?" asked the other.

"Ay, sir, ever so many," returned the old man.

"Is his memory impaired with age? It is to be expected now," said Mr. Redlaw, turning to the son, and speaking lower.

"Not a morsel of it, sir," replied Mr. William. "That's exactly what I say myself, sir. There never was such a memory as my father's. He's the most wonderful man in the world. He don't know what forgetting means. It's the very observation I'm always making to Mrs. William, sir, if you'll believe me!"

Mr. Swidger, in his polite desire to seem to acquiesce at all events, delivered this as if there were no iota of contradiction in it, and it were all said in unbounded and unqualified assent.

The Chemist pushed his plate away, and rising from the table, walked across the room to where the old man stood looking at a little sprig of holly in his hand.

"It recalls the time when many of those years were old and new, then?" he said, observing him attentively, and touching him on the shoulder. "Does it?"

"Oh, many, many!" said Philip, half awakening from his reverie. "I'm eighty-seven!"

"Merry and happy, was it?" asked the Chemist, in a low voice. "Merry and happy, old man?"

"May be as high as that, no higher," said the old man, holding out his hand a little way above the level of his knee, and looking retrospectively at his questioner, "when I first remember 'em! Cold, sunshiny day it was, out a walking, when some one—it was my mother as sure as you stand there, though I don't know what her blessed face was like, for she took ill and died that Christmas-time— told me they were food for birds. The pretty little fellow thought— that's me, you understand—that birds' eyes were so bright, perhaps, because the berries that they lived on in the winter were so bright. I recollect that. And I'm eighty-seven!"

"Merry and happy!" mused the other, bending his dark eyes upon the stooping figure, with a smile of compassion. "Merry and happy— and remember well?"

"Ay, ay, ay!" resumed the old man, catching the last words. "I remember 'em well in my school-time, year after year, and all the merry-making that used to come along with them. I was a strong chap then, Mr. Redlaw; and, if you'll believe me, hadn't my match at foot-ball within ten mile. Where's my son William? Hadn't my match at foot-ball, William, within ten mile!"

"That's what I always say, father!" returned the son promptly, and with great respect. "You ARE a Swidger, if ever there was one of the family!"

"Dear!" said the old man, shaking his head as he again looked at the holly. "His mother—my son William's my youngest son—and I have set among 'em all, boys and girls, little children and babies, many a year, when the berries like these were not shining half so bright all round us as their bright faces. Many of 'em are gone; she's gone; and my son George (our eldest, who was her pride more than all the rest!) is fallen very low; but I can see them, when I look here, alive and healthy, as they used to be in those days; and I can see him, thank God! in his innocence. It's a blessed thing to me, at eighty-seven."

The keen look that had been fixed upon him with so much earnestness had gradually sought the ground.

"When my circumstances got to be not so good as formerly, through not being honestly dealt by, and I first come here to be custodian," said the old man,—"which was upwards of fifty years ago—where's my son William? More than half a century ago, William!"

"That's what I say, father," replied the son, as promptly and dutifully as before; "that's exactly where it is. Two times ought's an ought, and twice five ten, and there's a hundred of 'em."

"It was quite a pleasure to know that one of our founders—or more correctly speaking," said the old man, with a great glory in his subject and his knowledge of it, "one of the learned gentlemen that helped endow us in Queen Elizabeth's time, for we were founded afore her day—left in his will, among the other bequests he made us, so much to buy holly, for garnishing the walls and windows, come Christmas. There was something homely and friendly in it. Being but strange here, then, and coming at Christmas-time, we took a liking for his very picter that hangs in what used to be, anciently, afore our ten poor gentlemen commuted for an annual stipend in money, our great Dinner Hall.—A sedate gentleman in a peaked beard, with a ruff round his neck, and a scroll below him, in old English letters, 'Lord, keep my memory green!' You know all about him, Mr. Redlaw?"

"I know the portrait hangs there, Philip."

"Yes, sure, it's the second on the right, above the panelling. I was going to say—he has helped to keep *my* memory green, I thank him; for going round the building every year, as I'm a doing now, and freshening up the bare rooms with these branches and berries, freshens up my bare old brain. One year brings back another, and that year another, and those others numbers! At last, it seems to me as if the birth-time of our Lord was the birth-time of all I have ever had affection for, or mourned for, or delighted in,—and they're a pretty many, for I'm eighty-seven!"

"Merry and happy," murmured Redlaw to himself.

The room began to darken strangely.

"So you see, sir," pursued old Philip, whose hale wintry cheek had warmed into a ruddier glow, and whose blue eyes had brightened while he spoke, "I have plenty to keep, when I keep this present season. Now where's my quiet Mouse? Chattering's the sin of my time of life, and there's half the building to do yet, if the cold don't freeze us first, or the wind don't blow us away, or the darkness don't swallow us up."

The quiet Mouse had brought her calm face to his side, and silently taken his arm, before he finished speaking.

"Come away, my dear," said the old man. "Mr. Redlaw won't settle to his dinner, otherwise, till it's cold as the winter. I hope you'll excuse me rambling on, sir, and I wish you good night, and, once again, a Merry—"

"Stay!" said Mr. Redlaw, resuming his place at the table, more, it would have seemed from his manner, to reassure the old keeper, than in any remembrance of his own appetite. "Spare me another moment, Philip. William, you were going to tell me something to your excellent wife's honour. It will not be disagreeable to her to hear you praise her. What was it?"

"Why, that's where it is, you see, sir," returned Mr. William Swidger, looking towards his wife in considerable embarrassment. "Mrs. William's got her eye upon me."

"But you're not afraid of Mrs. William's eye?"

"Why, no, sir," returned Mr. Swidger, "that's what I say myself. It wasn't made to be afraid of. It wouldn't have been made so mild, if that was the intention. But I wouldn't like to—Milly!—him, you know. Down in the Buildings."

Mr. William, standing behind the table, and rummaging disconcertedly among the objects upon it, directed persuasive glances at Mrs. William, and secret jerks of his head and thumb at Mr. Redlaw, as alluring her towards him.

"Him, you know, my love," said Mr. William. "Down in the

Buildings. Tell, my dear! You're the works of Shakespeare in comparison with myself. Down in the Buildings, you know, my love.—
Student."

"Student!" repeated Mr. Redlaw, raising his head.

"That's what I say, sir!" cried Mr. William, in the utmost animation of assent. "If it wasn't the poor student down in the Buildings,
why should you wish to hear it from Mrs. William's lips? Mrs.
William, my dear—Buildings."

"I didn't know," said Milly, with a quiet frankness, free from any
haste or confusion, "that William had said anything about it, or I
wouldn't have come. I asked him not to. It's a sick young gentleman,
sir—and very poor, I am afraid—who is too ill to go home this
holiday-time, and lives, unknown to any one, in but a common kind
of lodging for a gentleman, down in Jerusalem Buildings. That's all,
sir."

"Why have I never heard of him?" said the Chemist, rising
hurriedly. "Why has he not made his situation known to me? Sick!—
give me my hat and cloak. Poor!—what house?—what number?"

"Oh, you mustn't go there, sir," said Milly, leaving her father-in-
law, and calmly confronting him with her collected little face and
folded hands.

"Not go there?"

"Oh, dear, no!" said Milly, shaking her head as at a most manifest
and self-evident impossibility. "It couldn't be thought of!"

"What do you mean? Why not?"

"Why, you see, sir," said Mr. William Swidger, persuasively and
confidentially, "that's what I say. Depend upon it, the young gentleman would never have made his situation known to one of his own
sex. Mrs. William has got into his confidence, but that's quite different. They all confide in Mrs. William; they all trust *her*. A man, sir,
couldn't have got a whisper out of him; but woman, sir, and Mrs.
William combined—"

"There is good sense and delicacy in what you say, William,"
returned Mr. Redlaw, observant of the gentle and composed face at

his shoulder. And laying his finger on his lip, he secretly put his purse into her hand.

"Oh, dear, no, sir!" cried Milly, giving it back again. "Worse and worse! Couldn't be dreamed of!"

Such a staid matter-of-fact housewife she was, and so unruffled by the momentary haste of this rejection, that, an instant afterwards, she was tidily picking up a few leaves which had strayed from between her scissors and her apron, when she had arranged the holly.

Finding, when she rose from her stooping posture, that Mr. Redlaw was still regarding her with doubt and astonishment, she quietly repeated—looking about, the while, for any other fragments that might have escaped her observation:—

"Oh, dear, no, sir! He said that of all the world he would not be known to you, or receive help from you—though he is a student in your class. I have made no terms of secrecy with you, but I trust to your honour completely."

"Why did he say so?"

"Indeed I can't tell, sir," said Milly, after thinking a little, "because I am not at all clever, you know; and I wanted to be useful to him in making things neat and comfortable about him, and employed myself that way. But I know he is poor, and lonely, and I think he is somehow neglected too.—How dark it is!"

The room had darkened more and more. There was a very heavy gloom and shadow gathering behind the Chemist's chair.

"What more about him?" he asked.

"He is engaged to be married when he can afford it," said Milly, "and is studying, I think, to qualify himself to earn a living. I have seen, a long time, that he has studied hard and denied himself much.—How very dark it is!"

"It's turned colder, too," said the old man, rubbing his hands. "There's a chill and dismal feeling in the room. Where's my son William? William, my boy, turn the lamp, and rouse the fire!"

Milly's voice resumed, like quiet music very softly played:—

"He muttered in his broken sleep yesterday afternoon, after talking to me" (this was to herself) "about some one dead, and some great wrong done that could never be forgotten; but whether to him or to another person, I don't know. Not *by* him, I am sure."

"And, in short, Mrs. William, you see,—which she wouldn't say herself, Mr. Redlaw, if she was to stop here till the new year after this next one," said Mr. William, coming up to him to speak in his ear,— "has done him worlds of good! Bless you, worlds of good! All at home just the same as ever—my father made as snug and comfortable—not a crumb of litter to be found in the house, if you were to offer fifty pounds ready money for it—Mrs. William apparently never out of the way—yet Mrs. William backwards and forwards, backwards and forwards, up and down, up and down, a mother to him!"

The room turned darker and colder, and the gloom and shadow gathering behind the chair were heavier.

"Not content with this, sir, Mrs. William goes and finds, this very night, when she was coming home (why, it's not above a couple of hours ago), a creature more like a young wild beast than a young child, shivering upon a door-step. What does Mrs. William do, but brings it home to dry it, and feed it, and keep it till our old Bounty of food and flannel is given away on Christmas morning! If it ever felt a fire before, it's as much as it ever did; for it's sitting in the old Lodge chimney, staring at ours as if its ravenous eyes would never shut again. It's sitting there, at least," said Mr. William, correcting himself, on reflection, "unless it's bolted!"

"Heaven keep her happy!" said the Chemist aloud, "and you, too, Philip! and you, William! I must consider what to do in this. I may desire to see this student; I'll not detain you longer now. Good night!"

"I thankee, sir, I thankee!" said the old man, "for Mouse, and for my son William, and for myself. Where's my son William? William, you take the lantern and go on first, through them long dark passages, as you did last year and the year afore. Ha, ha! *I* remember—though I'm eighty-seven! 'Lord, keep my memory green!' It's a very good prayer, Mr. Redlaw, that of the learned gentleman in the peaked beard, with a ruff round his neck—hangs up, second on the right above the panelling, in what used to be, afore our ten poor gentlemen commuted, our great Dinner Hall. 'Lord, keep my memory green!' It's very good and pious, sir. Amen! Amen!"

As they passed out and shut the heavy door, which, however carefully withheld, fired a long train of thundering reverberations when it shut at last, the room turned darker.

As he fell a musing in his chair alone, the healthy holly withered on the wall, and dropped—dead branches.

As the gloom and shadow thickened behind him, in that place where it had been gathering so darkly, it took, by slow degrees,—or out of it there came, by some unreal, unsubstantial process,—not to be traced by any human sense, an awful likeness of himself.

Ghastly and cold, colourless in its leaden face and hands, but with his features, and his bright eyes, and his grizzled hair, and dressed in the gloomy shadow of his dress, it came into its terrible appearance of existence, motionless, without a sound. As *he* leaned his arm upon the elbow of his chair, ruminating before the fire, *it* leaned upon the chair-back, close above him, with its appalling copy of his face looking where his face looked, and bearing the expression his face bore.

This, then, was the Something that had passed and gone already. This was the dread companion of the haunted man!

It took, for some moments, no more apparent heed of him, than he of it. The Christmas Waits were playing somewhere in the distance, and, through his thoughtfulness, he seemed to listen to the music. It seemed to listen too.

At length he spoke; without moving or lifting up his face.

"Here again!" he said.

"Here again!" replied the Phantom.

"I see you in the fire," said the haunted man; "I hear you in music, in the wind, in the dead stillness of the night."

The Phantom moved his head, assenting.

"Why do you come, to haunt me thus?"

"I come as I am called," replied the Ghost.

"No. Unbidden," exclaimed the Chemist.

"Unbidden be it," said the Spectre. "It is enough. I am here."

Hitherto the light of the fire had shone on the two faces—if the dread lineaments behind the chair might be called a face—both addressed towards it, as at first, and neither looking at the other. But, now, the haunted man turned, suddenly, and stared upon the Ghost. The Ghost, as sudden in its motion, passed to before the chair, and stared on him.

The living man and the animated image of himself dead might so have looked, the one upon the other. An awful survey, in a lonely and remote part of an empty old pile of building, on a winter night, with the loud wind going by upon its journey of mystery—whence, or whither, no man knowing since the world began—and the stars, in unimaginable millions, glittering through it, from eternal space, where the world's bulk is as a grain, and its hoary age is infancy.

"Look upon me!" said the Spectre. "I am he, neglected in my youth, and miserably poor, who strove and suffered, and still strove and suffered, until I hewed out knowledge from the mine where it was buried, and made rugged steps thereof, for my worn feet to rest and rise on."

"I *am* that man," returned the Chemist.

"No mother's self-denying love," pursued the Phantom, "no father's counsel, aided *me*. A stranger came into my father's place when I was but a child, and I was easily an alien from my mother's heart. My parents, at the best, were of that sort whose care soon ends, and whose duty is soon done; who cast their offspring loose, early, as birds do theirs, and, if they do well, claim the merit; and if ill, the pity."

It paused, and seemed to tempt and goad him with its look, and with the manner of its speech, and with its smile.

"I am he," pursued the Phantom, "who, in this struggle upward, found a friend. I made him—won him—bound him to me! We worked together, side by side. All the love and confidence that in my earlier youth had had no outlet, and found no expression, I bestowed on him."

"Not all," said Redlaw hoarsely.

"No, not all," returned the Phantom. "I had a sister."

The haunted man, with his head resting on his hands, replied, "I had!" The Phantom, with an evil smile, drew closer to the chair, and resting its chin upon its folded hands, its folded hands upon the back, and looking down into his face with searching eyes, that seemed instinct with fire, went on:—

"Such glimpses of the light of home as I had ever known, had streamed from her. How young she was, how fair, how loving! I took her to the first poor roof that I was master of, and made it rich. She came into the darkness of my life, and made it bright.—She is before me!"

"I saw her, in the fire, but now. I hear her in music, in the wind, in the dead stillness of the night," returned the haunted man.

"*Did* he love her?" said the Phantom, echoing his contemplative tone. "I think he did once. I am sure he did. Better had she loved him less—less secretly, less dearly, from the shallower depths of a more divided heart!"

"Let me forget it," said the Chemist, with an angry motion of his hand. "Let me blot it from my memory!"

The Spectre, without stirring, and with its unwinking, cruel eyes still fixed upon his face, went on:—

"A dream, like hers, stole upon my own life."

"It did," said Redlaw.

"A love, as like hers," pursued the Phantom, "as my inferior nature might cherish, arose in my own heart. I was too poor to bind its object to my fortune then, by any thread of promise or entreaty. I loved her far too well, to seek to do it. But more than ever I had striven in my life, I strove to climb! Only an inch gained, brought me something nearer to the height. I toiled up! In the late pauses of my labour at that time,—my sister (sweet companion!) still sharing with me the expiring embers and the cooling hearth,—when day was breaking, what pictures of the future did I see!"

"I saw them in the fire, but now," he murmured. "They come back to me in music, in the wind, in the dead stillness of the night, in the revolving years."

"—Pictures of my own domestic life, in after-time, with her who was the inspiration of my toil. Pictures of my sister, made the wife of my dear friend, on equal terms—for he had some inheritance, we none—pictures of our sobered age and mellowed happiness, and of the golden links, extending back so far, that should bind us, and our children, in a radiant garland," said the Phantom.

"Pictures," said the haunted man, "that were delusions. Why is it my doom to remember them too well!"

"Delusions," echoed the Phantom in its changeless voice, and glaring on him with its changeless eyes. "For my friend (in whose breast my confidence was locked as in my own), passing between me and the centre of the system of my hopes and struggles, won her to himself, and shattered my frail universe. My sister, doubly dear, doubly devoted, doubly cheerful in my home, lived on to see me famous, and my old ambition so rewarded when its spring was broken, and then—"

"Then died," he interposed. "Died, gentle as ever, happy, and with no concern but for her brother. Peace!"

The Phantom watched him silently.

"Remembered!" said the haunted man, after a pause. "Yes. So well remembered, that even now, when years have passed, and nothing is more idle or more visionary to me than the boyish love so long outlived, I think of it with sympathy, as if it were a younger brother's or a son's. Sometimes I even wonder when her heart first inclined to him, and how it had been affected towards me.—Not lightly, once, I think.—But that is nothing. Early unhappiness, a wound from a hand I loved and trusted, and a loss that nothing can replace outlive such fancies."

"Thus," said the Phantom, "I bear within me a Sorrow and a Wrong. Thus I prey upon myself. Thus memory is my curse; and if I could forget my sorrow and my wrong, I would!"

"Mocker!" said the Chemist, leaping up, and making, with a wrathful hand, at the throat of his other self. "Why have I always that taunt in my ears?"

"Forbear!" exclaimed the Spectre in an awful voice. "Lay a hand on me, and die!"

He stopped midway, as if its words had paralysed him, and stood looking on it. It had glided from him; it had its arm raised high in warning; and a smile passed over its unearthly features, as it reared its dark figure in triumph.

"If I could forget my sorrow and wrong, I would," the Ghost repeated. "If I could forget my sorrow and my wrong, I would!"

"Evil spirit of myself," returned the haunted man, in a low, trembling tone, "my life is darkened by that incessant whisper."

"It is an echo," said the Phantom.

"If it be an echo of my thoughts—as now, indeed, I know it is," rejoined the haunted man, "why should I, therefore, be tormented? It is not a selfish thought. I suffer it to range beyond myself. All men and women have their sorrows,—most of them their wrongs; ingratitude, and sordid jealousy, and interest, besetting all degrees of life. Who would not forget their sorrows and their wrongs?"

"Who would not, truly, and be the happier and better for it?" said the Phantom.

"These revolutions of years, which we commemorate," proceeded Redlaw, "what do *they* recall! Are there any minds in which they do not reawaken some sorrow, or some trouble? What is the remembrance of the old man who was here tonight? A tissue of sorrow and trouble."

"But common natures," said the Phantom, with its evil smile upon its glassy face, "unenlightened minds and ordinary spirits, do not feel or reason on these things like men of higher cultivation and profounder thought."

"Tempter," answered Redlaw, "whose hollow look and voice I dread more than words can express, and from whom some dim foreshadowing of greater fear is stealing over me while I speak, I hear again an echo of my own mind."

"Receive it as a proof that I am powerful," returned the Ghost. "Hear what I offer! Forget the sorrow, wrong, and trouble you have known!"

"Forget them!" he repeated.

"I have the power to cancel their remembrance—to leave but very faint, confused traces of them, that will die out soon," returned the Spectre. "Say! Is it done?"

"Stay!" cried the haunted man, arresting by a terrified gesture the uplifted hand. "I tremble with distrust and doubt of you; and the dim fear you cast upon me deepens into a nameless horror I can hardly bear.—I would not deprive myself of any kindly recollection, or any sympathy that is good for me, or others. What shall I lose, if I assent to this? What else will pass from my remembrance?"

"No knowledge; no result of study; nothing but the inter-twisted chain of feelings and associations, each in its turn dependent on, and nourished by, the banished recollections. Those will go."

"Are they so many?" said the haunted man, reflecting in alarm.

"They have been wont to show themselves in the fire, in music, in the wind, in the dead stillness of the night, in the revolving years," returned the Phantom scornfully.

"In nothing else?"

The Phantom held its peace.

But having stood before him, silent, for a little while, it moved towards the fire; then stopped.

"Decide!" it said, "before the opportunity is lost!"

"A moment! I call Heaven to witness," said the agitated man, "that I have never been a hater of my kind,—never morose, indifferent, or hard, to anything around me. If, living here alone, I have made too much of all that was and might have been, and too little of what is, the evil, I believe, has fallen on me, and not on others. But if there were poison in my body, should I not, possessed of antidotes and knowledge how to use them, use them? If there be poison in my mind, and through this fearful shadow I can cast it out, shall I not cast it out?"

"Say," said the Spectre, "is it done?"

"A moment longer!" he answered hurriedly. *"I would forget it if I could!* Have *I* thought that, alone, or has it been the thought of thousands upon thousands, generation after generation? All human memory is fraught with sorrow and trouble. My memory is as the memory of other men, but other men have not this choice. Yes, I close the bargain. Yes! I WILL forget my sorrow, wrong, and trouble!"

"Say," said the Spectre, "is it done?"

"It is!"

"IT IS. And take this with you, man whom I here renounce! The gift that I have given, you shall give again, go where you will. Without recovering yourself the power that you have yielded up, you shall henceforth destroy its like in all whom you approach. Your wisdom has discovered that the memory of sorrow, wrong, and trouble is the lot of all mankind, and that mankind would be the happier in its other memories without it. Go! Be its benefactor! Freed from such remembrance, from this hour, carry involuntarily the blessing of such freedom with you. Its diffusion is inseparable and inalienable from you. Go! Be happy in the good you have won, and in the good you do!"

The Phantom, which had held its bloodless hand above him while it spoke, as if in some unholy invocation, or some ban; and which had gradually advanced its eyes so close to his that he could see how they did not participate in the terrible smile upon its face, but were a fixed, unalterable, steady horror, melted from before him, and was gone.

As he stood rooted to the spot, possessed by fear and wonder, and imagining he heard repeated in melancholy echoes, dying away fainter and fainter, the words, "Destroy its like in all whom you approach!" a shrill cry reached his ears. It came, not from the passages beyond the door, but from another part of the old building, and sounded like the cry of some one in the dark who had lost the way.

He looked confusedly upon his hands and limbs, as if to be assured of his identity, and then shouted in reply, loudly and wildly; for there was a strangeness and terror upon him, as if he, too, were lost.

The cry responding, and being nearer, he caught up the lamp, and raised a heavy curtain in the wall, by which he was accustomed to pass into and out of the theatre where he lectured,—which adjoined his room. Associated with youth and animation, and a high amphitheatre of faces which his entrance charmed to interest in a moment, it was a ghostly place when all this life was faded out of it, and stared upon him like an emblem of Death.

"Halloa!" he cried. "Halloa! This way! Come to the light!" When, as he held the curtain with one hand, and with the other raised the lamp and tried to pierce the gloom that filled the place, something rushed past him into the room like a wild-cat, and crouched down in a corner.

"What is it?" he said hastily.

He might have asked, "What is it?" even had he seen it well, as presently he did when he stood looking at it gathered up in its corner.

A bundle of tatters, held together by a hand, in size and form almost an infant's, but, in its greedy, desperate, little clutch, a bad old man's. A face rounded and smoothed by some half-dozen years, but pinched and twisted by the experiences of a life. Bright eyes, but not youthful. Naked feet, beautiful in their childish delicacy,—ugly in the blood and dirt that cracked upon them. A baby savage, a young monster, a child who had never been a child, a creature who might live to take the outward form of man, but who, within, would live and perish a mere beast.

Used, already, to be worried and hunted like a beast, the boy crouched down as he was looked at, and looked back again, and interposed his arm to ward off the expected blow.

"I'll bite," he said, "if you hit me!"

The time had been, and not many minutes since, when such a sight as this would have wrung the Chemist's heart. He looked upon it now, coldly; but with a heavy effort to remember something—he did not know what—he asked the boy what he did there, and whence he came.

"Where's the woman?" he replied. "I want to find the woman."

"Who?"

"The woman. Her that brought me here, and set me by the large fire. She was so long gone that I went to look for her, and lost myself. I don't want you. I want the woman."

He made a spring, so suddenly, to get away, that the dull sound of his naked feet upon the floor was near the curtain, when Redlaw caught him by his rags.

"Come! you let me go!" muttered the boy, struggling, and clenching his teeth. "I've done nothing to you. Let me go, will you, to the woman!"

"That is not the way. There is a nearer one," said Redlaw, detaining him, in the same blank effort to remember some association that ought of right to bear upon this monstrous object. "What is your name?"

"Got none."

"Where do you live?"

"Live! What's that?"

The boy shook his hair from his eyes to look at him for a moment, and then, twisting round his legs and wrestling with him, broke again into his repetition of "You let me go, will you? I want to find the woman."

The Chemist led him to the door. "This way," he said, looking at him still confusedly, but with repugnance and avoidance, growing out of his coldness. "I'll take you to her."

The sharp eyes in the child's head, wandering round the room, lighted on the table where the remnants of the dinner were.

"Give me some of that!" he said covetously.

"Has she not fed you?"

"I shall be hungry again to-morrow, shan't I? Ain't I hungry every day?"

Finding himself released, he bounded at the table like some small animal of prey, and hugging to his breast bread and meat, and his own rags, all together, said:—

"There! Now take me to the woman!"

As the Chemist, with a new-born dislike to touch him, sternly motioned him to follow, and was going out of the door, he trembled and stopped.

"The gift that I have given, you shall give again, go where you will!"

The Phantom's word blowing in the wind, and the wind blew chill upon him.

"I'll not go there to-night," he murmured faintly. "I'll go nowhere to-night. Boy! straight down this long-arched passage, and past the great dark door into the yard,—you will see the fire shining on a window there."

"The woman's fire?" inquired the boy.

He nodded, and the naked feet had sprung away. He came back with his lamp, locked his door hastily, and sat down in his chair, covering his face like one who was frightened at himself.

For now he was, indeed, alone. Alone, alone.

CHAPTER II

THE GIFT DIFFUSED

A SMALL man sat in a small parlour, partitioned off from a small shop by a small screen, pasted all over with small scraps of newspapers. In company with the small man was almost any amount of small children you may please to name—at least, it seemed so; they made, in that very limited sphere of action, such an imposing effect, in point of numbers.

Of these small fry, two had, by some strong machinery, been got into bed in a corner, where they might have reposed snugly enough in the sleep of innocence, but for a constitutional propensity to keep awake, and also to scuffle in and out of bed. The immediate occasion of these predatory dashes at the waking world was the construction of an oyster-shell wall in a corner, by two other youths of tender age; on which fortification the two in bed made harassing descents (like those accursed Picts and Scots who beleaguer the early historical studies of most young Britons), and then withdrew to their own territory.

In addition to the stir attendant on these inroads, and the retorts of the invaded, who pursued hotly, and made lunges at the bed-clothes, under which the marauders took refuge, another little boy, in another little bed, contributed his mite of confusion to the family stock, by casting his boots upon the waters; in other words, by launching these and several small objects, inoffensive in themselves, though of a hard substance, considered as missiles, at the disturbers of his repose,—who were not slow to return these compliments.

Besides which, another little boy—the biggest there, but still lit-tle—was tottering to and fro, bent on one side, and considerably affected in his knees by the weight of a large baby, which he was supposed, by a fiction that obtains sometimes in sanguine families, to be hushing to sleep. But oh! the inexhaustible regions of contempla-tion and watchfulness into which this baby's eyes were then only beginning to compose themselves to stare, over his unconscious shoulder!

It was a very Moloch of a baby, on whose insatiate altar the whole existence of this particular young brother was offered up a daily sacrifice. Its personality may be said to have consisted in its never being quiet, in any one place, for five consecutive minutes, and never going to sleep when required. "Tetterby's baby" was as well known in the neighbourhood as the postman or the pot-boy. It roved from door-step to door-step, in the arms of little Johnny Tetterby, and lagged heavily at the rear of troops of juveniles who followed the Tumblers or the Monkey, and came up, all on one side, a little too late for everything that was attractive, from Monday morning until Saturday night. Wherever childhood congregated to play, there was little Moloch making Johnny fag and toil. Wherever Johnny desired to stay, little Moloch became fractious and would not remain. Whenever Johnny wanted to go out, Moloch was asleep, and must be watched. Whenever Johnny wanted to stay at home, Moloch was awake, and must be taken out. Yet Johnny was verily persuaded that it was a faultless baby, without its peer in the realm of England; and was quite content to catch meek glimpses of things in general from behind its skirts, or over its limp, flapping bonnet, and to go staggering about with it like a very little porter with a very large parcel, which was not directed to anybody, and could never be delivered anywhere.

The small man who sat in the small parlour, making fruitless attempts to read his newspaper peaceably in the midst of this disturbance, was the father of the family, and the chief of the firm described in the inscription over the little shop front, by the name and title of A. TETTERBY AND CO., NEWSMEN. Indeed, strictly speaking, he was the only personage answering to that designation; as "Co." was a mere poetical abstraction, altogether baseless and impersonal.

Tetterby's was the corner shop in Jerusalem Buildings. There was a good show of literature in the window, chiefly consisting of picture newspapers out of date, and serial pirates, and footpads. Walking-sticks, likewise, and marbles, were included in the stock in trade. It had once extended into the light confectionery line; but it would seem that those elegancies of life were not in demand about Jerusalem Buildings, for nothing connected with that branch of commerce remained in the window, except a sort of small glass lantern containing a languishing mass of bull's-eyes, which had melted in the summer and congealed in the winter until all hope of ever getting them out, or of eating them without eating the lantern, too, was gone for ever. Tetterby's had tried its hand at several things. It had once made a feeble little dart at the toy business; for in another lantern, there was a heap of minute wax dolls, all sticking together upside down, in the direst confusion, with the feet on one another's heads, and a precipitate of broken arms and legs at the bottom. It had made a move in the millinery direction, which a few dry, wiry bonnet-shapes remained in a corner of the window to attest. It had fancied that a living might lie hidden in the tobacco trade, and had stuck up a representation of a native of each of the three integral portions of the British empire, in the act of consuming that fragrant weed; with a poetic legend attached, importing that united in one cause they sat and joked, one chewed tobacco, one took snuff, one smoked; but nothing seemed to have come of it—except flies. Time had been when it had put a forlorn trust in imitative jewellery, for in one pane of glass there was a card of cheap seals, and another of pencil-cases, and a mysterious black amulet of inscrutable intention labelled nine-pence. But to that hour, Jerusalem Buildings had bought none of them. In short, Tetterby's had tried so hard to get a livelihood out of Jerusalem Buildings in one way or other, and appeared to have done so indifferently in all that the best position in the firm was too evidently Co.'s; Co., as a bodiless creation, being untroubled with the vulgar inconveniences of hunger and thirst, being chargeable neither to the poor's-rates nor the assessed taxes, and having no young family to provide for.

Tetterby himself, however, in his little parlour, as already mentioned, having the presence of a young family impressed upon his mind in a manner too clamorous to be disregarded, or to comport with the quiet perusal of a newspaper, laid down his paper, wheeled in his distraction a few times round the parlour, like an undecided carrier-pigeon, made an ineffectual rush at one or two flying little figures in bed-gowns that skimmed past him, and then, bearing suddenly down upon the only unoffending member of the family, boxed the ears of little Moloch's nurse.

"You bad boy!" said Mr. Tetterby . . . —by E. A. Abbey

"You bad boy!" said Mr. Tetterby, "haven't you any feeling for your poor father after the fatigues and anxieties of a hard winter's day, since five o'clock in the morning, but must you wither his rest, and corrode his latest intelligence, with *your* wicious tricks? Isn't it enough, sir, that your brother 'Dolphus is toiling and moiling in the fog and cold, and you rolling in the lap of luxury with a—with a baby, and every-think you can wish for," said Mr. Tetterby, heaping this up as a great climax of blessings, "but must you make a wilderness of home, and maniacs of your parents? Must you, Johnny? Hey?" At each interrogation, Mr. Tetterby made a feint of boxing his ears again, but thought better of it, and held his hand.

"Oh, father!" whimpered Johnny, "when I wasn't doing anything, I'm sure, but taking such care of Sally, and getting her to sleep. Oh, father!"

"I wish my little woman would come home!" said Mr. Tetterby, relenting and repenting. "I only wish my little woman would come home! I ain't fit to deal with 'em. They make my head go round, and get the better of me. Oh, Johnny! Isn't it enough that your dear mother has provided you with that sweet sister?" indicating Moloch; "isn't it enough that you were seven boys before, without a ray of gal, and that your dear mother went through what she *did* go through, on purpose that you might all of you have a little sister, but must you so behave yourself as to make my head swim?"

Softening more and more, as his own tender feelings and those of his injured son were worked on, Mr. Tetterby concluded by embracing him, and immediately breaking away to catch one of the real delinquents. A reasonably good start occurring, he succeeded, after a short but smart run, and some rather severe cross-country work under and over the bedsteads, and in and out among the intricacies of the chairs, in capturing this infant, whom he condignly punished, and bore to bed. This example had a powerful, and apparently, mesmeric influence on him of the boots, who instantly fell into a deep sleep, though he had been, but a moment before, broad awake, and in the highest possible feather. Nor was it lost upon the two young architects, who retired to bed, in an adjoining closet, with great privacy and speed. The comrade of the Intercepted One also shrinking into his nest with similar discretion, Mr. Tetterby, when he paused for breath, found himself unexpectedly in a scene of peace.

"My little woman herself," said Mr. Tetterby, wiping his flushed face, "could hardly have done it better! I only wish my little woman had had it to do, I do, indeed!"

Mr. Tetterby sought upon his screen for a passage appropriate to be impressed upon his children's minds on the occasion, and read the following:—

" 'It is an undoubted fact that all remarkable men have had remarkable mothers, and have respected them in after life as their best friends.' Think of your own remarkable mother, my boys," said Mr. Tetterby, "and know her value while she is still among you!"

He sat down again in his chair by the fire, and composed himself, cross-legged, over his newspaper.

"Let anybody, I don't care who it is, get out of bed again," said Tetterby, as a general proclamation, delivered in a very soft-hearted manner, "and astonishment will be the portion of that respected contemporary!"—which expression Mr. Tetterby selected from his screen. "Johnny, my child, take care of your only sister, Sally; for she's the brightest gem that ever sparkled on your early brow."

Johnny sat down on a little stool, and devotedly crushed himself beneath the weight of Moloch.

"Ah, what a gift that baby is to you, Johnny!" said his father, "and how thankful you ought to be! 'It is not generally known,' Johnny,"—he was now referring to the screen again,—" 'but it is a fact ascertained, by accurate calculations, that the following immense percentage of babies never attain to two years old; that is to say—' "

"Oh, don't, father, please!" cried Johnny. "I can't bear it, when I think of Sally."

Mr. Tetterby desisting, Johnny, with a profounder sense of his trust, wiped his eyes, and hushed his sister.

"Your brother 'Dolphus," said his father, poking the fire, "is late tonight, Johnny, and will come home like a lump of ice. What's got your precious mother?"

"Here's mother, and 'Dolphus, too, father!" exclaimed Johnny, "I think."

"You're right!" returned his father, listening. "Yes, that's the footstep of my little woman."

The process of induction, by which Mr. Tetterby had come to the conclusion that his wife was a little woman, was his own secret. She would have made two editions of himself, very easily. Considered as an individual, she was rather remarkable for being robust and portly; but considered with reference to her husband, her dimensions became magnificent. Nor did they assume a less imposing proportion when studied with reference to the size of her seven sons, who were but diminutive. In the case of Sally, however, Mrs. Tetterby had asserted herself, at last; as nobody knew better than the victim Johnny, who weighed and measured that exacting idol every hour in the day.

Mrs. Tetterby, who had been marketing, and carried a basket, threw back her bonnet and shawl, and sitting down, fatigued, commanded Johnny to bring his sweet charge to her straightway, for a kiss. Johnny having complied, and gone back to his stool, and again crushed himself, Master Adolphus Tetterby, who had by this time unwound his torso out of a prismatic comforter, apparently interminable, requested the same favour. Johnny having again complied, and again gone back to his stool, and again crushed himself, Mr. Tetterby, struck by a sudden thought, preferred the same claim on his own parental part. The satisfaction of this third desire completely exhausted the sacrifice, who had hardly breath enough left to get back to his stool, crush himself again, and pant at his relations.

"Whatever you do, Johnny," said Mrs. Tetterby, shaking her head, "take care of her, or never look your mother in the face again."

"Nor your brother," said Adolphus.

"Nor your father, Johnny," added Mr. Tetterby.

Johnny, much affected by this conditional renunciation of him, looked down at Moloch's eyes to see that they were all right, so far, and skilfully patted her back (which was uppermost), and rocked her with his foot.

"Are you wet, 'Dolphus, my boy?" said his father. "Come and take my chair, and dry yourself."

"No, father, thankee," said Adolphus, smoothing himself down with his hands. "I ain't very wet, I don't think. Does my face shine much, father?"

"Well, it *does* look waxy, my boy," returned Mr. Tetterby.

"It's the weather, father," said Adolphus, polishing his cheeks on the worn sleeve of his jacket. "What with rain, and sleet, and wind, and snow, and fog, my face gets quite brought out into a rash some-times. And shines, it does—oh, don't it, though!"

Master Adolphus was also in the newspaper line of life, being employed, by a more thriving firm than his father and Co., to vend newspapers at a railway station, where his chubby little person, like a shabbily disguised Cupid, and his shrill little voice (he was not much more than ten years old), were as well known as the hoarse panting of the locomotives, running in and out. His juvenility might have been at some loss for a harmless outlet in this early application to traffic, but for a fortunate discovery he made of a means of entertain-ing himself, and of dividing the long day into stages of interest, without neglecting business. This ingenious invention, remarkable, like many great discoveries, for its simplicity, consisted in varying the first vowel in the word "paper," and substituting in its stead, at different periods of the day, all the other vowels in grammatical succession. Thus, before daylight in the winter-time, he went to and fro, in his little oilskin cap and cape, and his big comforter, piercing the heavy air with his cry of "Morn-ing Pa-per!" which, about an hour before noon, changed to "Morn-ing Pep-per!" which, at about two, changed to "Morn-ing Pip-per;" which, in a couple of hours, changed to "Morn-ing Pop-per!" and so declined with the sun into "Eve-ning Pup-per!" to the great relief and comfort of this young gentleman's spirits.

Mrs. Tetterby, his lady-mother, who had been sitting with her bonnet and shawl thrown back, as aforesaid, thoughtfully turning her wedding ring round and round upon her finger, now rose, and, divesting herself of her out-of-door attire, began to lay the cloth for supper.

"Ah, dear me, dear me, dear me!" said Mrs. Tetterby. "That's the way the world goes!"

"Which is the way the world goes, my dear?" asked Mr. Tetterby, looking round.

"Oh, nothing," said Mrs. Tetterby.

Mr. Tetterby elevated his eyebrows, folded his newspaper afresh, and carried his eyes up it, and down it, and across it, but was wandering in his attention, and not reading it.

Mrs. Tetterby, at the same time, laid the cloth, but rather as if she were punishing the table than preparing the family supper; hitting it unnecessarily hard with the knives and forks, slapping it with the plates, dinting it with the salt-cellar, and coming heavily down upon it with the loaf.

"Ah, dear me, dear me, dear me!" said Mrs. Tetterby. "That's the way the world goes!"

"My duck," returned her husband, looking round again, "you said that before. Which is the way the world goes?"

"Oh, nothing," said Mrs. Tetterby.

"Sophia!" remonstrated her husband, "you said *that* before, too."

"Well, I'll say it again if you like," returned Mrs. Tetterby. "Oh, nothing—there! And again if you like, oh, nothing—there! And again if you like, oh, nothing—now then!"

Mr. Tetterby brought his eye to bear upon the partner of his bosom, and said, in mild astonishment:—

"My little woman, what has put you out?"

"I'm sure *I* don't know," she retorted. "Don't ask me. Who said I was put out at all? *I* never did."

Mr. Tetterby gave up the perusal of his newspaper as a bad job, and taking a slow walk across the room, with his hands behind him, and his shoulders raised,—his gait according perfectly with the resignation of his manner,—addressed himself to his two eldest offspring.

"Your supper will be ready in a minute, 'Dolphus," said Mr. Tetterby. "Your mother has been out in the wet, to the cook's shop, to buy it. It was very good of your mother so to do. *You* shall get some supper too, very soon, Johnny. Your mother's pleased with you, my man, for being so attentive to your precious sister."

Mrs. Tetterby, without any remark, but with a decided subsidence of her animosity towards the table, finished her preparations, and took, from her ample basket, a substantial slab of hot pease pudding wrapped in paper, and a basin covered with a saucer, which, on being uncovered, sent forth an odour so agreeable, that the three pair of eyes in the two beds opened wide and fixed themselves upon the banquet. Mr. Tetterby, without regarding this tacit invitation to be seated, stood repeating slowly, "Yes, yes, your supper will be ready in a minute, 'Dolphus—your mother went out in the wet, to the cook's shop, to buy it. It was very good of your mother so to do,"—until Mrs. Tetterby, who had been exhibiting sundry tokens of contrition behind him, caught him round the neck, and wept.

"Oh, 'Dolphus!" said Mrs. Tetterby, "how could I go and behave so!"

This reconciliation affected Adolphus the younger and Johnny to that degree, that they both, as with one accord, raised a dismal cry, which had the effect of immediately shutting up the round eyes in the beds, and utterly routing the two remaining little Tetterbys, just then stealing in from the adjoining closet to see what was going on in the eating way.

"I am sure, 'Dolphus," sobbed Mrs. Tetterby, "coming home, I had no more idea than a child unborn—"

Mr. Tetterby seemed to dislike this figure of speech, and observed, "Say than the baby, my dear."

"—had no more idea than the baby," said Mrs. Tetterby,— "Johnny, don't look at me, but look at her, or she'll fall out of your lap and be killed, and then you'll die in agonies of a broken heart, and serve you right.—No more idea I hadn't than that darling, of being cross when I came home; but somehow, 'Dolphus"—Mrs. Tetterby paused, and again turned her wedding-ring round and round upon her finger.

"I see!" said Mr. Tetterby. "I understand! My little woman was put out. Hard times, and hard weather, and hard work make it trying now and then. I see, bless your soul! No wonder! Dolf, my man," continued Mr. Tetterby, exploring the basin with a fork, "here's your mother been and bought, at the cook's shop, besides pease pudding, a whole knuckle of a lovely roast leg of pork, with lots of crackling left upon it, and with seasoning gravy and mustard quite unlimited. Hand in your plate, my boy, and begin while it's simmering."

Master Adolphus, needing no second summons, received his portion with eyes rendered moist by appetite, and withdrawing to his particular stool, fell upon his supper tooth and nail. Johnny was not forgotten, but received his rations on bread, lest he should, in a flush of gravy, trickle any on the baby. He was required, for similar reasons, to keep his pudding, when not on active service, in his pocket.

There might have been more pork on the knucklebone,—which knucklebone the carver at the cook's shop had assuredly not forgotten in carving for previous customers,—but there was no stint of seasoning, and that is an accessory dreamily suggesting pork, and pleasantly cheating the sense of taste. The pease pudding, too, the gravy and mustard, like the Eastern rose in respect of the nightingale, if they were not absolutely pork, had lived near it; so, upon the whole, there was the flavour of a middle-sized pig. It was irresistible to the Tetterbys in bed, who, though professing to slumber peacefully, crawled out when unseen by their parents, and silently appealed to their brothers for any gastronomic token of fraternal affection. They, not hard of heart, presenting scraps in return, it resulted that a party of light skirmishers in nightgowns were careering about the parlour all through supper, which harassed Mr. Tetterby exceedingly, and once or twice imposed upon him the necessity of a charge, before which these guerilla troops retired in all directions and in great confusion.

Mrs. Tetterby did not enjoy her supper. There seemed to be something on Mrs. Tetterby's mind. At one time she laughed without reason, and at another time she cried without reason, and at last she laughed and cried together in a manner so very unreasonable that her husband was confounded.

"My little woman," said Mr. Tetterby, "if the world goes that way, it appears to go the wrong way, and to choke you."

"Give me a drop of water," said Mrs. Tetterby, struggling with herself, "and don't speak to me for the present, or take any notice of me. Don't do it!"

Mr. Tetterby, having administered the water, turned suddenly on the unlucky Johnny (who was full of sympathy), and demanded why he was wallowing there, in gluttony and idleness, instead of coming forward with the baby, that the sight of her might revive his mother. Johnny immediately approached, borne down by its weight; but Mrs. Tetterby holding out her hand to signify that she was not in a condition to bear that trying appeal to her feelings, he was interdicted from advancing another inch, on pain of perpetual hatred from all his dearest connections; and accordingly retired to his stool again, and crushed himself as before.

After a pause, Mrs. Tetterby said she was better now, and began to laugh.

"My little woman," said her husband dubiously, "are you quite sure you're better? Or are you, Sophia, about to break out in a fresh direction?"

"No, 'Dolphus, no," replied his wife. "I'm quite myself." With that, settling her hair, and pressing the palms of her hands upon her eyes, she laughed again.

"What a wicked fool I was, to think so for a moment," said Mrs. Tetterby. "Come nearer, 'Dolphus, and let me ease my mind, and tell you what I mean. Let me tell you all about it."

Mr. Tetterby bringing his chair closer, Mrs. Tetterby laughed again, gave him a hug, and wiped her eyes.

"You know, 'Dolphus, my dear," said Mrs. Tetterby, "that when I was single, I might have given myself away in several directions. At one time, four after me at once; two of them were sons of Mars."

"We're all sons of Ma's, my dear," said Mr. Tetterby, "jointly with Pa's."

"I don't mean that," replied his wife, "I mean soldiers—serjeants."

"Oh!" said Mr. Tetterby.

"Well, 'Dolphus, I'm sure I never think of such things now, to regret them; and I'm sure I've got as good a husband, and would do as much to prove that I was fond of him, as—"

"As any little woman in the world," said Mr. Tetterby. "Very good. *Very* good."

If Mr. Tetterby had been ten feet high, he could not have expressed a greater consideration for Mrs. Tetterby's fairy-like stature; and if Mrs. Tetterby had been two feet high, she could not have felt it more appropriately her due.

"But you see, 'Dolphus," said Mrs. Tetterby, "this being Christmas-time, when all people who can, make holiday, and when all people who have got money, like to spend some, I did, somehow, get a little out of sorts when I was in the streets just now. There were so many things to be sold—such delicious things to eat, such fine things to look at, such delightful things to have—and there was so much calculating and calculating necessary, before I durst lay out a sixpence for the commonest thing; and the basket was so large, and wanted so much in it; and my stock of money was so small, and would go such a little way;—you hate me, don't you, 'Dolphus?"

"Not quite," said Mr. Tetterby, "as yet."

"Well! I'll tell you the whole truth," pursued his wife penitently, "and then perhaps you will. I felt all this, so much, when I was trudging about in the cold, and when I saw a lot of other calculating faces and large baskets trudging about, too, that I began to think whether I mightn't have done better, and been happier, if—I—hadn't''—the wedding-ring went round again, and Mrs. Tetterby shook her downcast head as she turned it.

"I see," said her husband quietly; "if you hadn't married at all, or if you had married somebody else?"

"Yes," sobbed Mrs. Tetterby. "That's really what I thought. Do you hate me now, 'Dolphus?"

"Why, no," said Mr. Tetterby, "I don't find that I do as yet."

Mrs. Tetterby gave him a thankful kiss, and went on.

"I begin to hope you won't, now, 'Dolphus, though I am afraid I haven't told you the worst. I can't think what came over me. I don't know whether I was ill, or mad, or what I was, but I couldn't call up anything that seemed to bind us to each other, or to reconcile me to my fortune. All the pleasures and enjoyments we had ever had—*they* seemed so poor and insignificant, I hated them. I could have trodden on them. And I could think of nothing else except our being poor, and the number of mouths there were at home."

"Well, well, my dear," said Mr. Tetterby, shaking her hand encouragingly, "that's truth, after all. We *are* poor, and there *are* a number of mouths at home here."

"Ah! but, Dolf, Dolf!" cried his wife, laying her hands upon his neck, "my good, kind, patient fellow, when I had been at home a very little while—how different! Oh, Dolf, dear, how different it was! I felt as if there was a rush of recollection on me, all at once, that softened my hard heart, and filled it up till it was bursting. All our struggles for a livelihood, all our cares and wants since we have been married, all the times of sickness, all the hours of watching, we have ever had, by one another, or by the children, seemed to speak to me, and say that they had made us one, and that I never might have been, or could have been, or would have been, any other than the wife and mother I am. Then, the cheap enjoyments that I could have trodden on so cruelly, got to be so precious to me—oh, so priceless, and dear!—that I couldn't bear to think how much I had wronged them; and I said, and say again a hundred times, how could I ever behave so, 'Dolphus, how could I ever have the heart to do it!"

The good woman, quite carried away by her honest tenderness and remorse, was weeping with all her heart, when she started up with a scream, and ran behind her husband. Her cry was so terrified, that the children started from their sleep and from their beds, and clung about her. Nor did her gaze belie her voice, as she pointed to a pale man in a black cloak who had come into the room.

"Look at that man! Look there! What does he want?"

"My dear," returned her husband, "I'll ask him if you'll let me go. What's the matter? How you shake!"

"I saw him in the street when I was out just now. He looked at me, and stood near me. I am afraid of him."

"Afraid of him! Why?"

"I don't know why—I—stop! husband!" for he was going towards the stranger.

She had one hand pressed upon her forehead, and one upon her breast; and there was a peculiar fluttering all over her, and a hurried, unsteady motion of her eyes, as if she had lost something.

"Are you ill, my dear?"

"What is it that is going from me again?" she muttered in a low voice. "What *is* this that is going away?"

Then she abruptly answered, "Ill? No, I am quite well," and stood looking vacantly at the floor.

Her husband, who had not been altogether free from the infection of her fear at first, and whom the present strangeness of her manner did not tend to reassure, addressed himself to the pale visitor in the black cloak, who stood still, and whose eyes were bent upon the ground.

"What may be your pleasure, sir," he asked, "with us?"

"I fear that my coming in unperceived," returned the visitor, "has alarmed you; but you were talking and did not hear me."

"My little woman says—perhaps you heard her say it," returned

Mr. Tetterby, "that it's not the first time you have alarmed her to-night."

"I am sorry for it. I remember to have observed her, for a few moments only, in the street. I had no intention of frightening her."

As he raised his eyes in speaking, she raised hers. It was extraordinary to see what dread she had of him, and with what dread he observed it—and yet how narrowly and closely.

"My name," he said, "is Redlaw. I come from the old college hard by. A young gentleman who is a student there, lodges in your house, does he not?"

"Mr. Denham?" said Tetterby.

"Yes."

It was a natural action, and so slight as to be hardly noticeable; but the little man, before speaking again, passed his hand across his forehead, and looked quickly round the room, as though he were sensible of some change in its atmosphere. The Chemist, instantly transferring to him the look of dread he had directed towards the wife, stepped back, and his face turned paler.

"The gentleman's room," said Tetterby, "is up stairs, sir. There's a more convenient private entrance; but as you have come in here, it will save your going out into the cold, if you'll take this little staircase," showing one communicating directly with the parlour, "and go up to him that way, if you wish to see him."

"Yes, I wish to see him," said the Chemist. "Can you spare a light?"

The watchfulness of his haggard look, and the inexplicable distrust that darkened it, seemed to trouble Mr. Tetterby. He paused; and looking fixedly at him in return, stood for a minute or so, like a man stupefied or fascinated.

At length he said, "I'll light you, sir, if you'll follow me."

"No," replied the Chemist, "I don't wish to be attended, or announced to him. He does not expect me. I would rather go alone. Please to give me the light, if you can spare it, and I'll find the way."

In the quickness of his expression of this desire, and in taking the candle from the newsman, he touched him on the breast. Withdrawing his hand hastily, almost as though he had wounded him by accident (for he did not know in what part of himself his new power resided, or how it was communicated, or how the manner of its reception varied in different persons), he turned and ascended the stair.

But when he reached the top, he stopped and looked down. The wife was standing in the same place, twisting her ring round and round upon her finger. The husband, with his head bent forward on his breast, was musing heavily and sullenly. The children, still clustering about the mother, gazed timidly after the visitor, and nestled together when they saw him looking down.

"Come!" said the father roughly. "There's enough of this. Get to bed here!"

"The place is inconvenient and small enough," the mother added, "without you. Get to bed!"

The whole brood, scared and sad, crept away; little Johnny and the baby lagging last. The mother, glancing contemptuously round the sordid room, and tossing from her the fragments of their meal, stopped on the threshold of her task of clearing the table, and sat down, pondering idly and dejectedly. The father betook himself to the chimney corner, and impatiently raking the small fire together, bent over it as if he would monopolise it all. They did not interchange a word.

The Chemist, paler than before, stole upward like a thief; looking back upon the change below, and dreading equally to go on or return.

"What have I done!" he said confusedly. "What am I going to do!"

"To be the benefactor of mankind," he thought he heard a voice reply.

He looked round, but there was nothing there; and a passage now shutting out the little parlour from his view, he went on, directing his eyes before him at the way he went.

"It is only since last night," he muttered gloomily, "that I have remained shut up, and yet all things are strange to me. I am strange to myself. I am here, as in a dream. What interest have I in this place, or in any place that I can bring to my remembrance? My mind is going blind!"

There was a door before him, and he knocked at it. Being invited, by a voice within, to enter, he complied.

"Is that my kind nurse?" said the voice. "But I need not ask her. There is no one else to come here."

It spoke cheerfully, though in a languid tone, and attracted his attention to a young man lying on a couch, drawn before the chimney-piece, with the back towards the door. A meagre, scanty stove, pinched and hollowed like a sick man's cheeks, and bricked into the centre of a hearth that it could scarcely warm, contained the fire, to which his face was turned. Being so near the windy housetop, it wasted quickly, and with a busy sound, and the burning ashes dropped down fast.

"They chink when they shoot out here," said the student, smiling; "so, according to the gossips, they are not coffins, but purses. I shall be well and rich yet, some day, if it please God, and shall live perhaps to love a daughter Milly, in remembrance of the kindest nature and the gentlest heart in the world."

He put up his hand as if expecting her to take it, but, being weakened, he lay still, with his face resting on his other hand, and did not turn round.

The Chemist glanced about the room;—at the student's books and papers, piled upon a table in a corner, where they, and his extinguished reading-lamp, now prohibited and put away, told of the attentive hours that had gone before this illness, and perhaps caused it;—at such signs of his old health and freedom, as the out-of-door attire that hung idle on the wall;—at those remembrances of other and less solitary scenes, the little miniatures upon the chimney-piece, and the drawing of home;—at that token of his emulation, perhaps, in some sort, of his personal attachment too, the framed engraving of himself, the looker-on. The time had been, only yesterday, when not one of these objects, in its remotest association of interest with the living figure before him, would have been lost on Redlaw. Now, they were but objects; or, if any gleam of such connection shot upon him, it perplexed, and not enlightened him, as he stood looking round with a dull wonder.

The student, recalling the thin hand which had remained so long untouched, raised himself on the couch, and turned his head.

"Mr. Redlaw!" he exclaimed, and started up.

Redlaw put out his arm.

"Don't come near to me. I will sit here. Remain you, where you are!"

He sat down on a chair near the door, and having glanced at the young man standing leaning with his hand upon the couch, spoke with his eyes averted towards the ground.

"I heard, by an accident, by what accident is no matter, that one of my class was ill and solitary. I received no other description of him, than that he lived in this street. Beginning my inquiries at the first house in it, I have found him."

"I have been ill, sir," returned the student, not merely with a modest hesitation, but with a kind of awe of him, "but am greatly better. An attack of fever—of the brain, I believe—has weakened me, but I am much better. I cannot say I have been solitary in my illness, or I should forget the ministering hand that has been near me."

"You are speaking of the keeper's wife," said Redlaw.

"Yes." The student bent his head, as if he rendered her some silent homage.

The Chemist, in whom there was a cold, monotonous apathy, which rendered him more like a marble image on the tomb of the man who had started from his dinner yesterday at the first mention of this student's case, than the breathing man himself, glanced again at the student leaning with his hand upon the couch, and looked upon the ground, and in the air, as if for light for his blinded mind.

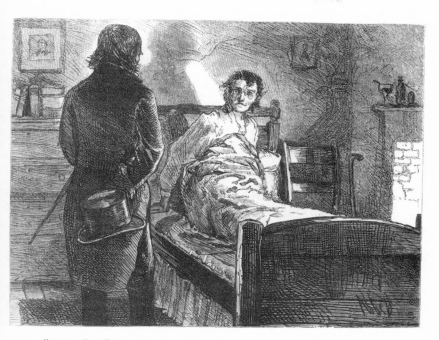

"Mr. Redlaw!" he exclaimed, and started up. —by E. A. Abbey

"I remembered your name," he said, "when it was mentioned to me down stairs, just now; and I recollect your face. We have held but very little personal communication together?"

"Very little."

"You have retired and withdrawn from me, more than any of the rest, I think?"

The student signified assent.

"And why?" said the Chemist; not with the least expression of interest, but with a moody, wayward kind of curiosity. "Why? How comes it that you have sought to keep, especially from me, the knowledge of your remaining here, at this season, when all the rest have dispersed, and of your being ill? I want to know why this is."

The young man, who had heard him with increasing agitation, raised his downcast eyes to his face, and clasping his hands together, cried with sudden earnestness, and with trembling lips:—

"Mr. Redlaw! You have discovered me. You know my secret!"

"Secret?" said the Chemist harshly. "*I* know?"

"Yes! Your manner, so different from the interest and sympathy which endear you to so many hearts, your altered voice, the constraint there is in everything you say, and in your looks," replied the student, "warn me that you know me. That you would conceal it, even now, is but a proof to me (God knows I need none!) of your natural kindness, and of the bar there is between us."

A vacant and contemptuous laugh was all his answer.

"But, Mr. Redlaw," said the student, "as a just man, and a good man, think how innocent I am, except in name and descent, of participation in any wrong inflicted on you, or in any sorrow you have borne."

"Sorrow!" said Redlaw, laughing. "Wrong! What are those to me?"

"For Heaven's sake," entreated the shrinking student, "do not let the mere interchange of a few words with me change you like this, sir! Let me pass again from your knowledge and notice. Let me occupy my old reserved and distant place among those whom you

instruct. Know me only by the name I have assumed, and not by that
of Longford—"

"Longford!" exclaimed the other.

He clasped his head with both his hands, and for a moment
turned upon the young man his own intelligent and thoughtful face.
But the light passed from it, like the sunbeam of an instant, and it
clouded as before.

"The name my mother bears, sir," faltered the young man; "the
name she took, when she might, perhaps, have taken one more honoured. Mr. Redlaw," hesitating, "I believe I know that history.
Where my information halts, my guesses at what is wanting may
supply something not remote from the truth. I am the child of a
marriage that has not proved itself a well assorted or a happy one.
From infancy, I have heard you spoken of with honour and respect—
with something that was almost reverence. I have heard of such
devotion, of such fortitude and tenderness, of such rising up against
the obstacles which press men down, that my fancy, since I learnt my
little lesson from my mother, has shed a lustre on your name. At last,
a poor student myself, from whom could I learn but you?"

Redlaw, unmoved, unchanged, and looking at him with a staring
frown, answered by no word or sign.

"I cannot say," pursued the other, "I should try in vain to say,
how much it has impressed me, and affected me, to find the gracious
traces of the past, in that certain power of winning gratitude and
confidence which is associated among us students (among the hum-
blest of us, most) with Mr. Redlaw's generous name. Our ages and
positions are so different, sir, and I am so accustomed to regard you
from a distance, that I wonder at my own presumption when I touch,
however lightly, on that theme. But to one who—I may say, who felt
no common interest in my mother once—it may be something to
hear, now that is all past, with what indescribable feelings of affection
I have, in my obscurity, regarded him; with what pain and reluctance
I have kept aloof from his encouragement, when a word of it would
have made me rich; yet how I have felt it fit that I should hold my

course, content to know him, and to be unknown. Mr. Redlaw," said the student faintly, "what I would have said, I have said ill, for my strength is strange to me as yet; but for anything unworthy in this fraud of mine, forgive me, and for all the rest forget me!"

The staring frown remained on Redlaw's face, and yielded to no other expression until the student, with these words, advanced towards him, as if to touch his hand, when he drew back and cried to him:—

"Don't come nearer to me!"

The young man stopped, shocked by the eagerness of his recoil, and by the sternness of his repulsion; and he passed his hand, thoughtfully, across his forehead.

"The past is past," said the Chemist. "It dies like the brutes. Who talks to me of its traces in my life? He raves or lies! What have I to do with your distempered dreams? If you want money, here it is. I came to offer it; and that is all I came for. There can be nothing else that brings me here," he muttered, holding his head again, with both his hands. "There *can* be nothing else, and yet—"

He had tossed his purse upon the table. As he fell into this dim cogitation with himself, the student took it up, and held it out to him.

"Take it back, sir," he said proudly, though not angrily. "I wish you could take from me, with it, the remembrance of your words and offer."

"You do?" he retorted, with a wild light in his eyes. "You do?"

"I do!"

The Chemist went close to him, for the first time, and took the purse, and turned him by the arm, and looked him in the face.

"There is sorrow and trouble in sickness, is there not?" he demanded, with a laugh.

The wondering student answered, "Yes."

"In its unrest, in its anxiety, in its suspense, in all its train of physical and mental miseries?" said the Chemist, with a wild, unearthly exultation. "All best forgotten, are they not?"

The student did not answer, but again passed his hand, confusedly, across his forehead. Redlaw still held him by the sleeve, when Milly's voice was heard outside.

"I can see very well now," she said, "thank you, Dolf. Don't cry, dear. Father and mother will be comfortable again, to-morrow, and home will be comfortable, too. A gentleman with him, is there!"

Redlaw released his hold, as he listened.

"I have feared, from the first moment," he murmured to himself, "to meet her. There is a steady quality of goodness in her that I dread to influence. I may be the murderer of what is tenderest and best within her bosom."

She was knocking at the door.

"Shall I dismiss it as an idle foreboding, or still avoid her?" he muttered, looking uneasily around.

She was knocking at the door again.

"Of all the visitors who could come here," he said, in a hoarse, alarmed voice, turning to his companion, "this is the one I should desire most to avoid. Hide me!"

The student opened a frail door in the wall, communicating, where the garret roof began to slope towards the floor, with a small inner room. Redlaw passed in hastily, and shut it after him.

The student then resumed his place upon the couch, and called to her to enter.

"Dear Mr. Edmund," said Milly, looking round, "they told me there was a gentleman here."

"There is no one here but I."

"There has been some one?"

"Yes, yes, there has been some one."

She put her little basket on the table, and went up to the back of the couch, as if to take the extended hand—but it was not there. A little surprised, in her quiet way, she leaned over to look at his face, and gently touched him on the brow.

"Are you quite as well to-night? Your head is not so cool as in the afternoon."

"Tut!" said the student petulantly, "very little ails me."

A little more surprise, but no reproach, was expressed in her face, as she withdrew to the other side of the table, and took a small packet of needle-work from her basket. But she laid it down again, on second thoughts, and, going noiselessly about the room, set everything exactly in its place, and in the neatest order; even to the cushions on the couch, which she touched with so light a hand that he hardly seemed to know it, as he lay looking at the fire. When all this was done, and she had swept the hearth, she sat down, in her modest little bonnet, to her work, and was quietly busy on it directly.

"It's the new muslin curtain for the window, Mr. Edmund," said Milly, stitching away as she talked. "It will look very clean and nice, though it costs very little, and will save your eyes, too, from the light. My William says the room should not be too light just now, when you are recovering so well, or the glare might make you giddy."

He said nothing; but there was something so fretful and impatient in his change of position that her quick fingers stopped, and she looked at him anxiously.

"The pillows are not comfortable," she said, laying down her work and rising. "I will soon put them right."

"They are very well," he answered. "Leave them alone, pray. You make so much of everything."

He raised his head to say this, and looked at her so thanklessly that, after he had thrown himself down again, she stood timidly pausing. However, she resumed her seat, and her needle, without having directed even a murmuring look towards him, and was soon as busy as before.

"I have been thinking, Mr. Edmund, that *you* have been often thinking of late, when I have been sitting by, how true the saying is that adversity is a good teacher. Health will be more precious to you, after this illness, than it has ever been. And years hence, when this time of year comes round, and you remember the days when you lay here sick, alone, that the knowledge of your illness might not afflict those who are dearest to you, your home will be doubly dear and doubly blest. Now, isn't that a good, true thing?"

She was too intent upon her work, and too earnest in what she said, and too composed and quiet altogether, to be on the watch for any look he might direct towards her in reply; so the shaft of his ungrateful glance fell harmless, and did not wound her.

"Ah!" said Milly, with her pretty head inclining thoughtfully on one side, as she looked down, following her busy fingers with her eyes. "Even on me—and I am very different from you, Mr. Edmund, for I have no learning, and don't know how to think properly—this view of such things has made a great impression, since you have been lying ill. When I have seen you so touched by the kindness and attention of the poor people down stairs, I have felt that you thought even that experience some repayment for the loss of health, and I have read in your face, as plain as if it was a book, that but for some trouble and sorrow we should never know half the good there is about us."

His getting up from the couch interrupted her, or she was going on to say more.

"We needn't magnify the merit, Mrs. William," he rejoined slightingly. "The people down stairs will be paid in good time, I dare say, for any little extra service they may have rendered me; and perhaps they anticipate no less. I am much obliged to you, too."

Her fingers stopped, and she looked at him.

"I can't be made to feel the more obliged by your exaggerating the case," he said. "I am sensible that you have been interested in me, and I say I am much obliged to you. What more would you have?"

Her work fell on her lap, as she still looked at him walking to and fro with an intolerant air, and stopping now and then.

"I say again, I am much obliged to you. Why weaken my sense of what is your due in obligation, by preferring enormous claims upon me? Trouble, sorrow, affliction, adversity! One might suppose I had been dying a score of deaths here!"

"Do you believe, Mr. Edmund," she asked, rising and going nearer to him, "that I spoke of the poor people of the house, with any reference to myself? To me?" laying her hand upon her bosom with a simple and innocent smile of astonishment.

"Oh! I think nothing about it, my good creature," he returned. "I have had an indisposition, which your solicitude—observe! I say solicitude—makes a great deal more of than it merits; and it's over, and we can't perpetuate it."

He coldly took a book and sat down at the table.

She watched him for a little while, until her smile was quite gone, and then, returning to where her basket was, said gently:—

"Mr. Edmund, would you rather be alone?"

"There is no reason why I should detain you here," he replied.

"Except—" said Milly, hesitating, and showing her work.

"Oh! the curtain," he answered, with a supercilious laugh. "That's not worth staying for."

She made up the little packet again, and put it in her basket. Then, standing before him with such an air of patient entreaty that he could not choose but look at her, she said:—

"If you should want me, I will come back willingly. When you did want me, I was quite happy to come; there was no merit in it. I think you must be afraid that, now you are getting well, I may be troublesome to you; but I should not have been, indeed. I should have come no longer than your weakness and confinement lasted. You owe me nothing; but it is right that you should deal as justly by me as if I was a lady—even the very lady that you love; and if you suspect me of meanly making much of the little I have tried to do to comfort your sick room, you do yourself more wrong than ever you can do me. That is why I am sorry. That is why I am very sorry."

If she had been as passionate as she was quiet, as indignant as she was calm, as angry in her look as she was gentle, as loud of tone as she was low and clear, she might have left no sense of her departure in the room, compared with that which fell upon the lonely student when she went away.

He was gazing drearily upon the place where she had been, when Redlaw came out of his concealment, and came to the door.

"When sickness lays its hand on you again," he said, looking fiercely back at him, "—may it be soon!—Die here! Rot here!"

"What have you done?" returned the other, catching at his cloak. "What change have you wrought in me? What curse have you brought upon me? Give me back myself!"

"Give me back *my*self!" exclaimed Redlaw, like a madman. "I am infected! I am infectious! I am charged with poison for my own mind, and the minds of all mankind. Where I felt interest, compassion, sympathy, I am turning into stone. Selfishness and ingratitude spring up in my blighting footsteps. I am only so much less base than the wretches whom I make so, that in the moment of their transformation I can hate them."

As he spoke—the young man still holding to his cloak—he cast him off, and struck him; then wildly hurried out into the night air where the wind was blowing, the snow falling, the cloud-drift sweeping on, the moon dimly shining; and where, blowing in the wind, falling with the snow, drifting with the clouds, shining in the moonlight, and heavily looming in the darkness, were the Phantom's words, "The gift that I have given, you shall give again, go where you will!"

Whither he went he neither knew nor cared, so that he avoided company. The change he felt within him made the busy streets a desert, and himself a desert, and the multitude around him, in their manifold endurances and ways of life, a mighty waste of sand, which the winds tossed into unintelligible heaps and made a ruinous confusion of. Those traces in his breast which the Phantom had told him would "die out soon" were not, as yet, so far upon their way to death, but that he understood enough of what he was, and what he made of others, to desire to be alone.

This put it in his mind—he suddenly bethought himself, as he was going along, of the boy who had rushed into his room. And then he recollected that, of those with whom he had communicated since the Phantom's disappearance, that boy alone had shown no sign of being changed.

Monstrous and odious as the wild thing was to him, he determined to seek it out, and prove if this were really so; and also to seek it with another intention, which came into his thoughts at the same time.

So, resolving with some difficulty where he was, he directed his steps back to the old college, and to that part of it where the general porch was, and where, alone, the pavement was worn by the tread of the students' feet.

The keeper's house stood just within the iron gates, forming a part of the chief quadrangle. There was a little cloister outside, and from that sheltered place he knew he could look in at the window of their ordinary room, and see who was within. The iron gates were shut, but his hand was familiar with the fastening, and, drawing it back by thrusting in his wrist between the bars, he passed through softly, shut it again, and crept up to the window, crumbling the thin crust of snow with his feet.

The fire, to which he had directed the boy last night, shining brightly through the glass, made an illuminated place upon the ground. Instinctively avoiding this, and going round it, he looked in at the window. At first, he thought that there was no one there, and that the blaze was reddening only the old beams in the ceiling and the dark walls; but peering in more narrowly, he saw the object of his search coiled asleep before it on the floor. He passed quickly to the door, opened it, and went in.

The creature lay in such a fiery heat that, as the Chemist stooped to rouse him, it scorched his head. So soon as he was touched, the boy, not half awake, clutched his rags together with the instinct of flight upon him, half rolled and half ran into a distant corner of the room, where, heaped upon the ground, he struck his foot out to defend himself.

"Get up!" said the Chemist. "You have not forgotten me?"

"You let me alone!" returned the boy. "This is the woman's house—not yours."

The Chemist's steady eye controlled him somewhat, or inspired him with enough submission to be raised upon his feet, and looked at.

"Who washed them, and put those bandages where they were bruised and cracked?" asked the Chemist, pointing to their altered state.

"The woman did."

"And is it she who has made you cleaner in the face, too?"

"Yes; the woman."

Redlaw asked these questions to attract his eyes towards himself, and with the same intent now held him by the chin, and threw his wild hair back, though he loathed to touch him. The boy watched his eyes keenly, as if he thought it needful to his own defence, not knowing what he might do next; and Redlaw could see well that no change came over him.

"Where are they?" he inquired.

"The woman's out."

"I know she is. Where is the old man with the white hair, and his son?"

"The woman's husband, d'ye mean?" inquired the boy.

"Ay. Where are those two?"

"Out. Something's the matter, somewhere. They were fetched out in a hurry, and told me to stop here."

"Come with me," said the Chemist, "and I'll give you money."

"Come where? and how much will you give?"

"I'll give you more shillings than you ever saw, and bring you back soon. Do you know your way to where you came from?"

"You let me go," returned the boy, suddenly twisting out of his grasp. "I'm not a going to take you there. Let me be, or I'll heave some fire at you!"

He was down before it, and ready, with his savage little hand, to pluck the burning coals out.

What the Chemist had felt, in observing the effect of his charmed influence stealing over those with whom he came in contact, was not nearly equal to the cold, vague terror with which he saw this baby-monster put it at defiance. It chilled his blood to look on the immovable, impenetrable thing, in the likeness of a child, with its sharp, malignant face turned up to his, and its almost infant hand, ready at the bars.

"Listen, boy!" he said. "You shall take me where you please, so that you take me where the people are very miserable or very wicked. I want to do them good, and not to harm them. You shall have money, as I have told you, and I will bring you back. Get up! Come quickly!" He made a hasty step towards the door, afraid of her returning.

"Will you let me walk by myself, and never hold me, nor yet touch me?" said the boy, slowly withdrawing the hand with which he threatened, and beginning to get up.

"I will!"

"And let me go before, behind, or anyways I like?"

"I will!"

"Give me some money first, then, and I'll go."

The Chemist laid a few shillings, one by one, in his extended hand. To count them was beyond the boy's knowledge, but he said "one," every time, and avariciously looked at each as it was given, and at the donor. He had nowhere to put them, out of his hand, but in his mouth; and he put them there.

Redlaw then wrote with his pencil on a leaf of his pocket-book, that the boy was with him; and laying it on the table, signed to him to follow. Keeping his rags together, as usual, the boy complied, and went out with his bare head and his naked feet into the winter night.

Preferring not to depart by the iron gate by which he had entered, where they were in danger of meeting her whom he so anxiously avoided, the Chemist led the way, through some of those passages among which the boy had lost himself, and by that portion of the building where he lived, to a small door of which he had the key. When they got into the street, he stopped to ask his guide—who instantly retreated from him—if he knew where they were.

The savage thing looked here and there, and at length, nodding his head, pointed in the direction he designed to take. Redlaw going on at once, he followed, somewhat less suspiciously; shifting his money from his mouth into his hand, and back again into his mouth, and stealthily rubbing it bright upon his shreds of dress, as he went along.

Three times, in their progress, they were side by side. Three times they stopped, being side by side. Three times the Chemist glanced down at his face, and shuddered as it forced upon him one reflection.

The first occasion was when they were crossing an old church-yard, and Redlaw stopped among the graves, utterly at a loss how to connect them with any tender, softening, or consolatory thought.

The second was when the breaking forth of the moon induced him to look up at the Heavens, where he saw her in her glory, surrounded by a host of stars he still knew by the names and histories which human science has appended to them; but where he saw nothing else he had been wont to see, felt nothing he had been wont to feel, in looking up there, on a bright night.

The third was when he stopped to listen to a plaintive strain of music, but could only hear a tune, made manifest to him by the dry mechanism of the instruments and his own ears, with no address to any mystery within him, without a whisper in it of the past, or of the future, powerless upon him as the sound of last year's running water, or the rushing of last year's wind.

At each of these three times, he saw with horror that in spite of the vast intellectual distance between them, and their being unlike each other in all physical respects, the expression on the boy's face was the expression on his own.

They journeyed on for some time—now through such crowded

places that he often looked over his shoulder, thinking he had lost his guide, but generally finding him within his shadow on his other side; now by ways so quiet that he could have counted his short, quick, naked footsteps coming on behind—until they arrived at a ruinous collection of houses, and the boy touched him and stopped.

"In there!" he said, pointing out one house where there were scattered lights in the windows, and a dim lantern in the doorway, with "Lodgings for Travellers" painted on it.

Redlaw looked about him; from the houses to the waste piece of ground on which the houses stood, or rather did not altogether tumble down, unfenced, undrained, unlighted, and bordered by a sluggish ditch; from that to the sloping line of arches, part of some neighbouring viaduct or bridge with which it was surrounded, and which lessened gradually towards them, until the last but one was a mere kennel for a dog, the last a plundered little heap of bricks; from that to the child, close to him, cowering and trembling with the cold, and limping on one little foot, while he coiled the other round his leg to warm it, yet staring at all these things with that frightful likeness of expression, so apparent in his face, that Redlaw started from him.

"In there!" said the boy, pointing out the house again. "I'll wait."

"Will they let me in?" asked Redlaw.

"Say you're a doctor," he answered with a nod. "There's plenty ill here."

Looking back on his way to the house door, Redlaw saw him trail himself upon the dust and crawl within the shelter of the smallest arch, as if he were a rat. He had no pity for the thing, but he was afraid of it; and when it looked out of its den at him, he hurried to the house as a retreat.

"Sorrow, wrong, and trouble," said the Chemist, with a painful effort at some more distinct remembrance, "at least haunt this place, darkly. He can do no harm, who brings forgetfulness of such things here!"

With these words, he pushed the yielding door, and went in.

There was a woman sitting on the stairs, either asleep or forlorn, whose head was bent down on her hands and knees. As it was not easy to pass without treading on her, and as she was perfectly regardless of his near approach, he stopped, and touched her on the shoulder. Looking up, she showed him quite a young face, but one whose bloom and promise were all swept away, as if the haggard winter should unnaturally kill the spring.

With little or no show of concern on his account, she moved nearer to the wall to leave him a wider passage.

"What are you?" said Redlaw, pausing, with his hand upon the broken stair-rail.

"What do you think I am?" she answered, showing him her face again.

He looked upon the ruined temple of God, so lately made, so soon disfigured; and something, which was not compassion—for the springs in which a true compassion for such miseries has its rise were dried up in his breast—but which was nearer to it, for the moment, than any feeling that had lately struggled into the darkening, but not yet wholly darkened, night of his mind—mingled a touch of softness with his next words.

"I am come here to give relief, if I can," he said. "Are you thinking of any wrong?"

She frowned at him, and then laughed; and then her laugh prolonged itself into a shivering sigh, as she dropped her head again, and hid her fingers in her hair.

"Are you thinking of a wrong?" he asked, once more.

"I am thinking of my life," she said, with a momentary look at him.

He had a perception that she was one of many, and that he saw the type of thousands when he saw her, drooping at his feet.

"What are your parents?" he demanded.

"I had a good home once. My father was a gardener, far away, in the country."

"Is he dead?"

"He's dead to me. All such things are dead to me. You a gentleman, and not know that?" She raised her eyes again, and laughed at him.

"Girl!" said Redlaw sternly, "before this death, of all such things, was brought about, was there no wrong done to you? In spite of all that you can do, does no remembrance of wrong cleave to you? Are there not times upon times when it is misery to you?"

So little of what was womanly was left in her appearance, that now, when she burst into tears, he stood amazed. But he was more amazed, and much disquieted, to note that in her awakened recollection of this wrong, the first trace of her old humanity and frozen tenderness appeared to show itself.

He drew a little off, and in doing so, observed that her arms were black, her face cut, and her bosom bruised.

"What brutal hand has hurt you so?" he asked.

"My own. I did it myself!" she answered quickly.

"It is impossible."

"I'll swear I did! He didn't touch me. I did it to myself in a passion, and threw myself down here. He wasn't near me. He never laid a hand upon me!"

In the white determination of her face, confronting him with this untruth, he saw enough of the last perversion and distortion of good surviving in that miserable breast, to be stricken with remorse that he had ever come near her.

"Sorrow, wrong, and trouble!" he muttered, turning his fearful gaze away. "All that connects her with the state from which she has fallen has those roots! In the name of God, let me go by!"

Afraid to look at her again, afraid to touch her, afraid to think of having sundered the last thread by which she held upon the mercy of Heaven, he gathered his cloak about him, and glided swiftly up the stairs.

Opposite to him, on the landing, was a door, which stood partly open, and which, as he ascended, a man with a candle in his hand came forward from within to shut. But this man, on seeing him, drew back, with much emotion in his manner, and, as if by a sudden impulse, mentioned his name aloud.

In the surprise of such a recognition there, he stopped, endeavouring to recollect the wan and startled face. He had no time to consider it, for to his yet greater amazement, old Philip came out of the room, and took him by the hand.

"Mr. Redlaw," said the old man, "this is like you, this is like you, sir! you have heard of it, and have come after us to render any help you can. Ah, too late, too late!"

Redlaw, with a bewildered look, submitted to be led into the room. A man lay there, on a truckle-bed, and William Swidger stood at the bedside.

"Too late!" murmured the old man, looking wistfully into the Chemist's face; and the tears stole down his cheeks.

"That's what I say, father," interposed his son in a low voice. "That's where it is, exactly. To keep as quiet as ever we can while he's a dozing is the only thing to do. You're right, father!"

Redlaw paused at the bedside, and looked down on the figure that was stretched upon the mattress. It was that of a man, who should have been in the vigour of his life, but on whom it was not likely that the sun would ever shine again. The vices of his forty or fifty years' career had so branded him, that, in comparison with their effects upon his face, the heavy hand of time upon the old man's face who watched him had been merciful and beautifying.

"Who is this?" asked the Chemist, looking round.

"My son George, Mr. Redlaw," said the old man, wringing his hands. "My eldest son, George, who was more his mother's pride than all the rest!"

Redlaw's eyes wandered from the old man's grey head, as he laid it down upon the bed, to the person who had recognised him, and who had kept aloof, in the remotest corner of the room. He seemed to be about his own age; and although he knew no such hopeless decay and broken man as he appeared to be, there was something in the turn of his figure, as he stood with his back towards him, and now went out at the door, that made him pass his hand uneasily across his brow.

"William," he said in a gloomy whisper, "who is that man?"

"Why, you see, sir," returned Mr. William, "that's what I say, myself. Why should a man ever go and gamble, and the like of that, and let himself down inch by inch till he can't let himself down any lower!"

"Has *he* done so?" asked Redlaw, glancing after him with the same uneasy action as before.

"Just exactly that, sir," returned William Swidger, "as I'm told. He knows a little about medicine, sir, it seems; and having been wayfaring towards London with my unhappy brother that you see here," Mr. William passed his coat-sleeve across his eyes, "and being lodging up stairs for the night,—what I say, you see, is that strange companions come together here sometimes,—he looked in to attend upon him, and came for us at his request. What a mournful spectacle, sir! But that's where it is. It's enough to kill my father!"

Redlaw looked up, at these words, and, recalling where he was and with whom, and the spell he carried with him,—which his surprise had obscured,—retired a little, hurriedly, debating with himself whether to shun the house that moment or remain.

Yielding to a certain sullen doggedness, which it seemed to be part of his condition to struggle with, he argued for remaining.

"Was it only yesterday," he said, "when I observed the memory of this old man to be a tissue of sorrow and trouble, and shall I be afraid, to-night, to shake it? Are such remembrances as I can drive away so precious to this dying man that I need fear for *him?* No, I'll stay here."

But he stayed, in fear and trembling none the less for these words; and shrouded in his black cloak, with his face turned from them, stood away from the bedside, listening to what they said, as if he felt himself a demon in the place.

"Father!" murmured the sick man, rallying a little from his stupor.

"My boy! My son George!" said old Philip.

"You spoke, just now, of my being mother's favourite, long ago. It's a dreadful thing to think now of long ago!"

"No, no, no," returned the old man. "Think of it. Don't say it's dreadful. It's not dreadful to me, my son."

"It cuts you to the heart, father." For the old man's tears were falling on him.

"Yes, yes," said Philip, "so it does; but it does me good. It's a heavy sorrow to think of that time, but it does me good, George. Oh, think of it, too, think of it, too, and your heart will be softened more and more! Where's my son William? William, my boy, your mother loved him dearly to the last, and with her latest breath said, 'Tell him I forgave him, blessed him, and prayed for him.' Those were her words to me. I have never forgotten them, and I'm eighty-seven!"

"Father!" said the man upon the bed, "I am dying, I know. I am so far gone that I can hardly speak, even of what my mind most runs on. Is there any hope for me, beyond this bed?"

"There is hope," returned the old man, "for all who are softened and penitent. There is hope for all such. Oh!" he exclaimed, clasping his hands and looking up, "I was thankful, only yesterday, that I could remember this unhappy son when he was an innocent child. But what a comfort is it now to think that even God himself has that remembrance of him!"

Redlaw spread his hands upon his face, and shrunk like a murderer.

"Ah!" feebly moaned the man upon the bed. "The waste since then, the waste of life, since then!"

"But he was a child once," said the old man. "He played with children. Before he lay down on his bed at night, and fell into his guiltless rest, he said his prayers at his poor mother's knee. I have seen him do it, many a time; and seen her lay his head upon her breast, and kiss him. Sorrowful as it was to her, and to me, to think of this, when he went so wrong, and when our hopes and plans for him were all broken, this gave him still a hold upon us that nothing else could have given. O Father, so much better than the fathers upon earth! O Father, so much more afflicted by the errors of thy children! take this wanderer back! Not as he is, but as he was then, let him cry to thee, as he has so often seemed to cry to us!"

As the old man lifted up his trembling hands, the son, for whom he made the supplication, laid his sinking head against him for support and comfort, as if he were, indeed, the child of whom he spoke.

When did man ever tremble, as Redlaw trembled, in the silence that ensued! He knew it must come upon them, knew that it was coming fast.

"My time is very short, my breath is shorter," said the sick man, supporting himself on one arm, and with the other groping in the air, "and I remember there is something on my mind concerning the man who was here just now. Father and William—wait!—is there really anything in black, out there?"

"Yes, yes, it is real," said his aged father.

"Is it a man?"

"What I say myself, George," interposed his brother, bending kindly over him. "It's Mr. Redlaw."

"I thought I had dreamed of him. Ask him to come here."

The Chemist, whiter than the dying man, appeared before him. Obedient to the motion of his hand, he sat upon the bed.

"It has been so ripped up to-night, sir," said the sick man, laying his hand upon his heart, with a look in which the mute, imploring agony of his condition was concentrated, "by the sight of my poor old father, and the thought of all the trouble I have been the cause of, and all the wrong and sorrow lying at my door, that—"

Was it the extremity to which he had come, or was it the dawning of another change, that made him stop?

"—that what I *can* do right, with my mind running on so much, so fast, I'll try to do. There was another man here. Did you see him?"

Redlaw could not reply by any word; for when he saw that fatal sign he knew so well now, of the wandering hand upon the forehead, his voice died at his lips. But he made some indication of assent.

"He is penniless, hungry, and destitute. He is completely beaten down, and has no resource at all. Look after him! Lose no time! I know he has it in his mind to kill himself."

It was working. It was on his face. His face was changing, hardening, deepening in all its shades, and losing all its sorrow.

"Don't you remember! Don't you know him?" he pursued.

He shut his face out for a moment, with the hand that again wandered over his forehead, and then it lowered on Redlaw, reckless, ruffianly, and callous.

"Why, d—n you!" he said, scowling round, "what have you been doing to me here! I have lived bold, and I mean to die bold. To the Devil with you!"

And so lay down upon his bed, and put his arms up, over his head and ears, as resolute from that time to keep out all access, and to die in his indifference.

If Redlaw had been struck by lightning, it could not have struck him from the bedside with a more tremendous shock. But the old man, who had left the bed while his son was speaking to him, now returning, avoided it quickly likewise, and with abhorrence.

"Where's my boy William?" said the old man hurriedly. "William, come away from here. We'll go home."

"Home, father!" returned William. "Are you going to leave your own son?"

"Where's my own son?" replied the old man.

"Where? why, there!"

"That's no son of mine," said Philip, trembling with resentment. "No such wretch as that has any claim on me. My children are pleasant to look at, and they wait upon me, and get my meat and drink ready, and are useful to me. I've a right to it! I'm eighty-seven!"

"You're old enough to be no older," muttered William, looking at him grudgingly, with his hands in his pockets. "I don't know what good you are, myself. We could have a deal more pleasant without you."

"*My* son, Mr. Redlaw!" said the old man. "*My* son, too! The boy talking to me of *my* son! Why, what has he ever done to give me any pleasure, I should like to know?"

"I don't know what you have ever done to give *me* any pleasure," said William sulkily.

"Let me think," said the old man. "For how many Christmas-times running have I sat in my warm place, and never had to come out in the cold night air; and have made good cheer, without being disturbed by any such uncomfortable, wretched sight as him there? Is it twenty, William?"

"Nigher forty, it seems," he muttered. "Why, when I look at my father, sir, and come to think of it," addressing Redlaw, with an impatience and irritation that were quite new, "I'm whipped if I can see anything in him but a calendar of ever so many years of eating, and drinking, and making himself comfortable, over and over again."

"I—I'm eighty-seven," said the old man, rambling on, childishly and weakly, "and I don't know as I ever was much put out by anything. I'm not a going to begin now, because of what he calls my son. He's not my son. I've had a power of pleasant times. I recollect once—no, I don't—no, it's broken off. It was something about a game of cricket and a friend of mine, but it's somehow broken off. I wonder who he was—I suppose I liked him? And I wonder what became of him—I suppose he died? But I don't know. And I don't care, neither; I don't care a bit."

In his drowsy chuckling, and shaking his head, he put his hands into his waistcoat pockets. In one of them he found a bit of holly (left there probably last night), which he now took out, and looked at.

"Berries, eh?" said the old man. "Ah! It's a pity they're not good to eat. I recollect when I was a little chap about as high as that, and out a walking with—let me see—who was I out a walking with?— no, I don't remember how that was. I don't remember as I ever walked with any one particular, or cared for any one, or any one for me. Berries, eh? There's good cheer when there's berries. Well; I ought to have my share of it, and to be waited on, and kept warm and comfortable; for I'm eighty-seven, and a poor old man. I'm eigh-ty-seven. Eigh-ty-seven!"

The drivelling, pitiable manner in which, as he repeated this, he nibbled at the leaves, and spat the morsels out; the cold, uninterested eye with which his youngest son (so changed) regarded him; the determined apathy with which his eldest son lay hardened in his sin;—impressed themselves no more on Redlaw's observation; for he broke his way from the spot to which his feet seemed to have been fixed, and ran out of the house.

His guide came crawling forth from his place of refuge, and was ready for him before he reached the arches.

"Back to the woman's?" he inquired.

"Back, quickly!" answered Redlaw. "Stop nowhere on the way!"

For a short distance the boy went on before; but their return was more like a flight than a walk, and it was as much as his bare feet could do to keep pace with the Chemist's rapid strides. Shrinking from all who passed, shrouded in his cloak, and keeping it drawn closely about him, as though there were mortal contagion in any fluttering touch of his garments, he made no pause until they reached the door by which they had come out. He unlocked it with his key, went in, accompanied by the boy, and hastened through the dark passages to his own chamber.

The boy watched him as he made the door fast, and withdrew behind the table, when he looked round.

"Come!" he said. "Don't you touch me! You've not brought me here to take my money away."

Redlaw threw some more upon the ground. He flung his body on it immediately, as if to hide it from him, lest the sight of it should tempt him to reclaim it; and not until he saw him seated by his lamp, with his face hidden in his hands, began furtively to pick it up. When he had done so, he crept near the fire, and, sitting down in a great chair before it, took from his breast some broken scraps of food, and fell to munching, and to staring at the blaze, and now and then to glancing at his shillings, which he kept clenched up in a bunch, in one hand.

"And this," said Redlaw, gazing on him with increasing repugnance and fear, "is the only one companion I have left on earth!"

How long it was before he was aroused from his contemplation of this creature whom he dreaded so—whether half an hour, or half the night—he knew not. But the stillness of the room was broken by the boy (whom he had not seen listening) starting up and running towards the door.

"Here's the woman coming!" he exclaimed.

The Chemist stopped him on his way, at the moment when she knocked.

"Let me go to her, will you?" said the boy.

"Not now," returned the Chemist. "Stay here. Nobody must pass in or out of the room now. Who's that?"

"It's I, sir," cried Milly. "Pray, sir, let me in."

"No! not for the world!" he said.

"Mr. Redlaw, Mr. Redlaw, pray, sir, let me in."

"What is the matter?" he said, holding the boy.

"The miserable man you saw is worse, and nothing I can say will wake him from his terrible infatuation. William's father has turned childish in a moment. William himself is changed. The shock has been too sudden for him; I cannot understand him; he is not like himself. Oh, Mr. Redlaw, pray advise me, help me!"

"No! No! No!" he answered.

"Mr. Redlaw! Dear sir! George has been muttering in his doze about the man you saw there, who, he fears, will kill himself."

"Better he should do it than come near me!"

"He says, in his wandering, that you know him; that he was your friend once, long ago; that he is the ruined father of a student here— my mind misgives me, of the young gentleman who has been ill. What is to be done? How is he to be followed? How is he to be saved? Mr. Redlaw, pray, oh, pray advise me! Help me!"

All this time he held the boy, who was half mad to pass him, and let her in.

"Phantoms! Punishers of impious thoughts!" cried Redlaw, gazing round in anguish, "look upon me! From the darkness of my mind, let the glimmering of contrition that I know is there shine up, and show my misery! In the material world, as I have long taught, nothing can be spared; no step or atom in the wondrous structure could be lost, without a blank being made in the great universe. I know, now, that it is the same with good and evil, happiness and sorrow, in the memories of men. Pity me! Relieve me!"

There was no response, but her "Help me, help me, let me in!" and the boy's struggling to get to her.

"Shadow of myself! Spirit of my darker hours!" cried Redlaw, in distraction, "come back, and haunt me day and night, but take this gift away! Or, if it must still rest with me, deprive me of the dreadful power of giving it to others. Undo what I have done. Leave me benighted, but restore the day to those whom I have cursed. As I have spared this woman from the first, and as I never will go forth again, but will die here, with no hand to tend me, save this creature's who is proof against me,—hear me!"

The only reply still was, the boy struggling to get to her, while he held him back; and the cry increasing in its energy, "Help! let me in. He was your friend once, how shall he be followed, how shall he be saved? They are all changed, there is no one else to help me, pray, pray, let me in!"

CHAPTER III

THE GIFT REVERSED

NIGHT was still heavy in the sky. On open plains, from hilltops and from the decks of solitary ships at sea, a distant low-lying line, that promised by and by to change to light, was visible in the dim horizon; but its promise was remote and doubtful, and the moon was striving with the night-clouds busily.

The shadows upon Redlaw's mind succeeded thick and fast to one another, and obscured its light as the night-clouds hovered between the moon and earth, and kept the latter veiled in darkness. Fitful and uncertain as the shadows which the night-clouds cast were their concealments from him, and imperfect revelations to him; and, like the night-clouds still, if the clear light broke forth for a moment, it was only that they might sweep over it, and make the darkness deeper than before.

Without, there was a profound and solemn hush upon the ancient pile of building, and its buttresses and angles made dark shapes of mystery upon the ground, which now seemed to retire into the smooth white snow and now seemed to come out of it, as the moon's path was more or less beset. Within, the Chemist's room was indistinct and murky, by the light of the expiring lamp; a ghostly silence had succeeded to the knocking and the voice outside; nothing was audible but, now and then, a low sound among the whitened ashes of the fire, as of its yielding up its last breath. Before it on the ground the boy lay fast asleep. In his chair, the Chemist sat, as he had sat there since the calling at his door had ceased—like a man turned to stone.

At such a time, the Christmas music he had heard before began to play. He listened to it at first, as he had listened in the churchyard; but presently—it playing still, and being borne towards him on the night-air, in a low, sweet, melancholy strain—he rose, and stood stretching his hands about him, as if there were some friend approaching within his reach, on whom his desolate touch might rest, yet do no harm. As he did this, his face became less fixed and wondering; a gentle trembling came upon him; and at last his eyes filled with tears, and he put his hands before them, and bowed down his head.

His memory of sorrow, wrong, and trouble, had not come back to him; he knew that it was not restored; he had no passing belief or hope that it was. But some dumb stir within him made him capable, again, of being moved by what was hidden, afar off, in the music. If it were only that it told him sorrowfully the value of what he had lost, he thanked Heaven for it with a fervent gratitude.

As the last chord died upon his ear, he raised his head to listen to its lingering vibration. Beyond the boy, so that his sleeping figure lay at its feet, the Phantom stood, immovable and silent, with its eyes upon him.

Ghastly it was, as it had ever been, but not so cruel and relentless in its aspect—or he thought or hoped so, as he looked upon it, trembling. It was not alone, but in its shadowy hand it held another hand.

And whose was that? Was the form that stood beside it indeed Milly's, or but her shade and picture? The quiet head was bent a little, as her manner was, and her eyes were looking down, as if in pity, on the sleeping child. A radiant light fell on her face, but did not touch the Phantom; for though close beside her, it was dark and colourless as ever.

"Spectre!" said the Chemist, newly troubled as he looked, "I have not been stubborn or presumptuous in respect of her. Oh, do not bring her here. Spare me that!"

"This is but a shadow," said the Phantom; "when the morning shines, seek out the reality whose image I present before you."

"Is it my inexorable doom to do so?" cried the Chemist.

"It is," replied the Phantom.

"To destroy her peace, her goodness; to make her what I am myself, and what I have made of others!"

"I have said, 'seek her out,' " returned the Phantom. "I have said no more."

"Oh, tell me," exclaimed Redlaw, catching at the hope which he fancied might lie hidden in the words. "Can I undo what I have done?"

"No," returned the Phantom.

"I do not ask for restoration to myself," said Redlaw. "What I abandoned, I abandoned of my own will, and have justly lost. But for those to whom I have transferred the fatal gift; who never sought it; who unknowingly received a curse of which they had no warning, and which they had no power to shun, can I do nothing?"

"Nothing," said the Phantom.

"If I cannot, can any one?"

The Phantom, standing like a statue, kept its gaze upon him for a while; then turned its head suddenly, and looked upon the shadow at its side.

"Ah! Can she?" cried Redlaw, still looking upon the shade.

The Phantom released the hand it had retained until now, and softly raised its own with a gesture of dismissal. Upon that, her shadow, still preserving the same attitude, began to move or melt away.

"Stay," cried Redlaw, with an earnestness to which he could not give enough expression. "For a moment! As an act of mercy! I know that some change fell upon me when those sounds were in the air just now. Tell me have I lost the power of harming her? May I go near her without dread? Oh, let her give me any sign of hope!"

The Phantom looked upon the shade as he did—not at him—and gave no answer.

"At least, say this—has she, henceforth, the consciousness of any power to set right what I have done?"

"She has not," the Phantom answered.

"Has she the power bestowed on her without the consciousness?"

The Phantom answered: "Seek her out." And her shadow slowly vanished.

They were face to face again, and looking on each other as intently and awfully as at the time of the bestowal of the gift, across the boy who still lay on the ground between them, at the Phantom's feet.

"Terrible instructor," said the Chemist, sinking on his knee before it, in an attitude of supplication, "by whom I was renounced, but by whom I am revisited (in which, and in whose milder aspect, I would fain believe I have a gleam of hope), I will obey without inquiry, praying that the cry I have sent up in the anguish of my soul has been, or will be heard, in behalf of those whom I have injured beyond human reparation. But there is one thing—"

"You speak to me of what is lying here," the Phantom interposed, and pointed with its finger to the boy.

"I do," returned the Chemist. "You know what I would ask. Why has this child alone been proof against my influence, and why, why have I detected in its thoughts a terrible companionship with mine?"

"This," said the Phantom, pointing to the boy, "is the last, completest illustration of a human creature, utterly bereft of such remembrances as you have yielded up. No softening memory of sorrow, wrong, or trouble enters here, because this wretched mortal from his birth has been abandoned to a worse condition than the beasts, and has, within his knowledge, no one contrast, no humanising touch, to make a grain of such a memory spring up in his hardened breast. All within this desolate creature is barren wilderness. All within the man bereft of what you have resigned is the same barren wilderness. Woe to such a man! Woe, tenfold, to the nation that shall count its monsters such as this, lying here by hundreds and by thousands!"

Redlaw shrunk, appalled, from what he heard.

"There is not," said the Phantom, "one of these—not one—but

SOWS a harvest that mankind MUST reap. From every seed of evil in this boy, a field of ruin is grown that shall be gathered in, and garnered up, and sown again in many places in the world, until regions are overspread with wickedness enough to raise the waters of another Deluge. Open and unpunished murder in a city's streets would be less guilty in its daily toleration than one such spectacle as this."

It seemed to look down upon the boy in his sleep. Redlaw, too, looked down upon him with a new emotion.

"There is not a father," said the Phantom, "by whose side in his daily or his nightly walk these creatures pass; there is not a mother among all the ranks of loving mothers in this land; there is no one risen from the state of childhood, but shall be responsible in his or her degree for this enormity. There is not a country throughout the earth on which it would not bring a curse. There is no religion upon earth that it would not deny; there is no people upon earth it would not put to shame."

The Chemist clasped his hands and looked, with trembling fear and pity, from the sleeping boy to the Phantom, standing above him with its finger pointing down.

"Behold, I say," pursued the Spectre, "the perfect type of what it was your choice to be. Your influence is powerless here because from this child's bosom you can banish nothing. His thoughts have been in 'terrible companionship' with yours, because you have gone down to his unnatural level. He is the growth of man's indifference; you are the growth of man's presumption. The beneficent design of Heaven is, in each case, overthrown, and from the two poles of the immaterial world you come together."

The Chemist stooped upon the ground beside the boy, and, with the same kind of compassion for him that he now felt for himself, covered him as he slept, and no longer shrunk from him with abhorrence or indifference.

Soon, now, the distant line on the horizon brightened, the darkness faded, the sun rose red and glorious, and the chimney stacks and gables of the ancient building gleamed in the clear air, which turned the smoke and vapour of the city into a cloud of gold. The very sundial in his shady corner, where the wind was used to spin with such un-windy constancy, shook off the finer particles of snow that had accumulated on his dull old face in the night, and looked out at the little white wreaths eddying round and round him. Doubtless some blind groping of the morning made its way down into the forgotten crypt so cold and earthy, where the Norman arches were half buried in the ground, and stirred the dull sap in the lazy vegetation hanging to the walls, and quickened the slow principle of life within the little world of wonderful and delicate creation which existed there, with some faint knowledge that the sun was up.

The Tetterbys were up, and doing. Mr. Tetterby took down the shutters of the shop, and, strip by strip, revealed the treasures of the window to the eyes, so proof against their seductions, of Jerusalem Buildings. Adolphus had been out so long already that he was halfway on to Morning Pepper. Five small Tetterbys, whose ten round eyes were much inflamed by soap and friction, were in the tortures of a cool wash in the back kitchen; Mrs. Tetterby presiding. Johnny, who was pushed and hustled through his toilet with great rapidity when Moloch chanced to be in an exacting frame of mind (which was always the case), staggered up and down with his charge before the shop door, under greater difficulties than usual; the weight of Moloch being much increased by a complication of defences against the cold, composed of knitted worsted-work, and forming a complete suit of chain-armour with a headpiece and blue gaiters.

It was a peculiarity of this baby to be always cutting teeth. Whether they never came, or whether they came and went away again, is not in evidence; but it had certainly cut enough, on the showing of Mrs. Tetterby, to make a handsome dental provision for the sign of the Bull and Mouth. All sorts of objects were impressed for the rubbing of its gums, notwithstanding that it always carried, dangling at its waist (which was immediately under its chin), a bone ring, large enough to have represented the rosary of a young nun.

Knife-handles, umbrella-tops, the heads of walking-sticks selected from the stock, the fingers of the family in general, but especially of Johnny, nutmeg-graters, crusts, the handles of doors, and the cool knobs on the tops of pokers, were among the commonest instruments indiscriminately applied for this baby's relief. The amount of electricity that must have been rubbed out of it in a week is not to be calculated. Still Mrs. Tetterby always said "it was coming through, and then the child would be herself;" and still it never did come through, and the child continued to be somebody else.

The tempers of the little Tetterbys had sadly changed with a few hours. Mr. and Mrs. Tetterby themselves were not more altered than their offspring. Usually they were an unselfish, good-natured, yielding little race, sharing short-commons when it happened (which was pretty often) contentedly and even generously, and taking a great deal of enjoyment out of a very little meat. But they were fighting now, not only for the soap and water, but even for the breakfast, which was yet in perspective. The hand of every little Tetterby was against the other little Tetterbys; and even Johnny's hand—the patient, much-enduring, and devoted Johnny—rose against the baby! Yes. Mrs. Tetterby, going to the door by a mere accident, saw him viciously pick out a weak place in the suit of armour, where a slap would tell, and slap that blessed child.

Mrs. Tetterby led him into the parlour, by the collar, in that same flash of time, and repaid him the assault with usury thereto.

"You brute, you murdering little boy," said Mrs. Tetterby. "Had you the heart to do it?"

"Why don't her teeth come through, then," retorted Johnny, in a loud, rebellious voice, "instead of bothering me? How would you like it yourself?"

"Like it, sir!" said Mrs. Tetterby, relieving him of his dishonoured load.

"Yes, like it," said Johnny. "How would you? Not at all. If you was me, you'd go for a soldier. I will, too. There ain't no babies in the army."

Mr. Tetterby, who had arrived upon the scene of action, rubbed his chin thoughtfully, instead of correcting the rebel, and seemed rather struck by this view of a military life.

"I wish I was in the army myself, if the child's in the right," said Mrs. Tetterby, looking at her husband, "for I have no peace of my life here. I'm a slave—a Virginia slave;" some indistinct association with their weak descent on the tobacco trade perhaps suggested this aggravated expression to Mrs. Tetterby. "I never have a holiday, or any pleasure at all, from year's end to year's end! Why, Lord bless and save the child," said Mrs. Tetterby, shaking the baby with an irritability hardly suited to so pious an aspiration, "what's the matter with her now?"

Not being able to discover, and not rendering the subject much clearer by shaking it, Mrs. Tetterby put the baby away in a cradle, and, folding her arms, sat rocking it angrily with her foot.

"How you stand there, 'Dolphus," said Mrs. Tetterby to her husband. "Why don't you do something?"

"Because I don't care about doing anything," Mr. Tetterby replied.

"I'm sure *I* don't," said Mrs. Tetterby.

"I'll take my oath *I* don't," said Mr. Tetterby.

A diversion arose here among Johnny and his five younger brothers, who, in preparing the family breakfast-table, had fallen to skirmishing for the temporary possession of the loaf, and were buffeting one another with great heartiness; the smallest boy of all, with precocious discretion, hovering outside the knot of combatants, and harassing their legs. Into the midst of this fray, Mr. and Mrs. Tetterby both precipitated themselves with great ardour, as if such ground were the only ground on which they could now agree; and having, with no visible remains of their late soft-heartedness, laid about them without any lenity, and, done much execution, resumed their former relative positions.

"You had better read your paper than do nothing at all," said Mrs. Tetterby.

"What's there to read in a paper?" returned Mr. Tetterby, with excessive discontent.

"What?" said Mrs. Tetterby. "Police."

"It's nothing to me," said Tetterby. "What do I care what people do, or are done to?"

"Suicides," suggested Mrs. Tetterby.

"No business of mine," replied her husband.

"Births, deaths, and marriages, are those nothing to you?" said Mrs. Tetterby.

"If the births were all over for good, and all to-day, and the deaths were all to begin to come off to-morrow, I don't see why it should interest me, till I thought it was a coming to my turn," grumbled Tetterby. "As to marriages, I've done it myself. I know quite enough about *them*."

To judge from the dissatisfied expression of her face and manner, Mrs. Tetterby appeared to entertain the same opinions as her husband; but she opposed him, nevertheless, for the gratification of quarrelling with him.

"Oh, you're a consistent man," said Mrs. Tetterby, "ain't you? You, with the screen of your own making there, made of nothing else but bits of newspapers, which you sit and read to the children by the half hour together!"

"Say used to, if you please," returned her husband. "You won't find me doing so any more. I'm wiser now."

"Bah! wiser, indeed!" said Mrs. Tetterby. "Are you better?"

The question sounded some discordant note in Mr. Tetterby's breast. He ruminated dejectedly, and passed his hand across and across his forehead.

"Better!" murmured Mr. Tetterby. "I don't know as any of us are better, or happier either. Better, is it?"

He turned to the screen, and traced about it with his finger, until he found a certain paragraph of which he was in quest.

"This used to be one of the family favourites, I recollect," said Tetterby, in a forlorn and stupid way, "and used to draw tears from the children, and make 'em good, if there was any little bickering or discontent among 'em, next to the story of the robin redbreasts in the wood. 'Melancholy case of destitution. Yesterday a small man, with a baby in his arms, and surrounded by half a dozen ragged little ones, of various ages between ten and two, the whole of whom were evidently in a famishing condition, appeared before the worthy magistrate, and made the following recital:'—Ha! I don't understand it, I'm sure," said Tetterby; "I don't see what it has got to do with us."

"How old and shabby he looks," said Mrs. Tetterby, watching him. "I never saw such a change in a man. Ah! dear me, dear me, dear me, it was a sacrifice!"

"What was a sacrifice?" her husband sourly inquired.

Mrs. Tetterby shook her head; and without replying in words, raised a complete sea-storm about the baby, by her violent agitation of the cradle.

"If you mean your marriage was a sacrifice, my good woman—" said her husband.

"I *do* mean it," said his wife.

"Why, then, I mean to say," pursued Mr. Tetterby, as sulkily and surlily as she, "that there are two sides to that affair; and that *I* was the sacrifice; and that I wish the sacrifice hadn't been accepted."

"I wish it hadn't, Tetterby, with all my heart and soul, I do assure you," said his wife. "You can't wish it more than I do, Tetterby."

"I don't know what I saw in her," muttered the newsman, "I'm sure;—certainly, if I saw anything, it's not there now. I was thinking so, last night, after supper, by the fire. She's fat, she's aging, she won't bear comparison with most other women."

"He's common-looking, he has no air with him, he's small, he's beginning to stoop, and he's getting bald," muttered Mrs. Tetterby.

"I must have been half out of my mind when I did it," muttered Mr. Tetterby.

"My senses must have forsook me. That's the only way in which I can explain it to myself," said Mrs. Tetterby, with elaboration.

In this mood they sat down to breakfast. The little Tetterbys were not habituated to regard that meal in the light of a sedentary occupation, but discussed it as a dance or trot; rather resembling a savage ceremony, in the occasional shrill whoops, and brandishings of bread and butter, with which it was accompanied, as well as in the intricate filings off into the street and back again, and the hoppings up and down the door-steps, which were incidental to the performance. In the present instance, the contentions between these Tetterby children for the milk and water jug, common to all, which stood upon the table, presented so lamentable an instance of angry passions risen very high, indeed, that it was an outrage on the memory of Doctor Watts. It was not until Mr. Tetterby had driven the whole herd out of the front door that a moment's peace was secured; and even that was broken by the discovery that Johnny had surreptitiously come back, and was at that instant choking in the jug like a ventriloquist, in his indecent and rapacious haste.

"These children will be the death of me at last!" said Mrs. Tetterby, after banishing the culprit. "And the sooner the better, I think."

"Poor people," said Mr. Tetterby, "ought not to have children at all. They give *us* no pleasure."

He was at that moment taking up the cup which Mrs. Tetterby had rudely pushed towards him, and Mrs. Tetterby was lifting her own cup to her lips, when they both stopped, as if they were transfixed.

"Here! Mother! Father!" cried Johnny, running into the room. "Here's Mrs. William coming down the street!"

And if ever, since the world began, a young boy took a baby from a cradle with the care of an old nurse, and hushed and soothed it tenderly, and tottered away with it cheerfully, Johnny was that boy, and Moloch was that baby, as they went out together.

Mr. Tetterby put down his cup; Mrs. Tetterby put down her cup. Mr. Tetterby rubbed his forehead; Mrs. Tetterby rubbed hers. Mr. Tetterby's face began to smooth and brighten; Mrs. Tetterby's began to smooth and brighten.

"Why, Lord forgive me," said Mr. Tetterby to himself, "what evil tempers have I been giving way to? What has been the matter here!"

"How could I ever treat him ill again, after all I said and felt last night!" sobbed Mrs. Tetterby, with her apron to her eyes.

"Am I a brute," said Mr. Tetterby, "or is there any good in me at all? Sophia! My little woman!"

" 'Dolphus, dear," returned his wife.

"I—I've been in a state of mind," said Mr. Tetterby, "that I can't abear to think of, Sophy."

"Oh! It's nothing to what I've been in, Dolf," cried his wife, in a great burst of grief.

"My Sophia," said Mr. Tetterby, "don't take on. I never shall forgive myself. I must have nearly broke your heart, I know."

"No, Dolf, no. It was me! Me!" cried Mrs. Tetterby.

"My little woman," said her husband, "don't. You make me reproach myself dreadful, when you show such a noble spirit. Sophia, my dear, you don't know what I thought. I showed it bad enough, no doubt; but what I thought, my little woman!—"

"Oh, dear Dolf, don't! Don't!" cried his wife.

"Sophia," said Mr. Tetterby, "I must reveal it. I couldn't rest in my conscience unless I mentioned it. My little woman—"

"Mrs. William's very nearly here!" screamed Johnny at the door.

"My little woman, I wondered how," gasped Mr. Tetterby, supporting himself by his chair, "I wondered how I had ever admired you—I forgot the precious children you have brought about me—and thought you didn't look as slim as I could wish. I—I never gave a recollection," said Mr. Tetterby, with severe self-accusation, "to the cares you've had as my wife, and along of me and mine, when you might have had hardly any with another man, who got on better and was luckier than me (anybody might have found such a man easily, I am sure); and I quarrelled with you for having aged a little in the rough years you've lightened for me. Can you believe it, my little woman? I hardly can myself."

Mrs. Tetterby, in a whirlwind of laughing and crying, caught his face within her hands, and held it there.

"O Dolf!" she cried. "I am so happy that you thought so; I am so grateful that you thought so! For I thought that you were common-looking, Dolf; and so you are, my dear, and may you be the commonest of all sights in my eyes till you close them with your own good hands. I thought that you were small; and so you are, and I'll make much of you because you are, and more of you because I love my husband. I thought that you began to stoop; and so you do, and you shall lean on me, and I'll do all I can to keep you up. I thought there was no air about you; but there is, and it's the air of home, and that's the purest and the best there is, and GOD bless home once more, and all belonging to it, Dolf!"

"Hurrah! Here's Mrs. William!" cried Johnny.

So she was, and all the children with her; and as she came in, they kissed her, and kissed one another, and kissed the baby, and kissed their father and mother, and then ran back and flocked and danced about her, trooping on with her in triumph.

Mr. and Mrs. Tetterby were not a bit behind-hand in the warmth of their reception. They were as much attracted to her as the children were; they ran towards her, kissed her hands, pressed around her, could not receive her ardently or enthusiastically enough. She came among them like the spirit of all goodness, affection, gentle consideration, love, and domesticity.

"What! are *you* all so glad to see me, too, this bright Christmas morning?" said Milly, clapping her hands in a pleasant wonder. "Oh, dear, how delightful this is!"

More shouting from the children, more kissing, more trooping round her, more happiness, more love, more joy, more honour, on all sides, than she could bear.

"Oh, dear," said Milly, "what delicious tears you make me shed. How can I ever have deserved this! What have I done to be so loved!"

"Who can help it!" cried Mr. Tetterby.

"Who can help it!" cried Mrs. Tetterby.

"Who can help it!" echoed the children, in a joyful chorus. And they danced and trooped about her again, and clung to her, and laid their rosy faces against her dress, and kissed and fondled it, and could not fondle it, or her, enough.

"I never was so moved," said Milly, drying her eyes, "as I have been this morning. I must tell you, as soon as I can speak. Mr. Redlaw came to me at sunrise, and with a tenderness in his manner, more as if I had been his darling daughter than myself, implored me to go with him to where William's brother George is lying ill. We went together, and all the way along he was so kind, and so subdued, and seemed to put such trust and hope in me, that I could not help crying with pleasure. When we got to the house we met a woman at the door (somebody had bruised and hurt her, I am afraid) who caught me by the hand, and blessed me as I passed."

"She was right," said Mr. Tetterby. Mrs. Tetterby said she was right. All the children cried out she was right.

"Ah, but there's more than that," said Milly. "When we got up stairs, into the room, the sick man, who had lain for hours in a state from which no effort could rouse him, rose up in his bed, and, bursting into tears, stretched out his arms to me, and said that he had led a misspent life, but that he was truly repentant now, in his sorrow for the past, which was all as plain to him as a great prospect from which a dense black cloud had cleared away, and that he entreated me to ask his poor old father for his pardon and his blessing, and to say a prayer beside his bed. And when I did so, Mr. Redlaw joined in it so fervently, and then so thanked and thanked me, and thanked Heaven, that my heart quite overflowed, and I could have done nothing but sob and cry, if the sick man had not begged me to sit down by him,—which made me quiet, of course. As I sat there, he held my hand in his until he sunk in a doze; and even then, when I withdrew my hand to leave him to come here (which Mr. Redlaw was very earnest indeed in wishing me to do), his hand felt for mine, so that some one else was obliged to take my place and make believe to give him my hand back. Oh, dear, oh, dear," said Milly, sobbing. "How thankful and how happy I should feel, and do feel, for all this!"

While she was speaking, Redlaw had come in, and, after pausing for a moment to observe the group of which she was the centre, had silently ascended the stairs. Upon those stairs he now appeared again; remaining there, while the young student passed him, and came running down.

"Kind nurse, gentlest, best of creatures," he said, falling on his knee to her, and catching at her hand, "forgive my cruel ingratitude!"

"Oh, dear, oh, dear," cried Milly, innocently, "here's another of them! Oh, dear, here's somebody else who likes me. What shall I ever do!"

The guileless, simple way in which she said it, and in which she put her hands before her eyes and wept for very happiness, was as touching as it was delightful.

"I was not myself," he said. "I don't know what it was,—it was some consequence of my disorder, perhaps,—I was mad. But I am so no longer. Almost as I speak, I am restored. I heard the children crying out your name, and the shade passed from me at the very sound of it. Oh, don't weep! Dear Milly, if you could read my heart, and only know with what affection and what grateful homage it is glowing, you would not let me see you weep. It is such deep reproach."

"No, no," said Milly; "it's not that. It's not, indeed. It's joy. It's wonder that you should think it necessary to ask me to forgive so little, and yet it's pleasure that you do."

"And will you come again? and will you finish the little curtain?"

"No," said Milly, drying her eyes, and shaking her head. "You won't care for *my* needlework now."

"Is it forgiving me, to say that?"

She beckoned him aside, and whispered in his ear.

"There is news from your home, Mr. Edmund."

"News? How?"

"Either your not writing when you were very ill, or the change in your handwriting when you began to be better, created some suspicion of the truth; however, that is—but you're sure you'll not be the worse for any news, if it's not bad news?"

"Sure."

"Then there's some one come!" said Milly.

"My mother?" asked the student, glancing round involuntarily towards Redlaw, who had come down from the stairs.

"Hush! No," said Milly.

"It can be no one else."

"Indeed?" said Milly; "are you sure?"

"It is not—" Before he could say more, she put her hand upon his mouth.

"Yes, it is!" said Milly. "The young lady (she is very like the miniature, Mr. Edmund, but she is prettier) was too unhappy to rest without satisfying her doubts, and came up, last night, with a little servant-maid. As you always dated your letters from the college, she came there; and before I saw Mr. Redlaw this morning, I saw her.— *She* likes me, too!" said Milly. "Oh, dear, that's another!"

"This morning! Where is she now?"

"Why, she is now," said Milly, advancing her lips to his ear, "in my little parlour in the Lodge, and waiting to see you."

He pressed her hand, and was darting off, but she detained him.

"Mr. Redlaw is much altered, and has told me this morning that his memory is impaired. Be very considerate to him, Mr. Edmund; he needs that from us all."

The young man assured her, by a look, that her caution was not ill-bestowed; and as he passed the Chemist on his way out, bent respectfully and with an obvious interest before him.

Redlaw returned the salutation courteously and even humbly, and looked after him as he passed on. He drooped his head upon his hand too, as trying to reawaken something he had lost. But it was gone.

The abiding change that had come upon him since the influence of the music, and the Phantom's reappearance, was, that now he truly felt how much he had lost, and could compassionate his own condition, and contrast it, clearly, with the natural state of those who were around him. In this, an interest in those who were around him was revived, and a meek, submissive sense of his calamity was bred, resembling that which sometimes obtains in age, when its mental powers are weakened, without insensibility or sullenness being added to the list of its infirmities.

He was conscious, that, as he redeemed, through Milly, more and more of the evil he had done, and as he was more and more with her, this change ripened itself within him. Therefore, and because of the attachment she inspired him with (but without other hope), he felt that he was quite dependent on her, and that she was his staff in his affliction.

So, when she asked him whether they should go home now, to where the old man and her husband were, and he readily replied "yes"—being anxious in that regard—he put his arm through hers, and walked beside her; not as if he were the wise and learned man to whom the wonders of nature were an open book, and hers were the uninstructed mind, but as if their two positions were reversed, and he knew nothing, and she all.

He saw the children throng about her, and caress her, as he and she went away together thus, out of the house; he heard the ringing of their laughter, and their merry voices; he saw their bright faces, clustering round him like flowers; he witnessed the renewed contentment and affection of their parents; he breathed the simple air of their poor home, restored to its tranquillity; he thought of the unwholesome blight he had shed upon it, and might, but for her, have been diffusing then; and perhaps it is no wonder that he walked submissively beside her, and drew her gentle bosom nearer to his own.

When they arrived at the Lodge, the old man was sitting in his chair in the chimney corner, with his eyes fixed on the ground, and his son was leaning against the opposite side of the fireplace, looking at him. As she came in at the door, both started and turned round towards her, and a radiant change came upon their faces.

"Oh, dear, dear, dear, they are pleased to see me like the rest!" cried Milly, clapping her hands in an ecstasy, and stopping short. "Here are two more!"

Pleased to see her! Pleasure was no word for it. She ran into her husband's arms, thrown wide open to receive her, and he would have been glad to have her there, with her head lying on his shoulder, through the short winter's day. But the old man couldn't spare her. He had arms for her too, and he locked her in them.

"Why, where has my quiet Mouse been all this time?" said the old man. "She has been a long while away. I find that it's impossible for me to get on without Mouse. I—where's my son William?—I fancy I have been dreaming, William."

"That's what I say myself, father," returned his son. "*I* have been in an ugly sort of dream, I think.—How are you, father? Are you pretty well?"

"Strong and brave, my boy," returned the old man.

It was quite a sight to see Mr. William shaking hands with his father, and patting him on the back, and rubbing him gently down with his hand, as if he could not possibly do enough to show an interest in him.

"What a wonderful man you are, father!—How are you, father? Are you really pretty hearty, though?" said William, shaking hands with him again, and patting him again, and rubbing him gently down again.

"I never was fresher or stouter in my life, my boy."

"What a wonderful man you are, father! But that's exactly where it is," said Mr. William, with enthusiasm. "When I think of all that my father's gone through, and all the chances and changes, and sorrows and troubles, that have happened to him in the course of his long life, and under which his head has grown grey, and years upon years have gathered on it, I feel as if we couldn't do enough to honour the old gentleman, and make his old age easy.—How are you, father? Are you really pretty well, though?"

Mr. William might never have left off repeating this inquiry and shaking hands with him again, and patting him again, and rubbing him down again, if the old man had not espied the Chemist, whom until now he had not seen.

"I ask your pardon, Mr. Redlaw," said Philip, "but didn't know you were here, sir, or should have made less free. It reminds me, Mr. Redlaw, seeing you here on a Christmas morning, of the time when you was a student yourself, and worked so hard that you was backwards and forwards in our library even at Christmas-time. Ha, ha! I'm old enough to remember that; and I remember it right well, I do, though I am eighty-seven. It was after you left here that my poor wife died. You remember my poor wife, Mr. Redlaw?"

The Chemist answered yes.

"Yes," said the old man. "She was a dear creetur.—I recollect you come here one Christmas morning with a young lady—I ask your pardon, Mr. Redlaw, but I think it was a sister you was very much attached to?"

The Chemist looked at him, and shook his head. "I had a sister," he said vacantly. He knew no more.

"One Christmas morning," pursued the old man, "that you come here with her—and it began to snow, and my wife invited the young lady to walk in, and sit by the fire that is always a burning on Christmas Day in what used to be, before our ten poor gentlemen commuted, our great Dinner Hall. I was there; and I recollect, as I was stirring up the blaze for the young lady to warm her pretty feet by, she read the scroll out loud, that is underneath that picter. 'Lord, keep my memory green!' She and my poor wife fell a talking about it; and it's a strange thing to think of, now, that they both said (both being so unlike to die) that it was a good prayer, and that it was one they would put up very earnestly, if they were called away young, with reference to those who were dearest to them. 'My brother,' says the young lady—'My husband,' says my poor wife.—'Lord, keep his memory of me green, and do not let me be forgotten!'"

Tears more painful, and more bitter than he had ever shed in all his life, coursed down Redlaw's face. Philip, fully occupied in recalling his story, had not observed him until now, nor Milly's anxiety that he should not proceed.

"Philip!" said Redlaw, laying his hand upon his arm, "I am a stricken man, on whom the hand of Providence has fallen heavily, although deservedly. You speak to me, my friend, of what I cannot follow; my memory is gone."

"Merciful Power!" cried the old man.

"I have lost my memory of sorrow, wrong, and trouble," said the Chemist; "and with that I have lost all man would remember!"

To see old Philip's pity for him, to see him wheel his own great chair for him to rest in, and look down upon him with a solemn sense of his bereavement, was to know, in some degree, how precious to old age such recollections are.

The boy came running in, and ran to Milly.

"Here's the man," he said, "in the other room. I don't want *him*."

"What man does he mean?" asked Mr. William.

"Hush!" said Milly.

Obedient to a sign from her, he and his old father softly withdrew. As they went out, unnoticed, Redlaw beckoned to the boy to come to him.

"I like the woman best," he answered, holding to her skirts.

"You are right," said Redlaw, with a faint smile. "But you needn't fear to come to me. I am gentler than I was. Of all the world, to you poor child!"

The boy still held back at first; but yielding little by little to her urging, he consented to approach, and even to sit down at his feet. As Redlaw laid his hand upon the shoulder of the child, looking on him with compassion and a fellow-feeling, he put out his other hand to Milly. She stooped down on that side of him, so that she could look into his face; and after silence, said:—

"Mr. Redlaw, may I speak to you?"

"Yes," he answered, fixing his eyes upon her. "Your voice and music are the same to me."

"May I ask you something?"

"What you will."

"Do you remember what I said, when I knocked at your door last night? About one who was your friend once, and who stood on the verge of destruction?"

"Yes. I remember," he said with some hesitation.

"Do you understand it?"

He smoothed the boy's hair—looking at her fixedly the while, and shook his head.

"This person," said Milly, in her clear, soft voice, which her mild eyes, looking at him, made clearer and softer, "I found soon afterwards. I went back to the house, and, with Heaven's help, traced him. I was not too soon. A very little, and I should have been too late."

He took his hand from the boy, and laying it on the back of that hand of hers, whose timid and yet earnest touch addressed him no less appealingly than her voice and eyes, looked more intently on her.

"He *is* the father of Mr. Edmund, the young gentleman we saw just now. His real name is Longford.—You recollect the name?"

"I recollect the name."

"And the man?"

"No, not the man. Did he ever wrong me?"

"Yes!"

"Ah! Then it's hopeless—hopeless."

He shook his head, and softly beat upon the hand he held, as though mutely asking her commiseration.

"I did not go to Mr. Edmund last night," said Milly.—"You will listen to me just the same as if you did remember all?"

"To every syllable you say."

"Both, because I did not know, then, that this really was his father, and because I was fearful of the effect of such intelligence upon him, after his illness, if it should be. Since I have known who this person is, I have not gone either; but that is for another reason. He has long been separated from his wife and son,—has been a stranger to his home almost from his son's infancy, I learn from him,—and has abandoned and deserted what he should have held most dear. In all that time, he has been falling from the state of a gentleman more and more, until"—she rose up, hastily, and going out for a moment, returned, accompanied by the wreck that Redlaw had beheld last night.

"Do you know me?" asked the Chemist.

"I should be glad," returned the other, "and that is an unwonted word for me to use, if I could answer no."

The Chemist looked at the man, standing in self-abasement and degradation before him, and would have looked longer, in an ineffectual struggle for enlightenment, but that Milly resumed her late position by his side, and attracted his attentive gaze to her own face.

"See how low he is sunk, how lost he is!" she whispered, stretching out her arm towards him, without looking from the Chemist's face. "If you could remember all that is connected with him, do you not think it would move your pity to reflect that one you ever loved (do not let us mind how long ago, or in what belief that he has forfeited) should come to this?"

"I hope it would," he answered. "I believe it would."

His eyes wandered to the figure standing near the door, but came back speedily to her, on whom he gazed intently, as if he strove to learn some lesson from every tone of her voice, and every beam of her eyes.

"I have no learning, and you have much," said Milly; "I am not used to think, and you are always thinking. May I tell you why it seems to me a good thing for us to remember wrong that has been done us?"

"Yes."

"That we may forgive it."

"Pardon me, great Heaven!" said Redlaw, lifting up his eyes, "for having thrown away thine own high attribute!"

"And if," said Milly,—"if your memory should one day be restored, as we will hope and pray it may be, would it not be a blessing to you to recall at once a wrong and its forgiveness?"

He looked at the figure by the door, and fastened his attentive eyes on her again; a ray of clearer light appeared to him to shine into his mind from her bright face.

"He cannot go to his abandoned home. He does not seek to go there. He knows that he could only carry shame and trouble to those he has so cruelly neglected; and that the best reparation he can make them now is to avoid them. A very little money carefully bestowed would remove him to some distant place, where he might live and do no wrong, and make such atonement as if left within his power for the wrong he has done. To the unfortunate lady who is his wife, and to his son, this would be the best and kindest boon that their best friend could give them—one, too, that they need never know of; and to him, shattered in reputation, mind, and body, it might be salvation."

He took her head between his hands, and kissed it, and said, "It shall be done. I trust to you to do it for me, now and secretly; and to tell him that I would forgive him, if I were so happy as to know for what."

As she rose, and turned her beaming face towards the fallen man, implying that her mediation had been successful, he advanced a step, and, without raising his eyes, addressed himself to Redlaw.

"You are so generous," he said,—"you ever were—that you will try to banish your rising sense of retribution, in the spectacle that is before you. I do not try to banish it from myself, Redlaw. If you can, believe me."

The Chemist entreated Milly, by a gesture, to come nearer to him; and, as he listened, looked in her face, as if to find in it the clue to what he heard.

"I am too decayed a wretch to make professions; I recollect my own career too well to array any such before you. But from the day on which I made my first step downward, in dealing falsely by you, I have gone down with a certain, steady, doomed progression. That I say."

Redlaw, keeping her close at his side, turned his face towards the speaker, and there was sorrow in it. Something like mournful recognition, too.

"I might have been another man, my life might have been another life, if I had avoided that first fatal step. I don't know that it would have been. I claim nothing for the possibility. Your sister is at rest, and better than she could have been with me, if I had continued even what you thought me; even what I once supposed myself to be."

Redlaw made a hasty motion with his hand, as if he would have put that subject on one side.

"I speak," the other went on, "like a man taken from the grave. I should have made my own grave last night, had it not been for this blessed hand."

"Oh, dear, he likes me, too!" sobbed Milly, under her breath. "That's another!"

"I could not have put myself in your way, last night, even for bread. But to-day, my recollection of what has been between us is so strongly stirred, and is presented to me, I don't know how, so vividly, that I have dared to come at her suggestion, and to take your bounty, and to thank you for it, and to beg you, Redlaw, in your dying hour, to be as merciful to me in your thoughts as you are in your deeds."

He turned towards the door, and stopped a moment on his way forth.

"I hope my son may interest you, for his mother's sake. I hope he may deserve to do so. Unless my life should be preserved a long time, and I should know that I have not misused your aid, I shall never look upon him more."

Going out, he raised his eyes to Redlaw for the first time. Redlaw, whose steadfast gaze was fixed upon him, dreamily held out his hand. He returned and touched it—little more—with both his own—and bending down his head, went slowly out.

In the few moments that elapsed, while Milly silently took him to the gate, the Chemist dropped into his chair, and covered his face with his hands. Seeing him thus, when she came back, accompanied by her husband and his father (who were both greatly concerned for him), she avoided disturbing him, or permitting him to be disturbed; and kneeled down near the chair, to put some warm clothing on the boy.

"That's exactly where it is. That's what I always say, father!" exclaimed her admiring husband. "There's a motherly feeling in Mrs. William's breast that must and will have went!"

"Ay, ay," said the old man; "you're right. My son William's right!"

"It happens all for the best, Milly dear, no doubt," said Mr. William tenderly, "that we have no children of our own; and yet I sometimes wish you had one to love and cherish. Our little dead child that you built such hopes upon, and that never breathed the breath of life—it has made you quiet-like, Milly."

"I am very happy in the recollection of it, William dear," she answered. "I think of it every day."

"I was afraid you thought of it a good deal."

"Don't say afraid; it is a comfort to me; it speaks to me in so many ways. The innocent thing that never lived on earth is like an angel to me, William."

"You are like an angel to father and me," said Mr. William softly. "I know that."

"When I think of all those hopes I built upon it, and the many times I sat and pictured to myself the little smiling face upon my bosom that never lay there, and the sweet eyes turned up to mine that never opened to the light," said Milly, "I can feel a greater tenderness, I think, for all the disappointed hopes in which there is no harm. When I see a beautiful child in its fond mother's arms, I love it all the better, thinking that my child might have been like that, and might have made my heart as proud and happy."

Redlaw raised his head, and looked towards her.

"All through life, it seems by me," she continued, "to tell me something. For poor neglected children, my little child pleads as if it were alive, and had a voice I knew, with which to speak to me. When I hear of youth in suffering or shame, I think that my child might have come to that, perhaps, and that God took it from me in his mercy. Even in age and grey hair, such as father's, it is present; saying that it too might have lived to be old, long and long after you and I were gone, and to have needed the respect and love of younger people."

Her quiet voice was quieter than ever, as she took her husband's arm, and laid her head against it.

"Children love me so, that sometimes I half fancy—it's a silly fancy, William—they have some way I don't know of, of feeling for my little child, and me, and understanding why their love is precious to me. If I have been quiet since, I have been more happy, William, in a hundred ways. Not least happy, dear, in this—that even when my little child was born and dead but a few days, and I was weak and sorrowful, and could not help grieving a little, the thought arose, that if I tried to lead a good life, I should meet in heaven a bright creature, who would call me, Mother!"

Redlaw fell upon his knees, with a loud cry.

"O Thou," he said, "who, through the teaching of pure love, has graciously restored me to the memory which was the memory of Christ upon the cross, and of all the good who perished in His cause, receive my thanks, and bless her!"

Then he folded her to his heart; and Milly, sobbing more than ever, cried, as she laughed, "He is come back to himself. He likes me very much, indeed, too? Oh, dear, dear, dear me, here's another!"

Then the student entered, leading by the hand a lovely girl, who was afraid to come. And Redlaw so changed towards him, seeing in him and in his youthful choice the softened shadow of that chastening passage in his own life, to which, as to a shady tree, the dove so long imprisoned in his solitary ark might fly for rest and company, fell upon his neck, entreating them to be his children.

Then, as Christmas is a time in which, of all times in the year, the memory of every remediable sorrow, wrong, and trouble in the world around us should be active with us, not less than our own experiences, for all good, he laid his hand upon the boy, and, silently calling Him to witness who laid His hand on children in old time, rebuking, in the majesty of His prophetic knowledge, those who kept them from Him, vowed to protect him, teach him, and reclaim him.

Then he gave his right hand cheerily to Philip, and said that they would that day hold a Christmas dinner in what used to be, before the ten poor gentlemen commuted, their great Dinner Hall; and that they would bid to it as many of that Swidger family, who, his son had told him, were so numerous that they might join hands and make a ring round England, as could be brought together on so short a notice.

And it was that day done. There were so many Swidgers there, grown up and children, that an attempt to state them in round numbers might engender doubts, in the distrustful, of the veracity of this history. Therefore the attempt shall not be made. But there they were, by dozens and scores—and there was good news and good hope there, ready for them, of George, who had been visited again by his father and brother, and by Milly, and again left in a quiet sleep. There, present at the dinner, too, were the Tetterbys, including young Adolphus, who arrived in his prismatic comforter, in good time for the beef. Johnny and the baby were too late, of course, and came in all on one side, the one exhausted, the other in a supposed state of double-tooth; but that was customary, and not alarming.

It was sad to see the child who had no name or lineage, watching the other children as they played, not knowing how to talk with them, or sport with them, and more strange to the ways of childhood than a rough dog. It was sad, though in a different way, to see what an instinctive knowledge the youngest children there had of his being different from all the rest, and how they made timid approaches to him with soft words and touches, and with little presents, that he might not be unhappy. But he kept by Milly, and began to love her— that was another, as she said!—and, as they all liked her dearly, they were glad of that; and when they saw him peeping at them from behind her chair, they were pleased that he was so close to it.

All this the Chemist, sitting with the student and his bride that was to be, and Philip, and the rest, saw.

Some people have said since that he only thought what has been herein set down; others that he read it in the fire, one winter night about the twilight time; others that the Ghost was but the representation of his gloomy thoughts, and Milly the embodiment of his better wisdom. *I* say nothing.

—Except this. That as they were assembled in the old Hall, by no other light than that of a great fire (having dined early), the shadows once more stole out of their hiding-places, and danced about the room, showing the children marvellous shapes and faces on the walls, and gradually changing what was real and familiar there to what was wild and magical. But that there was one thing in the Hall to which the eyes of Redlaw, and of Milly and her husband, and of the old man, and of the student, and his bride that was to be, were often turned, which the shadows did not obscure or change. Deepened in its gravity by the firelight, and gazing from the darkness of the panelled wall like life, the sedate face in the portrait, with the beard and ruff, looked down at them from under its verdant wreath of holly, as they looked up at it; and, clear and plain below, as if a voice had uttered them, were the words:—

"Lord, keep my Memory Green."

To Be Read at Dusk:

A Gathering of

Ghostly Tales

NURSE'S STORIES

THERE are not many places that I find it more agreeable to revisit, when I am in an idle mood, than some places to which I have never been. For, my acquaintance with those spots is of such long standing, and has ripened into an intimacy of so affectionate a nature, that I take a particular interest in assuring myself that they are unchanged.

I never was in Robinson Crusoe's Island, yet I frequently return there. The colony he established on it soon faded away, and it is uninhabited by any descendants of the grave and courteous Spaniards, or of Will Atkins and the other mutineers, and has relapsed into its original condition. Not a twig of its wicker houses remains, its goats have long run wild again, its screaming parrots would darken the sun with a cloud of many flaming colours if a gun were fired there, no face is ever reflected in the waters of the little creek which Friday swam across when pursued by his two brother cannibals with sharpened stomachs. After comparing notes with other travellers who have similarly revisited the Island, and conscientiously inspected it, I have satisfied myself that it contains no vestige of Mr. Atkins's domesticity or theology, though his track on the memorable evening of his landing to set his captain ashore, when he was decoyed about and round about until it was dark, and his boat was stove, and his strength and spirits failed him, is yet plainly to be traced. So is the hill-top on which Robinson was struck dumb with joy when the reinstated captain pointed to the ship, riding within half a mile of the shore, that was to bear him away, in the nine and twentieth year of his seclusion in that lonely place. So is the sandy beach on which the memorable footstep was impressed, and where the savages hauled up their canoes when they came ashore for those dreadful public dinners, which led to a dancing worse than speech-making. So is the cave where the flaring eyes of the old goat made such a goblin appearance in the dark. So is the site of the hut where Robinson lived with the dog and the parrot and the cat, and where he endured those first agonies of solitude, which—strange to say—never involved any ghostly fancies; a circumstance so very remarkable, that perhaps he left out something in writing his record? Round hundreds of such objects, hidden in the dense tropical foliage, the tropical sea breaks evermore; and over them the tropical sky, saving in the short rainy season, shines bright and cloudless.

Neither was I ever belated among wolves, on the borders of France and Spain; nor did I ever, when night was closing in and the ground was covered with snow, draw up my little company among some felled trees which served as a breastwork, and there fire a train of gunpowder so dexterously that suddenly we had three or four score blazing wolves illuminating the darkness around us. Nevertheless, I occasionally go back to that dismal region, and perform the feat again; when, indeed, to smell the singeing and the frying of the wolves afire, and to see them setting one another alight as they rush and tumble, and to behold them rolling in the snow vainly attempting to put themselves out, and to hear their howlings taken up by all the echoes as well as by all the unseen wolves within the woods, makes me tremble.

I was never in the robbers' cave where Gil Blas lived, but I often go back there, and find the trap-door just as heavy to raise as it used to be, while that wicked old disabled Black lies everlastingly cursing in bed. I was never in Don Quixote's study, where he read his books of chivalry until he rose and hacked at imaginary giants, and then refreshed himself with great draughts of water, yet you couldn't move a book in it without my knowledge, or with my consent. I was never (thank Heaven!) in company with the little old woman who hobbled out of the chest, and told the merchant Abudah to go in search of the Talisman of Oromanes, yet I make it my business to know that she is well preserved, and as intolerable as ever. I was never at the school where the boy Horatio Nelson got out of bed to steal the pears; not because he wanted any, but because every other boy was afraid: yet I have several times been back to this Academy, to see him let down out of window with a sheet. So with Damascus, and Bagdad, and Brobdingnag (which has the curious fate of being usually misspelt when written), and Lilliput, and Laputa, and the Nile, and Abyssinia, and the Ganges, and the North Pole, and many hundreds of places—I was never at them, yet it is an affair of my life to keep them intact, and I am always going back to them.

But, when I was in Dullborough one day, revisiting the associations of my childhood, as recorded in previous pages of these notes, my experience in this wise was made quite inconsiderable and of no account, by the quantity of places and people—utterly impossible places and people, but none the less alarmingly real—that I found I had been introduced to by my nurse before I was six years old, and used to be forced to go back to at night without at all wanting to go. If we all knew our own minds (in a more enlarged sense than the popular acceptation of that phrase), I suspect we should find our nurses responsible for most of the dark corners we are forced to go back to against our wills.

The first diabolical character who intruded himself on my peaceful youth (as I called to mind that day at Dullborough) was a certain Captain Murderer. This wretch must have been an offshoot of the Blue Beard family, but I had no suspicion of the consanguinity in those times. His warning name would seem to have awakened no general prejudice against him, for he was admitted into the best society, and possessed immense wealth. Captain Murderer's mission was matrimony, and the gratification of a cannibal appetite with tender brides. On his marriage morning, he always caused both sides of the way to church to be planted with curious flowers; and when his bride said, "Dear Captain Murderer, I never saw flowers like these before: what are they called?" he answered, "They are called Garnish for house-lamb," and laughed at his ferocious practical joke in a horrid manner, disquieting the minds of the noble bridal company, with a very sharp show of teeth, then displayed for the first time. He made love in a coach and six, and married in a coach and twelve, and all his horses were milk-white horses with one red spot on the back, which he caused to be hidden by the harness. For, the spot *would* come there, though every horse was milk-white when Captain Murderer bought him. And the spot was young bride's blood. (To this terrific point I am indebted for my first personal experience of a shudder and cold beads on the forehead.) When Captain Murderer had made an end of feasting and revelry, and had dismissed the noble guests, and was alone with his wife on the day month after their marriage, it was his whimsical custom to produce a golden rolling-pin and a silver pie-board. Now, there was this special feature in the Captain's courtships, that he always asked if the young lady could make pie-crust; and, if she couldn't by nature or education, she was taught. Well! When the bride saw Captain Murderer produce the golden rolling-pin and silver pie-board, she remembered this, and turned up her laced silk sleeves to make a pie. The Captain brought out a silver pie-dish of immense capacity, and the Captain brought out flour and butter and eggs and all things needful, except the inside of the pie; of materials for the staple of the pie itself, the Captain brought out none. Then said the lovely bride, "Dear Captain Murderer, what pie is this to be?" He replied, "A meat-pie." Then said the lovely bride, "Dear Captain Murderer, I see no meat." The Captain humorously retorted, "Look in the glass." She looked in the glass, but still she saw no meat, and then the Captain roared with laughter, and, suddenly frowning and drawing his sword, bade her roll out the crust. So she rolled out the crust, dropping large tears upon it all the time because he was so cross, and when she had lined the dish with crust and had cut the crust all ready to fit the top, the Captain called out, "*I* see the meat in the glass!" And the bride looked up at the glass just in time to see the Captain cutting her head off; and he chopped her in pieces, and peppered her, and salted her, and put her in the pie, and sent it to the baker's, and ate it all, and picked the bones.

Captain Murderer went on in this way, prospering exceedingly, until he came to choose a bride from two twin sisters, and at first didn't know which to choose. For, though one was fair and the other dark, they were both equally beautiful. But the fair twin loved him, and the dark twin hated him, so he chose the fair one. The dark twin would have prevented the marriage if she could, but she couldn't; however, on the night before it, much suspecting Captain Murderer, she stole out and climbed his garden wall, and looked in at his window through a chink in the shutter, and saw him having his teeth filed sharp. Next day she listened all day, and heard him make his joke about the house-lamb. And that day month he had the paste rolled out, and cut the fair twin's head off, and chopped her in pieces, and peppered her, and salted her, and put her in the pie, and sent it to the baker's, and ate it all, and picked the bones.

Now, the dark twin had had her suspicions much increased by the filing of the Captain's teeth, and again by the house-lamb joke. Putting all things together when he gave out that her sister was dead, she divined the truth, and determined to be revenged. So, she went up to Captain Murderer's house, and knocked at the knocker, and pulled at the bell, and, when the Captain came to the door, said: "Dear Captain Murderer, marry me next, for I always loved you, and was jealous of my sister." The Captain took it as a compliment, and made a polite answer, and the marriage was quickly arranged. On the night before it, the bride again climbed to his window, and again saw him having his teeth filed sharp. At this sight she laughed such a terrible laugh at the chink in the shutter, that the Captain's blood curdled,

And the bride looked up at the glass just in time to see the Captain cutting her head off . . . —by C. S. Reinhart

and he said: "I hope nothing has disagreed with me!" At that, she laughed again, a still more terrible laugh, and the shutter was opened and search made, but she was nimbly gone, and there was no one. Next day they went to church in a coach and twelve, and were married. And that day month she rolled the pie-crust out, and Captain Murderer cut her head off, and chopped her in pieces, and peppered her, and salted her, and put her in the pie, and sent it to the baker's, and ate it all, and picked the bones.

But, before she began to roll out the paste, she had taken a deadly poison of a most awful character, distilled from toads' eyes and spiders' knees; and Captain Murderer had hardly picked her last bone, when he began to swell, and to turn blue, and to be all over spots, and to scream. And he went on swelling and turning bluer, and being more all over spots and screaming, until he reached from floor to ceiling, and from wall to wall; and then, at one o'clock in the morning, he blew up with a loud explosion. At the sound of it, all the milk-white horses in the stables broke their halters and went mad, and then they galloped over everybody in Captain Murderer's house (beginning with the family blacksmith who had filed his teeth) until the whole were dead, and then they galloped away.

Hundreds of times did I hear this legend of Captain Murderer in my early youth, and added hundreds of times was there a mental compulsion upon me, in bed, to peep in at his window as the dark twin peeped, and to revisit his horrible house, and look at him in his blue and spotty and screaming stage, as he reached from floor to ceiling, and from wall to wall. The young woman who brought me acquainted with Captain Murderer had a fiendish enjoyment of my terrors, and used to begin, I remember—as a sort of introductory overture—by clawing the air with both hands, and uttering a long low hollow groan. So acutely did I suffer from this ceremony in combination with this infernal Captain, that I sometimes used to plead, I thought I was hardly strong enough and old enough to hear the story again just yet. But, she never spared me one word of it, and, indeed, commended the awful chalice to my lips as the only preservative known to science against "The Black Cat"—a weird and glaring-eyed supernatural Tom, who was reputed to prowl about the world by night, sucking the breath of infancy, and who was endowed with a special thirst (as I was given to understand) for mine.

This female bard—may she have been repaid my debt of obligation to her in the matter of nightmares and perspirations!—reappears in my memory as the daughter of a shipwright. Her name was Mercy, though she had none on me. There was something of a ship-building flavour in the following story. As it always recurs to me in a vague association with calomel pills, I believe it to have been reserved for dull nights when I was low with medicine.

There was once a shipwright, and he wrought in a Government Yard, and his name was Chips. And his father's name before him was Chips, and *his* father's name before *him* was Chips, and they were all Chipses. And Chips the father had sold himself to the Devil for an iron pot and a bushel of tenpenny nails and half a ton of copper and a rat that could speak; and Chips the grandfather had sold himself to the Devil for an iron pot and a bushel of tenpenny nails and half a ton of copper and a rat that could speak; and Chips the great-grandfather had disposed of himself in the same direction on the same terms; and the bargain had run in the family for a long, long time. So, one day, when young Chips was at work in the Dock Slip all alone, down in the dark hold of an old Seventy-four that was haled up for repairs, the Devil presented himself, and remarked:—

> *"A Lemon has pips,*
> *And a Yard has ships,*
> *And I'll have Chips!"*

(I don't know why, but this fact of the Devil's expressing himself in rhyme was peculiarly trying to me.) Chips looked up when he heard the words, and there he saw the Devil with saucer eyes that squinted on a terrible great scale, and that struck out sparks of blue fire continually. And, whenever he winked his eyes, showers of blue sparks came out, and his eyelashes made a clattering like flints and steels striking lights. And hanging over one of his arms by the handle was an iron pot, and under that arm was a bushel of tenpenny nails, and under his other arm was half a ton of copper, and sitting on one of his shoulders was a rat that could speak. So, the Devil said again:—

"A Lemon has pips,
And a Yard has ships,
And I'll have Chips!"

(The invariable effect of this alarming tautology on the part of the Evil Spirit was to deprive me of my senses for some moments.) So, Chips answered never a word, but went on with his work. "What are you doing, Chips?" said the rat that could speak. "I am putting in new planks where you and your gang have eaten old away," said Chips. "But we'll eat them too," said the rat that could speak; "and we'll let in the water and drown the crew, and we'll eat them too." Chips, being only a shipwright, and not a man-of-war's man, said, "You are welcome to it." But he couldn't keep his eyes off the half a ton of copper, or the bushel of tenpenny nails; for nails and copper are a shipwright's sweethearts, and shipwrights will run away with them whenever they can. So, the Devil said, "I see what you are looking at, Chips. You had better strike the bargain. You know the terms. Your father before you was well acquainted with them, and so were your grandfather and great-grandfather before him." Says Chips, "I like the copper, and I like the nails, and I don't mind the pot, but I don't like the rat." Says the Devil fiercely, "You can't have the metal without him—and *he's* a curiosity. I'm going." Chips, afraid of losing the half a ton of copper and the bushel of nails, then said, "Give us hold!" So, he got the copper and the nails and the pot and the rat that could speak, and the Devil vanished. Chips sold the copper, and he sold the nails, and he would have sold the pot; but, whenever he offered it for sale, the rat was in it, and the dealers dropped it, and would have nothing to say to the bargain. So, Chips resolved to kill the rat, and being at work in the Yard one day with a great kettle of hot pitch on one side of him, and the iron pot with the rat in it on the other, he turned the scalding pitch into the pot, and filled it full. Then, he kept his eye upon it till it cooled and hardened, and then he let it stand for twenty days, and then he heated the pitch again, and turned it back into the kettle, and then he sank the pot in water for twenty days more, and then he got the smelters to put it in the furnace for twenty days more, and then they gave it him out, red-hot, and looking like red-hot glass instead of iron—yet there was the rat in it, just the same as ever! And the moment it caught his eye, it said with a jeer,—

> "*A Lemon has pips,*
> *And a Yard has ships,*
> *And I'll have Chips!*"

(For this Refrain I had waited, since its last appearance, with inexpressible horror, which now culminated.) Chips now felt certain in his own mind that the rat would stick to him; the rat, answering his thought, said, "I will—like pitch!"

Now, as the rat leaped out of the pot when it had spoken, and made off, Chips began to hope that it wouldn't keep its word. But, a terrible thing happened next day. For, when dinner-time came, and the Dock bell rang to strike work, he put his rule into the long pocket at the side of his trousers, and there he found a rat—not that rat, but another rat. And in his hat he found another; and in his pocket-handkerchief another; and in the sleeves of his coat, when he pulled it on to go to dinner, two more. And from that time he found himself so frightfully intimate with all the rats in the Yard, that they climbed up his legs when he was at work, and sat on his tools while he used them. And they could all speak to one another, and he understood what they said. And they got into his lodging, and into his bed, and into his teapot, and into his beer, and into his boots. And he was

going to be married to a corn-chandler's daughter; and when he gave
her a workbox he had himself made for her, a rat jumped out of it;
and when he put his arm round her waist, a rat clung about her; so
the marriage was broken off, though the banns were already twice
put up—which the parish clerk well remembers, for, as he handed
the book to the clergyman for the second time of asking, a large fat
rat ran over the leaf. (By this time a special cascade of rats was
rolling down my back, and the whole of my small listening person
was overrun with them. At intervals ever since, I have been morbidly
afraid of my own pocket, lest my exploring hand should find a speci-
men or two of those vermin in it.)

You may believe that all this was very terrible to Chips; but even
all this was not the worst. He knew, besides, what the rats were
doing, wherever they were. So, sometimes he would cry aloud when
he was at his club at night, "Oh! Keep the rats out of the convicts'
burying-ground! Don't let them do that!" Or "There's one of them
at the cheese down-stairs!" Or "There's two of them smelling at the
baby in the garret!" Or, other things of that sort. At last he was
voted mad, and lost his work in the Yard, and could get no other
work. But, King George wanted men, so before very long he got
pressed for a sailor. And so he was taken off in a boat one evening to
his ship, lying at Spithead, ready to sail. And so the first thing he
made out in her, as he got near her, was the figure-head of the old
Seventy-four, where he had seen the Devil. She was called the Argonaut, and they rowed right under the bowsprit, where the figure-head
of the Argonaut, with a sheepskin in his hand and a blue gown on,
was looking out to sea; and sitting staring on his forehead was the rat
who could speak, and his exact words were these: "Chips ahoy! Old
boy! We've pretty well eat them too, and we'll drown the crew, and
will eat them too!" (Here I always became exceedingly faint, and
would have asked for water, but that I was speechless.)

The ship was bound for the Indies; and if you don't know where
that is, you ought to, and angels will never love you. (Here I felt
myself an outcast from a future state.) The ship set sail that very

night, and she sailed, and sailed, and sailed. Chips's feelings were dreadful. Nothing ever equalled his terrors. No wonder. At last, one day, he asked leave to speak to the Admiral. The Admiral giv' leave. Chips went down on his knees in the Great State Cabin. "Your Honour, unless your Honour, without a moment's loss of time, makes sail for the nearest shore, this is a doomed ship, and her name is the Coffin!" "Young man, your words are a madman's words." "Your Honour, no; they are nibbling us away." "They?" "Your Honour, them dreadful rats. Dust and hollowness where solid oak ought to be! Rats nibbling a grave for every man on board! Oh! Does your Honour love your Lady and your pretty children?" "Yes, my man, to be sure." "Then, for God's sake, make for the nearest shore, for at this present moment the rats are all stopping in their work, and are all looking straight towards you with bare teeth, and are all saying to one another that you shall never, never, never, never see your Lady and your children more." "My poor fellow, you are a case for the doctor. Sentry, take care of this man!"

So, he was bled and he was blistered, and he was this and that for six whole days and nights. So, then he again asked leave to speak to the Admiral. The Admiral giv' leave. He went down on his knees in the Great State Cabin. "Now, Admiral, you must die! You took no warning; you must die! The rats are never wrong in their calculations, and they make out that they'll be through at twelve to-night. So, you must die!—With me and all the rest!" And so at twelve o'clock there was a great leak reported in the ship, and a torrent of water rushed in, and nothing could stop it, and they all went down, every living soul. And what the rats—being water-rats—left of Chips at last floated to shore, and sitting on him was an immense overgrown rat, laughing, that dived when the corpse touched the beach, and never came up. And there was a deal of seaweed on the remains. And if you get thirteen bits of seaweed, and dry them, and burn them in the fire, they will go off like in these thirteen words as plain as plain can be:—

"A Lemon has pips,
And a Yard has ships,
And I've got Chips!"

The same female bard—descended, possibly, from those terrible old scalds who seem to have existed for the express purpose of addling the brains of mankind when they begin to investigate languages—made a standing pretence which greatly assisted in forcing me back to a number of hideous places that I would by all means have avoided. This pretence was, that all her ghost stories had occurred to her own relations. Politeness towards a meritorious family, therefore, forbade my doubting them, and they acquired an air of authentication that impaired my digestive powers for life. There was a narrative concerning an unearthly animal foreboding death, which appeared in the open street to a parlour-maid who "went to fetch the beer" for supper; first (as I now recall it) assuming the likeness of a black dog, and gradually rising on its hind-legs, and swelling into the semblance of some quadruped greatly surpassing a hippopotamus: which apparition—not because I deemed it in the least improbable, but because I felt it to be really too large to bear—I feebly endeavoured to explain away. But, on Mercy's retorting with wounded dignity that the parlour-maid was her own sister-in-law, I perceived there was no hope, and resigned myself to this zoölogical phenomenon as one of my many pursuers. There was another narrative describing the apparition of a young woman who came out of a glass case, and haunted another young woman until the other young woman questioned it, and elicited that its bones (Lord! to think of its being so particular about its bones!) were buried under the glass case, whereas she required them to be interred, with every Undertaking solemnity up to twenty-four pound ten, in another particular place. This narrative I considered I had a personal interest in disproving, because we had glass cases at home, and how otherwise was I to be guaranteed from the intrusion of young women requiring *me* to bury them up to twenty-four pound ten, when I had only twopence a week? But my remorseless nurse cut the ground from under my tender feet, by informing me that She was the other young woman; and I couldn't say, "I don't believe you;" it was not possible.

Such are a few of the uncommercial journeys that I was forced to make, against my will, when I was very young and unreasoning. And really, as to the latter part of them, it is not so very long ago—now I come to think of it—that I was asked to undertake them once again with a steady countenance.

THE SIGNAL-MAN

ALLOA! Below there!"

When he heard a voice thus calling to him, he was standing at the door of his box, with a flag in his hand, furled round its short pole. One would have thought, considering the nature of the ground, that he could not have doubted from what quarter the voice came; but, instead of looking up to where I stood on the top of the steep cutting nearly over his head, he turned himself about and looked down the Line. There was something remarkable in his manner of doing so, though I could not have said for my life what. But I know it was remarkable enough to attract my notice, even though his figure was foreshortened and shadowed, down in the deep trench, and mine was high above him, so steeped in the glow of an angry sunset, that I had shaded my eyes with my hand before I saw him at all.

"Halloa! Below!"

From looking down the Line, he turned himself about again, and, raising his eyes, saw my figure high above him.

"Is there any path by which I can come down and speak to you?"

He looked up at me without replying, and I looked down at him without pressing him too soon with a repetition of my idle question.

Just then there came a vague vibration in the earth and air, quickly changing into a violent pulsation, and an on-coming rush that caused me to start back, as though it had force to draw me down. When such vapour as rose to my height from this rapid train had passed me, and was skimming away over the landscape, I looked down again, and saw him refurling the flag he had shown while the train went by.

I repeated my inquiry. After a pause, during which he seemed to regard me with fixed attention, he motioned with his rolled-up flag towards a point on my level, some two or three hundred yards distant. I called down to him, "All right!" and made for that point. There, by dint of looking closely about me, I found a rough zigzag descending path notched out, which I followed.

The cutting was extremely deep, and unusually precipitate. It was made through a clammy stone, that became oozier and wetter as I went down. For these reasons, I found the way long enough to give me time to recall a singular air of reluctance or compulsion with which he had pointed out the path.

When I came down low enough upon the zigzag descent to see him again, I saw that he was standing between the rails on the way by which the train had lately passed, in an attitude as if he were waiting for me to appear. He had his left hand at his chin, and that left elbow rested on his right hand, crossed over his breast. His attitude was one of such expectation and watchfulness, that I stopped a moment, wondering at it.

I resumed my downward way, and stepping out upon the level of the railroad, and drawing nearer to him, saw that he was a dark sallow man, with a dark beard and rather heavy eyebrows. His post was in as solitary and dismal a place as ever I saw. On either side, a dripping wet wall of jagged stone, excluding all view but a strip of sky; the perspective one way only a crooked prolongation of this great dungeon; the shorter perspective in the other direction terminating in a gloomy red light, and the gloomier entrance to a black tunnel, in whose massive architecture there was a barbarous, depressing, and forbidding air. So little sunlight ever found its way to this spot, that it had an earthy, deadly smell; and so much cold wind rushed through it, that it struck chill to me, as if I had left the natural world.

Before he stirred, I was near enough to him to have touched him. Not even then removing his eyes from mine, he stepped back one step, and lifted his hand.

This was a lonesome post to occupy (I said), and it had riveted my attention when I looked down from up yonder. A visitor was a rarity, I should suppose; not an unwelcome rarity, I hoped? In me he merely saw a man who had been shut up within narrow limits all his life, and who, being at last set free, had a newly awakened interest in these great works. To such purpose I spoke to him; but I am far from sure of the terms I used; for, besides that I am not happy in opening any conversation, there was something in the man that daunted me.

He directed a most curious look towards the red light near the tunnel's mouth, and looked all about it, as if something were missing from it, and then looked at me.

That light was part of his charge? Was it not?

He answered in a low voice, "Don't you know it is?"

The monstrous thought came into my mind, as I perused the fixed eyes and the saturnine face, that this was a spirit, not a man. I have speculated since whether there may have been infection in his mind.

In my turn, I stepped back. But, in making the action, I detected in his eyes some latent fear of me. This put the monstrous thought to flight.

"You look at me," I said, forcing a smile, "as if you had a dread of me."

"I was doubtful," he returned, "whether I had seen you before."

"Where?"

He pointed to the red light he had looked at.

"There?" I said.

Intently watchful of me, he replied (but without sound), "Yes."

"My good fellow, what should I do there? However, be that as it may, I never was there, you may swear."

"I think I may," he rejoined. "Yes; I am sure I may."

His manner cleared, like my own. He replied to my remarks with readiness, and in well-chosen words. Had he much to do there? Yes; that was to say, he had enough responsibility to bear; but exactness and watchfulness were what was required of him, and of actual work—manual labour—he had next to none. To change that signal, to trim those lights, and to turn his iron handle now and then, was all he had to do under that head. Regarding those many long and lonely hours of which I seemed to make so much, he could only say that the routine of his life had shaped itself into that form, and he had grown used to it. He had taught himself a language down here,—if only to know it by sight, and to have formed his own crude ideas of its pronunciation, could be called learning it. He had also worked at fractions and decimals, and tried a little algebra; but he was, and had been as a boy, a poor hand at figures. Was it necessary for him when on duty always to remain in that channel of damp air, and could he never rise into the sunshine from between those high stone walls? Why, that depended upon times and circumstances. Under some conditions there would be less upon the Line than under others, and the same held good as to certain hours of the day and night. In bright weather he did choose occasions for getting a little above these lower shadows; but being at all times liable to be called by his electric bell, and at such times listening for it with redoubled anxiety, the relief was less than I would suppose.

He took me into his box, where there was a fire, a desk for an official book in which he had to make certain entries, a telegraphic instrument with its dial, face, and needles, and the little bell of which he had spoken. On my trusting that he would excuse the remark that he had been well educated, and (I hoped I might say without offence) perhaps educated above that station, he observed that instances of slight incongruity in such wise would rarely be found wanting among large bodies of men; that he had heard it was so in workhouses, in the police force, even in that last desperate resource, the army; and that he knew it was so, more or less, in any great railway staff. He had been, when young (if I could believe it, sitting in that hut,—he scarcely could), a student of natural philosophy, and had attended lectures; but he had run wild, misused his opportunities, gone down, and never risen again. He had no complaint to offer about that. He had made his bed, and he lay upon it. It was far too late to make another.

All that I have here condensed he said in a quiet manner, with his grave dark regards divided between me and the fire. He threw in the word "Sir" from time to time, and especially when he referred to his youth,—as though to request me to understand that he claimed to be nothing but what I found him. He was several times interrupted by the little bell, and had to read off messages and send replies. Once he had to stand without the door, and display a flag as a train passed, and made some verbal communication to the driver. In the discharge of his duties, I observed him to be remarkably exact and vigilant, breaking off his discourse at a syllable, and remaining silent until what he had to do was done.

In a word, I should have set this man down as one of the safest of men to be employed in that capacity, but for the circumstance that while he was speaking to me he twice broke off with a fallen colour, turned his face towards the little bell when it did NOT ring, opened the door of the hut (which was kept shut to exclude the unhealthy damp), and looked out towards the red light near the mouth of the tunnel. On both of those occasions he came back to the fire with the inexplicable air upon him which I had remarked, without being able to define, when we were so far asunder.

Said I, when I rose to leave him, "You almost make me think that I have met with a contented man."

(I am afraid I must acknowledge that I said it to lead him on.)

"I believe I used to be so," he rejoined in the low voice in which he had first spoken; "but I am troubled, sir, I am troubled."

He would have recalled the words if he could. He had said them, however, and I took them up quickly.

"With what? What is your trouble?"

"It is very difficult to impart, sir. It is very, very difficult to speak of. If ever you make me another visit, I will try to tell you."

"But I expressly intend to make you another visit. Say, when shall it be?"

"I go off early in the morning, and I shall be on again at ten to-morrow night, sir."

"I will come at eleven."

He thanked me, and went out at the door with me. "I'll show my white light, sir," he said in his peculiar low voice, "till you have found the way up. When you have found it, don't call out! And when you are at the top, don't call out!"

His manner seemed to make the place strike colder to me, but I said no more than, "Very well."

"And when you come down to-morrow night, don't call out! Let me ask you a parting question. What made you cry, 'Halloa! Below there!' to-night?"

"Heaven knows," said I. "I cried something to that effect—"

"Not to that effect, sir. Those were the very words. I know them well."

"Admit those were the very words. I said them, no doubt, because I saw you below."

"For no other reason?"

"What other reason could I possibly have?"

"You had no feeling that they were conveyed to you in any supernatural way?"

"No."

He wished me good night, and held up his light. I walked by the side of the down Line of rails (with a very disagreeable sensation of a train coming behind me) until I found the path. It was easier to mount than to descend, and I got back to my inn without any adventure.

Punctual to my appointment, I placed my foot on the first notch of the zigzag next night as the distant clocks were striking eleven. He was waiting for me at the bottom, with his white light on. "I have not called out," I said when we came close together; "may I speak now?" "By all means, sir." "Good night, then, and here's my hand." "Good night, sir, and here's mine." With that we walked side by side to his box, entered it, closed the door, and sat down by the fire.

"I have made up my mind sir," he began, bending forward as soon as we were seated, and speaking in a tone but a little above a whisper, "that you shall not have to ask me twice what troubles me. I took you for some one else yesterday evening. That troubles me."

"That mistake?"

"No. That some one else."

"Who is it?"

"I don't know."

"Like me?"

"I don't know. I never saw the face. The left arm is across the face, and the right arm is waved,—violently waved. This way."

I followed his action with my eyes, and it was the action of an arm gesticulating, with the utmost passion and vehemence, "For God's sake, clear the way!"

"One moonlight night," said the man, "I was sitting here, when I heard a voice cry, 'Halloa! Below there!' I started up, looked from that door, and saw this Some one else standing by the red light near the tunnel, waving as I just now showed you. The voice seemed hoarse with shouting, and it cried, 'Look out! Look out!' And then again, 'Halloa! Below there! Look out!' I caught up my lamp, turned it on red, and ran towards the figure, calling, 'What's wrong? What has happened? Where?' It stood just outside the blackness of the tunnel. I advanced so close upon it that I wondered at its keeping the sleeve across its eyes. I ran right up at it, and had my hand stretched out to pull the sleeve away, when it was gone."

"Into the tunnel?" said I.

"No. I ran on into the tunnel, five hundred yards. I stopped, and held my lamp above my head, and saw the figures of the measured distance, and saw the wet stains stealing down the walls and trickling through the arch. I ran out again faster than I had run in (for I had a mortal abhorrence of the place upon me), and I looked all round the red light with my own red light, and I went up the iron ladder to the gallery atop of it, and I came down again, and ran back here. I telegraphed both ways, 'An alarm has been given. Is anything wrong?' The answer came back, both ways, 'All well.'"

Resisting the slow touch of a frozen finger tracing out my spine, I showed him how that this figure must be a deception of his sense of sight; and how that figures, originating in disease of the delicate nerves that minister to the functions of the eye, were known to have often troubled patients, some of whom had become conscious of the nature of their affliction, and had even proved it by experiments upon themselves. "As to an imaginary cry," said I, "do but listen for a moment to the wind in this unnatural valley while we speak so low, and to the wild harp it makes of the telegraph wires!"

That was all very well, he returned, after we had sat listening for a while, and he ought to know something of the wind and the wires,—he who so often passed long winter nights there, alone and watching. But he would beg to remark that he had not finished.

I asked his pardon, and he slowly added these words, touching my arm:—

"Within six hours after the Appearance, the memorable accident on this Line happened, and within ten hours the dead and wounded were brought along through the tunnel over the spot where the figure had stood."

A disagreeable shudder crept over me, but I did my best against it. It was not to be denied, I rejoined, that this was a remarkable coincidence, calculated deeply to impress his mind. But it was unquestionable that remarkable coincidences did continually occur, and they must be taken into account in dealing with such a subject. Though to be sure I must admit, I added (for I thought I saw that he was going to bring the objection to bear upon me), men of common sense did not allow much for coincidences in making the ordinary calculations of life.

He again begged to remark that he had not finished.

I again begged his pardon for being betrayed into interruptions.

"This," he said, again laying his hand upon my arm, and glancing over his shoulder with hollow eyes, "was just a year ago. Six or seven months passed, and I had recovered from the surprise and shock, when one morning, as the day was breaking, I, standing at the door, looked towards the red light, and saw the spectre again." He stopped with a fixed look at me.

"Did it cry out?"

"No. I was silent."

"Did it wave its arm?"

"No. It leaned against the shaft of the light, with both hands before the face. Like this."

Once more I followed his action with my eyes. It was an action of mourning. I have seen such an attitude in stone figures on tombs.

"Did you go up to it?"

"I came in and sat down, partly to collect my thoughts, partly because it had turned me faint. When I went to the door again, daylight was above me, and the ghost was gone."

"But nothing followed? Nothing came of this?"

He touched me on the arm with his forefinger twice or thrice, giving a ghastly nod each time.

"That very day, as a train came out of the tunnel, I noticed, at a carriage window on my side, what looked like a confusion of hands and heads, and something waved. I saw it just in time to signal the driver, Stop! He shut off, and put his brake on, but the train drifted past here a hundred and fifty yards or more. I ran after it, and, as I went along, heard terrible screams and cries. A beautiful young lady had died instantaneously in one of the compartments, and was brought in here, and laid down on this floor between us."

Involuntarily I pushed my chair back, as I looked from the boards at which he pointed to himself.

"True, sir. True. Precisely as it happened, so I tell it you."

I could think of nothing to say to any purpose, and my mouth was very dry. The wind and the wires took up the story with a long lamenting wail.

He resumed. "Now, sir, mark this, and judge how my mind is troubled. The spectre came back a week ago. Ever since, it has been there, now and again, by fits and starts."

"At the light?"

"At the danger-light."

"What does it seem to do?"

He repeated, if possible with increased passion and vehemence, that former gesticulation of, "For God's sake, clear the way!"

Then he went on. "I have no peace or rest for it. It calls to me, for many minutes together, in an agonised manner, 'Below there! Look out! Look out!' It stands waving to me. It rings my little bell—"

I caught at that. "Did it ring your bell yesterday evening when I was here, and you went to the door?"

"Twice."

"Why, see," said I, "how your imagination misleads you! My eyes were on the bell, and my ears were open to the bell, and, if I am a living man, it did NOT ring at those times. No, nor at any other time, except when it was rung in the natural course of physical things by the station communicating with you."

He shook his head. "I have never made a mistake as to that yet, sir. I have never confused the spectre's ring with the man's. The ghost's ring is a strange vibration in the bell that it derives from nothing else, and I have not asserted that the bell stirs to the eye. I don't wonder that you failed to hear it. But *I* heard it."

"And did the spectre seem to be there when you looked out?"

"It WAS there."

"Both times?"

He repeated firmly: "Both times."

"Will you come to the door with me, and look for it now?"

He bit his under lip as though he were somewhat unwilling, but arose. I opened the door, and stood on the step, while he stood in the doorway. There was the danger-light. There was the dismal mouth of the tunnel. There were the high, wet stone walls of the cutting. There were the stars above them.

"Do you see it?" I asked him, taking particular note of his face. His eyes were prominent and strained, but not very much more so, perhaps, than my own had been when I had directed them earnestly towards the same spot.

"No," he answered. "It is not there."

"Agreed," said I.

We went in again, shut the door, and resumed our seats. I was thinking how best to improve this advantage, if it might be called one, when he took up the conversation in such a matter of course way, so assuming that there could be no serious question of fact between us, that I felt myself placed in the weakest of positions.

"By this time you will fully understand, sir," he said, "that what troubles me so dreadfully is the question, What does the spectre mean?"

I was not sure, I told him, that I did fully understand.

"What is its warning against?" he said, ruminating, with his eyes on the fire, and only by times turning them on me. "What is the danger? Where is the danger? There is danger overhanging somewhere on the Line. Some dreadful calamity will happen. It is not to be doubted this third time after what has gone before. But surely this is a cruel haunting of *me*. What can *I* do?"

He pulled out his handkerchief, and wiped the drops from his heated forehead.

"If I telegraph Danger on either side of me, or on both, I can give no reason for it," he went on, wiping the palms of his hands. "I should get into trouble, and do no good. They would think I was mad. This is the way it would work,—Message: 'Danger! Take care!'

Answer: 'What Danger? Where?' Message: 'Don't know. But, for God's sake, take care!' They would displace me. What else could they do?"

His pain of mind was most pitiable to see. It was the mental torture of a conscientious man, oppressed beyond endurance by an unintelligible responsibility involving life.

"When it first stood under the danger-light," he went on, putting his dark hair back from his head, and drawing his hands outward across and across his temples in an extremity of feverish distress, "why not tell me where that accident was to happen,—if it must happen? Why not tell me how it could be averted,—if it could have been averted? When on its second coming it hid its face, why not tell me, instead, 'She is going to die. Let them keep her at home'? If it came, on those two occasions, only to show me that its warnings were true, and so to prepare me for the third, why not warn me plainly now? And I, Lord help me! A mere poor signal-man on this solitary station! Why not go to somebody with credit to be believed, and power to act?"

When I saw him in this state, I saw that for the poor man's sake, as well as for the public safety, what I had to do for the time was to compose his mind. Therefore, setting aside all question of reality or unreality between us, I represented to him that whoever thoroughly discharged his duty, must do well, and that at least it was his comfort that he understood his duty, though he did not understand these confounding Appearances. In this effort I succeeded far better than in the attempt to reason him out of his conviction. He became calm; the occupations incidental to his post as the night advanced began to make larger demands on his attention; and I left him at two in the morning. I had offered to stay through the night, but he would not hear of it.

That I more than once looked back at the red light as I ascended the pathway, that I did not like the red light, and that I should have slept but poorly if my bed had been under it, I see no reason to conceal. Nor did I like the two sequences of the accident and the dead girl. I see no reason to conceal that either.

But what ran most in my thoughts was the consideration, how ought I to act, having become the recipient of this disclosure? I had proved the man to be intelligent, vigilant, painstaking, and exact; but how long might he remain so, in his state of mind? Though in a subordinate position, still he held a most important trust, and would I (for instance) like to stake my own life on the chances of his continuing to execute it with precision?

Unable to overcome a feeling that there would be something treacherous in my communicating what he had told me to his superiors in the Company, without first being plain with himself and proposing a middle course to him, I ultimately resolved to offer to accompany him (otherwise keeping his secret for the present) to the wisest medical practitioner we could hear of in those parts, and to take his opinion. A change in his time of duty would come round next night, he had apprised me, and he would be off an hour or two after sunrise, and on again soon after sunset. I had appointed to return accordingly.

Next evening was a lovely evening, and I walked out early to enjoy it. The sun was not yet quite down when I traversed the field path near the top of the deep cutting. I would extend my walk for an hour, I said to myself, half an hour on and half an hour back, and it would then be time to go to my signal-man's box.

Before pursuing my stroll, I stepped to the brink, and mechanically looked down, from the point from which I had first seen him. I cannot describe the thrill that seized upon me when, close at the mouth of the tunnel, I saw the appearance of a man, with his left sleeve across his eyes, passionately waving his right arm.

The nameless horror that oppressed me passed in a moment, for in a moment I saw that this appearance of a man was a man indeed, and that there was a little group of other men, standing at a short distance, to whom he seemed to be rehearsing the gesture he made.

The danger-light was not yet lighted. Against its shaft, a little low hut, entirely new to me, had been made of some wooden supports and tarpaulin. It looked no bigger than a bed.

With an irresistible sense that something was wrong,—with a flashing, self-reproachful fear that fatal mischief had come of my leaving the man there, and causing no one to be sent to overlook or correct what he did,—I descended the notched path with all the speed I could make.

"What is the matter?" I asked the men.

"Signal-man killed this morning, sir."

"Not the man belonging to that box?"

"Yes, sir."

"Not the man I know?"

"You will recognise him, sir, if you knew him," said the man who spoke for the others, solemnly uncovering his own head, and raising an end of the tarpaulin, "for his face is quite composed."

"Oh, how did this happen, how did this happen?" I asked, turning from one to another as the hut closed in again.

"He was cut down by an engine, sir. No man in England knew his work better. But somehow he was not clear of the outer rail. It was just at broad day. He had struck the light, and had the lamp in his hand. As the engine came out of the tunnel, his back was towards her, and she cut him down. That man drove her, and was showing how it happened. Show the gentleman, Tom."

The man, who wore a rough dark dress, stepped back to his former place at the mouth of the tunnel.

"Coming round the curve in the tunnel, sir," he said, "I saw him at the end, like as if I saw him down a perspective-glass. There was no time to check speed, and I knew him to be very careful. As he didn't seem to take heed of the whistle, I shut it off when we were running down upon him, and called to him as loud as I could call."

"What did you say?"

"I said, 'Below there! Look out! Look out! For God's sake, clear the way!'"

I started.

"Ah! it was a dreadful time, sir. I never left off calling to him. I put this arm before my eyes not to see, and I waved this arm to the last; but it was no use."

Without prolonging the narrative to dwell on any one of its curious circumstances more than on any other, I may, in closing it, point out the coincidence that the warning of the engine-driver included, not only the words which the unfortunate signal-man had repeated to me as haunting him, but also the words which I myself—not he—had attached, and that only in my own mind, to the gesticulation he had imitated.

THE STORY OF THE
BAGMAN'S UNCLE

M Y UNCLE, gentlemen," said the bagman, "was one of the merriest, pleasantest, cleverest fellows that ever lived. I wish you had known him, gentlemen. On second thoughts, gentlemen, I *don't* wish you had known him, for if you had, you would have been all by this time in the ordinary course of nature, if not dead, at all events so near it, as to have taken to stopping at home and giving up company: which would have deprived me of the inestimable pleasure of addressing you at this moment. Gentlemen, I wish your fathers and mothers had known my uncle. They would have been amazingly fond of him, especially your respectable mothers; I know they would. If any two of his numerous virtues predominated over the many that adorned his character, I should say they were his mixed punch and his after-supper song. Excuse my dwelling upon these melancholy recollections of departed worth; you won't see a man like my uncle every day in the week.

"I have always considered it a great point in my uncle's character, gentlemen, that he was the intimate friend and companion of Tom Smart, of the great house of Bilson and Slum, Cateaton Street, City. My uncle collected for Tiggin and Welps, but for a long time he went pretty near the same journey as Tom; and the very first night they met, my uncle took a fancy for Tom, and Tom took a fancy for my uncle. They made a bet of a new hat before they had known each other half an hour, who should brew the best quart of punch and drink it the quickest. My uncle was judged to have won the making, but Tom Smart beat him in the drinking by about half a salt-spoon-full. They took another quart a-piece to drink each other's health in, and were staunch friends ever afterwards. There's a destiny in these things, gentlemen; we can't help it.

"In personal appearance, my uncle was a trifle shorter than the middle size; he was a thought stouter too, than the ordinary run of people, and perhaps his face might be a shade redder. He had the jolliest face you ever saw, gentlemen: something like Punch, with a handsomer nose and chin; his eyes were always twinkling and sparkling with good humour; and a smile—not one of your unmeaning wooden grins, but a real, merry, hearty, good-tempered smile, was perpetually on his countenance. He was pitched out of his gig once, and knocked head first against a mile-stone. There he lay, stunned, and so cut about the face with some gravel which had been heaped up alongside it, that, to use my uncle's own strong expression, if his mother could have revisited the earth, she wouldn't have known him. Indeed, when I come to think of the matter, gentlemen, I feel pretty sure she wouldn't, for she died when my uncle was two years and seven months old, and I think it's very likely that even without the gravel, his top-boots would have puzzled the good lady not a little: to say nothing of his jolly red face. However, there he lay, and I have heard my uncle say, many a time, that the man said who picked him up that he was smiling as merrily as if he had tumbled out for a treat, and that after they had bled him, the first faint glimmerings of returning animation, were, his jumping up in bed, bursting out into a loud laugh, kissing the young woman who held the basin, and demanding a mutton chop and a pickled walnut instantly. He was very fond of pickled walnuts, gentlemen. He said he always found that, taken without vinegar, they relished the beer.

"My uncle's great journey was in the fall of the leaf, at which time he collected debts and took orders in the north: going from London to Edinburgh, from Edinburgh to Glasgow, from Glasgow back to Edinburgh, and thence to London by the smack. You are to understand that this second visit to Edinburgh was for his own pleasure. He used to go back for a week, just to look up his old friends; and what with breakfasting with this one, and lunching with that, and dining with a third, and supping with another, a pretty tight week he used to make of it. I don't know whether any of you, gentlemen, ever partook of a real substantial hospitable Scotch breakfast, and then went out to a slight lunch of a bushel of oysters, a dozen or so of bottled ale, and a noggin or two of whiskey to close up with. If you ever did, you will agree with me that it requires a pretty strong head to go out to dinner and supper afterwards.

"But, bless your hearts and eyebrows, all this sort of thing was nothing to my uncle! He was so well seasoned, that it was mere child's play. I have heard him say that he could see the Dundee people out, any day, and walk home afterwards without staggering; and yet the Dundee people have as strong heads and as strong punch, gentlemen, as you are likely to meet with, between the poles. I have heard of a Glasgow man and a Dundee man drinking against each other for fifteen hours at a sitting. They were both suffocated, as nearly as could be ascertained, at the same moment, but with this trifling exception, gentlemen, they were not a bit the worse for it.

"One night, within four-and-twenty hours of the time when he had settled to take shipping for London, my uncle supped at the house of a very old friend of his, a Baillie Mac something, and four syllables after it, who lived in the old town of Edinburgh. There were the baillie's wife, and the baillie's three daughters, and the baillie's grown-up son, and three or four stout, bushy-eyebrowed, canty old Scotch fellows that the baillie had got together to do honour to my uncle, and help to make merry. It was a glorious supper. There was kippered salmon, and Finnan haddocks, and a lamb's head, and a haggis; a celebrated Scotch dish, gentlemen, which my uncle used to say always looked to him, when it came to table, very much like a cupid's stomach; and a great many other things besides, that I forget the names of, but very good things notwithstanding. The lassies were pretty and agreeable; the baillie's wife one of the best creatures that ever lived; and my uncle in thoroughly good cue: the consequence of which was, that the young ladies tittered and giggled, and the old lady laughed out loud, and the baillie and the other old fellows roared till they were red in the face, the whole mortal time. I don't quite recollect how many tumblers of whiskey toddy each man drank after supper, but this I know, that about one o'clock in the morning, the baillie's grown-up son became insensible while attempting the first verse of 'Willie brewed a peck o' maut'; and he having been, for half an hour before, the only other man visible above the mahogany, it occurred to my uncle that it was almost time to think about going: especially as drinking had set in at seven o'clock, in order that he might get home at a decent hour. But, thinking it might not be quite polite to go just then, my uncle voted himself into the chair, mixed another glass, rose to propose his own health, addressed himself in a neat and complimentary speech, and drank the toast with great enthusiasm. Still nobody woke; so my uncle took a little drop more— neat this time, to prevent the toddy disagreeing with him—and, laying violent hands on his hat, sallied forth into the street.

"It was a wild gusty night when my uncle closed the baillie's door; and settling his hat firmly on his head, to prevent the wind from taking it, thrust his hands into his pockets, and looking upwards, took a short survey of the state of the weather. The clouds were drifting over the moon at their giddiest speed: at one time wholly obscuring her: at another, suffering her to burst forth in full splendour and shed her light on all the objects around: anon, driving over her again, with increased velocity, and shrouding everything in darkness. 'Really, this won't do,' said my uncle, addressing himself to the weather, as if he felt himself personally offended. 'This is not the kind of thing for my voyage. It will not do at any price,' said my uncle, very impressively. And having repeated this, several times, he recovered his balance with some difficulty—for he was rather giddy with looking up into the sky so long—and walked merrily on.

"The baillie's house was in the Canongate, and my uncle was going to the other end of Leith Walk, rather better than a mile's journey. On either side of him, there shot up against the dark sky, tall, gaunt, straggling houses, with time-stained fronts, and windows that seemed to have shared the lot of eyes in mortals, and to have grown dim and sunken with age. Six, seven, eight stories high were the houses; story piled above story, as children build with cards—throwing their dark shadows over the roughly paved road, and making the night darker. A few oil lamps were scattered, at long distances, but they only served to mark the dirty entrance to some narrow close, or to show where a common stair communicated, by steep and intricate windings, with the various flats above. Glancing at all these things with the air of a man who had seen them too often before, to think them worthy of much notice now, my uncle walked up the middle of the street, with a thumb in each waistcoat pocket, indulging from time to time in various snatches of song, chaunted forth with such good-will and spirit, that the quiet honest folk started from their first sleep and lay trembling in bed till the sound died away in the distance; when, satisfying themselves that it was only some drunken ne'er-do-weel finding his way home, they covered themselves up warm and fell asleep again.

"I am particular in describing how my uncle walked up the middle of the street, with his thumbs in his waistcoat pockets, gentlemen, because, as he often used to say (and with great reason too) there is nothing at all extraordinary in this story, unless you distinctly understand at the beginning, that he was not by any means of a marvellous or romantic turn.

"Gentlemen, my uncle walked on with his thumbs in his waistcoat pockets, taking the middle of the street to himself, and singing, now a verse of a love song, and then a verse of a drinking one; and when he was tired of both, whistling melodiously, until he reached the North

Bridge, which at this point connects the old and new towns of Edinburgh. Here he stopped for a minute, to look at the strange irregular clusters of lights piled one above the other, and twinkling afar off, so high in the air, that they looked like stars, gleaming from the castle walls on the one side and the Calton Hill on the other, as if they illuminated veritable castles in the air: while the old picturesque town slept heavily on in gloom and darkness below; its palace and chapel of Holyrood, guarded day and night, as a friend of my uncle's used to say, by old Arthur's Seat, towering, surly and dark like some gruff genius, over the ancient city he has watched so long. I say, gentlemen, my uncle stopped here, for a minute, to look about him; and then, paying a compliment to the weather which had a little cleared up, though the moon was sinking, walked on again as royally as before: keeping the middle of the road with great dignity, and looking as if he should very much like to meet with somebody who would dispute possession of it with him. There was nobody at all disposed to contest the point, as it happened; and so on he went, with his thumbs in his waistcoat pockets, as peaceable as a lamb.

"When my uncle reached the end of Leith Walk, he had to cross a pretty large piece of waste ground which separated him from a short street which he had to turn down, to go direct to his lodging. Now, in this piece of waste ground, there was at that time, an inclosure belonging to some wheelwright, who contracted with the Post-office for the purchase of old worn-out mail-coaches; and my uncle, being very fond of coaches, old, young, or middle-aged, all at once took it into his head to step out of his road for no other purpose than to peep between the palings at these mails; about a dozen of which, he remembered to have seen, crowded together in a very forlorn and dismantled state, inside. My uncle was a very enthusiastic, emphatic sort of person, gentlemen; so, finding that he could not obtain a good peep between the palings, he got over them, and sitting himself quietly down on an old axletree, began to contemplate the mail coaches with a great deal of gravity.

"There might be a dozen of them, or there might be more—my

uncle was never quite certain upon this point, and being a man of very scrupulous veracity about numbers, didn't like to say—but there they stood, all huddled together in the most desolate condition imaginable. The doors had been torn from their hinges and removed, the linings had been stripped off: only a shred hanging here and there by a rusty nail; the lamps were gone, the poles had long since vanished, the iron-work was rusty, the paint worn away; the wind whistled through the chinks in the bare wood-work; and the rain, which had collected on the roofs, fell drop by drop into the insides, with a hollow and melancholy sound. They were the decaying skeletons of departed mails, and in that lonely place, at that time of night, they looked chill and dismal.

"My uncle rested his head upon his hands, and thought of the busy bustling people who had rattled about, years before, in the old coaches, and were now as silent and changed; he thought of the numbers of people to whom one of those crazy, mouldering vehicles had borne, night after night, for many years, and through all weathers, the anxiously expected intelligence, the eagerly looked-for remittance, the promised assurance of health and safety, the sudden announcement of sickness and death. The merchant, the lover, the wife, the widow, the mother, the schoolboy, the very child who tottered to the door at the postman's knock—how had they all looked forward to the arrival of the old coach. And where were they all now!

"Gentlemen, my uncle used to *say* that he thought all this at the time, but I rather suspect he learnt it out of some book afterwards, for he distinctly stated that he fell into a kind of doze, as he sat on the old axletree looking at the decayed mail-coaches, and that he was suddenly awakened by some deep church-bell striking two. Now, my uncle was never a fast thinker, and if he had thought all these things, I am quite certain it would have taken him till full half-past two o'clock at the very least. I am, therefore, decidedly of opinion, gentlemen, that my uncle fell into the kind of doze, without having thought about anything at all.

"Be this as it may, a church-bell struck two. My uncle woke, rubbed his eyes, and jumped up in astonishment.

"In one instant, after the clock struck two, the whole of this deserted and quiet spot had become a scene of the most extraordinary life and animation. The mail-coach doors were on their hinges, the lining was replaced, the iron-work was as good as new, the paint was restored, the lamps were alight; cushions and great coats were on every coach-box, porters were thrusting parcels into every boot, guards were stowing away letter-bags, hostlers were dashing pails of water against the renovated wheels; numbers of men were rushing about, fixing poles into every coach; passengers arrived, portmanteaus were handed up, horses were put to; and in short, it was perfectly clear that every mail there was to be off directly. Gentlemen, my uncle opened his eyes so wide at all this, that, to the very last moment of his life, he used to wonder how it fell out that he had ever been able to shut 'em again.

" 'Now then!' said a voice, as my uncle felt a hand on his shoulder, 'You're booked for one inside. You'd better get in.'

" '*I* booked!' said my uncle, turning round.

" 'Yes, certainly.'

"My uncle, gentlemen, could say nothing; he was so very much astonished. The queerest thing of all, was, that although there was such a crowd of persons, and although fresh faces were pouring in every moment, there was no telling where they came from; they seemed to start up in some strange manner, from the ground or the air, and to disappear in the same way. When a porter had put his luggage in the coach, and received his fare, he turned round and was gone; and before my uncle had well begun to wonder what had become of him, half-a-dozen fresh ones started up, and staggered along under the weight of parcels which seemed big enough to crush them. The passengers were all dressed so oddly too—large, broad-skirted laced coats with great cuffs and no collars; and wigs, gentlemen,—great formal wigs with a tie behind. My uncle could make nothing of it.

" 'Now, *are* you going to get in?' said the person who had addressed my uncle before. He was dressed as a mail guard, with a wig on his head and most enormous cuffs to his coat, and had got a lantern in one hand and a huge blunderbuss in the other, which he was going to stow away in his little arm-chest. '*Are* you going to get in, Jack Martin?' said the guard, holding the lantern to my uncle's face.

" 'Hallo!' said my uncle, falling back a step or two. 'That's familiar!'

" 'It's so on the way-bill,' replied the guard.

" 'Isn't there a "Mister" before it?' said my uncle—for he felt, gentlemen, that for a guard he didn't know, to call him Jack Martin, was a liberty which the Post-office wouldn't have sanctioned if they had known it.

" 'No; there is not,' rejoined the guard coolly.

" 'Is the fare paid?' inquired my uncle.

" 'Of course it is,' rejoined the guard.

" 'It is, is it?' said my uncle. 'Then here goes—which coach?'

" 'This,' said the guard, pointing to an old-fashioned Edinburgh and London Mail, which had got the steps down, and the door open. 'Stop—here are the other passengers. Let them get in first.'

"As the guard spoke, there all at once appeared, right in front of my uncle, a young gentleman in a powdered wig and a sky-blue coat trimmed with silver, made very full and broad in the skirts, which were lined with buckram. Tiggin and Welps were in the printed calico and waistcoat piece line, gentlemen, so my uncle knew all the materials at once. He wore knee breeches and a kind of leggings rolled up over his silk stockings, and shoes with buckles; he had ruffles at his wrists, a three-cornered hat on his head, and a long taper sword by his side. The flaps of his waistcoat came half way down his thighs, and the ends of his cravat reached to his waist. He stalked gravely to the coach-door, pulled off his hat, and held it out above his head at arm's length, cocking his little finger in the air at the same time, as some affected people do when they take a cup of

T. Sibson

"Then he drew his feet together, and made a low grave bow, and then put out his left hand. My uncle was just going to step forward and shake it heartily, when he perceived that these attentions were directed, not towards him, but to a young lady, who just then appeared" &c.

He stalked gravely to the coach-door, pulled off his hat, and held it out above his head at arm's length, cocking his little finger in the air at the same time, as some affected people do when they take a cup of tea . . . —by Thomas Sibson tea: then drew his feet together, and made a low grave bow, and then put out his left hand. My uncle was just going to step forward, and shake it heartily, when he perceived that these attentions were directed not towards him, but to a young lady, who just then appeared at the foot of the steps, attired in an old-fashioned green velvet dress, with a long waist and stomacher. She had no bonnet on her head, gentlemen, which was muffled in a black silk hood, but she looked round for an instant as she prepared to get into the coach, and such a beautiful face as she discovered my uncle had never seen—not even in a picture. She got into the coach, holding up her dress with one hand, and as my uncle always said with a round oath, when he told the story, he wouldn't have believed it possible that legs and feet could have been brought to such a state of perfection unless he had seen them with his own eyes.

"But in this one glimpse of the beautiful face, my uncle saw that the young lady had cast an imploring look upon him, and that she appeared terrified and distressed. He noticed, too, that the young fellow in the powdered wig, notwithstanding his show of gallantry, which was all very fine and grand, clasped her tight by the wrist when she got in, and followed himself immediately afterwards. An uncommonly ill-looking fellow in a close brown wig, and a plum-coloured suit, wearing a very large sword and boots up to his hips, belonged to the party; and when he sat himself down next to the young lady, who shrunk into a corner at his approach, my uncle was confirmed in his original impression that something dark and mysterious was going forward, or, as he always said himself, that 'there was a screw loose somewhere.' It's quite surprising how quickly he made up his mind to help the lady at any peril, if she needed help.

" 'Death and lightning!' exclaimed the young gentleman, laying his hand upon his sword, as my uncle entered the coach.

" 'Blood and thunder!' roared the other gentleman. With this he whipped his sword out, and made a lunge at my uncle without further ceremony. My uncle had no weapon about him, but with great dexterity he snatched the ill-looking gentleman's three-cornered hat from his head, and receiving the point of his sword right through the crown squeezed the sides together, and held it tight.

" 'Pink him behind,' cried the ill-looking gentleman to his companion, as he struggled to regain his sword.

" 'He had better not,' cried my uncle, displaying the heel of one of his shoes in a threatening manner. 'I'll kick his brains out if he has any, or fracture his skull if he hasn't.' Exerting all his strength at this moment, my uncle wrenched the ill-looking man's sword from his grasp, and flung it clean out of the coach-window, upon which the younger vociferated 'Death and lightning!' again, and laid his hand upon the hilt of his sword in a very fierce manner, but didn't draw it. Perhaps, gentlemen, as my uncle used to say, with a smile, perhaps he was afraid of alarming the lady.

" 'Now, gentlemen,' said my uncle, taking his place deliberately, 'I don't want to have any death with or without lightning in a lady's presence, and we have had quite blood and thundering enough for one journey; so if you please, we'll sit in our places like quiet insides—here, guard, pick up that gentleman's carving-knife.'

"As quickly as my uncle said these words, the guard appeared at the coach-window with the gentleman's sword in his hand. He held up his lantern, and looked earnestly in my uncle's face as he handed it in, when by its light my uncle saw, to his great surprise, that an immense crowd of mail-coach guards swarmed round the window, every one of whom had his eyes earnestly fixed upon him too. He had never seen such a sea of white faces, and red bodies, and earnest eyes, in all his born days.

" 'This is the strangest sort of thing I ever had anything to do with,' thought my uncle—'allow me to return you your hat, Sir.'

"The ill-looking gentleman received his three-cornered hat in silence—looked at the hole in the middle with an inquiring air, and finally stuck it on the top of his wig, with a solemnity the effect of which was a trifle impaired by his sneezing violently at the moment, and jerking it off again.

" 'All right!' cried the guard with the lantern, mounting into his little seat behind. Away they went. My uncle peeped out of the coach-window as they emerged from the yard, and observed that the other mails, with coachmen, guards, horses, and passengers complete, were driving round and round in circles, at a slow trot of about five miles an hour. My uncle burnt with indignation, gentlemen. As a commercial man, he felt that the mail bags were not to be trifled with, and he resolved to memorialise the Post-office upon the subject, the very instant he reached London.

"At present, however, his thoughts were occupied with the young lady who sat in the furthest corner of the coach, with her face muffled closely in her hood: the gentleman with the sky-blue coat sitting opposite to her, and the other man in the plum-coloured suit, by her side, and both watching her intently. If she so much as rustled the folds of her hood, he could hear the ill-looking man clap his hand upon his sword, and tell by the other's breathing (it was so dark he couldn't see his face) that he was looking as big as if he were going to devour her at a mouthful. This roused my uncle more and more, and he resolved, come what come might, to see the end of it. He had a great admiration for bright eyes, and sweet faces, and pretty legs and feet; in short he was fond of the whole sex. It runs in our family, gentlemen—so am I.

"Many were the devices which my uncle practised to attract the lady's attention, or at all events, to engage the mysterious gentlemen in conversation. They were all in vain; the gentlemen wouldn't talk, and the lady didn't dare. He thrust his head out of the coach-window at intervals, and bawled out to know why they didn't go faster. But he called till he was hoarse—nobody paid the least attention to him. He leant back in the coach, and thought of the beautiful face, and the feet and legs. This answered better; it wiled away the time, and kept him from wondering where he was going to, and how it was he found himself in such an odd situation. Not that this would have worried him much any way—he was a mighty free and easy, roving, devil-may-care sort of person, was my uncle, gentlemen.

"All of a sudden the coach stopped. 'Hallo!' said my uncle, 'what's in the wind now?'

" 'Alight here,' said the guard, letting down the steps.

" 'Here!' cried my uncle.

" 'Here,' rejoined the guard.

" 'I'll do nothing of the sort,' said my uncle.

" 'Very well—then stop where you are,' said the guard.

" 'I will,' said my uncle.

" 'Do,' said the guard.

"The other passengers had regarded this colloquy with great attention; and finding that my uncle was determined not to alight, the younger man squeezed past him, to hand the lady out. At this moment the ill-looking man was inspecting the hole in the crown of his three-cornered hat. As the young lady brushed past, she dropped one of her gloves into my uncle's hand, and softly whispered with her lips, so close to his face that he felt her warm breath on his nose, the single word, 'Help!' Gentlemen, my uncle leaped out of the coach at once with such violence that it rocked on the springs again.

" 'Oh! you've thought better of it, have you?' said the guard, when he saw my uncle standing on the ground.

"My uncle looked at the guard for a few seconds, in some doubt whether it wouldn't be better to wrench his blunderbuss from him, fire it in the face of the man with the big sword, knock the rest of the company over the head with the stock, snatch up the young lady, and go off in the smoke. On second thoughts, however, he abandoned this plan as being a shade too melodramatic in the execution, and followed the two mysterious men, who, keeping the lady between them, were now entering an old house in front of which the coach had stopped. They turned into the passage, and my uncle followed.

"Of all the ruinous and desolate places my uncle had ever beheld, this was the most so. It looked as if it had once been a large house of entertainment, but the roof had fallen in, in many places, and the stairs were steep, rugged, and broken. There was a huge fire-place in the room into which they walked, and the chimney was blackened with smoke, but no warm blaze lighted it up now. The white feathery dust of burnt wood was still strewed over the hearth, but the stove was cold, and all was dark and gloomy.

" 'Well,' said my uncle as he looked about him, 'a mail travelling at the rate of six miles and a half an hour, and stopping for an indefinite time at such a hole as this, is rather an irregular sort of proceeding, I fancy. This shall be made known; I'll write to the papers.'

"My uncle said this in a pretty loud voice, and in an open unreserved sort of manner, with the view of engaging the two strangers in conversation if he could. But neither of them took any more notice of him than whispering to each other, and scowling at him as they did so. The lady was at the further end of the room, and once she ventured to wave her hand, as if beseeching my uncle's assistance.

"At length the two strangers advanced a little, and the conversation began in earnest.

" 'You don't know this is a private room, I suppose, fellow,' said the gentleman in sky-blue.

" 'No, I do not, fellow,' rejoined my uncle. 'Only if this is a private room specially ordered for the occasion, I should think the public room must be a very comfortable one;' with this, my uncle sat himself down in a high-backed chair and took such an accurate measure of the gentleman with his eyes, that Tiggin and Welps could have supplied him with printed calico for a suit, and not an inch too much or too little, from that estimate alone.

" 'Quit this room,' said both the men together, grasping their swords.

" 'Eh?' said my uncle, not at all appearing to comprehend their meaning.

" 'Quit the room, or you are a dead man,' said the ill-looking fellow with the large sword, drawing it at the same time and flourishing it in the air.

" 'Down with him!' said the gentleman in sky-blue, drawing his sword also, and falling back two or three yards. 'Down with him!' The lady gave a scream.

"Now, my uncle was always remarkable for great boldness and great presence of mind. All the time that he had appeared so indifferent to what was going on, he had been looking slyly about for some missile or weapon of defence, and at the very instant when the swords were drawn he espied standing in the chimney corner, an old basket-hilted rapier in a rusty scabbard. At one bound, my uncle caught it in his hand, drew it, flourished it gallantly above his head, called aloud to the lady to keep out of the way, hurled the chair at the man in sky-blue, and the scabbard at the man in plum-colour, and taking advantage of the confusion, fell upon them both, pell-mell.

"Gentlemen, there is an old story—none the worse for being true—regarding a fine young Irish gentleman, who being asked if he could play the fiddle, replied he had no doubt he could, but he couldn't exactly say for certain, because he had never tried. This is not inapplicable to my uncle and his fencing. He had never had a sword in his hand before, except once when he played Richard the Third at a private theatre, upon which occasion it was arranged with Richmond that he was to be run through from behind without shewing fight at all; but here he was, cutting and slashing with two experienced swordsmen, thrusting, and guarding, and poking, and slicing, and acquitting himself in the most manful and dexterous manner possible, although up to that time he had never been aware that he had the least notion of the science. It only shows how true the old saying is, that a man never knows what he can do, till he tries, gentlemen.

"The noise of the combat was terrific, each of the three combatants swearing like troopers, and their swords clashing with as much noise as if all the knives and steels in Newport market were rattling together at the same time. When it was at its very height, the lady, to encourage my uncle, most probably, withdrew her hood entirely from her face, and disclosed a countenance of such dazzling beauty, that he would have fought against fifty men to win one smile from it and die. He had done wonders before, but now he began to powder away like a raving mad giant.

"At this very moment, the gentleman in sky-blue turning round, and seeing the young lady with her face uncovered, vented an exclamation of rage and jealousy; and turning his weapon against her beautiful bosom, pointed a thrust at her heart, which caused my uncle to utter a cry of apprehension that made the building ring. The lady stepped lightly aside, and snatching the young man's sword from his hand before he had recovered his balance, drove him to the wall, and running it through him and the panelling up to the very hilt, pinned him there hard and fast. It was a splendid example. My uncle, with a loud shout of triumph and a strength that was irresistible, made his adversary retreat in the same direction, and plunging the old rapier into the very centre of a large red flower in the pattern of his waistcoat, nailed him beside his friend; there they both stood, gentlemen, jerking their arms and legs about in agony, like the toy-shop figures that are moved by a piece of packthread. My uncle always said afterwards, that this was one of the surest means he knew of, for disposing of an enemy; but it was liable to one objection on the ground of expense, inasmuch as it involved the loss of a sword for every man disabled.

" 'The mail, the mail!' cried the lady, running up to my uncle and throwing her beautiful arms round his neck; 'we may escape yet.'

" '*May!*' said my uncle. 'Why, my dear, there's nobody else to kill, is there?' My uncle was rather disappointed, gentlemen, for he thought a little quiet bit of love-making would be agreeable after the slaughtering, if it were only to change the subject.

" 'We have not an instant to lose here,' said the young lady. 'He (pointing to the young gentleman in sky-blue) is the only son of the powerful Marquess of Filletoville.'

" 'Well then, my dear, I'm afraid he'll never come to the title,' said my uncle, looking coolly at the young gentleman as he stood fixed up against the wall, in the cockchafer fashion I have described. 'You have cut off the entail, my love.'

" 'I have been torn from my home and friends by these villains,' said the young lady, her features glowing with indignation. 'That wretch would have married me by violence in another hour.'

" 'Confound his impudence!' said my uncle, bestowing a very contemptuous look on the dying heir of Filletoville.

" 'As you may guess from what you have seen,' said the young lady, 'the party were prepared to murder me if I appealed to any one for assistance. If their accomplices find us here, we are lost. Two minutes hence may be too late. The mail!'—and with these words, overpowered by her feelings, and the exertion of sticking the young Marquess of Filletoville, she sunk into my uncle's arms. My uncle caught her up and bore her to the house-door. There stood the mail with four long-tailed, flowing-maned, black horses, ready harnessed; but no coachman, no guard, no hostler even, at the horses' heads.

"Gentlemen, I hope I do no injustice to my uncle's memory, when I express my opinion, that although he was a bachelor, he *had* held some ladies in his arms before this time; I believe, indeed, that he had rather a habit of kissing barmaids; and I know that, in one or two instances, he had been seen by credible witnesses, to hug a landlady in a very perceptible manner. I mention the circumstance, to show what a very uncommon sort of person this beautiful young lady must have been, to have affected my uncle in the way she did; he used to say, that as her long dark hair trailed over his arm, and her beautiful dark eyes fixed themselves upon his face when she recovered, he felt so strange and nervous, that his legs trembled beneath him. But who can look into a sweet soft pair of dark eyes, without feeling queer? I can't, gentlemen. I am afraid to look at some eyes I know, and that's the truth of it.

" 'You will never leave me,' murmured the young lady.

" 'Never,' said my uncle. And he meant it too.

" 'My dear preserver!' exclaimed the young lady. 'My dear, kind, brave preserver!'

" 'Don't,' said my uncle, interrupting her.

" 'Why?' inquired the young lady.

" 'Because your mouth looks so beautiful when you speak,' rejoined my uncle, 'that I am afraid I shall be rude enough to kiss it.'

"The young lady put up her hand as if to caution my uncle not to do so, and said—no, she didn't say anything—she smiled. When you are looking at a pair of the most delicious lips in all the world, and see them gently break into a roguish smile—if you are very near them, and nobody else by—you cannot better testify your admiration of their beautiful form and colour than by kissing them at once. My uncle did so, and I honour him for it.

" 'Hark!' cried the young lady, starting. 'The noise of wheels and horses!'

" 'So it is,' said my uncle, listening. He had a good ear for wheels and the tramping of hoofs; but there appeared to be so many horses and carriages rattling towards them from a distance, that it was impossible to form a guess at their number. The sound was like that of fifty breaks, with six blood cattle in each.

" 'We are pursued!' cried the young lady, clasping her hands. 'We are pursued. I have no hope but in you!'

"There was such an expression of fear in her beautiful face, that my uncle made up his mind at once. He lifted her into the coach, told her not to be frightened, pressed his lips to hers once more, and then advising her to draw up the window to keep the cold air out, mounted to the box.

" 'Stay, love,' cried the young lady.

" 'What's the matter?' said my uncle, from the coach-box.

" 'I want to speak to you,' said the young lady; 'only a word—only one word, dearest.'

" 'Must I get down?' inquired my uncle. The lady made no answer, but she smiled again. Such a smile, gentlemen!—it beat the other one all to nothing. My uncle descended from his perch in a twinkling.

" 'What is it, my dear?' said my uncle, looking in at the coach window. The lady happened to bend forward at the same time, and my uncle thought she looked more beautiful than she had done yet.

He was very close to her just then, gentlemen, so he really ought to know.

" 'What is it, my love?' said my uncle.

" 'Will you never love any one but me—never marry any one beside?' said the young lady.

"My uncle swore a great oath that he never would marry anybody else, and the young lady drew in her head, and pulled up the window. He jumped upon the box, squared his elbows, adjusted the ribands, seized the whip which lay on the roof, gave one flick to the off leader, and away went the four long-tailed, flowing-maned black horses, at fifteen good English miles an hour, with the old mail coach behind them—whew! how they tore along!

"But the noise behind grew louder. The faster went the old mail, the faster came the pursuers—men, horses, dogs, were leagued in the pursuit. The noise was frightful, but above all, rose the voice of the young lady, urging my uncle on, and shrieking, 'Faster! faster!'

"They whirled past the dark trees, as feathers would be swept before a hurricane. Houses, gates, churches, haystacks, objects of every kind they shot by, with a velocity and noise like roaring waters suddenly let loose. But still the noise of pursuit grew louder, and still my uncle could hear the young lady wildly screaming, 'Faster! faster!'

"My uncle plied whip and rein, and the horses flew onward till they were white with foam; and yet the noise behind increased, and yet the young lady cried, 'Faster! faster!' My uncle gave a loud stamp upon the boot in the energy of the moment, and—found that it was grey morning, and he was sitting in the wheelwright's yard on the box of an old Edinburgh mail, shivering with the cold and wet, and stamping his feet to warm them! He got down, and looked eagerly inside for the beautiful young lady—alas! there was neither door nor seat to the coach—it was a mere shell.

"Of course my uncle knew very well that there was some mystery in the matter, and that everything had passed exactly as he used to relate it. He remained staunch to the great oath he had sworn to the beautiful young lady, refusing several eligible landladies on her account, and died a bachelor at last. He always said, what a curious thing it was that he should have found out, by such a mere accident as his clambering over the palings, that the ghosts of mail-coaches and horses, guards, coachmen, and passengers, were in the habit of making journeys regularly every night; he used to add, that he believed he was the only living person who had ever been taken as a passenger on one of these excursions; and I think he was right, gentlemen—at least I never heard of any other."

"I wonder what these ghosts of mail-coaches carry in their bags," said the landlord, who had listened to the whole story with profound attention.

"The dead letters, of course," said the Bagman.

"Oh, ah—to be sure," rejoined the landlord. "I never thought of that."

TO BE TAKEN WITH A GRAIN OF SALT

I HAVE always noticed a prevalent want of courage, even among persons of superior intelligence and culture, as to imparting their own psychological experiences when those have been of a strange sort. Almost all men are afraid that what they could relate in such wise would find no parallel or response in a listener's internal life, and might be suspected or laughed at. A truthful traveller, who should have seen some extraordinary creature in the likeness of a sea-serpent, would have no fear of mentioning it; but the same traveller, having had some singular presentiment, impulse, vagary of thought, vision (so called), dream, or other remarkable mental impression, would hesitate considerably before he would own to it. To this reticence I attribute much of the obscurity in which such subjects are involved. We do not habitually communicate our experiences of these subjective things as we do our experiences of objective creation. The consequence is that the general stock of experience in this regard appears exceptional, and really is so, in respect of being miserably imperfect.

In what I am going to relate, I have no intention of setting up, opposing, or supporting any theory whatever. I know the history of the Bookseller of Berlin, I have studied the case of the wife of a late

Astronomer Royal as related by Sir David Brewster, and I have followed the minutest details of a much more remarkable case of Spectral Illusion occurring within my private circle of friends. It may be necessary to state, as to this last, that the sufferer (a lady) was in no degreee, however distant, related to me. A mistaken assumption on that head might suggest an explanation of a part of my own case,—but only a part,—which would be wholly without foundation. It cannot be referred to my inheritance of any developed peculiarity, nor had I ever before any at all similar experience, nor have I ever had any at all similar experience since.

It does not signify how many years ago, or how few, a certain murder was committed in England, which attracted great attention. We hear of more than enough of murderers as they rise in succession to their atrocious eminence, and I would bury the memory of this particular brute, if I could, as his body was buried, in Newgate Jail. I purposely abstain from giving any direct clue to the criminal's individuality.

When the murder was first discovered, no suspicion fell—or I ought rather to say, for I cannot be too precise in my facts, it was nowhere publicly hinted that any suspicion fell—on the man who was afterwards brought to trial. As no reference was at that time made to him in the newspapers, it is obviously impossible that any description of him can at that time have been given in the newspapers. It is essential that this fact be remembered.

Unfolding at breakfast my morning paper, containing the account of that first discovery, I found it to be deeply interesting, and I read it with close attention. I read it twice, if not three times. The discovery had been made in a bedroom, and, when I laid down the paper, I was aware of a flash—rush—flow—I do not know what to call it,—no word I can find is satisfactorily descriptive,—in which I seemed to see that bedroom passing through my room, like a picture impossibly painted on a running river. Though almost instantaneous in its passing, it was perfectly clear; so clear that I distinctly, and with a sense of relief, observed the absence of the dead body from the bed.

It was in no romantic place that I had this curious sensation, but in chambers in Piccadilly, very near to the corner of St. James's Street. It was entirely new to me. I was in my easy-chair at the moment, and the sensation was accompanied with a peculiar shiver which started the chair from its position. (But it is to be noted that the chair ran easily on casters.) I went to one of the windows (there are two in the room, and the room is on the second floor) to refresh my eyes with the moving objects down in Piccadilly. It was a bright autumn morning, and the street was sparkling and cheerful. The wind was high. As I looked out, it brought down from the Park a quantity of fallen leaves, which a gust took, and whirled into a spiral pillar. As the pillar fell and the leaves dispersed, I saw two men on the opposite side of the way, going from West to East. They were one behind the other. The foremost man often looked back over his shoulder. The second man followed him, at a distance of some thirty paces, with his right hand menacingly raised. First, the singularity and steadiness of this threatening gesture in so public a thoroughfare attracted my attention; and next, the more remarkable circumstance that nobody heeded it. Both men threaded their way among the other passengers with a smoothness hardly consistent even with the action of walking on a pavement; and no single creature, that I could see, gave them place, touched them, or looked after them. In passing before my windows, they both stared up at me. I saw their two faces very distinctly, and I knew that I could recognise them anywhere. Not that I had consciously noticed anything very remarkable in either face, except that the man who went first had an unusually lowering appearance, and that the face of the man who followed him was of the colour of impure wax.

I am a bachelor, and my valet and his wife constitute my whole establishment. My occupation is in a certain Branch Bank, and I wish that my duties as head of a Department were as light as they are popularly supposed to be. They kept me in town that autumn, when I stood in need of change. I was not ill, but I was not well. My reader is to make the most that can be reasonably made of my feeling jaded, having a depressing sense upon me of a monotonous life, and being "slightly dyspeptic." I am assured by my renowned doctor that my real state of health at that time justifies no stronger description, and I quote his own from his written answer to my request for it.

As the circumstances of the murder, gradually unravelling, took stronger and stronger possession of the public mind, I kept them away from mine by knowing as little about them as was possible in the midst of the universal excitement. But I knew that a verdict of Wilful Murder had been found against the suspected murderer, and that he had been committed to Newgate for trial. I also knew that his trial had been postponed over one Sessions of the Central Criminal Court, on the ground of general prejudice and want of time for the preparation of the defence. I may further have known, but I believe I did not, when, or about when, the Sessions to which his trial stood postponed would come on.

My sitting-room, bedroom, and dressing-room are all on one floor. With the last there is no communication but through the bedroom. True, there is a door in it, once communicating with the staircase; but a part of the fitting of my bath has been—and had then been for some years—fixed across it. At the same period, and as a part of the same arrangement, the door has been nailed up and canvassed over.

I was standing in my bedroom late one night, giving some directions to my servant before he went to bed. My face was towards the only available door of communication with the dressing-room, and it was closed. My servant's back was towards that door. While I was speaking to him, I saw it open, and a man look in, who very earnestly and mysteriously beckoned to me. That man was the man who had gone second of the two along Piccadilly, and whose face was of the colour of impure wax.

The figure, having beckoned, drew back, and closed the door. With no longer pause than was made by my crossing the bedroom, I opened the dressing-room door, and looked in. I had a lighted candle

While I was speaking to him, I saw it open, and a man look in, who very earnestly and mysteriously beckoned to me. —by E. G. Dalziel

already in my hand. I felt no inward expectation of seeing the figure in the dressing-room, and I did not see it there.

Conscious that my servant stood amazed, I turned round to him, and said: "Derrick, could you believe that in my cool senses I fancied I saw a—" As I there laid my hand upon his breast, with a sudden start he trembled violently, and said, "O Lord, yes, sir! A dead man beckoning."

Now, I do not believe that this John Derrick, my trusty and attached servant for more than twenty years, had any impression whatever of having seen any such figure until I touched him. The change in him was so startling when I touched him that I fully believe he derived his impression in some occult manner from me at that instant.

I bade John Derrick bring some brandy, and I gave him a dram, and was glad to take one myself. Of what had preceded that night's phenomenon, I told him not a single word. Reflecting on it, I was absolutely certain that I had never seen that face before, except on the one occasion in Piccadilly. Comparing its expression when beckoning at the door with its expression when it had stared up at me as I stood at my window, I came to the conclusion that on the first occasion it had sought to fasten itself upon my memory, and that on the second occasion it had made sure of being immediately remembered.

I was not very comfortable that night, though I felt a certainty, difficult to explain, that the figure would not return. At daylight I fell into a heavy sleep, from which I was awakened by John Derrick's coming to my bedside with a paper in his hand.

This paper, it appeared, had been the subject of an altercation at the door between its bearer and my servant. It was a summons to me to serve upon a Jury at the forthcoming Sessions of the Central Criminal Court at the Old Bailey. I had never before been summoned on such a Jury, as John Derrick well knew. He believed—I am not certain at this hour whether with reason or otherwise—that that class of Jurors were customarily chosen on a lower qualification than mine, and he had at first refused to accept the summons. The man who served it had taken the matter very coolly. He had said that my attendance or non-attendance was nothing to him; there the summons was; and I should deal with it at my own peril, and not at his.

For a day or two I was undecided whether to respond to this call, or take no notice of it. I was not conscious of the slightest mysterious bias, influence, or attraction, one way or other. Of that I am as strictly sure as of every other statement that I make here. Ultimately I decided, as a break in the monotony of my life, that I would go.

The appointed morning was a raw morning in the month of November. There was a dense brown fog in Piccadilly, and it became positively black and in the last degree oppressive east of Temple Bar. I found the passages and staircases of the Courthouse flaringly lighted with gas, and the Court itself similarly illuminated. I *think* that, until I was conducted by officers into the Old Court and saw its crowded state, I did not know that the Murderer was to be tried that day. I *think* that, until I was so helped into the Old Court with considerable difficulty, I did not know into which of the two Courts sitting my summons would take me. But this must not be received as a positive assertion, for I am not completely satisfied in my mind on either point.

I took my seat in the place appropriated to Jurors in waiting, and I looked about the Court as well as I could through the cloud of fog and breath that was heavy in it. I noticed the black vapour hanging like a murky curtain outside the great windows, and I noticed the stifled sound of wheels on the straw or tan that was littered in the street; also, the hum of the people gathered there, which a shrill whistle, or a louder song or hail than the rest, occasionally pierced. Soon afterwards the Judges, two in number, entered, and took their seats. The buzz in the Court was awfully hushed. The direction was given to put the Murderer to the bar. He appeared there. And in that same instant I recognised in him the first of the two men who had gone down Piccadilly.

If my name had been called then, I doubt if I could have answered to it audibly. But it was called about sixth or eighth in the panel, and I was by that time able to say, "Here!" Now, observe. As I stepped into the box, the prisoner, who had been looking on attentively, but with no sign of concern, became violently agitated, and beckoned to his attorney. The prisoner's wish to challenge me was so manifest that it occasioned a pause, during which the attorney, with his hand upon the dock, whispered with his client, and shook his head. I afterwards had it from that gentleman, that the prisoner's first affrighted words to him were, *"At all hazards, challenge that man!"* But that, as he would give no reason for it, and admitted that he had not even known my name until he heard it called and I appeared, it was not done.

Both on the ground already explained, that I wish to avoid reviving the unwholesome memory of that Murderer, and also because a detailed account of his long trial is by no means indispensable to my narrative, I shall confine myself closely to such incidents in the ten days and nights during which we, the Jury, were kept together, as directly bear on my own curious personal experience. It is in that, and not in the Murderer, that I seek to interest my reader. It is to that, and not to a page of the Newgate Calendar, that I beg attention.

I was chosen Foreman of the Jury. On the second morning of the trial, after evidence had been taken for two hours (I heard the church clocks strike), happening to cast my eyes over my brother jurymen, I found an inexplicable difficulty in counting them. I counted them several times, yet always with the same difficulty. In short, I made them one too many.

I touched the brother juryman whose place was next me, and I whispered to him, "Oblige me by counting us." He looked surprised by the request, but turned his head and counted. "Why," says he suddenly, "we are Thirt—; but no, it's not possible. No. We are twelve."

According to my counting that day, we were always right in detail, but in the gross we were always one too many. There was no appearance—no figure—to account for it; but I had now an inward foreshadowing of the figure that was surely coming.

The Jury were housed at the London Tavern. We all slept in one large room on separate tables, and we were constantly in the charge and under the eye of the officer sworn to hold us in safe keeping. I see no reason for suppressing the real name of that officer. He was intelligent, highly polite, and obliging, and (I was glad to hear) much respected in the City. He had an agreeable presence, good eyes, enviable black whiskers, and a fine sonorous voice. His name was Mr. Harker.

When we turned into our twelve beds at night, Mr. Harker's bed was drawn across the door. On the night of the second day, not being disposed to lie down, and seeing Mr. Harker sitting on his bed, I went and sat beside him, and offered him a pinch of snuff. As Mr. Harker's hand touched mine in taking it from my box, a peculiar shiver crossed him, and he said, "Who is this?"

Following Mr. Harker's eyes, and looking along the room, I saw again the figure I expected,—the second of the two men who had gone down Piccadilly. I rose, and advanced a few steps; then stopped, and looked round at Mr. Harker. He was quite unconcerned, laughed, and said in a pleasant way, "I thought for a moment we had a thirteenth juryman without a bed. But I see it is the moonlight."

Making no revelation to Mr. Harker, but inviting him to take a walk with me to the end of the room, I watched what the figure did. It stood for a few moments by the bedside of each of my eleven brother jurymen, close to the pillow. It always went to the right-hand side of the bed, and always passed out crossing the foot of the next bed. It seemed, from the action of the head, merely to look down pensively at each recumbent figure. It took no notice of me, or of my bed, which was that nearest to Mr. Harker's. It seemed to go out where the moonlight came in, through a high window, as by an aerial flight of stairs.

Next morning, at breakfast, it appeared that everybody present had dreamed of the murdered man last night, except myself and Mr. Harker.

I now felt as convinced that the second man who had gone down Piccadilly was the murdered man (so to speak), as if it had been borne into my comprehension by his immediate testimony. But even this took place, and in a manner for which I was not at all prepared.

On the fifth day of the trial, when the case for the prosecution was drawing to a close, a miniature of the murdered man, missing from his bedroom upon the discovery of the deed, and afterwards found in a hiding-place where the Murderer had been seen digging, was put in evidence. Having been identified by the witness under examination, it was handed up to the Bench, and thence handed down to be inspected by the Jury. As an officer in a black gown was making his way with it across to me, the figure of the second man who had gone down Piccadilly impetuously started from the crowd, caught the miniature from the officer, and gave it to me with his own hands, at the same time saying, in a low and hollow tone,—before I saw the miniature, which was in a locket,— *"I was younger then, and my face was not then drained of blood."* It also came between me and the brother juryman to whom I would have given the miniature, and between him and the brother juryman to whom he would have given it, and so passed it on through the whole of our number, and back into my possession. Not one of them, however, detected this.

At table, and generally when we were shut up together in Mr. Harker's custody, we had from the first naturally discussed the day's proceedings a good deal. On that fifth day, the case for the prosecution being closed, and we having that side of the question in a completed shape before us, our discussion was more animated and serious. Among our number was a vestryman,—the densest idiot I have ever seen at large,—who met the plainest evidence with the most preposterous objections, and who was sided with by two flabby parochial parasites; all the three impanelled from a district so delivered over to Fever, that they ought to have been upon their own trial for five hundred Murders. When these mischievous blockheads were at their loudest, which was towards midnight, while some of us were already preparing for bed, I again saw the murdered man. He stood grimly behind them, beckoning to me. On my going towards them, and striking into the conversation, he immediately retired. This was the beginning of a separate series of appearances, confined to that long room in which *we* were confined. Whenever a knot of my brother jurymen laid their heads together, I saw the head of the murdered man among theirs. Whenever their comparison of notes was going against him, he would solemnly and irresistibly beckon to me.

It will be borne in mind that down to the production of the miniature, on the fifth day of the trial, I had never seen the Appearance in Court. Three changes occurred now that we entered on the case for the defence. Two of them I will mention together, first. The figure was now in Court continually, and it never there addressed itself to me, but always to the person who was speaking at the time. For instance: the throat of the murdered man had been cut straight across. In the opening speech for the defence, it was suggested that the deceased might have cut his own throat. At that very moment, the figure, with its throat in the dreadful condition referred to (this it had concealed before), stood at the speaker's elbow, motioning across and across its windpipe, now with the right hand, now with the left, vigorously suggesting to the speaker himself the impossibility of such a wound having been self-inflicted by either hand. For another instance: a witness to character, a woman, deposed to the prisoner's being the most amiable of mankind. The figure at that instant stood on the floor before her, looking her full in the face, and pointing out the prisoner's evil countenance with an extended arm and an outstretched finger.

The third change now to be added impressed me strongly as the most marked and striking of all. I do not theorise upon it; I accurately state it, and there leave it. Although the Appearance was not itself perceived by those whom it addressed, its coming close to such persons was invariably attended by some trepidation or disturbance on their part. It seemed to me as if it were prevented, by laws to which I was not amenable, from fully revealing itself to others, and yet as if it could invisibly, dumbly, and darkly overshadow their minds. When the leading counsel for the defence suggested that hypothesis of suicide, and the figure stood at the learned gentleman's elbow, frightfully sawing at its severed throat, it is undeniable that the counsel faltered in his speech, lost for a few seconds the thread of his ingenuous discourse, wiped his forehead with his handkerchief, and turned extremely pale. When the witness to character was confronted by the Appearance, her eyes most certainly did follow the direction of its pointed finger, and rest in great hesitation and trouble upon the prisoner's face. Two additional illustrations will suffice. On the eighth day of the trial, after the pause which was every day made early in the afternoon for a few minutes' rest and refreshment, I came back into Court with the rest of the Jury some little time before the return of the Judges. Standing up in the box and looking about me, I thought the figure was not there, until, chancing to raise my eyes to the gallery, I saw it bending forward, and leaning over a very decent woman, as if to assure itself whether the Judges had resumed their seats or not. Immediately afterwards that woman screamed, fainted, and was carried out. So with the venerable, sagacious, and patient Judge who conducted the trial. When the case was over, and he settled himself and his papers to sum up, the murdered man, entering by the Judge's door, advanced to his Lordship's desk, and looked eagerly over his shoulder at the pages of his notes which he was turning. A change came over his Lordship's face; his hand stopped; the peculiar shiver, that I knew so well, passed over him; he faltered, "Excuse me, gentlemen, for a few moments. I am somewhat oppressed by the vitiated air;" and did not recover until he had drunk a glass of water.

Through all the monotony of six of those interminable ten days,—the same Judges and others on the bench, the same Murderer in the dock, the same lawyers at the table, the same tones of question and answer rising to the roof of the Court, the same scratching of the

Judge's pen, the same ushers going in and out, the same lights kindled at the same hour when there had been any natural light of day,
the same foggy curtain outside the great windows when it was foggy,
the same rain pattering and dripping when it was rainy, the same
footmarks of turnkeys and prisoner day after day on the same saw-
dust, the same keys locking and unlocking the same heavy doors,—
through all the wearisome monotony which made me feel as if I had
been Foreman of the Jury for a vast period of time, and Piccadilly
had flourished coevally with Babylon, the murdered man never lost
one trace of his distinctness in my eyes, nor was he at any moment
less distinct than anybody else. I must not omit, as a matter of fact,
that I never once saw the Appearance which I call by the name of the
murdered man look at the Murderer. Again and again I wondered,
"Why does he not?" But he never did.

Nor did he look at me, after the production of the miniature, until
the last closing minutes of the trial arrived. We retired to consider at
seven minutes before ten at night. The idiotic vestryman and his two
parochial parasites gave us so much trouble that we twice returned
into Court to beg to have certain extracts from the Judge's notes re-
read. Nine of us had not the smallest doubt about those passages;
neither, I believe, had any one in the Court; the dunder-headed
triumvirate, however, having no idea but obstruction, disputed them
for that very reason. At length we prevailed, and finally the Jury
returned into Court at ten minutes past twelve.

The murdered man at that time stood directly opposite the Jury-
box, on the other side of the Court. As I took my place, his eyes
rested on me with great attention; he seemed satisfied, and slowly
shook a great grey veil, which he carried on his arm for the first time,
over his head and whole form. As I gave in our verdict, "Guilty,"
the veil collapsed, all was gone, and his place was empty.

The Murderer, being asked by the Judge, according to usage,
whether he had anything to say before sentence of Death should be
passed upon him, indistinctly muttered something which was described in the leading newspapers of the following day as "a few

rambling, incoherent, and half-audible words, in which he was understood to complain that he had not had a fair trial, because the Foreman of the Jury was prepossessed against him." The remarkable declaration that he really made was this: *"My Lord, I knew I was a doomed man when the Foreman of my Jury came into the box. My Lord, I knew he would never let me off, because, before I was taken, he somehow got to my bedside in the night, woke me, and put a rope round my neck."*

THE STORY OF THE GOBLINS WHO STOLE A SEXTON

I N AN old Abbey town, down in this part of the country, a long, long while ago—so long, that the story must be a true one, because our great grandfathers implicitly believed it—there officiated as sexton and grave-digger in the churchyard, one Gabriel Grub. It by no means follows that because a man is a sexton, and constantly surrounded by emblems of mortality, therefore he should be a morose and melancholy man; your undertakers are the merriest fellows in the world, and I once had the honour of being on intimate terms with a mute, who in private life, and off duty, was as comical and jocose a little fellow as ever chirped out a devil-may-care song, without a hitch in his memory, or drained off a good stiff glass of grog without stopping for breath. But notwithstanding these precedents to the contrary, Gabriel Grub was an ill-conditioned, cross-grained, surly fellow—a morose and lonely man, who consorted with nobody but himself, and an old wicker bottle which fitted into his large deep waistcoat pocket; and who eyed each merry face as it passed him by, with such a deep scowl of malice and ill-humour, as it was difficult to meet without feeling something the worse for.

"A little before twilight one Christmas eve, Gabriel shouldered his spade, lighted his lantern, and betook himself towards the old churchyard, for he had got a grave to finish by next morning, and feeling very low he thought it might raise his spirits perhaps, if he went on with his work at once. As he wended his way up the ancient street, he saw the cheerful light of the blazing fires gleam through the old casements, and heard the loud laugh and the cheerful shouts of those who were assembled around them; he marked the bustling preparations for next day's good cheer, and smelt the numerous savoury odours consequent thereupon, as they steamed up from the kitchen windows in clouds. All this was gall and wormwood to the heart of Gabriel Grub; and as groups of children bounded out of the houses, tripped across the road, and were met, before they could knock at the opposite door, by half a dozen curly-headed little rascals who crowded round them as they flocked up-stairs to spend the evening in their Christmas games, Gabriel smiled grimly, and clutched the handle of his spade with a firmer grasp, as he thought of measles, scarlet-fever, thrush, whooping-cough, and a good many other sources of consolation beside.

"In this happy frame of mind, Gabriel strode along, returning a short sullen growl to the good-humoured greetings of such of his neighbours as now and then passed him, until he turned into the dark lane which led to the churchyard. Now Gabriel had been looking forward to reaching the dark lane, because it was, generally speaking, a nice gloomy mournful place, into which the towns-people did not much care to go, except in broad day-light, and when the sun was shining; consequently he was not a little indignant to hear a young urchin roaring out some jolly song about a merry Christmas, in this very sanctuary, which had been called Coffin Lane ever since the days of the old abbey, and the time of the shaven-headed monks. As Gabriel walked on, and the voice drew nearer, he found it proceeded from a small boy, who was hurrying along, to join one of the little parties in the old street, and who, partly to keep himself company, and partly to prepare himself for the occasion, was shouting out the song at the highest pitch of his lungs. So Gabriel waited till the boy came up, and then dodged him into a corner, and rapped him over the head with his lantern five or six times, just to teach him to modulate his voice. And as the boy hurried away with his hand to his head, singing quite a different sort of tune, Gabriel Grub chuckled very heartily to himself, and entered the churchyard, locking the gate behind him.

"He took off his coat, set down his lantern, and getting into the unfinished grave, worked at it for an hour or so, with right good will. But the earth was hardened with the frost, and it was no easy matter to break it up, and shovel it out; and although there was a moon, it was a very young one, and shed little light upon the grave, which was in the shadow of the church. At any other time, these obstacles would have made Gabriel Grub very moody and miserable, but he was so well pleased with having stopped the small boy's singing, that he took little heed of the scanty progress he had made, and looked down into the grave when he had finished work for the night, with grim satisfaction, murmuring as he gathered up his things—

> 'Brave lodgings for one, brave lodgings for one,
> A few feet of cold earth, when life is done;
> A stone at the head, a stone at the feet,
> A rich, juicy meal for the worms to eat;
> Rank grass over head, and damp clay around,
> Brave lodgings for one, these, in holy ground!

" 'Ho! ho!' laughed Gabriel Grub, as he sat himself down on a flat tombstone which was a favourite resting place of his; and drew forth his wicker bottle. 'A coffin at Christmas—a Christmas Box. Ho! ho! ho!'

" 'Ho! ho! ho!' repeated a voice which sounded close behind him.

"Gabriel paused in some alarm, in the act of raising the wicker bottle to his lips, and looked round. The bottom of the oldest grave about him, was not more still and quiet, than the churchyard in the pale moonlight. The cold hoar-frost glistened on the tombstones, and sparkled like rows of gems among the stone carvings of the old church. The snow lay hard and crisp upon the ground, and spread over the thickly-strewn mounds of earth so white and smooth a cover that it seemed as if corpses lay there, hidden only by their winding sheets. Not the faintest rustle broke the profound tranquillity of the solemn scene. Sound itself appeared to be frozen up, all was so cold and still.

" 'It was the echoes,' said Gabriel Grub, raising the bottle to his lips again.

" 'It was *not*,' said a deep voice.

"Gabriel started up, and stood rooted to the spot with astonishment and terror; for his eyes rested on a form which made his blood run cold.

"Seated on an upright tombstone, close to him, was a strange unearthly figure, whom Gabriel felt at once, was no being of this world. His long fantastic legs, which might have reached the ground, were cocked up, and crossed after a quaint, fantastic fashion; his sinewy arms were bare, and his hands rested on his knees. On his short round body he wore a close covering, ornamented with small slashes; and a short cloak dangled at his back; the collar was cut into curious peaks, which served the goblin in lieu of ruff or neckerchief; and his shoes curled up at the toes into long points. On his head he wore a broad-brimmed sugar-loaf hat, garnished with a single feather. The hat was covered with the white frost, and the goblin looked as if he had sat on the same tombstone very comfortably, for two or three hundred years. He was sitting perfectly still; his tongue was put out, as if in derision; and he was grinning at Gabriel Grub with such a grin as only a goblin could call up.

" 'It was *not* the echoes,' said the goblin.

"Gabriel Grub was paralysed, and could make no reply.

" 'What do you here on Christmas eve?' said the goblin sternly.

" 'I came to dig a grave, Sir,' stammered Gabriel Grub.

" 'What man wanders among graves and churchyards on such a night as this?' said the goblin.

" 'Gabriel Grub! Gabriel Grub!' screamed a wild chorus of voices that seemed to fill the churchyard. Gabriel looked fearfully round— nothing was to be seen.

" 'What have you got in that bottle?' said the goblin.

" 'Hollands, Sir,' replied the sexton, trembling more than ever; for he had bought it of the smugglers, and he thought that perhaps his questioner might be in the excise department of the goblins.

" 'Who drinks Hollands alone, and in a churchyard, on such a night as this?' said the goblin.

" 'Gabriel Grub! Gabriel Grub!' exclaimed the wild voices again.

"The goblin leered maliciously at the terrified sexton, and then raising his voice, exclaimed—

" 'And who, then, is our fair and lawful prize?'

"To this inquiry the invisible chorus replied, in a strain that sounded like the voices of many choristers singing to the mighty swell of the old church organ—a strain that seemed borne to the sexton's ears upon a gentle wind, and to die away as its soft breath passed onward—but the burden of the reply was still the same, 'Gabriel Grub! Gabriel Grub!'

"The goblin grinned a broader grin than before, as he said, 'Well, Gabriel, what do you say to this?'

"The sexton gasped for breath.

" 'What do you think of this, Gabriel?' said the goblin, kicking up his feet in the air on either side the tombstone, and looking at the turned-up points with as much complacency as if he had been con- templating the most fashionable pair of Wellingtons in all Bond Street.

" 'It's—it's—very curious, Sir,' replied the sexton, half dead with fright, 'very curious, and very pretty, but I think I'll go back and finish my work, Sir, if you please.'

" 'Work!' said the goblin, 'what work?'

" 'The grave, Sir, making the grave,' stammered the sexton.

" 'Oh, the grave, eh?' said the goblin. 'Who makes graves at a time when all other men are merry, and takes a pleasure in it?'

"Again the mysterious voices replied, 'Gabriel Grub! Gabriel Grub!'

" 'I'm afraid my friends want you, Gabriel,' said the goblin, thrusting his tongue further into his cheek than ever—and a most astonishing tongue it was—'I'm afraid my friends want you, Gabriel,' said the goblin.

" 'Under favour, Sir,' replied the horror-struck sexton, 'I don't think they can, Sir; they don't know me, Sir; I don't think the gentlemen have ever seen me, Sir.'

" 'Oh yes they have,' replied the goblin; 'we know the man with the sulky face and the grim scowl, that came down the street to-night, throwing his evil looks at the children, and grasping his burying spade the tighter. We know the man that struck the boy in the envious malice of his heart, because the boy could be merry, and he could not. We know him, we know him.'

"Here the goblin gave a loud shrill laugh, that the echoes returned twenty fold, and throwing his legs up in the air, stood upon his head, or rather upon the very point of his sugar-loaf hat, on the narrow edge of the tombstone, from whence he threw a summerset with extraordinary agility, right to the sexton's feet, at which he planted himself in the attitude in which tailors generally sit upon the shop-board.

" 'I—I—am afraid I must leave you, Sir,' said the sexton, making an effort to move.

" 'Leave us!' said the goblin, 'Gabriel Grub going to leave us. Ho! ho! ho!'

"As the goblin laughed, the sexton observed for one instant a brilliant illumination within the windows of the church, as if the whole building were lighted up; it disappeared, the organ pealed forth a lively air, and whole troops of goblins, the very counterpart of the first one, poured into the churchyard, and began playing at leap-frog with the tombstones, never stopping for an instant to take breath, but overing the highest among them, one after the other, with the most marvellous dexterity. The first goblin was a most astonish-

The front cover of an 1867 edition of "The Story of the Goblins Who Stole a Sexton."

ing leaper, and none of the others could come near him; even in the extremity of his terror the sexton could not help observing, that while his friends were content to leap over the common-sized gravestones, the first one took the family vaults, iron railings and all, with as much ease as if they had been so many street posts.

"At last the game reached to a most exciting pitch; the organ played quicker and quicker, and the goblins leaped faster and faster, coiling themselves up, rolling head over heels upon the ground, and bounding over the tombstones like foot-balls. The sexton's brain whirled round with the rapidity of the motion he beheld, and his legs reeled beneath him, as the spirits flew before his eyes, when the goblin king, suddenly darting towards him, laid his hand upon his collar, and sank with him through the earth.

"When Gabriel Grub had had time to fetch his breath, which the rapidity of his descent had for the moment taken away, he found himself in what appeared to be a large cavern, surrounded on all sides by crowds of goblins, ugly and grim; in the centre of the room, on an elevated seat, was stationed his friend of the churchyard; and close beside him stood Gabriel Grub himself, without the power of motion.

" 'Cold to-night,' said the king of the goblins, 'very cold. A glass of something warm, here.'

"At this command, half a dozen officious goblins, with a perpetual smile upon their faces, whom Gabriel Grub imagined to be courtiers, on that account, hastily disappeared, and presently returned with a goblet of liquid fire, which they presented to the king.

" 'Ah!' said the goblin, whose cheeks and throat were quite transparent, as he tossed down the flame, 'this warms one, indeed: bring a bumper of the same, for Mr. Grub.'

"It was in vain for the unfortunate sexton to protest that he was not in the habit of taking anything warm at night; for one of the goblins held him while another poured the blazing liquid down his throat, and the whole assembly screeched with laughter as he coughed and choked, and wiped away the tears which gushed plentifully from his eyes, after swallowing the burning draught.

" 'And now,' said the king, fantastically poking the taper corner of his sugar-loaf hat into the sexton's eye, and thereby occasioning him the most exquisite pain—'And now, show the man of misery and gloom a few of the pictures from our own great storehouse.'

"As the goblin said this, a thick cloud which obscured the further end of the cavern, rolled gradually away, and disclosed, apparently at a great distance, a small and scantily furnished, but neat and clean apartment. A crowd of little children were gathered round a bright fire, clinging to their mother's gown, and gamboling round her chair. The mother occasionally rose, and drew aside the window-curtain as if to look for some expected object; a frugal meal was ready spread upon the table, and an elbow chair was placed near the fire. A knock was heard at the door: the mother opened it, and the children crowded round her, and clapped their hands for joy, as their father entered. He was wet and weary, and shook the snow from his garments, as the children crowded round him, and seizing his cloak, hat, stick, and gloves, with busy zeal, ran with them from the room. Then as he sat down to his meal before the fire, the children climbed about his knee, and the mother sat by his side, and all seemed happiness and comfort.

"But a change came upon the view, almost imperceptibly. The scene was altered to a small bed-room, where the fairest and youngest child lay dying; the roses had fled from his cheek, and the light from his eye; and even as the sexton looked upon him with an interest he had never felt or known before, he died. His young brothers and sisters crowded round his little bed, and seized his tiny hand, so cold and heavy; but they shrunk back from its touch and looked with awe on his infant face; for calm and tranquil as it was, and sleeping in rest and peace as the beautiful child seemed to be, they saw that he was dead, and they knew that he was an angel looking down upon, and blessing them, from a bright and happy Heaven.

"Again the light cloud passed across the picture, and again the subject changed. The father and mother were old and helpless now, and the number of those about them was diminished more than half; but content and cheerfulness sat on every face, and beamed in every eye, as they crowded round the fireside, and told and listened to old stories of earlier and bygone days. Slowly and peacefully the father sank into the grave, and, soon after, the sharer of all his cares and troubles followed him to a place of rest and peace. The few, who yet survived them, knelt by their tomb, and watered the green turf which covered it with their tears; then rose and turned away, sadly and mournfully, but not with bitter cries, or despairing lamentations, for they knew that they should one day meet again; and once more they mixed with the busy world, and their content and cheerfulness were restored. The cloud settled upon the picture, and concealed it from the sexton's view.

" 'What do you think of *that?*' said the goblin, turning his large face towards Gabriel Grub.

"Gabriel murmured out something about its being very pretty, and looked somewhat ashamed, as the goblin bent his fiery eyes upon him.

" '*You* a miserable man!' said the goblin, in a tone of excessive contempt. 'You!' He appeared disposed to add more, but indignation choked his utterance, so he lifted up one of his very pliable legs, and flourishing it above his head a little, to insure his aim, administered a good sound kick to Gabriel Grub; immediately after which, all the goblins in waiting crowded round the wretched sexton, and kicked him without mercy, according to the established and invariable custom of courtiers upon earth, who kick whom royalty kicks, and hug whom royalty hugs.

" 'Show him some more,' said the king of the goblins.

"At these words the cloud was again dispelled, and a rich and beautiful landscape was disclosed to view—there is just such another to this day, within half a mile of the old abbey town. The sun shone from out the clear blue sky, the water sparkled beneath his rays, and the trees looked greener, and the flowers more gay, beneath his cheering influence. The water rippled on, with a pleasant sound, the trees rustled in the light wind that murmured among their leaves, the birds sang upon the boughs, and the lark carolled on high her welcome to the morning. Yes, it was morning, the bright, balmy morning of summer; the minutest leaf, the smallest blade of grass, was instinct with life. The ant crept forth to her daily toil, the butterfly fluttered and basked in the warm rays of the sun; myriads of insects spread their transparent wings, and revelled in their brief but happy existence. Man walked forth, elated with the scene; and all was brightness and splendour.

" '*You* a miserable man!' said the king of the goblins, in a more contemptuous tone than before. And again the king of the goblins gave his leg a flourish; again it descended on the shoulders of the sexton; and again the attendant goblins imitated the example of their chief.

"Many a time the cloud went and came, and many a lesson it taught to Gabriel Grub, who although his shoulders smarted with pain from the frequent applications of the goblin's feet thereunto, looked on with an interest which nothing could diminish. He saw that men who worked hard, and earned their scanty bread with lives of labour, were cheerful and happy; and that to the most ignorant, the sweet face of nature was a never-failing source of cheerfulness and joy. He saw those who had been delicately nurtured, and tenderly brought up, cheerful under privations, and superior to suffering that would have crushed many of a rougher grain, because they bore within their own bosoms the materials of happiness, contentment, and peace. He saw that women, the tenderest and most fragile of all God's creatures, were the oftenest superior to sorrow, adversity, and distress; and he saw that it was because they bore in their own hearts an inexhaustible well-spring of affection and devotedness. Above all, he saw that men like himself, who snarled at the mirth and cheerfulness of others, were the foulest weeds on the fair surface of the earth; and setting all the good of the world against the evil, he came to the conclusion that it was a very decent and respectable world after all. No sooner had he formed it, than the cloud which had closed over the last picture, seemed to settle on his senses, and lull him to repose. One by one, the goblins faded from his sight, and as the last one disappeared, he sunk to sleep.

"The day had broken when Gabriel Grub awoke, and found himself lying at full length on the flat grave-stone in the churchyard, with the wicker bottle lying empty by his side, and his coat, spade, and lantern, all well whitened by the last night's frost, scattered on the ground. The stone on which he had first seen the goblin seated, stood bolt upright before him, and the grave at which he had worked, the night before, was not far off. At first he began to doubt the reality of his adventures, but the acute pain in his shoulders when he attempted to rise, assured him that the kicking of the goblins was certainly not ideal. He was staggered again, by observing no traces of footsteps in the snow on which the goblins had played leap-frog with the gravestones, but he speedily accounted for this circumstance when he remembered that, being spirits, they would leave no visible impression behind them. So Gabriel Grub got on his feet as well as he could, for the pain in his back; and brushing the frost off his coat, put it on, and turned his face towards the town.

"But he was an altered man, and he could not bear the thought of returning to a place where his repentance would be scoffed at, and his reformation disbelieved. He hesitated for a few moments; and then turned away to wander where he might, and seek his bread elsewhere.

"The lantern, the spade, and the wicker bottle, were found that day in the churchyard. There were a great many speculations about the sexton's fate at first, but it was speedily determined that he had been carried away by the goblins; and there were not wanting some very credible witnesses who had distinctly seen him whisked through the air on the back of a chestnut horse blind of one eye, with the hind quarters of a lion, and the tail of a bear. At length all this was devoutly believed; and the new sexton used to exhibit to the curious, for a trifling emolument, a good-sized piece of the church weather-cock which had been accidentally kicked off by the aforesaid horse in his aërial flight, and picked up by himself in the churchyard, a year or two afterwards.

"Unfortunately these stories were somewhat disturbed by the un-looked-for re-appearance of Gabriel Grub himself, some ten years afterwards, a ragged, contented, rheumatic old man. He told his story to the clergyman, and also to the mayor; and in course of time it began to be received as a matter of history, in which form it has continued down to this very day. The believers in the weathercock tale, having misplaced their confidence once, were not easily pre-vailed upon to part with it again, so they looked as wise as they could, shrugged their shoulders, touched their foreheads, and mur-mured something about Gabriel Grub's having drunk all the Hol-lands, and then fallen asleep on the flat tombstone; and they affected to explain what he supposed he had witnessed in the goblin's cavern, by saying that he had seen the world, and grown wiser. But this opinion, which was by no means a popular one at any time, gradually died off; and be the matter how it may, as Gabriel Grub was afflicted with rheumatism to the end of his days, this story has at least one moral, if it teach no better one—and that is, that if a man turns sulky and drinks by himself at Christmas time, he may make up his mind to be not a bit the better for it, let the spirits be ever so good, or let them be even as many degrees beyond proof, as those which Gabriel Grub saw in the goblin's cavern."

"A Whole Tragic Comic Heroic Theatre": Dickens Onstage

"Sairey Gamp and Betsey Prig." —*by Sol Eytinge, Jr.*

MRS. GAMP

MR. Pecksniff was in a hackney-cabriolet, for Jonas Chuzzlewit had said, "Spare no expense." It should never be charged upon his father's son that he grudged the money for his father's funeral.

Mr. Pecksniff had been to the undertaker, and was now on his way to another officer in the train of mourning,—a female functionary, a nurse, and watcher, and performer of nameless offices about the persons of the dead,—whom the undertaker had recommended. Her name was Gamp; her residence, in Kingsgate Street, High Holborn. So Mr. Pecksniff, in a hackney-cab, was rattling over Holborn's stones, in quest of Mrs. Gamp.

This lady lodged at a bird-fancier's, next door but one to the celebrated mutton-pie shop, and directly opposite to the original cat's-meat warehouse. It was a little house, and this was the more convenient; for Mrs. Gamp being also a monthly nurse, and lodging in the first-floor front, her window was easily assailable at night by pebbles, walking-sticks, and fragments of tobacco-pipe,—all much more efficacious than the street-door knocker; which was so ingeniously constructed as to wake the street with ease, without making the smallest impression on the premises to which it was addressed.

It chanced on this particular occasion that Mrs. Gamp had been up with a distressed Lady all the previous night. It chanced that Mrs. Gamp had not been regularly engaged, but had been called in at a crisis, to assist another professional lady with her advice; and thus it happened that, all points of interest in the case being over, Mrs. Gamp had come home again to the bird-fancier's, and gone to bed. So, when Mr. Pecksniff drove up in the hackney-cab, Mrs. Gamp's curtains were drawn close, and Mrs. Gamp was fast asleep behind them.

Mr. Pecksniff, in the innocence of his heart, applied himself to the knocker; but at his first double-knock, every window in the street became alive with female heads; and before he could repeat it, whole troops of married ladies came flocking round the steps, all crying out with one accord, and with uncommon interest, "Knock at the winder, sir, knock at the winder. Lord bless you, don't lose no more time than you can help,—knock at the winder!"

Borrowing the driver's whip for the purpose, Mr. Pecksniff soon made a commotion among the first-floor flower-pots, and roused Mrs. Gamp, whose voice—to the great satisfaction of the matrons— was heard to say, "I'm coming."

"He's as pale as a muffin," said one lady in allusion to Mr. Pecksniff.

"So he ought to be, if he's the feelings of a man," observed another.

A third lady said she wished he had chosen any other time for fetching Mrs. Gamp, but it always happened so with *her*.

It gave Mr. Pecksniff much uneasiness to infer, from these re-marks, that he was supposed to have come to Mrs. Gamp upon an errand touching, not the close of life, but the other end. Mrs. Gamp herself was under the same impression, for, throwing open the window, she cried behind the curtains, as she hastily dressed herself:

"Is it Mrs. Perkins?"

"No! nothing of the sort."

"What, Mr. Whilks! Don't say it's you, Mr. Whilks, and that

poor creetur Mrs. Whilks with not even a pincushion ready. Don't say it's you, Mr. Whilks!"

"It isn't Mr. Whilks. I don't know the man. Nothing of the kind. A gentleman is dead; and some person being wanted in the house, you have been recommended by Mr. Mould the undertaker. You are also wanted to relieve Mrs. Prig, the day-nurse in attendance on the bookkeeper of the deceased,—one Mr. Chuffey,—whose grief seems to have affected his mind."

As she was by this time in a condition to appear, Mrs. Gamp, who had a face for all occasions, looked out of the window with her mourning countenance, and said she would be down directly.

But the matrons took it very ill that Mr. Pecksniff's mission was of so unimportant a kind; and rated him in good round terms, signifying that they would be glad to know what he meant by terrifying delicate females "with his corpses," and giving it as their opinion that he was ugly enough to know better.

So, when Mrs. Gamp appeared, the unoffending gentleman was glad to hustle her into the cabriolet, and drive off, overwhelmed with popular execration.

Mrs. Gamp had a large bundle with her, a pair of pattens, and a species of gig umbrella; the latter article in colour like a faded leaf, except where a circular patch of a lively blue had been let in at the top. She was much flurried by the haste she had made, and laboured under the most erroneous views of cabriolets, which she appeared to confound with mail-coaches or stage-wagons, insomuch that she was constantly endeavouring for the first half-mile to force her luggage through the little front window, and clamouring to the driver to "put it in the boot." When she was disabused of this idea, her whole being resolved itself into an obsorbing anxiety about her pattens, with which she played innumerable games of quoits on Mr. Pecksniff's legs. It was not until they were close upon the house of mourning that she had enough composure to observe:—

"And so the gentleman's dead, sir! Ah! The more's the pity,"— she didn't even know his name. "But it's what we must all come to.

It's as certain as being born, except that we can't make our calculations as exact. Ah! Poor dear!"

She was a fat old woman, with a husky voice and a moist eye. Having very little neck, it cost her some trouble to look over herself, if one may say so, at those to whom she talked. She wore a rusty black gown, rather the worse for snuff, and a shawl and bonnet to correspond. The face of Mrs. Gamp—the nose in particular—was somewhat red and swollen, and it was difficult to enjoy her society without becoming conscious of a smell of spirits.

"Ah!" repeated Mrs. Gamp, for that was always a safe sentiment in cases of mourning,—"ah, dear! When Gamp was summonsed to his long home, and I see him a lying in the hospital with a penny-piece on each eye, and his wooden leg under his left arm, I thought I should have fainted away. But I bore up."

If certain whispers current in the Kingsgate Street circles had any truth in them, Mrs. Gamp had borne up surprisingly, and had indeed exerted such uncommon fortitude as to dispose of Mr. Gamp's remains for the benefit of science.

"You have become indifferent since then, I suppose? Use is second nature, Mrs. Gamp."

"You may well say second natur, sir. One's first ways is to find sich things a trial to the feelings, and such is one's lasting custom. If it wasn't for the nerve a little sip of liquor gives me (which I was never able to do more than taste it), I never could go through with what I sometimes has to do. 'Mrs. Harris,' I says, at the wery last case as ever I acted in, which it was but a young person,—'Mrs. Harris,' I says, 'leave the bottle on the chimley-piece, and don't ask me to take none, but let me put my lips to it when I am so dispoged, and then I will do what I am engaged to do, according to the best of my ability.' 'Mrs. Gamp,' she says, in answer, 'if ever there was a sober creetur to be got at eighteen-pence a day for working people, and three and six for gentlefolks,—night watching being a extra charge—you are that inwallable person.' 'Mrs. Harris,' I says to her, 'don't name the charge, for if I could afford to lay all my fellow-

creeturs out for nothink, I would gladly do it, sich is the love I bears
'em.' "

At this point, she was fain to stop for breath. And advantage may
be taken of the circumstance, to state that a fearful mystery surrounded this lady of the name of Harris, whom no one in the circle
of Mrs. Gamp's acquaintance had ever seen; neither did any human
being know her place of residence. The prevalent opinion was that
she was a phantom of Mrs. Gamp's brain, created for the purpose of
holding complimentary dialogues with her on all manner of subjects.

"The bottle shall be duly placed on the chimney-piece, Mrs.
Gamp, and you shall put your lips to it at your own convenience."

"Thank you, sir. Which it is a thing as hardly ever occurs with
me, unless when I am indispoged, and find my half a pint o' porter
settling heavy on the chest. Mrs. Harris often and often says to me,
'Sairey Gamp,' she says, 'you raly do amaze me!' 'Mrs. Harris,' I says
to her, 'why so? Give it a name, I beg!' 'Telling the truth then,
ma'am,' says Mrs. Harris, 'and shaming him as shall be nameless
betwixt you and me, never did I think, till I know'd you, as any
woman could sick-nurse and monthly likeways, on the little that you
takes to drink.' 'Mrs. Harris,' I says to her, 'none on us knows what
we can do till we tries; and wunst *I* thought so, too. But now,' I says,
'my half a pint of porter fully satisfies; perwisin', Mrs. Harris, that it
is brought reg'lar, and draw'd mild.' "

The conclusion of this affecting narrative brought them to the
house. In the passage they encountered Mr. Mould, the undertaker, a
little elderly gentleman, bald, and in a suit of black; with a note-book
in his hand, and a face in which a queer attempt at melancholy was at
odds with a smirk of satisfaction.

"Well, Mrs. Gamp, and how are *you*, Mrs. Gamp?"

"Pretty well, I thank you, sir."

"You'll be very particular here, with the deceased party upstairs,
Mrs. Gamp. This is not a common case, Mrs. Gamp. Let everything
be very nice and comfortable, about the deceased, Mrs. Gamp, if you
please."

"It shall be so, sir; you knows me of old, I hope, and so does Mrs. Mould, your ansome pardner, sir; and so does the two sweet young ladies, your darters; although the blessing of a daughter was deniged myself, which, if we had had one, Gamp would certainly have drunk its little shoes right off its feet, as with our precious boy he did, and arterwards send the child a errand, to sell his wooden leg for any liquor it would fetch as matches in the rough; which was truly done beyond his years, for ev'ry individgle penny that child lost at tossing for kidney-pies, and come home arterwards quite bold, to break the news, and offering to drown himself if sech would be a satisfaction to his parents. But wery different is them two sweet young ladies o'yourn, Mister Mould, as I know'd afore a tooth in their pretty heads was cut, and have many a time seen—ah! the dear creeturs!—a playing at berryin's down in the shop, and a follerin' the order-book to its long home in the iron safe. Young ladies with such faces as your darters thinks of something else besides berryin's; don't they, sir? Thinks o' marryin's; don't they, sir?"

"I'm sure I don't know, Mrs. Gamp. Very shrewd woman, Mr. Pecksniff, sir. Woman whose intellect is immensely superior to her station in life; sort of woman one would really almost feel disposed to bury for nothing, and do it neatly, too. Mr. Pecksniff, sir. This Funeral is one of the most impressive cases, sir, that I have seen in the whole course of my professional experience."

"Indeed, Mr. Mould!"

"Such affectionate regret I never saw. There is no limitation; there is positively NO limitation in point of expense! I have orders, sir, in short, to turn out something absolutely gorgeous."

"My friend Mr. Jonas is an excellent man."

"Well, I have seen a good deal of what is filial in my time, sir, and of what is unfilial, too! It is the lot of parties in my line, sir. We come into the knowledge of those secrets. But anything so filial as this—anything so honourable to human nature, anything so expensive, so calculated to reconcile all of us to the world we live in—never yet came under my observation. It only proves, sir, what was so forcibly observed by the lamented poet,—buried at Stratford,—that there is good in everything."

"It is very pleasant to hear you say so, Mr. Mould."

"You are very kind, sir. And what a man the late Mr. Chuzzlewit was, sir! Ah! what a man he was. Mr. Pecksniff, sir, good morning!"

Mr. Pecksniff returned the compliment; and Mould was going away with a brisk smile, when he remembered the occasion. Quickly becoming depressed again, he sighed; looked into the crown of his hat, as if for comfort; put it on without finding any; and slowly departed.

Mrs. Gamp and Mr. Pecksniff then ascended the staircase; and Mrs. Gamp, having been shown to the chamber in which all that remained of old Anthony Chuzzlewit lay covered up, with but one loving heart, and that the heart of his old book-keeper, to mourn it, left Mr. Pecksniff free to enter the darkened room below in search of Mr. Jonas.

He found that example to bereaved sons, and pattern in the eyes of all performers of funerals, so subdued, that he could scarcely be heard to speak, and only seen to walk across the room.

"Pecksniff, you shall have the regulation of it all, mind! You shall be able to tell anybody who talks about it, that everything was correctly and freely done. There isn't any one you'd like to ask to the funeral, is there?"

"No, Mr. Jonas, I think not."

"Because if there is, you know, ask him. We don't want to make a secret of it."

"No; I am not the less obliged to you on that account, Mr. Jonas, for your liberal hospitality; but there really is no one."

"Very well; then you, and I, and the doctor, will be just an easy coachful. We'll have the doctor, Pecksniff, because he knows what was the matter with my father, and that it couldn't be helped."

With that, they went up to the room where the old book-keeper was, attended by Mrs. Betsey Prig. And to them entered Mrs. Gamp soon afterwards, who saluted Mrs. Prig as one of the sisterhood, and "the best of creeturs."

The old book-keeper sat beside the bed, with his head bowed down; until Mrs. Gamp took him by the arm, when he meekly rose, saying:—

"My old master died at threescore and ten,—ought and carry seven. Some men are so strong that they live to fourscore—four times ought's an ought, four times two's an eight—eighty. Oh! why—why—why—didn't he live to four times ought's an ought, and four times two's an eight—eighty? Why did he died before his poor old crazy servant! Take him from me, and what remains? I loved him. He was good to me. I took him down once, six boys, in the arithmetic class at school. God forgive me! Had I the heart to take him down!"

"Well I'm sure," said Mrs. Gamp, "you're a wearing old soul, and that's the blessed truth. You ought to know that you was born in a wale, and that you live in a wale, and that you must take the consequences of sich a sitivation. As a good friend of mine has frequent made remark to me, Mr. Jonage Chuzzlewit, which her name, sir,—I will not deceive you,—is Harris,—Mrs. Harris through the square and up the steps a turnin' round by the tobacker shop,— and which she said it the last Monday evening as ever dawned upon this Pilgrim's Progress of a mortal wale,—'O Sairey, Sairey, little do we know wot lays afore us!' 'Mrs. Harris, ma'am,' I says, 'not much, it's true, but more than you suppoge. Our calciations, ma'am,' I says, 'respectin' wot the number of a family will be, comes most times within one, and oftener than you would suppoge, exact.' 'Sairey,' says Mrs. Harris, in a awful way, 'tell me wot is my in-dividgle number.' 'No, Mrs. Harris,' I says to her, 'ex-cuge me, if you please. My own family,' I says, 'has fallen out of three-pair backs, and has had damp doorsteps settled on their lungs, and one was turned up smilin' in a bedstead unbeknown. Therefore, ma'am,' I says, 'seek not to protigipate, but take 'em as they come and as they go. Mine,' I says to her,—'mine is all gone, my dear young chick. And as to husbands, there's a wooden leg gone likewise home to its account, which, in its constancy of walking into public-'ouses, and never coming out again till fetched by force, was quite as weak as flesh, if not weaker.' "

Mrs. Gamp, now left to the live part of her task, formally relieved Mrs. Prig for the night. That interesting lady had a gruff voice and a beard, and straightway got her bonnet and shawl on.

"Anythink to tell afore you goes, Betsey, my dear?"

"The pickled salmon in this house is delicious. I can partickler recommend it. The drinks is all good. His physic and them things is on the drawers and mankleshelf. He took his last slime draught at seven. The easy-chair ain't soft enough. You'll want his piller."

Mrs. Gamp thanked Mrs. Prig for these friendly hints and gave her good night. She then entered on her official duties: firstly, she put on a yellow-white nightcap of prodigious size, in shape resembling a cabbage: having previously divested herself of a row of bald old curls, which could scarcely be called false, they were so innocent of anything approaching to deception; secondly, and lastly, she summoned the housemaid, to whom she delivered this official charge, in tones expressive of faintness:—

"I think, young woman, as I could peck a little bit o' pickled salmon, with a little sprig o' fennel, and a sprinkling o' white pepper. I takes new bread, my dear, with jest a little pat o' fredge butter and a mossel o' cheese. With respect to ale, if they draws the Brighton old tipper at any 'ouse nigh here, I takes that ale at night, my love; not as I cares for it myself, but on accounts of it being considered wakeful by the doctors; and whatever you do, young woman, don't bring me more than a shillingsworth of gin-and-water, warm, when I rings the bell a second time; for that is always my allowange, and I never takes a drop beyond. In case there should be sich a thing as a cowcumber in the 'ouse, I'm rather partial to 'em, though I am but a poor woman. Rich folks may ride on camels, but it ain't so easy for them to see out of a needle's eye. That is my comfort, and I hopes I knows it."

The supper and drink being brought and done full justice to, she administered the patient's medicine by the simple process of clutching his windpipe to make him gasp, and immediately pouring it down his throat.

"Drat the old wexagious creetur, I a'most forgot your piller, I declare!" she said, drawing it away. "There! Now you're as comfortable as you need be, I'm sure! and *I*'m a going to be comfortable too."

All her arrangements made, she lighted the rushlight, coiled herself up on her couch, and fell asleep.

Ghostly and dark the room, and full of shadows. The noises in the streets were hushed, the house was quiet, the dead of night was coffined in the silent city. When Mrs. Gamp awoke, she found that the busy day was broad awake too. Mrs. Prig relieved punctually, having passed a good night at another patient's. But Mrs. Prig relieved in an ill temper.

The best among us have their failings, and it must be conceded of Mrs. Prig, that if there were a blemish in the goodness of her disposition, it was a habit she had of not bestowing all its sharp and acid properties upon her patients (as a thoroughly amiable woman would have done), but of keeping a considerable remainder for the service of her friends. She looked offensively at Mrs. Gamp, and winked her eye. Mrs. Gamp felt it necessary that Mrs. Prig should know her place, and be made sensible of her exact station in society. So she began a remonstrance with:—

"Mrs. Harris, Betsey—"

"Bother Mrs. Harris!"

Mrs. Gamp looked at Betsey with amazement, incredulity, and indignation. Mrs. Prig, winking her eye tighter, folder her arms and uttered these tremendous words:—

"I don't believe there's no sich a person!"

With these expressions, she snapped her fingers once, twice, thrice, each time nearer to the face of Mrs. Gamp, and then turned away as one who felt that there was now a gulf between them which nothing could ever bridge across.

SIKES AND NANCY

CHAPTER I

FAGIN the receiver of stolen goods was up, betimes, one morning, and waited impatiently for the appearance of his new associate, Noah Claypole, otherwise Morris Bolter; who at length presented himself, and, cutting a monstrous slice of bread, commenced a voracious assault on the breakfast.

"Bolter, Bolter."

"Well, here I am. What's the matter? Don't yer ask me to do anything till I have done eating. That's a great fault in this place. Yer never get time enough over yer meals."

"You can talk as you eat, can't you?"

"Oh yes, I can talk. I get on better when I talk. Talk away. Yer won't interrupt me."

There seemed, indeed, no great fear of anything interrupting him, as he had evidently sat down with a determination to do a deal of business.

"I want you, Bolter," leaning over the table, "to do a piece of work for me, my dear, that needs great care and caution."

"I say, don't yer go a-shoving me into danger, yer know. That don't suit me, that don't; and so I tell yer."

"There's not the smallest danger in it—not the very smallest; it's only to dodge a woman."

"An old woman?"

"A young one."

"I can do that pretty well. I was a regular sneak when I was at school. What am I to dodge her for? Not to—"

"Not to do anything, but tell me where she goes, who she sees, and, if possible, what she says; to remember the street, if it is a street, or the house, if it is a house; and to bring me back all the information you can."

"What'll yer give me?"

"If you do it well, a pound, my dear. One pound. And that's what I never gave yet, for any job of work where there wasn't valuable consideration to be got."

"Who is she?"

"One of us."

"Oh Lor! Yer doubtful of her, are yer?"

"She has found out some new friends, my dear, and I must know who they are."

"I see. Ha! ha! ha! I'm your man. Where is she? Where am I to wait for her? Where am I to go?"

"All that, my dear, you shall hear from me. I'll point her out at the proper time. You keep ready, in the clothes I have got here for you, and leave the rest to me."

That night, and the next, and the next again, the spy sat booted and equipped in the disguise of a carter: ready to turn out at a word from Fagin. Six nights passed, and on each, Fagin came home with a disappointed face, and briefly intimated that it was not yet time. On the seventh he returned exultant. It was Sunday Night.

"She goes abroad to-night," said Fagin, "and on the right errand, I'm sure; for she has been alone all day, and the man she is afraid of will not be back much before daybreak. Come with me! Quick!"

They left the house, and, stealing through a labyrinth of streets, arrived at length before a public-house. It was past eleven o'clock, and the door was closed; but it opened softly as Fagin gave a low whistle. They entered, without noise.

Scarcely venturing to whisper, but substituting dumb show for words, Fagin pointed out a pane of glass high in the wall to Noah, and signed to him to climb up, on a piece of furniture below it, and observe the person in the adjoining room.

"Is that the woman?"

Fagin nodded "yes."

"I can't see her face well. She is looking down, and the candle is behind her."

"Stay there." He signed to the lad, who had opened the house-door to them; who withdrew—entered the room adjoining, and, under pretence of snuffing the candle, moved it in the required position; then he spoke to the girl, causing her to raise her face.

"I see her now!"

"Plainly?"

"I should know her among a thousand."

The spy descended, the room-door opened, and the girl came out. Fagin drew him behind a small partition, and they held their breath as she passed within a few feet of their place of concealment, and emerged by the door at which they had entered.

"After her!! To the left. Take the left hand, and keep on the other side. After her!!"

The spy darted off; and, by the light of the street lamps, saw the girl's retreating figure, already at some distance before him. He advanced as near as he considered prudent, and kept on the opposite side of the street. She looked nervously round. She seemed to gather courage as she advanced, and to walk with a steadier and firmer step. The spy preserved the same relative distance between them, and followed.

CHAPTER II

THE churches chimed three quarters past eleven, as the two figures emerged on London Bridge. The young woman advanced with a swift and rapid step, and looked about her as though in quest of some expected object; the young man, who slunk along in the deepest shadow he could find, and, at some distance, accommodated his pace to hers: stopping when she stopped: and as she moved again, creeping stealthily on: but never allowing himself, in the ardour of his pursuit, to gain upon her. Thus, they crossed the bridge, from the Middlesex to the Surrey shore, when the woman, disappointed in her anxious scrutiny of the foot-passengers, turned back. The movement was sudden; but the man was not thrown off his guard by it; for, shrinking into one of the recesses which surmount the piers of the bridge, and leaning over the parapet the better to conceal his figure, he suffered her to pass. When she was about the same distance in advance as she had been before, he slipped quietly down, and followed her again. At nearly the centre of the bridge she stopped. He stopped.

It was a very dark night. The day had been unfavourable, and at that hour and place there were few people stirring. Such as there were, hurried past: possibly without seeing, certainly without noticing, either the woman, or the man. Their appearance was not attractive of such of London's destitute population, as chanced to take their way over the bridge that night; and they stood there in silence: neither speaking nor spoken to.

The girl had taken a few turns to and fro—closely watched by her hidden observer—when the heavy bell of St. Paul's tolled for the death of another day. Midnight had come upon the crowded city. Upon the palace, the night-cellar, the jail, the madhouse: the chambers of birth and death, of health and sickness, upon the rigid face of the corpse and the calm sleep of the child.

A young lady, accompanied by a grey-haired gentleman, alighted from a hackney-carriage. They had scarcely set foot upon the pavement of the bridge, when the girl started, and joined them.

"Not here!! I am afraid to speak to you here. Come away—out of the public road—down the steps yonder!"

The steps to which she pointed, were those which, on the Surrey bank, and on the same side of the bridge as Saint Saviour's Church, form a landing-stairs from the river. To this spot the spy hastened unobserved; and after a moment's survey of the place, he began to descend.

These stairs are a part of the bridge; they consist of three flights. Just below the end of the second, going down, the stone wall on the left terminates in an ornamental pilaster facing towards the Thames. At this point the lower steps widen: so that a person turning that angle of the wall, is necessarily unseen by any others on the stairs who chance to be above, if only a step. The spy looked hastily round, when he reached this point; and as there seemed no better place of concealment, and as the tide being out there was plenty of room, he slipped aside, with his back to the pilaster, and there waited: pretty certain that they would come no lower down.

So tardily went the time in this lonely place, and so eager was the spy, that he was on the point of emerging from his hiding-place, and regaining the road above, when he heard the sound of footsteps, and directly afterwards of voices almost close at his ear.

He drew himself straight upright against the wall, and listened attentively.

"This is far enough," said a voice, which was evidently that of the gentleman. "I will not suffer the young lady to go any further. Many people would have distrusted you too much to have come even so far, but you see I am willing to humour you."

"To humour me!" cried the voice of the girl whom he had followed. "You're considerate, indeed, sir. To humour me! Well, well, it's no matter."

"Why, for what purpose can you have brought us to this strange place? Why not have let me speak to you, above there, where it is light, and there is something stirring, instead of bringing us to this dark and dismal hole?"

"I told you before, that I was afraid to speak to you there. I don't know why it is," said the girl shuddering, "but I have such a fear and dread upon me to-night that I can hardly stand."

"A fear of what?"

"I scarcely know of what—I wish I did. Horrible thoughts of death—and shrouds with blood upon them—and a fear that has made me burn as if I was on fire—have been upon me all day. I was reading a book to-night, to while the time away, and the same things came into the print."

"Imagination!"

"No imagination. I swear I saw 'coffin' written in every page of the book in large black letters,—aye, and they carried one close to me, in the streets to-night."

"There is nothing unusual in that. They have passed me often."

"Real ones. This was not."

"Pray speak to her kindly," said the young lady to the grey-haired gentleman. "Poor creature! She seems to need it."

"Bless you, miss, for that! Your haughty religious people would have held their heads up to see me as I am to-night, and would have preached of flames and vengeance. Oh, dear lady, why ar'n't those who claim to be God's own folks, as gentle and as kind to us poor wretches as you!"

—"You were not here last Sunday night, girl, as you appointed."

"I couldn't come. I was kept by force."

"By whom?"

"Bill—Sikes—him that I told the young lady of before."

"You were not suspected of holding any communication

with anybody on the subject which has brought us here to-night, I hope?"

"No," replied the girl, shaking her head. "It's not very easy for me to leave him unless he knows why; I couldn't have seen the lady when I did, but that I gave him a drink of laudanum before I came away."

"Did he awake before you returned?"

"No; and neither he nor any of them suspect me."

"Good. Now listen to me. I am Mr. Brownlow, this young lady's friend. I wish you, in this young lady's interest, and for her sake, to deliver up Fagin."

"Fagin! I will not do it! I will never do it! Devil that he is, and worse than devil as he has been to me, as my Teacher in all Devilry, I will never do it."

"Why?"

"For the reason that, bad life as he has led, I have led a bad life too; for the reason that there are many of us who have kept the same courses together, and I'll not turn upon them, who might—any of them—have turned upon me, but didn't, bad as they are. Last, for the reason—(how can I say it with the young lady here!)—that, among them, there is one—this Bill—this Sikes—the most desperate of all—that I can't leave. Whether it is God's wrath for the wrong I have done, I don't know, but I am drawn back to him through everything, and I should be, I believe, if I knew that I was to die by his hand!"

"But, put one man—not him—not one of the gang—the one man Monks into my hands, and leave him to me to deal with."

"What if he turns against the others?"

"I promise you that, in that case, there the matter shall rest; they shall go scot free."

"Have I the lady's promise for that?"

"You have," replied Rose Maylie, the young lady.

"I have been a liar, and among liars from a little child, but I will take your words."

After receiving an assurance from both, that she might safely do so, she proceeded in a voice so low that it was often difficult for the listener to discover even the purport of what she said, to describe the means by which this one man Monks might be found and taken. But nothing would have induced her to compromise one of her own companions; little reason though she had, poor wretch! to spare them.

"Now," said the gentleman, when she had finished, "you have given us most valuable assistance, young woman, and I wish you to be the better for it. What can I do to serve you?"

"Nothing."

"You will not persist in saying that; think now; take time. Tell me."

"Nothing, sir. You can do nothing to help me. I am past all hope."

"You put yourself beyond the pale of hope. The past has been a dreary waste with you, of youthful energies mis-spent, and such treasures lavished, as the Creator bestows but once and never grants again, but, for the future, you may hope! I do not say that it is in our power to offer you peace of heart and mind, for that must come as you seek it; but a quiet asylum, either in England, or, if you fear to remain here, in some foreign country, it is not only within the compass of our ability but our most anxious wish to secure you. Before the dawn of morning, before this river wakes to the first glimpse of daylight, you shall be placed as entirely beyond the reach of your former associates, and leave as complete an absence of all trace behind you, as if you were to disappear from the earth this moment. Come! I would not have you go back to exchange one word with any old companion, or take one look at any old haunt. Quit them all, while there is time and opportunity!"

"She will be persuaded now," cried the young lady.

"I fear not, my dear."

"No, sir—no, miss. I am chained to my old life. I loathe and hate it, but I cannot leave it.—When ladies as young and good, as happy and beautiful as you, miss, give away your hearts, love will carry even you all lengths. When such as I, who have no certain roof but the coffin-lid, and no friend in sickness or death but the hospital-nurse, set our rotten hearts on any man, who can hope to cure us!—This fear comes over me again. I must go home. Let us part. I shall be watched or seen. Go! Go! If I have done you any service, all I ask is, leave me, and let me go my way alone."

"Take this purse," cried the young lady. "Take it for my sake, that you may have some resource in an hour of need and trouble."

"No! I have not done this for money. Let me have that to think of. And yet—give me something that you have worn—I should like to have something—*no, no,* not a *ring*, they'd rob me of that—your gloves or handkerchief—anything that I can keep, as having belonged to you. There. Bless you! God bless you!! Good-night, good-night!"

The agitation of the girl, and the apprehension of some discovery which would subject her to violence, seemed to determine the gentleman to leave her. The sound of retreating footsteps followed, and the voices ceased.

After a time Nancy ascended to the street. The spy remained on his post for some minutes, and then, after peeping out, to make sure that he was unobserved, darted away, and made for Fagin's house as fast as his legs would carry him.

CHAPTER III

I T was nearly two hours before daybreak; that time which in the autumn of the year, may be truly called the dead of night; when the streets are silent and deserted; when even sound appears to slumber, and profligacy and riot have staggered home to dream; it was at this still and silent hour, that Fagin sat in his old lair. Stretched upon a mattress on the floor, lay Noah Claypole, otherwise Morris Bolter, fast asleep. Towards him the old man sometimes directed his eyes for an instant, and then brought them back again to the wasting candle.

He sat without changing his attitude, or appearing to take the smallest heed of time, until the door-bell rang. He crept up-stairs, and presently returned accompanied by a man muffled to the chin, who carried a bundle under one arm. Throwing back his outer coat, the man displayed the burly frame of Sikes, the housebreaker.

"There!" laying the bundle on the table. "Take care of that, and do the most you can with it. It's been trouble enough to get. I thought I should have been here three hours ago."

Fagin laid his hand upon the bundle, and locked it in the cupboard. But he did not take his eyes off the robber, for an instant.

"Wot now?" cried Sikes. "Wot do you look at a man, like that, for?"

Fagin raised his right hand, and shook his trembling forefinger in the air.

"Hallo!" feeling in his breast. "He's gone mad. I must look to myself here."

"No, no, it's not—you're not the person, Bill. I've no—no fault to find with you."

"Oh! you haven't, haven't you?" passing a pistol into a more convenient pocket. "That's lucky—for one of us. Which one that is, don't matter."

"I've got that to tell you, Bill, will make you worse than me."

"Aye? Tell away! Look sharp, or Nance will think I'm lost."

"Lost! She has pretty well settled that, in her own mind, already."

He looked, perplexed, into the old man's face, and reading no satisfactory explanation of the riddle there, clenched his coat collar in his huge hand and shook him soundly.

"Speak, will you? Or if you don't, it shall be for want of breath. Open your mouth and say wot you've got to say. Out with it, you thundering, blundering, wondering old cur, out with it!"

"Suppose that lad that's lying there—" Fagin began.

Sikes turned round to where Noah was sleeping, as if he had not previously observed him. "Well?"

"Suppose that lad was to peach—to blow upon us all. Suppose that lad was to do it, of his own fancy—not grabbed, tried, ear-wigged by the parson and brought to it on bread and water,—but of his own fancy; to please his own taste; stealing out at nights to do it. Do you hear me? Suppose he did all this, what then?"

"What then? If he was left alive till I came, I'd grind his skull under the iron heel of my boot into as many grains as there are hairs upon his head."

"What if *I* did it! *I*, that know so much, and could hang so many besides myself!"

"I don't know. I'd do something in the jail that 'ud get me put in irons; and, if I was tried along with you, I'd fall upon you with them in the open court, and beat your brains out afore the people. I'd smash your head as if a loaded waggon had gone over it."

Fagin looked hard at the robber; and, motioning him to be silent, stooped over the bed upon the floor, and shook the sleeper to rouse him.

"Bolter! Bolter! Poor lad!" said Fagin, looking up with an expression of devilish anticipation, and speaking slowly and with marked emphasis. "He's tired—tired with watching for *her* so long—watching for *her*, Bill."

"Wot d'ye mean?"

Fagin made no answer, but bending over the sleeper again, hauled him into a sitting posture. When his assumed name had been repeated several times, Noah rubbed his eyes, and, giving a heavy yawn, looked sleepily about him.

"Tell me that again—once again, just for him to hear," said the Jew, pointing to Sikes as he spoke.

"Tell yer what?" asked the sleepy Noah, shaking himself pettishly.

"That about—Nancy!! You followed her?"

"Yes."

"To London Bridge?"

"Yes."

"Where she met two people?"

"So she did."

"A gentleman and a lady that she had gone to of her own accord before, who asked her to give up all her pals, and Monks first, which she did—and to describe him, which she did—and to tell her what house it was that we meet at, and go to, which she did—and where it could be best watched from, which she did—and what time the people went there, which she did. She did all this. She told it all, every word, without a threat, without a murmur—she did—did she not?"

"All right," replied Noah, scratching his head. "That's just what it was!"

"What did they say about last Sunday?"

"About last Sunday! Why, I told yer that before."

"Again. Tell it again!"

"They asked her," as he grew more wakeful, and seemed to have a dawning perception who Sikes was, "they asked her why she didn't come, last Sunday, as she promised. She said she couldn't."

"Why? Tell him that."

"Because she was forcibly kept at home by Bill—Sikes—the man that she had told them of before."

"What more of him? What more of Bill—Sikes—the man she had told them of before? Tell him that, tell him that."

"Why, that she couldn't very easily get out of doors unless he knew where she was going to, and so the first time she went to see the lady, she—ha! ha! ha! it made me laugh when she said it, that did—she gave him, a drink of laudanum!! ha! ha! ha!"

Sikes rushed from the room, and darted up the stairs.

"Bill, Bill!" cried Fagin, following him, hastily. "A word. Only a word."

"Let me out. Don't speak to me! it's not safe. Let me out."

"Hear me speak a word," rejoined Fagin, laying his hand upon the lock. "You won't be—you won't be—too—violent, Bill?"

The day was breaking, and there was light enough for the men to see each other's faces. They exchanged a brief glance; there was the same fire in the eyes of both.

"I mean, not too—violent—for—for—safety. Be crafty, Bill, and not too bold."

The robber dashed into the silent streets.

Without one pause, or moment's consideration; without once turning his head to the right or left; without once raising his eyes to the sky, or lowering them to the ground, but looking straight before him with savage resolution: he muttered not a word, nor relaxed a muscle, until he reached his own house-door.—He opened it, softly, with a key; strode lightly up the stairs; and entering his own room, double-locked the door, and drew back the curtain of the bed.

The girl was lying, half-dressed, upon the bed. He had roused her from her sleep, for she raised herself with a hurried and startled look.

"Get up!"

"It *is* you, Bill!"

"Get up!!!"

There was a candle burning, but he drew it from the candlestick, and hurled it under the grate. Seeing the faint light of early day without, the girl rose to undraw the curtain.

"Let it be. There's light enough for wot I've got to do."—

"Bill, why do you look like that at me?"

The robber regarded her, for a few seconds, with dilated nostrils and heaving breast; then, grasping her by the head and throat, dragged her into the middle of the room, and placed his heavy hand upon her mouth.

"You were watched to-night, you she-devil; every word you said was heard."

"Then if every word I said was heard, it was heard that I spared you. Bill, dear Bill, you cannot have the heart to kill me. Oh! think of all I have given up, only this one night, for *you*. Bill, Bill! For dear

God's sake, for your own, for mine, stop before you spill my blood!!! I have been true to you, upon my guilty soul I have!!! The gentleman and that dear lady told me to-night of a home in some foreign country where I could end my days in solitude and peace. Let me see them again, and beg them, on my knees, to show the same mercy to you; and let us both leave this dreadful place, and far apart lead better lives, and forget how we have lived, except in prayers, and never see each other more. It is never too late to repent. They told me so—I feel it now. But we must have time—we must have a little, little time!"

The housebreaker freed one arm, and grasped his pistol. The certainty of immediate detection if he fired, flashed across his mind; and he beat it twice upon the upturned face that almost touched his own.

She staggered and fell, but raising herself on her knees, she drew from her bosom a white handkerchief—Rose Maylie's—and holding it up towards Heaven, breathed one prayer, for mercy to her Maker.

It was a ghastly figure to look upon. The murderer staggering backward to the wall, and shutting out the sight with his hand, seized a heavy club, and struck her down!!

The bright sun burst upon the crowded city in clear and radiant glory. Through costly-coloured glass and paper-mended window, through cathedral dome and rotten crevice, it shed its equal ray. It lighted up the room where the murdered woman lay. It did. He tried to shut it out, but it would stream in. If the sight had been a ghastly one in the dull morning, what was it, now, in all that brilliant light!!!

He had not moved; he had been afraid to stir. There had been a moan and motion of the hand; and, with terror added to rage, he had struck and struck again. Once he threw a rug over it; but it was worse to fancy the eyes, and imagine them moving towards him, than to see them glaring upward, as if watching the reflection of the pool of gore that quivered and danced in the sunlight on the ceiling. He had plucked it off again. And there was the body—mere flesh and blood, no more—but such flesh, and so much blood!!!

"A foul deed." —by F. W. Pailthorpe

He struck a light, kindled a fire, and thrust the club into it. There was hair upon the end, which shrunk into a light cinder, and whirled up the chimney. Even that frightened him; but he held the weapon till it broke, and then piled it on the coals to burn away, and smoulder into ashes. He washed himself, and rubbed his clothes; there were spots upon them that would not be removed, but he cut the pieces out, and burnt them. How those stains were dispersed about the room! The very feet of his dog were bloody!!!!

All this time he had, never once, turned his back upon the corpse. He now moved, backward, towards the door: dragging the dog with him, shut the door softly, locked it, took the key, and left the house.

As he gradually left the town behind him all that day, and plunged that night into the solitude and darkness of the country, he was haunted by that ghastly figure following at his heels. He could hear its garments rustle in the leaves; and every breath of wind came laden with that last low cry. If *he* stopped, *it* stopped. If *he* ran, *it* followed; not running too—that would have been a relief—but borne on one slow melancholy air that never rose or fell.

At times, he turned to beat this phantom off, though it should look him dead; but the hair rose on his head, and his blood stood still, for it had turned with him, and was behind him then. He leaned his back against a bank, and felt that it stood above him, visibly out against the cold night sky. He threw himself on his back upon the road. At his head it stood, silent, erect, and still: a human gravestone with its epitaph in Blood!!

Suddenly, towards daybreak, he took the desperate resolution of going back to London. "There's somebody to speak to there, at all events. A hiding-place, too, in our gang's old house in Jacob's Island.—I'll risk it."

Choosing the least frequented roads for his journey back, he resolved to lie concealed within a short distance of the city until it was dark night again, and then proceed to his destination. He did this, and limped in among three affrighted fellow-thieves, the ghost of himself—blanched face, sunken eyes, hollow cheeks—his dog at his heels covered with mud, lame, half blind, crawling as if those stains had poisoned him!!

All three men shrank away. Not one of them spake.

"You that keep this house.—Do you mean to sell me, or to let me lie here 'till the hunt is over?"

"You may stop if you think it safe. But what man ever escaped the men who are after you!"

Hark!!!! A great sound coming on like a rushing fire! What? Tracked so soon? The hunt was up already? Lights gleaming below, voices in loud and earnest talk, hurried tramp of footsteps on the wooden bridges over Folly Ditch, a beating on the heavy door and window-shutters of the house, a waving crowd in the outer darkness like a field of corn moved by an angry storm!

"The tide was in, as I come up. Give me a rope. I may drop from the top of the house, at the back into the Folly Ditch, and clear off that way, or be stifled. Give me a rope!"

No one stirred. They pointed to where they kept such things, and the murderer hurried with a strong cord to the housetop. Of all the terrific yells that ever fell on mortal ears, none could exceed the furious cry when he was seen. Some shouted to those who were nearest, to set the house on fire; others adjured the officers to shoot him dead; others, with execrations, clutched and tore at him in the empty air; some called for ladders, some for sledge-hammers; some ran with torches to and fro, to seek them. "I promise Fifty Pounds," cried Mr. Brownlow from the nearest bridge, "to the man who takes that murderer alive!"

He set his foot against the stack of chimneys, fastened one end of the rope firmly round it, and with the other made a strong running noose by the aid of his hands and teeth. With the cord round his back, he could let himself down to within a less distance of the ground than his own height, and had his knife ready in his hand to cut the cord, and drop.

At the instant that he brought the loop over his head before slipping it beneath his arm-pits, looking behind him on the roof he threw up his arms, and yelled, "The eyes again!" Staggering as if struck by lightning, he lost his balance and tumbled over the parapet. The noose was at his neck; it ran up with his weight; tight as a bowstring, and swift as the arrow it speeds. He fell five-and-thirty feet, and hung with his open knife clenched in his stiffening hand!!!

The dog which had lain concealed 'till now, ran backwards and forwards on the parapet with a dismal howl, and, collecting himself for a spring, jumped for the dead man's shoulders. Missing his aim, he fell into the ditch, turning over as he went, and striking against a stone, dashed out his brains!!

THE TRIAL FROM
PICKWICK

O N THE morning of the trial of the great action for breach of promise of marriage—Bardell against Pickwick—the defendant, Mr. Pickwick, being escorted into court, stood up in a state of agitation, and took a glance around him. There were already a pretty large sprinkling of spectators in the gallery, and a numerous muster of gentlemen in wigs, in the barristers' seats: who presented, as a body, all that pleasing and extensive variety of nose and whisker for which the bar of England is justly celebrated. Such of the gentlemen as had a brief to carry, carried it in as conspicuous a manner as possible, and occasionally scratched their noses with it, to impress it more strongly on the observation of the spectators. Other gentlemen who had no briefs, carried under their arms goodly octavos, with a red label behind, and that under-done-pie-crust-coloured cover, which is technically known as "law calf." Others, who had neither briefs nor books, thrust their hands into their pockets, and looked as wise as they could. The whole, to the great wonderment of Mr. Pickwick, were divided into little groups, who were chatting and discussing the news of the day in the most unfeeling manner possible,—just as if no trial at all were coming on.

A loud cry of "Silence!" announced the entrance of the judge:

who was most particularly short, and so fat, that he seemed all face and waistcoat. He rolled in, upon two little turned legs, and having bobbed to the bar, who bobbed to him, put his little legs underneath his table, and his little three-cornered hat upon it. A sensation was then perceptible in the body of the court; and immediately afterwards Mrs. Bardell, the plaintiff, supported by Mrs. Cluppins, her bosom friend number one, was led in in a drooping state. An extra-sized umbrella was then handed in by Mr. Dodson, and a pair of pattens by Mr. Fogg (Dodson and Fogg being the plaintiff's attornies), each of whom had prepared a sympathising and melancholy face for the occasion. Mrs. Sanders, bosom friend number two, then appeared, leading in Master Bardell, whom she placed on the floor of the court in front of his hysterical mother,—a commanding position in which he could not fail to awaken the sympathy of both judge and jury. This was not done without considerable opposition on the part of the young gentleman himself, who had misgivings that his being placed in the full glare of the judge's eye was only a formal prelude to his being immediately ordered away for instant execution.

"I am for the plaintiff, my Lord," said Mr. Serjeant Buzfuz.

COURT.—"Who is with you, brother Buzfuz?" Mr. Skimpin bowed, to intimate that he was.

"I appear for the defendant, my Lord," said Mr. Serjeant Snubbin.

COURT.—"Anybody with you, brother Snubbin?"

"Mr. Phunky, my Lord."

COURT.—"Go on."

Mr. Skimpin proceeded to "open the case"; and the case appeared to have very little inside it when he had opened it, for he kept such particulars as he knew, completely to himself.

Serjeant Buzfuz then rose with all the majesty and dignity which the grave nature of the proceedings demanded, and having whispered to Dodson, and conferred briefly with Fogg, pulled his gown over his shoulders, settled his wig, and addressed the jury.

Serjeant Buzfuz began by saying, that never, in the whole course of his professional experience—never, from the very first moment of his applying himself to the study and practice of the law—had he approached a case with such a heavy sense of the responsibility imposed upon him—a responsibility he could never have supported, were he not buoyed up and sustained by a conviction so strong, that it amounted to positive certainty that the cause of truth and justice, or, in other words, the cause of his much-injured and most oppressed client, *must* prevail with the high-minded and intelligent dozen of men whom he now saw in that box before him.

Counsel always begin in this way, because it puts the jury on the best terms with themselves, and makes them think what sharp fellows they must be. A visible effect was produced immediately; several jurymen beginning to take voluminous notes.

"You have heard from my learned friend, gentlemen," continued Serjeant Buzfuz, well knowing that, from the learned friend alluded to, the gentlemen of the jury had heard nothing at all—"you have heard from my learned friend, gentlemen, that this is an action for a breach of promise of marriage, in which the damages are laid at 1500£. But you have not heard from my learned friend, inasmuch as it did not come within my learned friend's province to tell you, what are the facts and circumstances of this case. Those facts and circumstances, gentlemen, you shall hear detailed by me, and proved by the unimpeachable female whom I will place in that box before you. The plaintiff is a widow; yes, gentlemen, a widow. The late Mr. Bardell, after enjoying, for many years, the esteem and confidence of his sovereign, as one of the guardians of his royal revenues, glided almost imperceptibly from the world, to seek elsewhere for that repose and peace which a custom-house can never afford."

This was a pathetic description of the decease of Mr. Bardell, who had been knocked on the head with a quart-pot in a public-house cellar.

"Some time before Mr. Bardell's death, he had stamped his likeness on a little boy. With this little boy, the only pledge of her departed exciseman, Mrs. Bardell shrunk from the world, and courted the retirement and tranquillity of Goswell Street; and here she placed in her front parlour-window a written placard, bearing this inscription—'Apartments furnished for a single gentleman. Inquire within.' " Here Serjeant Buzfuz paused, while several gentlemen of the jury took a note of the document.

"There is no date to that, is there, sir?" inquired a juror.

"There is no date, gentlemen, but I am instructed to say that it was put in the plaintiff's parlour-window just this time three years. Now, I entreat the attention of the jury to the wording of this document—'Apartments furnished for a single gentleman!' 'Mr. Bardell,' said the widow; 'Mr. Bardell was a man of honour—Mr. Bardell was a man of his word—Mr. Bardell was no deceiver—Mr. Bardell was once a single gentleman himself; *in* single gentlemen I shall perpetually see something to remind me of what Mr. Bardell was, when he first won my young and untried affections; to a single gentleman shall my lodgings be let.' Actuated by this beautiful and touching impulse, (among the best impulses of our imperfect nature, gentlemen,) the desolate widow dried her tears, furnished her first floor, caught her innocent boy to her maternal bosom, and put the bill up in her parlour-window. Did it remain there long? No. Before the bill had been in the parlour-window three days—three days, gentlemen—a Being, erect upon two legs, and bearing all the outward semblance of a man, and not of a monster, knocked at Mrs. Bardell's door. He inquired within; he took the lodgings; and on the very next day he entered into possession of them. This man was Pickwick—Pickwick the defendant."

Serjeant Buzfuz here paused for breath. The silence awoke Mr. Justice Stareleigh, who immediately wrote down something with a pen without any ink in it, and looked unusually profound, to impress the jury with the belief that he always thought most deeply with his eyes shut.

"Of this man Pickwick I will say little; the subject presents but few attractions; and I, gentlemen, am not the man, nor are you, gentlemen, the men, to delight in the contemplation of revolting heartlessness, and of systematic villany."

Here Mr. Pickwick, who had been writhing in silence, gave a violent start, as if some vague idea of assaulting Serjeant Buzfuz, in the august presence of justice and law, suggested itself to his mind.

"I say systematic villany, gentlemen," said Serjeant Buzfuz, looking through Mr. Pickwick, and talking *at* him; "and when I say systematic villany, let me tell the defendant Pickwick—if he be in court, as I am informed he is—that it would have been more decent in him, more becoming, in better judgment, and in better taste, if he had stopped away. I shall show you, gentlemen, that for two years Pickwick continued to reside without interruption or intermission, at Mrs. Bardell's house. I shall show you that, on many occasions, he gave halfpence, and on some occasions even sixpences, to her little boy; and I shall prove to you, by a witness whose testimony it will be impossible for my learned friend to weaken or controvert, that on one occasion he patted the boy on the head, and, after inquiring whether he had won any *alley tors* or *commoneys* lately (both of which I understand to be a particular species of marbles much prized by the youth of this town), made use of this remarkable expression—'How should you like to have another father?' I shall prove to you, gentlemen, on the testimony of three of his own friends—most unwilling witnesses, gentlemen—most unwilling witnesses—that on that morning he was discovered by them holding the plaintiff in his arms, and soothing her agitation by his caresses and endearments. And now, gentlemen, but one word more. Two letters have passed between these parties—letters which are admitted to be in the handwriting of the defendant. Let me read the first:—'Garraway's, twelve o'clock. Dear Mrs. B.—Chops and Tomata sauce. Yours, Pickwick.' Gentlemen, what does this mean? Chops! Gracious heavens! and Tomata sauce! Gentlemen, is the happiness of a sensitive and confiding female to be trifled away by such shallow artifices as these? The next has no date whatever, which is in itself suspicious.—'Dear Mrs. B., I shall not be at home till to-morrow. Slow coach.' And then follows this very remarkable expression—'Don't trouble yourself about the warming-pan.' Why, gentlemen, who *does* trouble himself about a warming-pan? Why is Mrs. Bardell so earnestly entreated not to agitate herself about this warming-pan, unless it is, as I assert it to be, a mere cover for hidden fire—a mere substitute for some endearing word or promise, agreeably to a preconcerted system of correspondence, artfully contrived by Pickwick with a view to his contemplated desertion, and which I am not in a condition to explain? Enough of this: my client's hopes and prospects are ruined. But Pickwick, gentlemen, Pickwick, the ruthless destroyer of this domestic oasis in the desert of Goswell Street—Pickwick, who has chocked up the well, and thrown ashes on the sward—Pickwick, who comes before you to-day with his heartless Tomata sauce and warming-pans—Pickwick still rears his head with unblushing effrontery, and gazes without a sigh on the ruin he has made. Damages, gentlemen—heavy damages—are the only punishment with which you can visit him; the only recompense you can award to my client. And for those damages she now appeals to an enlightened, a high-minded, a right-feeling, a conscientious, a dispassionate, a sympathising, a contemplative jury of her civilised countrymen."

With this beautiful peroration, Mr. Serjeant Buzfuz sat down, and Mr. Justice Stareleigh woke up.

"Call Elizabeth Cluppins," said Serjeant Buzfuz, rising a minute afterwards, with renewed vigour.

"Do you recollect, Mrs. Cluppins? Do you recollect being in Mrs. Bardell's back one pair of stairs, on one particular morning in July last, when she was dusting Pickwick's apartment?"

"Yes, my Lord and Jury, I do."

"Mr. Pickwick's sitting-room was the first floor front, I believe?"

"Yes, it were, sir."

COURT.—"What were you doing in the back room, ma'am?"

"My Lord and Jury, I will not deceive you."

COURT.—"You had better not, ma'am."

"I was there, unbeknown to Mrs. Bardell; I had been out with a little basket, gentlemen, to buy three pound of red kidney purtaties, which was three pound tuppence ha'penny, when I see Mrs. Bardell's street door on the jar."

COURT.—"On the what?"

"Partly open, my Lord."

COURT.—"She *said* on the jar."

"It's all the same, my Lord."

The little judge looked doubtful, and said he'd make a note of it.

"I walked in, gentlemen, just to say good mornin', and went, in a permiscuous manner, up stairs, and into the back room. Gentlemen, there was the sound of voices in the front room, and—"

"And you listened, I believe, Mrs. Cluppins?"

"Beggin' your pardon, sir, I would scorn the haction. The voices was very loud, sir, and forced themselves upon my ear."

"Well, Mrs. Cluppins, you were not listening, but you heard the voices. Was one of those voices, Pickwick's?"

"Yes, it were, sir."

And Mrs. Cluppins, after distinctly stating that Mr. Pickwick addressed himself to Mrs. Bardell, repeated, by slow degrees, and by dint of many questions, the conversation she had heard. Which, like many other conversations repeated under such circumstances, or indeed like many other conversations repeated under any circumstances, was of the smallest possible importance in itself, but looked big now.

Mrs. Cluppins having broken the ice, thought it a favourable opportunity for entering into a short dissertation on her own domestic affairs; so, she straightway proceeded to inform the court that she was the mother of eight children at that present speaking, and that she entertained confident expectations of presenting Mr. Cluppins with a ninth, somewhere about that day six months. At this interesting point, the little judge interposed most irascibly, and the worthy lady was taken out of court.

"Nathaniel Winkle!" said Mr. Skimpin.

"Here!" Mr. Winkle entered the witness-box, and having been duly sworn, bowed to the judge: who acknowledged the compliment by saying:

COURT.—"Don't look at me, sir; look at the jury."

Mr. Winkle obeyed the mandate, and looked at the place where he thought the jury might be.

Mr. Winkle was then examined by Mr. Skimpin.

"Now, sir, have the goodness to let his Lordship and the jury know what your name is, will you?" Mr. Skimpin inclined his head on one side and listened with great sharpness for the answer, as if to imply that he rather thought Mr. Winkle's natural taste for perjury would induce him to give some name which did not belong to him.

"Winkle."

COURT.—"Have you any Christian name, sir?"

"Nathaniel, sir."

COURT.—"Daniel,—any other name?"

"Nathaniel, Sir—my Lord, I mean."

COURT.—"Nathaniel Daniel, or Daniel Nathaniel?"

"No, my Lord, only Nathaniel—not Daniel at all."

COURT.—"What did you tell me it was Daniel for then, sir?"

"I didn't, my Lord."

COURT.—"You did, sir. How could I have got Daniel on my notes, unless you told me so, sir?"

"Mr. Winkle has rather a short memory, my Lord; we shall find means to refresh it before we have quite done with him, I dare say. Now, Mr. Winkle, attend to me, if you please, sir; and let me recommend you be careful. I believe you are a particular friend of Pickwick, the defendant, are you not?"

"I have known Mr. Pickwick now, as well as I recollect at this moment, nearly—"

"Pray, Mr. Winkle, do not evade the question. Are you, or are you not, a particular friend of the defendant's?"

"I was just about to say, that—"

"Will you, or will you not, answer my question, sir?"

Court.—"If you don't answer the question, you'll be committed to prison, sir."

"Yes, I am."

"Yes, you are. And couldn't you say that at once, sir? Perhaps you know the plaintiff too—eh, Mr. Winkle?"

"I don't know her; but I've seen her."

"Oh, you don't know her, but you've seen her? Now, have the goodness to tell the gentlemen of the jury what you mean by *that*, Mr. Winkle."

"I mean that I am not intimate with her, but that I have seen her when I went to call on Mr. Pickwick, in Goswell Street."

"How often have you seen her, sir?"

"How often?"

"Yes, Mr. Winkle, how often? I'll repeat the question for you a dozen times, if you require it, sir."

On this question there arose the edifying brow-beating, customary on such points. First of all, Mr. Winkle said it was quite impossible for him to say how many times he had seen Mrs. Bardell. Then he was asked if he had seen her twenty times, to which he replied, "Certainly,—more than that." Then he was asked whether he hadn't seen her a hundred times—whether he couldn't swear that he had seen her more than fifty times—whether he didn't know that he had seen her at least seventy-five times—and so forth.

"Pray, Mr. Winkle, do you remember calling on the defendant Pickwick at these apartments in the plaintiff's house in Goswell Street, on one particular morning, in the month of July last?"

"Yes, I do."

"Were you accompanied on that occasion by a friend of the name of Tupman, and another of the name of Snodgrass?"

"Yes, I was."

"Are they here?"

"Yes, they are," looking very earnestly towards the spot where his friends were stationed.

"Pray attend to me, Mr. Winkle, and never mind your friends,"

Mʀs BARDELL

Of false men ye damsels all beware,
For I so graceful, smart and slick,
Now wasted away as you can see,
By one so base and vile—Pickwick.

Mrs. Bardell and her son, Tommy. —*from* Sam Weller's Scrap Sheet *(1837)*

with an expressive look at the jury. "They must tell their stories without any previous consultation with you, if none has yet taken place (another look at the jury). Now, sir, tell the gentlemen of the jury what you saw on entering the defendant's room, on this particular morning. Come; out with it, sir; we must have it, sooner or later."

"The defendant, Mr. Pickwick, was holding the plaintiff in his arms, with his hands clasping her waist, and the plaintiff appeared to have fainted away."

"Did you hear the defendant say anything?"

"I heard him call Mrs. Bardell a good creature, and I heard him ask her to compose herself, for what a situation it was, if anybody should come, or words to that effect."

"Now, Mr. Winkle, I have only one more question to ask you. Will you undertake to swear that Pickwick, the defendant, did not say on the occasion in question, 'My dear Mrs. Bardell, you're a good creature; compose yourself to this situation, for to this situation you must come,' or words to *that* effect?"

"I—I didn't understand him so, certainly. I was on the staircase, and couldn't hear distinctly; the impression on my mind is—"

"The gentlemen of the jury want none of the impressions on your mind, Mr. Winkle, which I fear would be of little service to honest straightforward men. You were on the staircase, and didn't distinctly hear; but you will not swear that Pickwick did not make use of the expressions I have quoted? Do I understand that?"

"No I will not."

"You may leave the box, sir."

Tracy Tupman, and Augustus Snodgrass, were severally called into the box; both corroborated the testimony of their unhappy friend; and each was driven to the verge of desperation by excessive badgering.

Susannah Sanders was then called, and examined by Serjeant Buzfuz, and cross-examined by Serjeant Snubbin. Had always said and believed that Pickwick would marry Mrs. Bardell; knew that Mrs. Bardell's being engaged to Pickwick was the current topic of conversation in the neighbourhood, after the fainting in July. Had heard Pickwick ask the little boy how he should like to have another father. Did not know that Mrs. Bardell was at that time keeping company with the baker, but did know that the baker was then a single man and is now married. Thought Mrs. Bardell fainted away on the morning in July, because Pickwick asked her to name the day; knew that she (witness) fainted away stone dead when Mr. Sanders asked *her* to name the day, and believed that anybody as called herself a lady would do the same under similar circumstances. During the period of her keeping company with Mr. Sanders she had received love letters, like other ladies. In the course of their correspondence Mr. Sanders had often called her a "duck," but he had never called her "chops," nor yet "tomata sauce."

Serjeant Buzfuz now rose with more importance than he had yet exhibited, if that were possible, and said "Call Samuel Weller."

It was quite unnecessary to call Samuel Weller; for Samuel Weller stepped into the box the instant his name was pronounced; and placing his hat on the floor, and his arms on the rail, took a bird's-eye view of the bar, and a comprehensive survey of the bench with a remarkably cheerful and lively aspect.

COURT.—"What's your name, sir?"

"Sam Weller, my Lord."

COURT.—"Do you spell it with a 'V' or with a 'W'?"

"That depends upon the taste and fancy of the speller, my Lord. I never had occasion to spell it more than once or twice in my life, but I spells it with a 'V.' "

Here a voice in the gallery exclaimed, "Quite right too, Samivel; quite right. Put it down a we, my Lord, put it down a we."

COURT.—"Who is that, who dares to address the court? Usher."

"Yes, my Lord."

COURT.—"Bring that person here instantly."

"Yes, my Lord."

But as the usher didn't find the person, he didn't bring him; and, after a great commotion, all the people who had got up to look for the culprit, sat down again. The little judge turned to the witness as soon as his indignation would allow him to speak, and said,

COURT.—"Do you know who that was, sir?"

"I rayther suspect it was my father, my Lord."

COURT.—"Do you see him here now?"

Sam stared up into the lantern in the roof of the court, and said, "Why no, my Lord, I can't say that I *do* see him at the present moment."

COURT.—"If you could have pointed him out, I would have sent him to jail instantly."

Sam bowed his acknowledgments.

"Now, Mr. Weller," said Serjeant Buzfuz.

"Now, sir."

"I believe you are in the service of Mr. Pickwick, the defendant in this case. Speak up, if you please, Mr. Weller."

"I mean to speak up, sir. I am in the service o' that 'ere gen'l'man, and a wery good service it is."

"Little to do, and plenty to get, I suppose?"

"Oh, quite enough to get, sir, as the soldier said ven they ordered him three hundred and fifty lashes."

COURT.—"You must not tell us what the soldier said, unless the soldier is in court, and is examined in the usual way; it's not evidence."

"Wery good, my Lord."

"Do you recollect anything particular happening on the morning when you were first engaged by the defendant; eh, Mr. Weller?"

"Yes I do, sir."

"Have the goodness to tell the jury what it was."

"I had a reg'lar new fit out o' clothes that mornin', gen'l'men of the jury, and that was a wery partickler and uncommon circumstance vith me in those days."

The judge looked sternly at Sam, but Sam's features were so perfectly serene that the judge said nothing.

"Do you mean to tell me, Mr. Weller, that you saw nothing of this fainting on the part of the plaintiff in the arms of the defendant, which you have heard described by the witnesses?"

"Certainly not, sir, I was in the passage 'till they called me up; and then the old lady as you call the plaintiff, she warn't there, sir."

"You were in the passage and yet saw nothing of what was going forward. Have you a pair of eyes, Mr. Weller?"

"Yes, I have a pair of eyes, and that's just it. If they wos a pair o' patent double million magnifyin' gas microscopes of hextra power, p'r'aps I might be able to see through two flights o' stairs and a deal door; but bein' only eyes, you see, my wision's limited."

"Now, Mr. Weller, I'll ask you a question on another point, if you please."

"If you please, sir."

"Do you remember going up to Mrs. Bardell's house, one night in November?"

"Oh yes, very well."

"Oh, you *do* remember that, Mr. Weller. I thought we should get at something at last."

"I rayther thought that, too, sir."

"Well; I suppose you went up to have a little talk about the trial—eh, Mr. Weller?"

"I went up to pay the rent; but we *did* get a talkin' about the trial."

"Oh, you did get a talking about the trial. Now what passed about the trial; will you have the goodness to tell us, Mr. Weller?"

"Vith all the pleasure in life, sir. Arter a few unimportant obserwations from the two wirtuous females as has been examined here to-day, the ladies gets into a wery great state o' admiration at the honourable conduct of Mr. Dodson and Mr. Fogg—them two gen'l'men as is settin' near you now."

"The attornies for the plaintiff. Well, they spoke in high praise of the honourable conduct of Messrs. Dodson and Fogg, the attornies for the plaintiff, did they?"

"Yes; they said what a wery gen'rous thing it was o' them to have taken up the case on spec, and not to charge nothin' at all for costs, unless they got 'em out of Mr. Pickwick."

"It's perfectly useless, my Lord, attempting to get at any evidence through the impenetrable stupidity of this witness. I will not trouble the court by asking him any more questions. Stand down, sir. That's my case, my Lord."

Serjeant Snubbin then addressed the jury on behalf of the defendant; and did the best he could for Mr. Pickwick; and the best, as everybody knows, could do no more.

Mr. Justice Stareleigh summed up, in the old-established form. He read as much of his notes to the jury as he could decipher on so short a notice; he didn't read as much of them as he couldn't make out; and he made running comments on the evidence as he went along. If Mrs. Bardell were right, it was perfectly clear Mr. Pickwick was wrong; and if they thought the evidence of Mrs. Cluppins worthy of credence, they would believe it; and, if they didn't, why they wouldn't. The jury then retired to their private room to talk the matter over, and the judge retired to *his* private room to refresh himself with a mutton chop and a glass of sherry.

An anxious quarter of an hour elapsed; the jury came back; and the judge was fetched in. Mr. Pickwick put on his spectacles, and gazed at the foreman.

"Gentlemen, are you all agreed upon your verdict?"

"We are."

"Do you find for the plaintiff, gentlemen, or for the defendant?"

"For the plaintiff."

"With what damages, gentlemen?"

"Seven hundred and fifty pounds."

Mr. Pickwick having drawn on his gloves with great nicety, and stared at the foreman all the while, allowed himself to be assisted into a hackney-coach, which had been fetched for the purpose by the ever-watchful Sam Weller.

Sam had put up the steps, and was preparing to jump on the box, when he felt himself gently touched on the shoulder; and his father stood before him.

"Samivel! The gov'nor ought to have been got off with a alleybi. Ve got Tom Vildspark off o' that 'ere manslaughter (that come of hard driving) vith a alleybi, ven all the big vigs to a man, said as nothing couldn't save him. I know'd what 'ud come o' this here way o' doin' bisniss. O Sammy, Sammy, vy worn't there a alleybi!"

"To Every Man and Woman Who Reads It a Personal Kindness"

A CHRISTMAS CAROL

Being a Ghost Story
of Christmas

PREFACE

I have endeavoured in this Ghostly little book, to raise the Ghost of an Idea, which shall not put my readers out of humour with themselves, with each other, with the season, or with me. May it haunt their house pleasantly, and no one wish to lay it.

Their faithful Friend and Servant,

C.D.

December 1843.

Scrooge and the Ghosts of Christmas Past, Present, and Yet to Come.
—drawn (as are the sixteen illustrations that follow) by Sol Eytinge, Jr.

MARLEY'S GHOST

ARLEY was dead, to begin with. There is no doubt whatever about that. The register of his burial was signed by the clergyman, the clerk, the undertaker, and the chief mourner. Scrooge signed it. And Scrooge's name was good upon 'Change for anything he chose to put his hand to.

Old Marley was as dead as a door-nail.

Mind! I don't mean to say that I know, of my own knowledge, what there is particularly dead about a door-nail. I might have been inclined, myself, to regard a coffin-nail as the deadest piece of ironmongery in the trade. But the wisdom of our ancestors is in the simile; and my unhallowed hands shall not disturb it, or the Country's done for. You will therefore permit me to repeat, emphatically, that Marley was as dead as a door-nail.

Scrooge knew he was dead? Of course he did. How could it be otherwise? Scrooge and he were partners for I don't know how many years. Scrooge was his sole executor, his sole administrator, his sole assign, his sole residuary legatee, his sole friend, and sole mourner. And even Scrooge was not so dreadfully cut up by the sad event, but that he was an excellent man of business on the very day of the funeral, and solemnised it with an undoubted bargain.

The mention of Marley's funeral brings me back to the point I started from. There is no doubt that Marley was dead. This must be distinctly understood, or nothing wonderful can come of the story I am going to relate. If we were not perfectly convinced that Hamlet's Father died before the play began, there would be nothing more remarkable in his taking a stroll at night, in an easterly wind, upon his own ramparts, than there would be in any other middle-aged gentleman rashly turning out after dark in a breezy spot—say St. Paul's Churchyard, for instance—literally to astonish his son's weak mind.

Scrooge never painted out old Marley's name. There it stood, years afterwards, above the warehouse door: Scrooge and Marley. The firm was known as Scrooge and Marley. Sometimes people new to the business called Scrooge Scrooge, and sometimes Marley, but he answered to both names. It was all the same to him.

Oh! But he was a tight-fisted hand at the grindstone, Scrooge! a squeezing, wrenching, grasping, scraping, clutching, covetous, old sinner! Hard and sharp as flint, from which no steel had ever struck out generous fire; secret, and self-contained, and solitary as an oyster. The cold within him froze his old features, nipped his pointed nose, shrivelled his cheek, stiffened his gait; made his eyes red, his thin lips blue; and spoke out shrewdly in his grating voice. A frosty rime was on his head, and on his eyebrows, and his wiry chin. He carried his own low temperature always about with him; he iced his office in the dog-days; and didn't thaw it one degree at Christmas.

External heat and cold had little influence on Scrooge. No warmth could warm, no wintry weather chill him. No wind that blew was bitterer than he, no falling snow was more intent upon its purpose, no pelting rain less open to entreaty. Foul weather didn't know where to have him. The heaviest rain, and snow, and hail, and sleet, could boast of the advantage over him in only one respect. They often "came down" handsomely, and Scrooge never did.

Nobody ever stopped him in the street to say, with gladsome

looks, "My dear Scrooge, how are you? When will you come to see me?" No beggars implored him to bestow a trifle, no children asked him what it was o'clock, no man or woman ever once in all his life inquired the way to such and such a place, of Scrooge. Even the blindmen's dogs appeared to know him; and when they saw him coming on would tug their owners into doorways and up courts; and then would wag their tails as though they said, "No eye at all is better than an evil eye, dark master!"

But what did Scrooge care! It was the very thing he liked. To edge his way along the crowded paths of life, warning all human sympathy to keep its distance, was what the knowing ones call "nuts" to Scrooge.

Once upon a time—of all the good days in the year, on Christmas Eve—old Scrooge sat busy in his counting-house. It was cold, bleak, biting weather—foggy withal; and he could hear the people in the court outside go wheezing up and down, beating their hands upon their breasts, and stamping their feet upon the pavement stones to warm them. The city clocks had only just gone three, but it was quite dark already,—it had not been light all day,—and candles were flaring in the windows of the neighbouring offices, like ruddy smears upon the palpable brown air. The fog came pouring in at every chink and keyhole, and was so dense without that, although the court was of the narrowest, the houses opposite were mere phantoms. To see the dingy cloud come drooping down, obscuring everything, one might have thought that Nature lived hard by, and was brewing on a large scale.

The door of Scrooge's counting-house was open, that he might keep his eye upon his clerk, who in a dismal little cell beyond, a sort of tank, was copying letters. Scrooge had a very small fire, but the clerk's fire was so very much smaller that it looked like one coal. But he couldn't replenish it, for Scrooge kept the coal-box in his own room; and so surely as the clerk came in with the shovel, the master predicted that it would be necessary for them to part. Wherefore the clerk put on his white comforter, and tried to warm himself at the candle; in which effort, not being a man of strong imagination, he failed.

"A merry Christmas, uncle! God save you!" cried a cheerful voice. It was the voice of Scrooge's nephew, who came upon him so quickly that this was the first intimation he had of his approach.

"Bah!" said Scrooge. "Humbug!"

He had so heated himself with rapid walking in the fog and frost, this nephew of Scrooge's, that he was all in a glow; his face was ruddy and handsome; his eyes sparkled, and his breath smoked again.

"Christmas a humbug, uncle?" said Scrooge's nephew. "You don't mean that, I am sure!"

"I do," said Scrooge. "Merry Christmas! What right have you to be merry? What reason have you to be merry? You're poor enough."

"Come, then," returned the nephew gaily. "What right have you to be dismal? What reason have you to be morose? You're rich enough."

Scrooge, having no better answer ready on the spur of the moment, said, "Bah!" again; and followed it up with "Humbug!"

"Don't be cross, uncle!" said the nephew.

"What else can I be," returned the uncle, "when I live in such a world of fools as this? Merry Christmas! Out upon merry Christmas! What's Christmas-time to you but a time for paying bills without money; a time for finding yourself a year older, and not an hour richer; a time for balancing your books and having every item in 'em through a round dozen of months presented dead against you? If I could work my will," said Scrooge indignantly, "every idiot who goes about with 'Merry Christmas' on his lips should be boiled with his own pudding, and buried with a stake of holly through his heart. He should!"

"Uncle!" pleaded the nephew.

"Nephew!" returned the uncle sternly, "keep Christmas in your own way, and let me keep it in mine."

"Keep it!" repeated Scrooge's nephew. "But you don't keep it."

"Let me leave it alone, then," said Scrooge. "Much good may it do you! Much good it has ever done you!"

"There are many things from which I might have derived good, by which I have not profited, I dare say," returned the nephew, "Christmas among the rest. But I am sure I have always thought of Christmas-time, when it has come round,—apart from the veneration due to its sacred name and origin, if anything belonging to it can be apart from that,—as a good time; a kind, forgiving, charitable, pleasant time; the only time I know of, in the long calendar of the year, when men and women seem by one consent to open their shut-up hearts freely, and to think of people below them as if they really were fellow-passengers to the grave, and not another race of creatures bound on other journeys. And therefore, uncle, though it has never put a scrap of gold or silver in my pocket, I believe that it *has* done me good, and *will* do me good; and I say, God bless it!"

The clerk in the tank involuntarily applauded. Becoming immediately sensible of the impropriety, he poked the fire, and extinguished the last frail spark for ever.

"Let me hear another sound from *you*," said Scrooge, "and you'll keep your Christmas by losing your situation. You're quite a powerful speaker, sir," he added, turning to his nephew. "I wonder you don't go into Parliament."

"Don't be angry, uncle. Come! Dine with us to-morrow."

Scrooge said that he would see him,—yes, indeed, he did. He went the whole length of the expression, and said that he would see him in that extremity first.

"But why?" cried Scrooge's nephew. "Why?"

"Why did you get married?" said Scrooge.

"Because I fell in love."

"Because you fell in love!" growled Scrooge, as if that were the only one thing in the world more ridiculous than a merry Christmas. "Good afternoon!"

"Nay, uncle, but you never came to see me before that happened. Why give it as a reason for not coming now?"

. . . he poked the fire, and extinguished the last frail spark for ever.

"Good afternoon," said Scrooge.

"I want nothing from you; I ask nothing of you; why cannot we be friends?"

"Good afternoon," said Scrooge.

"I am sorry, with all my heart, to find you so resolute. We have never had any quarrel to which I have been a party. But I have made the trial in homage to Christmas, and I'll keep my Christmas humour to the last. So A Merry Christmas, uncle!"

"Good afternoon!" said Scrooge.

"And A Happy New Year!"

"Good afternoon," said Scrooge.

His nephew left the room without an angry word, notwithstanding. He stopped at the outer door to bestow the greetings of the season on the clerk, who, cold as he was, was warmer than Scrooge; for he returned them cordially.

"There's another fellow," muttered Scrooge, who overheard him; "my clerk, with fifteen shillings a week, and a wife and family, talking about a merry Christmas. I'll retire to Bedlam."

This lunatic, in letting Scrooge's nephew out, had let two other people in. They were portly gentlemen, pleasant to behold, and now stood, with their hats off, in Scrooge's office. They had books and papers in their hands, and bowed to him.

"Scrooge and Marley's, I believe," said one of the gentlemen, referring to his list. "Have I the pleasure of addressing Mr. Scrooge, or Mr. Marley?"

"Mr. Marley has been dead these seven years," Scrooge replied. "He died seven years ago, this very night."

"We have no doubt his liberality is well represented by his surviving partner," said the gentleman, presenting his credentials.

It certainly was; for they had been two kindred spirits. At the ominous word "liberality," Scrooge frowned, and shook his head, and handed the credentials back.

"At this festive season of the year, Mr. Scrooge," said the gentleman, taking up a pen, "it is more than usually desirable that we

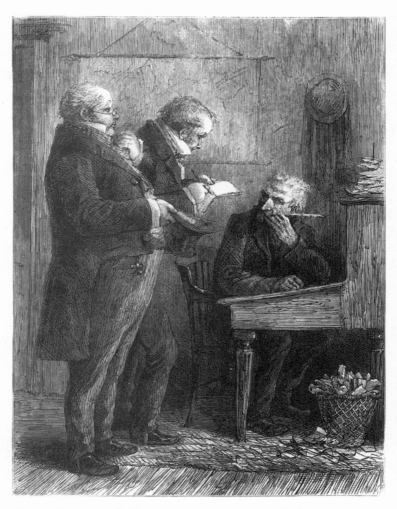

"Have I the pleasure of addressing Mr. Scrooge, or Mr. Marley?"

should make some slight provision for the Poor and destitute, who suffer greatly at the present time. Many thousands are in want of common necessaries; hundreds of thousands are in want of common comforts, sir."

"Are there no prisons?" asked Scrooge.

"Plenty of prisons," said the gentleman, laying down the pen again.

"And the Union workhouses?" demanded Scrooge. "Are they still in operation?"

"They are. Still," returned the gentleman, "I wish I could say they were not."

"The Treadmill and the Poor Law are in full vigour, then?" said Scrooge.

"Both very busy, sir."

"Oh! I was afraid, from what you said at first, that something had occurred to stop them in their useful course," said Scrooge. "I am very glad to hear it."

"Under the impression that they scarcely furnish Christian cheer of mind or body to the multitude," returned the gentleman, "a few of us are endeavouring to raise a fund to buy the Poor some meat and drink, and means of warmth. We choose this time, because it is a time, of all others, when Want is keenly felt, and Abundance rejoices. What shall I put you down for?"

"Nothing!" Scrooge replied.

"You wish to be anonymous?"

"I wish to be left alone," said Scrooge. "Since you ask me what I wish, gentlemen, that is my answer. I don't make merry myself at Christmas, and I can't afford to make idle people merry. I help to support the establishments I have mentioned—they cost enough; and those who are badly off must go there."

"Many can't go there; and many would rather die."

"If they would rather die," said Scrooge, "they had better do it, and decrease the surplus population. Besides—excuse me—I don't know that."

"But you might know it," observed the gentleman.

"It's not my business," Scrooge returned. "It's enough for a man to understand his own business, and not to interfere with other people's. Mine occupies me constantly. Good afternoon, gentlemen!"

Seeing clearly that it would be useless to pursue their point, the gentlemen withdrew. Scrooge resumed his labours with an improved opinion of himself, and in a more facetious temper than was usual with him.

Meanwhile the fog and darkness thickened so that people ran about with flaring links, proffering their services to go before horses and carriages, and conduct them on their way. The ancient tower of a church, whose gruff old bell was always peeping slily down at Scrooge out of a gothic window in the wall, became invisible, and struck the hours and quarters in the clouds, with tremulous vibrations afterwards, as if its teeth were chattering in its frozen head up there. The cold became intense. In the main street, at the corner of the court, some labourers were repairing the gas-pipes, and had lighted a great fire in a brazier, round which a party of ragged men and boys were gathered, warming their hands and winking their eyes before the blaze in rapture. The water-plug being left in solitude, its overflowings suddenly congealed, and turned to misanthropic ice. The brightness of the shops where holly sprigs and berries crackled in the lamp heat of the windows made pale faces ruddy as they passed. Poulterers' and grocers' trades became a splendid joke; a glorious pageant, with which it was next to impossible to believe that such dull principles as bargain and sale had anything to do. The Lord Mayor, in the stronghold of the mighty Mansion House, gave orders to his fifty cooks and butlers to keep Christmas as a Lord Mayor's household should; and even the little tailor whom he had fined five shillings on the previous Monday for being drunk and bloodthirsty in the streets stirred up to-morrow's pudding in his garret, while his lean wife and the baby sallied out to buy the beef.

Foggier yet, and colder! Piercing, searching, biting cold. If the good St. Dunstan had but nipped the Evil Spirit's nose with a touch of such weather as that, instead of using his familiar weapons, then indeed he would have roared to lusty purpose. The owner of one scant young nose, gnawed and mumbled by the hungry cold as bones are gnawed by dogs, stooped down at Scrooge's keyhole to regale him with a Christmas carol; but at the first sound of

> *"God bless you, merry gentleman,*
> *May nothing you dismay!"*

Scrooge seized the ruler with such energy of action that the singer fled in terror, leaving the keyhole to the fog, and even more congenial frost.

At length the hour of shutting up the counting-house arrived. With an ill-will Scrooge dismounted from his stool, and tacitly admitted the fact to the expectant clerk in the tank, who instantly snuffed his candle out, and put on his hat.

"You'll want all day to-morrow, I suppose," said Scrooge.

"If quite convenient, sir."

"It's not convenient," said Scrooge, "and it's not fair. If I was to stop half a crown for it, you'd think yourself ill-used, I'll be bound?"

The clerk smiled faintly.

"And yet," said Scrooge, "you don't think *me* ill-used, when I pay a day's wages for no work."

The clerk observed that it was only once a year.

"A poor excuse for picking a man's pocket every twenty-fifth of December!" said Scrooge, buttoning his great-coat to the chin. "But I suppose you must have the whole day. Be here all the earlier next morning."

The clerk promised that he would; and Scrooge walked out with a growl. The office was closed in a twinkling, and the clerk, with the long ends of his white comforter dangling below the waist (for he boasted no great-coat), went down a slide on Cornhill, at the end of a lane of boys, twenty times, in honour of its being Christmas Eve, and then ran home to Camden Town as hard as he could pelt, to play at blindman's bluff.

Scrooge took his melancholy dinner in his usual melancholy tavern; and having read all the newspapers, and beguiled the rest of the evening with his banker's book, went home to bed. He lived in chambers which had once belonged to his deceased partner. They were a gloomy suite of rooms, in a lowering pile of building up a yard, where it had so little business to be that one could scarcely help fancying it must have run there when it was a young house, playing at hide-and-seek with other houses, and have forgotten the way out again. It was old enough now, and dreary enough; for nobody lived in it but Scrooge, the other rooms being all let out as offices. The yard was so dark that even Scrooge, who knew its every stone, was fain to grope with his hands. The fog and frost so hung about the black old gateway of the house that it seemed as if the Genius of the Weather sat in mournful meditation on the threshold.

Now it is a fact that there was nothing at all particular about the knocker on the door, except that it was very large. It is also a fact that Scrooge had seen it, night and morning, during his whole residence in that place; also that Scrooge had as little of what is called fancy about him as any man in the city of London, even including— which is a bold word—the corporation, aldermen, and livery. Let it also be borne in mind that Scrooge had not bestowed one thought on Marley since his last mention of his seven-years' dead partner that afternoon. And then let any man explain to me, if he can, how it happened that Scrooge, having his key in the lock of the door, saw in the knocker, without its undergoing any intermediate process of change—not a knocker, but Marley's face.

Marley's face. It was not in impenetrable shadow, as the other objects in the yard were, but had a dismal light about it, like a bad lobster in a dark cellar. It was not angry or ferocious, but looked at Scrooge as Marley used to look; with ghostly spectacles turned up on its ghostly forehead. The hair was curiously stirred, as if by breath or hot air; and though the eyes were wide open, they were perfectly motionless. That, and its livid colour, made it horrible; but its horror seemed to be in spite of the face, and beyond its control, rather than a part of its own expression.

As Scrooge looked fixedly at this phenomenon, it was a knocker again.

To say that he was not startled, or that his blood was not conscious of a terrible sensation to which it had been a stranger from infancy, would be untrue. But he put his hand upon the key he had relinquished, turned it sturdily, walked in, and lighted his candle.

He *did* pause, with a moment's irresolution, before he shut the door; and he *did* look cautiously behind it first, as if he half expected to be terrified with the sight of Marley's pig-tail sticking out into the hall. But there was nothing on the back of the door, except the screws and nuts that held the knocker on, so he said, "Pooh, pooh!" and closed it with a bang.

The sound resounded through the house like thunder. Every room above, and every cask in the wine-merchant's cellars below, appeared to have a separate peal of echoes of its own. Scrooge was not a man to be frightened by echoes. He fastened the door, and walked across the hall, and up the stairs; slowly, too, trimming his candle as he went.

You may talk vaguely about driving a coach-and-six up a good old flight of stairs, or through a bad young Act of Parliament; but I mean to say you might have got a hearse up that staircase, and taken it broadside, with the splinter-bar towards the wall and the door towards the balustrades, and done it easy. There was plenty of width for that, and room to spare; which is perhaps the reason why Scrooge thought he saw a locomotive hearse going on before him in the gloom. Half a dozen gas-lamps out of the street wouldn't have lighted the entry too well, so you may suppose that it was pretty dark with Scrooge's dip.

Up Scrooge went, not caring a button for that. Darkness is cheap, and Scrooge liked it. But before he shut his heavy door, he walked through his rooms to see that all was right. He had just enough recollection of the face to desire to do that.

Sitting-room, bedroom, lumber-room. All as they should be. Nobody under the table, nobody under the sofa; a small fire in the grate; spoon and basin ready; and the little saucepan of gruel (Scrooge had a cold in his head) upon the hob. Nobody under the bed; nobody in the closet; nobody in his dressing-gown, which was hanging up in a suspicious attitude against the wall. Lumber-room as usual. Old fire-guard, old shoes, two fish-baskets, washing-stand on three legs, and a poker.

Quite satisfied, he closed his door, and locked himself in; double-locked himself in, which was not his custom. Thus secured against surprise, he took off his cravat; put on his dressing-gown and slippers, and his nightcap; and sat down before the fire to take his gruel.

It was a very low fire, indeed; nothing on such a bitter night. He was obliged to sit close to it, and brood over it, before he could extract the least sensation of warmth from such a handful of fuel. The fireplace was an old one, built by some Dutch merchant long ago, and paved all round with quaint Dutch tiles, designed to illustrate the Scriptures. There were Cains and Abels, Pharaoh's daughters, Queens of Sheba, Angelic messengers descending through the air on clouds like feather-beds, Abrahams, Belshazzars, Apostles putting off to sea in butter-boats, hundreds of figures to attract his thoughts; and yet that face of Marley, seven years dead, came like the ancient prophet's rod, and swallowed up the whole. If each smooth tile had been a blank at first, with power to shape some picture on its surface from the disjointed fragments of his thoughts, there would have been a copy of old Marley's head on every one.

"Humbug!" said Scrooge; and walked across the room.

After several turns, he sat down again. As he threw his head back in the chair, his glance happened to rest upon a bell, a disused bell, that hung in the room, and communicated for some purpose now forgotten with a chamber in the highest story of the building. It was with great astonishment, and with a strange, inexplicable dread, that, as he looked, he saw this bell begin to swing. It swung so softly in the outset that it scarcely made a sound; but soon it rang out loudly, and so did every bell in the house.

This might have lasted half a minute, or a minute, but it seemed an hour. The bells ceased as they had begun, together. They were succeeded by a clanking noise, deep down below, as if some person were dragging a heavy chain over the casks in the wine-merchant's cellar. Scrooge then remembered to have heard that ghosts in haunted houses were described as dragging chains.

The cellar door flew open with a booming sound, and then he heard the noise much louder, on the floors below; then coming up the stairs; then coming straight towards his door.

"It's humbug still!" said Scrooge. "I won't believe it."

His colour changed, though, when, without a pause, it came on through the heavy door, and passed into the room before his eyes. Upon its coming in, the dying flame leaped up, as though it cried, "I know him! Marley's ghost!" and fell again.

The same face—the very same. Marley in his pig-tail, usual waistcoat, tights, and boots; the tassels on the latter bristling like his pig-tail, and his coat-skirts, and the hair upon his head. The chain he drew was clasped about his middle. It was long and wound about him like a tail; and it was made (for Scrooge observed it closely) of cash-boxes, keys, padlocks, ledgers, deeds, and heavy purses wrought in steel. His body was transparent; so that Scrooge, observing him, and looking through his waistcoat, could see the two buttons on his coat behind.

Scrooge had often heard it said that Marley had no bowels, but he had never believed it until now.

No, nor did he believe it even now. Though he looked the phantom through and through, and saw it standing before him; though he felt the chilling influence of its death-cold eyes; and marked the very texture of the folded kerchief bound about its head and chin, which wrapper he had not observed before,—he was still incredulous, and fought against his senses.

"How now!" said Scrooge, caustic and cold as ever. "What do you want with me?"

"Much!"—Marley's voice, no doubt about it.

"Who are you?"

"Ask me who I *was*."

"Who *were* you, then?" said Scrooge, raising his voice. "You're particular for a shade." He was going to say "*to* a shade," but substituted this, as more appropriate.

"In life I was your partner, Jacob Marley."

"Can you—can you sit down?" asked Scrooge, looking doubtfully at him.

"I can."

"Do it, then."

Scrooge asked the question, because he didn't know whether a ghost so transparent might find himself in a condition to take a chair; and felt that, in the event of its being impossible, it might involve the necessity of an embarrassing explanation. But the Ghost sat down on the opposite side of the fireplace, as if he were quite used to it.

"You don't believe in me," observed the Ghost.

"I don't," said Scrooge.

"What evidence would you have of my reality beyond that of your own senses?"

"I don't know," said Scrooge.

"Why do you doubt your senses?"

"Because," said Scrooge, "a little thing affects them. A slight disorder of the stomach makes them cheats. You may be an undigested bit of beef, a blot of mustard, a crumb of cheese, a fragment of an underdone potato. There's more of gravy than of grave about you, whatever you are!"

Scrooge was not much in the habit of cracking jokes, nor did he feel in his heart by any means waggish then. The truth is that he tried to be smart, as a means of distracting his own attention, and keeping down his terror; for the spectre's voice disturbed the very marrow in his bones.

To sit staring at those fixed, glazed eyes, in silence for a moment, would play, Scrooge felt, the very deuce with him. There was something very awful, too, in the spectre's being provided with an infernal atmosphere of his own. Scrooge could not feel it himself, but this was clearly the case; for though the Ghost sat perfectly motionless, its hair, and skirts, and tassels, were still agitated as by the hot vapour from an oven.

"You see this toothpick?" said Scrooge, returning quickly to the charge, for the reason just assigned; and wishing, though it were only for a second, to divert the vision's stony gaze from himself.

"I do," replied the Ghost.

"You are not looking at it," said Scrooge.

"But I see it," said the Ghost, "notwithstanding."

"Well!" returned Scrooge; "I have but to swallow this, and be for the rest of my days persecuted by a legion of goblins, all of my own creation. Humbug, I tell you; humbug!"

At this the spirit raised a frightful cry, and shook its chain with such a dismal and appalling noise that Scrooge held on tight to his chair, to save himself from falling in a swoon. But how much greater was his horror, when the phantom, taking off the bandage round his head, as if it were too warm to wear in doors, its lower jaw dropped down upon its breast!

Scrooge fell upon his knees, and clasped his hands before his face.

"Mercy!" he said. "Dreadful apparition, why do you trouble me?"

"Man of the worldly mind," replied the Ghost, "do you believe in me or not?"

"I do," said Scrooge. "I must. But why do spirits walk the earth, and why do they come to me?"

"It is required of every man," the Ghost returned, "that the spirit within him should walk abroad among his fellow-men, and travel far

. . . the spirit raised a *frightful cry*, and shook its chain with such a dismal and appalling noise that Scrooge held on tight to his chair, to save himself from falling in a swoon.

and wide; and if that spirit goes not forth in life, it is condemned to do so after death. It is doomed to wander through the world—oh, woe is me!—and witness what it cannot share, but might have shared on earth, and turned to happiness!"

Again the spectre raised a cry, and shook its chain and wrung its shadowy hands.

"You are fettered," said Scrooge, trembling. "Tell me why?"

"I wear the chain I forged in life," replied the Ghost. "I made it link by link, and yard by yard; I girded it on of my own free will, and of my own free will I wore it. Is its pattern strange to *you?*"

Scrooge trembled more and more.

"Or would you know," pursued the Ghost, "the weight and length of the strong coil you bear yourself? It was full as heavy and as long as this, seven Christmas Eves ago. You have laboured on it since. It is a ponderous chain!"

Scrooge glanced about him on the floor, in the expectation of finding himself surrounded by some fifty or sixty fathoms of iron cable; but he could see nothing.

"Jacob," he said imploringly. "Old Jacob Marley, tell me more. Speak comfort to me, Jacob!"

"I have none to give," the Ghost replied. "It comes from other regions, Ebenezer Scrooge, and is conveyed by other ministers, to other kinds of men. Nor can I tell you what I would. A very little more is all permitted to me. I cannot rest, I cannot stay, I cannot linger anywhere. My spirit never walked beyond our counting-house—mark me!—in life my spirit never roved beyond the narrow limits of our money-changing hole; and weary journeys lie before me!"

It was a habit with Scrooge, whenever he became thoughtful, to put his hands in his breeches' pockets. Pondering on what the Ghost had said, he did so now, but without lifting up his eyes, or getting off his knees.

"You must have been very slow about it, Jacob," Scrooge observed, in a business-like manner, though with humility and deference.

"Slow!" the Ghost repeated.

"Seven years dead," mused Scrooge. "And travelling all the time?"

"The whole time," said the Ghost. "No rest, no peace. Incessant torture of remorse."

"You travel fast?" said Scrooge.

"On the wings of the wind," replied the Ghost.

"You might have got over a great quantity of ground in seven years," said Scrooge.

The Ghost, on hearing this, set up another cry, and clanked its chain so hideously in the dead silence of the night that the Ward would have been justified in indicting it for a nuisance.

"Oh! captive, bound, and double-ironed," cried the phantom, "not to know that ages of incessant labour, by immortal creatures, for this earth must pass into eternity before the good of which it is susceptible is all developed. Not to know that any Christian spirit working kindly in its little sphere, whatever it may be, will find its mortal life too short for its vast means of usefulness. Not to know that no space of regret can make amends for one life's opportunities misused! Yet such was I! Oh! such was I!"

"But you were always a good man of business, Jacob," faltered Scrooge, who now began to apply this to himself.

"Business!" cried the Ghost, wringing its hands again. "Mankind was my business. The common welfare was my business; charity, mercy, forbearance, and benevolence were, all, my business. The dealings of my trade were but a drop of water in the comprehensive ocean of my business!"

It held up its chain at arm's length, as if that were the cause of all its unavailing grief, and flung it heavily upon the ground again.

"At this time of the rolling year," the spectre said, "I suffer most. Why did I walk through crowds of fellow-beings with my eyes turned down, and never raise them to that blessed Star which led the

Wise Men to a poor abode! Were there no poor homes to which its light would have conducted *me!*"

Scrooge was very much dismayed to hear the spectre going on at this rate, and began to quake exceedingly.

"Hear me!" cried the Ghost. "My time is nearly gone."

"I will," said Scrooge. "But don't be hard upon me! Don't be flowery, Jacob! Pray!"

"How it is that I appear before you in a shape that you can see, I may not tell. I have sat invisible beside you many and many a day."

It was not an agreeable idea. Scrooge shivered, and wiped the perspiration from his brow.

"That is no light part of my penance," pursued the Ghost. "I am here to-night to warn you, that you have yet a chance and hope of escaping my fate. A chance and hope of my procuring, Ebenezer."

"You were always a good friend to me," said Scrooge. "Thankee!"

"You will be haunted," resumed the Ghost, "by Three Spirits."

Scrooge's countenance fell almost as low as the Ghost's had done.

"Is that the chance and hope you mentioned, Jacob?" he demanded, in a faltering voice.

"It is."

"I—I think I'd rather not," said Scrooge.

"Without their visits," said the Ghost, "you cannot hope to shun the path I tread. Expect the first to-morrow, when the bell tolls One."

"Couldn't I take 'em all at once, and have it over, Jacob?" hinted Scrooge.

"Expect the second on the next night at the same hour. The third, upon the next night when the last stroke of Twelve has ceased to vibrate. Look to see me no more; and look that, for your own sake, you remember what has passed between us!"

When it had said these words, the spectre took its wrapper from the table, and bound it round its head, as before. Scrooge knew this by the smart sound its teeth made, when the jaws were brought together by the bandage. He ventured to raise his eyes again, and found his supernatural visitor confronting him in an erect attitude, with its chain wound over and about its arm.

The apparition walked backwards from him; and at every step it took, the window raised itself a little, so that when the spectre reached it, it was wide open. It beckoned Scrooge to approach, which he did. When they were within two paces of each other, Marley's Ghost held up its hand, warning him to come no nearer. Scrooge stopped.

Not so much in obedience, as in surprise and fear; for on the raising of the hand, he became sensible of confused noises in the air; incoherent sounds of lamentation and regret; wailings inexpressibly sorrowful and self-accusatory. The spectre, after listening for a moment, joined in the mournful dirge, and floated out upon the bleak, dark night.

Scrooge followed to the window, desperate in his curiosity. He looked out.

The air was filled with phantoms, wandering hither and thither in restless haste, and moaning as they went. Every one of them wore chains like Marley's Ghost; some few (they might be guilty governments) were linked together; none were free. Many had been personally known to Scrooge in their lives. He had been quite familiar with one old ghost in a white waistcoat, with a monstrous iron safe attached to its ankle, who cried piteously at being unable to assist a wretched woman with an infant, whom it saw below upon a doorstep. The misery with them all was, clearly, that they sought to interfere, for good, in human matters and had lost the power for ever.

Whether these creatures faded into mist, or mist enshrouded them, he could not tell. But they and their spirit voices faded together; and the night became as it had been when he walked home.

Scrooge closed the window, and examined the door by which the Ghost had entered. It was double-locked, as he had locked it with his own hands, and the bolts were undisturbed. He tried to say "Humbug!" but stopped at the first syllable. And being, from the emotion he had undergone, or the fatigues of the day, or his glimpse of the Invisible World, or the dull conversation of the Ghost, or the lateness of the hour, much in need of repose, went straight to bed, without undressing, and fell asleep upon the instant.

STAVE II

THE FIRST OF THE THREE SPIRITS

WHEN Scrooge awoke, it was so dark, that, looking out of bed, he could scarcely distinguish the transparent window from the opaque walls of his chamber. He was endeavouring to pierce the darkness with his ferret eyes, when the chimes of a neighbouring church struck the four quarters. So he listened for the hour.

To his great astonishment, the heavy bell went on from six to seven, and from seven to eight, and regularly up to twelve; then stopped. Twelve! It was past two when he went to bed. The clock was wrong. An icicle must have got into the works. Twelve!

He touched the spring of his repeater, to correct this most preposterous clock. Its rapid little pulse beat twelve, and stopped.

"Why, it isn't possible," said Scrooge, "that I can have slept through a whole day and far into another night. It isn't possible that anything has happened to the sun, and this is twelve at noon!"

The idea being an alarming one, he scrambled out of bed, and groped his way to the window. He was obliged to rub the frost off with the sleeve of his dressing-gown before he could see anything; and could see very little then. All he could make out was, that it was still very foggy and extremely cold, and that there was no noise of people running to and fro, and making a great stir, as there unquestionably would have been if night had beaten off bright day, and taken possession of the world. This was a great relief, because "Three days after sight of this First of Exchange pay to Mr. Ebenezer Scrooge or his order," and so forth, would have become a mere United States' security if there were no days to count by.

Scrooge went to bed again, and thought, and thought, and thought it over and over, and could make nothing of it. The more he thought, the more perplexed he was; and the more he endeavoured not to think, the more he thought.

Marley's Ghost bothered him exceedingly. Every time he resolved within himself, after mature inquiry, that it was all a dream, his mind flew back again, like a strong spring released, to its first position, and presented the same problem to be worked all through, "Was it a dream or not?"

Scrooge lay in this state until the chime had gone three quarters more, when he remembered, on a sudden, that the Ghost had warned him of a visitation when the bell tolled one. He resolved to lie awake until the hour was passed; and, considering that he could no more go to sleep than go to Heaven, this was perhaps the wisest resolution in his power.

The quarter was so long, that he was more than once convinced he must have sunk into a doze unconsciously, and missed the clock. At length it broke upon his listening ear.

"Ding, dong!"

"A quarter past," said Scrooge, counting.

"Ding, dong!"

"Half-past!" said Scrooge.

"Ding, dong!"

"A quarter to it," said Scrooge.

"Ding, dong!"

"The hour itself," said Scrooge triumphantly, "and nothing else!"

He spoke before the hour bell sounded, which it now did with a deep, dull, hollow, melancholy ONE. Light flashed up in the room upon the instant, and the curtains of his bed were drawn.

The curtains of his bed were drawn aside, I tell you, by a hand.

The curtains of his bed were drawn aside . . . and Scrooge, starting up into a half-recumbent attitude, found himself face to face with the unearthly visitor . . .

Not the curtains at his feet, nor the curtains at his back, but those to which his face was addressed. The curtains of his bed were drawn aside; and Scrooge, starting up into a half-recumbent attitude, found himself face to face with the unearthly visitor who drew them—as close to it as I am now to you, and I am standing in the spirit at your elbow.

It was a strange figure—like a child; yet not so like a child as like an old man, viewed through some supernatural medium, which gave him the appearance of having receded from the view, and being diminished to a child's proportions. Its hair, which hung about its neck and down its back, was white as if with age; and yet the face had not a wrinkle in it, and the tenderest bloom was on the skin. The arms were very long and muscular; the hands the same, as if its hold were of uncommon strength. Its legs and feet, most delicately formed, were, like those upper members, bare. It wore a tunic of the purest white; and round its waist was bound a lustrous belt, the sheen of which was beautiful. It held a branch of fresh green holly in its hand; and, in singular contradiction of that wintry emblem, had its dress trimmed with summer flowers. But the strangest thing about it was, that from the crown of its head there sprung a bright clear jet of light, by which all this was visible; and which was doubtless the occasion of its using, in its duller moments, a great extinguisher for a cap, which it now held under its arm.

Even this, though, when Scrooge looked at it with increasing steadiness, was *not* its strangest quality. For as its belt sparkled and glittered now in one part and now in another, and what was light one instant at another time was dark, so the figure itself fluctuated in its distinctness, being now a thing with one arm, now with one leg, now with twenty legs, now a pair of legs without a head, now a head without a body, of which dissolving parts, no outline would be visible in the dense gloom wherein they melted away. And in the very wonder of this, it would be itself again; distinct and clear as ever.

"Are you the Spirit, sir, whose coming was foretold to me?" asked Scrooge.

"I am!"

The voice was soft and gentle. Singularly low, as if instead of being so close beside him, it were at a distance.

"Who and what are you?" Scrooge demanded.

"I am the Ghost of Christmas Past."

"Long Past?" inquired Scrooge, observant of its dwarfish stature.

"No. Your past."

Perhaps Scrooge could not have told anybody why, if anybody could have asked him; but he had a special desire to see the Spirit in his cap, and begged him to be covered.

"What!" exclaimed the Ghost, "would you so soon put out, with worldly hands, the light I give? Is it not enough that you are one of those whose passions made this cap, and force me through whole trains of years to wear it low upon my brow!"

Scrooge reverently disclaimed all intention to offend or any knowledge of having wilfully "bonneted" the Spirit at any period of his life. He then made bold to inquire what business brought him there.

"Your welfare!" said the Ghost.

Scrooge expressed himself much obliged, but could not help thinking that a night of unbroken rest would have been more conducive to that end. The Spirit must have heard him thinking, for it said immediately:—

"Your reclamation, then. Take heed!"

It put out its strong hand as it spoke, and clasped him gently by the arm.

"Rise! and walk with me!"

It would have been in vain for Scrooge to plead that the weather and the hour were not adapted to pedestrian purposes; that the bed was warm, and the thermometer a long way below freezing; that he was clad but lightly in his slippers, dressing-gown, and nightcap; and that he had a cold upon him at that time. The grasp, though gentle as a woman's hand, was not to be resisted. He rose; but finding that the Spirit made towards the window, clasped its robe in supplication.

"I am a mortal," Scrooge remonstrated, "and liable to fall."

"Bear but a touch of my hand *there,*" said the Spirit, laying it upon his heart, "and you shall be upheld in more than this."

As the words were spoken, they passed through the wall, and stood upon an open country road, with fields on either hand. The city had entirely vanished. Not a vestige of it was to be seen. The darkness and the mist had vanished with it, for it was a clear, cold, winter day, with snow upon the ground.

"Good Heaven!" said Scrooge, clasping his hands together, as he looked about him. "I was bred in this place. I was a boy here!"

The Spirit gazed upon him mildly. Its gentle touch, though it had been light and instantaneous, appeared still present to the old man's sense of feeling. He was conscious of a thousand odours floating in the air, each one connected with a thousand thoughts, and hopes, and joys, and cares long, long forgotten!

"Your lip is trembling," said the Ghost. "And what is that upon your cheek?"

Scrooge muttered, with an unusual catching in his voice, that it was a pimple; and begged the Ghost to lead him where he would.

"You recollect the way?" inquired the Spirit.

"Remember it!" cried Scrooge, with fervour; "I could walk it blindfold."

"Strange to have forgotten it for so many years!" observed the Ghost. "Let us go on."

They walked along the road, Scrooge recognising every gate, and post, and tree; until a little market-town appeared in the distance, with its bridge, its church, and winding river. Some shaggy ponies now were seen trotting towards them with boys upon their backs, who called to other boys in country gigs and carts, driven by farmers. All these boys were in great spirits, and shouted to each other, until the broad fields were so full of merry music that the crisp air laughed to hear it.

"These are but shadows of the things that have been," said the Ghost. "They have no consciousness of us."

The jocund travellers came on; and as they came, Scrooge knew and named them every one. Why was he rejoiced beyond all bounds to see them! Why did his cold eye glisten, and his heart leap up as they went past! Why was he filled with gladness when he heard them give each other Merry Christmas, as they parted at cross-roads and byways for their several homes? What was Merry Christmas to Scrooge? Out upon Merry Christmas! What good had it ever done to him?

"The school is not quite deserted," said the Ghost. "A solitary child, neglected by his friends, is left there still."

Scrooge said he knew it. And he sobbed.

They left the high-road, by a well-remembered lane, and soon approached a mansion of dull red brick, with a little weathercock-surmounted cupola on the roof, and a bell hanging in it. It was a large house, but one of broken fortunes; for the spacious offices were little used, their walls were damp and mossy, their windows broken, and their gates decayed. Fowls clucked and strutted in the stables; and the coach-houses and sheds were overrun with grass. Nor was it more retentive of its ancient state within; for entering the dreary hall, and glancing through the open doors of many rooms, they found them poorly furnished, cold, and vast. There was an earthy savour in the air, a chilly bareness in the place which associated itself some-how with too much getting up by candle-light, and not too much to eat.

They went, the Ghost and Scrooge, across the hall, to a door at the back of the house. It opened before them, and disclosed a long, bare, melancholy room, made barer still by lines of plain deal forms and desks. At one of these a lonely boy was reading near a feeble fire; and Scrooge sat down upon a form, and wept to see his poor forgotten self as he had used to be.

Not a latent echo in the house, not a squeak and scuffle from the mice behind the panelling, not a drip from the half-thawed water-spout in the dull yard behind, not a sigh among the leafless boughs of one despondent poplar, not the idle swinging of an empty storehouse door, no, not a clicking in the fire, but fell upon the heart of Scrooge with softening influence, and gave a freer passage to his tears.

The Spirit touched him on the arm, and pointed to his younger self, intent upon his reading. Suddenly a man in foreign garments, wonderfully real and distinct to look at, stood outside the window, with an axe stuck in his belt, and leading by the bridle an ass laden with wood.

"Why, it's Ali Baba!" Scrooge exclaimed in ecstasy. "It's dear old honest Ali Baba! Yes, yes, I know. One Christmas-time, when yonder solitary child was left here all alone, he *did* come, for the first time, just like that. Poor boy! And Valentine," said Scrooge, "and his wild brother, Orson; there they go! And what's his name, who was put down in his drawers, asleep, at the gate of Damascus; don't you see him! And the Sultan's Groom turned upside down by the Genii, there he is upon his head! Serve him right. I'm glad of it. What business had *he* to be married to the Princess!"

To hear Scrooge expending all the earnestness of his nature on such subjects, in a most extraordinary voice between laughing and crying, and to see his heightened and excited face, would have been a surprise to his business friends in the city, indeed.

"There's the Parrot!" cried Scrooge. "Green body and yellow tail, with a thing like a lettuce growing out of the top of his head; there he is! Poor Robin Crusoe, he called him, when he came home again after sailing round the island. 'Poor Robin Crusoe, where have you been, Robin Crusoe?' The man thought he was dreaming, but he wasn't. It was the Parrot, you know. There goes Friday, running for his life to the little creek! Halloa! Hoop! Halloo!"

Then, with a rapidity of transition very foreign to his usual character, he said, in pity for his former self, "Poor boy!" and cried again.

"I wish," Scrooge muttered, putting his hand in his pocket, and looking about him, after drying his eyes with his cuff—"but it's too late now."

"What is the matter?" asked the Spirit.

"Nothing," said Scrooge. "Nothing. There was a boy singing a Christmas Carol at my door last night. I should like to have given him something; that's all."

The Ghost smiled thoughtfully, and waved its hand; saying as it did so, "Let us see another Christmas!"

Scrooge's former self grew larger at the words, and the room became a little darker and more dirty. The panels shrunk, the windows cracked; fragments of plaster fell out of the ceiling, and the naked laths were shown instead; but how all this was brought about, Scrooge knew no more than you do. He only knew that it was quite correct; that everything had happened so; that there he was, alone again, when all the other boys had gone home for the jolly holidays.

He was not reading now, but walking up and down despairingly. Scrooge looked at the Ghost, and, with a mournful shaking of his head, glanced anxiously towards the door.

It opened; and a little girl, much younger than the boy, came darting in, and putting her arms about his neck, and often kissing him, addressed him as her "Dear, dear brother."

"I have come to bring you home, dear brother!" said the child, clapping her tiny hands, and bending down to laugh. "To bring you home, home, home!"

"Home, little Fan?" returned the boy.

"Yes!" said the child, brimful of glee. "Home, for good and all. Home, for ever and ever. Father is so much kinder than he used to be that home's like Heaven! He spoke so gently to me one dear night when I was going to bed that I was not afraid to ask him once more if you might come home; and he said Yes, you should; and sent me in a coach to bring you. And you're to be a man!" said the child, opening her eyes; "and are never to come back here; but first, we're to be together all the Christmas long, and have the merriest time in all the world."

"You are quite a woman, little Fan!" exclaimed the boy.

She clapped her hands and laughed, and tried to touch his head; but being too little, laughed again, and stood on tiptoe to embrace him. Then she began to drag him, in her childish eagerness, towards the door; and he, nothing loth to go, accompanied her.

A terrible voice in the hall cried, "Bring down Master Scrooge's box, there!" and in the hall appeared the schoolmaster himself, who glared on Master Scrooge with a ferocious condescension, and threw him into a dreadful state of mind by shaking hands with him. He then conveyed him and his sister into the veriest old well of a shivering best parlour that ever was seen, where the maps upon the wall, and the celestial and terrestrial globes in the windows, were waxy with cold. Here he produced a decanter of curiously light wine, and a block of curiously heavy cake, and administered instalments of those dainties to the young people; at the same time sending out a meagre servant to offer a glass of "something" to the postboy, who answered that he thanked the gentleman, but if it was the same tap as he had tasted before he had rather not. Master Scrooge's trunk being by this time tied on to the top of the chaise, the children bade the schoolmaster good-bye right willingly; and getting into it, drove gaily down the garden-sweep, the quick wheels dashing the hoar-frost and snow from off the dark leaves of the evergreens like spray.

"Always a delicate creature, whom a breath might have withered," said the Ghost. "But she had a large heart!"

"So she had," cried Scrooge. "You're right. I will not gainsay it, Spirit. God forbid!"

"She died a woman," said the Ghost, "and had, as I think, children."

"One child," Scrooge returned.

"True," said the Ghost. "Your nephew!"

Scrooge seemed uneasy in his mind; and answered briefly, "Yes."

Although they had but that moment left the school behind them, they were now in the busy thoroughfares of a city, where shadowy passengers passed and repassed; where shadowy carts and coaches battled for the way, and all the strife and tumult of a real city were. It was made plain enough, by the dressing of the shops, that here, too, it was Christmas-time again; but it was evening, and the streets were lighted up.

The Ghost stopped at a certain warehouse door, and asked Scrooge if he knew it.

"Know it!" said Scrooge. "Was I apprenticed here!"

They went in. At sight of an old gentleman in a Welsh wig, sitting behind such a high desk that if he had been two inches taller he must have knocked his head against the ceiling, Scrooge cried in great excitement:—

"Why, it's old Fezziwig! Bless his heart; it's Fezziwig alive again!"

Old Fezziwig laid down his pen, and looked up at the clock, which pointed to the hour of seven. He rubbed his hands; adjusted his capacious waistcoat; laughed all over himself, from his shoes to his organ of benevolence, and called out in a comfortable, oily, rich, fat, jovial voice:—

"Yo ho, there! Ebenezer! Dick!"

Scrooge's former self, now grown a young man, came briskly in, accompanied by his fellow-'prentice.

"Dick Wilkins, to be sure!" said Scrooge to the Ghost. "Bless me, yes. There he is. He was very much attached to me, was Dick. Poor Dick! Dear, dear!"

"Yo ho, my boys!" said Fezziwig. "No more work to-night. Christmas Eve, Dick. Christmas, Ebenezer! Let's have the shutters up," cried old Fezziwig, with a sharp clap of his hands, "before a man can say Jack Robinson!"

You wouldn't believe how those two fellows went at it! They charged into the street with the shutters—one, two, three—had 'em up in their places—four, five, six—barred 'em and pinned 'em—seven, eight, nine—and came back before you could have got to twelve, panting like race-horses.

"Hilli-ho!" cried old Fezziwig, skipping down from the high desk, with wonderful agility. "Clear away, my lads, and let's have lots of room here! Hilli-ho, Dick! Chirrup, Ebenezer!"

Clear away! There was nothing they wouldn't have cleared away, or couldn't have cleared away, with old Fezziwig looking on. It was done in a minute. Every movable was packed off, as if it were dismissed from public life for evermore; the floor was swept and watered, the lamps were trimmed, fuel was heaped upon the fire; and the warehouse was as snug, and warm, and dry, and bright a ballroom, as you would desire to see upon a winter's night.

In came a fiddler with a music-book, and went up to the lofty desk, and made an orchestra of it, and tuned like fifty stomachaches. In came Mrs. Fezziwig, one vast substantial smile. In came the three Miss Fezziwigs, beaming and lovable. In came the six young followers whose hearts they broke. In came all the young men and women employed in the business. In came the housemaid, with her cousin the baker. In came the cook, with her brother's particular friend, the milkman. In came the boy from over the way, who was suspected of not having board enough from his master; trying to hide himself behind the girl from next door but one, who was proved to have had her ears pulled by her mistress. In they all came, one after another; some shyly, some boldly, some gracefully, some awkwardly, some pushing, some pulling,—in they all came, anyhow and everyhow. Away they all went, twenty couple at once; hands half round and back again the other way; down the middle and up again; round and round in various stages of affectionate grouping; old top couple always turning up in the wrong place; new top couple starting off again, as soon as they got there; all top couples at last, and not a bottom one to help them! When this result was brought about, old Fezziwig, clapping his hands to stop the dance, cried out, "Well done!" and the fiddler plunged his hot face into a pot of porter, especially provided for that purpose. But scorning rest upon his reappearance, he instantly began again, though there were no dancers yet, as if the other fiddler had been carried home, exhausted, on a shutter, and he were a bran-new man resolved to beat him out of sight or perish.

There were more dances, and there were forfeits, and more dances, and there was cake, and there was negus, and there was a great piece of Cold Roast, and there was a great piece of Cold Boiled, and there were mince-pies, and plenty of beer. But the great effect of the evening came after the Roast and Boiled, when the fiddler (an artful dog, mind! The sort of man who knew his business better than you or I could have told it him!) struck up "Sir Roger de Coverley." Then old Fezziwig stood out to dance with Mrs. Fezziwig. Top couple, too; with a good stiff piece of work cut out for them; three or four and twenty pair of partners; people who were not to be trifled with; people who *would* dance, and had no notion of walking.

But if they had been twice as many—ah, four times—old Fezziwig would have been a match for them, and so would Mrs. Fezziwig. As to *her*, she was worthy to be his partner in every sense of the term. If that's not high praise, tell me higher, and I'll use it. A positive light appeared to issue from Fezziwig's calves. They shone in every part of the dance like moons. You couldn't have predicted, at any given time, what would become of them next. And when old Fezziwig and Mrs. Fezziwig had gone all through the dance; advance and retire, both hands to your partner, bow and curtsey, corkscrew, thread-the-needle, and back again to your place; Fezziwig "cut"—cut so deftly that he appeared to wink with his legs, and came upon his feet again without a stagger.

When the clock struck eleven, this domestic ball broke up. Mr. and Mrs. Fezziwig took their stations, one on either side the door, and, shaking hands with every person individually as he or she went out, wished him or her a Merry Christmas. When everybody had retired but the two 'prentices, they did the same to them; and thus the cheerful voices died away, and the lads were left to their beds; which were under a counter in the back shop.

During the whole of this time Scrooge had acted like a man out of

A positive light appeared to issue from Fezziwig's calves. They shone in every part of the dance like moons. You couldn't have predicted, at any given time, what would have become of them next.

his wits. His heart and soul were in the scene, and with his former self. He corroborated everything, remembered everything, enjoyed everything, and underwent the strangest agitation. It was not until now, when the bright faces of his former self and Dick were turned from them, that he remembered the Ghost, and became conscious that it was looking full upon him, while the light upon its head burnt very clear.

"A small matter," said the Ghost, "to make these silly folks so full of gratitude."

"Small!" echoed Scrooge.

The Spirit signed to him to listen to the two apprentices, who were pouring out their hearts in praise of Fezziwig, and when he had done so said:—

"Why! Is it not? He has spent but a few pounds of your mortal money: three or four, perhaps. Is that so much that he deserves this praise?"

"It isn't that," said Scrooge, heated by the remark, and speaking unconsciously like his former, not his latter self. "It isn't that, Spirit. He has the power to render us happy or unhappy; to make our service light or burdensome; a pleasure or a toil. Say that his power lies in words and looks; in things so slight and insignificant that it is impossible to add and count 'em up; what, then? The happiness he gives is quite as great as if it cost a fortune."

He felt the Spirit's glance, and stopped.

"What is the matter?" asked the Ghost.

"Nothing particular," said Scrooge.

"Something, I think?" the Ghost insisted.

"No," said Scrooge, "no. I should like to be able to say a word or two to my clerk just now. That's all."

His former self turned down the lamps as he gave utterance to the wish; and Scrooge and the Ghost again stood side by side in the open air.

"My time grows short," observed the Spirit. "Quick!"

This was not addressed to Scrooge, or to any one whom he could

. . . again Scrooge saw himself. He was older now; a man in the prime of life.
His face had not the harsh and rigid lines of later years; but it had begun to wear
the signs of care and avarice . . . He was not alone.

see, but it produced an immediate effect. For again Scrooge saw himself. He was older now; a man in the prime of life. His face had not the harsh and rigid lines of later years; but it had begun to wear the signs of care and avarice. There was an eager, greedy, restless motion in the eye, which showed the passion that had taken root, and where the shadow of the growing tree would fall.

He was not alone, but sat by the side of a fair young girl in a mourning-dress; in whose eyes there were tears, which sparkled in the light that shone out of the Ghost of Christmas Past.

"It matters little," she said softly. "To you, very little. Another idol has displaced me; and if it can cheer and comfort you in time to come as I would have tried to do, I have no just cause to grieve."

"What idol has displaced you?" he rejoined.

"A golden one."

"This is the even-handed dealing of the world!" he said. "There is nothing on which it is so hard as poverty; and there is nothing it professes to condemn with such severity as the pursuit of wealth!"

"You fear the world too much," she answered gently. "All your other hopes have merged into the hope of being beyond the chance of its sordid reproach. I have seen your nobler aspirations fall off one by one, until the master-passion, Gain, engrosses you. Have I not?"

"What then?" he retorted. "Even if I had grown so much wiser, what then? I am not changed towards you."

She shook her head.

"Am I?"

"Our contract is an old one. It was made when we were both poor and content to be so, until, in good season, we could improve our worldly fortune by our patient industry. You *are* changed. When it was made, you were another man."

"I was a boy," he said impatiently.

"Your own feeling tells you that you were not what you are," she returned. "I am. That which promised happiness when we were one in heart is fraught with misery now that we are two. How often and how keenly I have thought of this, I will not say. It is enough that I *have* thought of it, and can release you."

"Have I ever sought release?"

"In words—no. Never."

"In what, then?"

"In a changed nature; in an altered spirit; in another atmosphere of life; another Hope as its great end. In everything that made my love of any worth or value in your sight. If this had never been between us," said the girl, looking mildly, but with steadiness, upon him, "tell me, would you seek me out and try to win me now? Ah, no!"

He seemed to yield to the justice of this supposition, in spite of himself. But he said, with a struggle, "You think not."

"I would gladly think otherwise if I could," she answered, "Heaven knows! When *I* have learned a Truth like this, I know how strong and irresistible it must be. But if you were free to-day, to-morrow, yesterday, can even I believe that you would choose a dowerless girl—you who, in your very confidence with her, weigh everything by Gain; or, choosing her, if for a moment you were false enough to your one guiding principle to do so, do I not know that your repentance and regret would surely follow? I do; and I release you. With a full heart, for the love of him you once were."

He was about to speak; but with her head turned from him, she resumed:—

"You may—the memory of what is past half makes me hope you will—have pain in this. A very, very brief time, and you will dismiss the recollection of it, gladly, as an unprofitable dream, from which it happened well that you awoke. May you be happy in the life you have chosen!"

She left him and they parted.

"Spirit!" said Scrooge, "show me no more! Conduct me home. Why do you delight to torture me?"

"One shadow more!" exclaimed the Ghost.

"No more!" cried Scrooge. "No more. I don't wish to see it. Show me no more!"

But the relentless Ghost pinioned him in both his arms, and forced him to observe what happened next.

They were in another scene and place; a room, not very large or handsome, but full of comfort. Near to the winter fire sat a beautiful young girl, so like that last that Scrooge believed it was the same, until he saw *her*, now a comely matron, sitting opposite her daughter. The noise in this room was perfectly tumultuous, for there were more children there than Scrooge in his agitated state of mind could count; and, unlike the celebrated herd in the poem, they were not forty children conducting themselves like one, but every child was conducting itself like forty. The consequences were uproarious beyond belief; but no one seemed to care; on the contrary, the mother and daughter laughed heartily, and enjoyed it very much; and the latter, soon beginning to mingle in the sports, got pillaged by the young brigands most ruthlessly. What would I not have given to be one of them! Though I never could have been so rude, no, no! I wouldn't for the wealth of all the world have crushed that braided hair, and torn it down; and for the precious little shoe, I wouldn't have plucked it off, God bless my soul! to save my life. As to measuring her waist in sport, as they did, bold young brood, I couldn't have done it; I should have expected my arm to have grown round it for a punishment, and never come straight again. And yet I should have dearly liked, I own, to have touched her lips; to have questioned her, that she might have opened them; to have looked upon the lashes of her downcast eyes, and never raised a blush; to have let loose waves of hair, an inch of which would be a keepsake beyond price; in short, I should have liked, I do confess, to have had the slightest licence of a child, and yet to have been man enough to know its value.

But now a knocking at the door was heard, and such a rush immediately ensued that she with laughing face and plundered dress was borne towards it in the centre of a flushed and boisterous group, just in time to greet the father, who came home attended by a man laden with Christmas toys and presents. Then the shouting and the struggling, and the onslaught that was made on the defenceless porter! The scaling him, with chairs for ladders, to dive into his pockets, despoil him of brown-paper parcels, hold on tight by his cravat, hug him round the neck, pommel his back, and kick his legs in irrepressible affection! The shouts of wonder and delight with which the development of every package was received! The terrible announcement that the baby had been taken in the act of putting a doll's frying-pan into his mouth, and was more than suspected of having swallowed a fictitious turkey, glued on a wooden platter! The immense relief of finding this a false alarm! The joy, and gratitude, and ecstasy! They are all indescribable alike. It is enough that, by degrees, the children and their emotions got out of the parlour, and, by one stair at a time, up to the top of the house, where they went to bed and so subsided.

And now Scrooge looked on more attentively than ever, when the master of the house, having his daughter leaning fondly on him, sat down with her and her mother at his own fireside; and when he thought that such another creature, quite as graceful and as full of promise, might have called him father, and been a spring-time in the haggard winter of his life, his sight grew very dim indeed.

"Belle," said the husband, turning to his wife with a smile, "I saw an old friend of yours this afternoon."

"Who was it?"

"Guess!"

"How can I? Tut, don't I know," she added, in the same breath, laughing as he laughed. "Mr. Scrooge."

"Mr. Scrooge it was. I passed his office window; and as it was not shut up, and he had a candle inside, I could scarcely help seeing him. His partner lies upon the point of death, I hear; and there he sat alone. Quite alone in the world, I do believe."

"Spirit!" said Scrooge, in a broken voice, "remove me from this place."

"I told you these were shadows of the things that have been," said the Ghost. "That they are what they are, do not blame me!"

"Remove me!" Scrooge exclaimed. "I cannot bear it!"

He turned upon the Ghost, and seeing that it looked upon him with a face in which in some strange way there were fragments of all the faces it had shown him, wrestled with it.

"Leave me! Take me back. Haunt me no longer!"

In the struggle—if that can be called a struggle in which the Ghost, with no visible resistance on its own part, was undisturbed by any effort of its adversary—Scrooge observed that its light was burning high and bright; and dimly connecting that with its influence over him, he seized the extinguisher cap, and by a sudden action pressed it down upon its head.

The Spirit dropped beneath it, so that the extinguisher covered its whole form; but though Scrooge pressed it down with all his force, he could not hide the light, which streamed from under it, in an unbroken flood upon the ground.

He was conscious of being exhausted, and overcome by an irresistible drowsiness; and futher, of being in his own bedroom. He gave the cap a parting squeeze, in which his hand relaxed; and had barely time to reel to bed, before he sank into a heavy sleep.

STAVE III

THE SECOND OF
THE THREE SPIRITS

A WAKING in the middle of a prodigiously tough snore, and sitting up in bed to get his thoughts together, Scrooge had no occasion to be told that the bell was again upon the stroke of One. He felt that he was restored to consciousness in the right nick of time, for the especial purpose of holding a conference with the second messenger despatched to him through Jacob Marley's intervention. But finding that he turned uncomfortably cold when he began to wonder which of his curtains this new spectre would draw back, he put them every one aside with his own hands, and lying down again, established a sharp look-out all round the bed. For he wished to challenge the Spirit on the moment of its appearance, and did not wish to be taken by surprise and made nervous.

Gentlemen of the free and easy sort, who plume themselves on being acquainted with a move or two, and being usually equal to the time of day, express the wide range of their capacity for adventure by observing that they are good for anything from pitch and toss to manslaughter; between which opposite extremes, no doubt, there lies a tolerably wide and comprehensive range of subjects. Without venturing for Scrooge quite as hardily as this, I don't mind calling on you to believe that he was ready for a good broad field of strange appearances, and that nothing between a baby and rhinoceros would have astonished him very much.

Now being prepared for almost anything, he was not by any means prepared for nothing; and, consequently, when the bell struck One, and no shape appeared, he was taken with a violent fit of trembling. Five minutes, ten minutes, a quarter of an hour went by, yet nothing came. All this time, he lay upon his bed, the very core and centre of a blaze of ruddy light, which streamed upon it when the clock proclaimed the hour; and which, being only light, was more alarming than a dozen ghosts, as he was powerless to make out what it meant, or would be at; and was sometimes apprehensive that he might be at that very moment an interesting case of spontaneous combustion, without having the consolation of knowing it. At last, however, he began to think—as you or I would have thought at first; for it is always the person not in the predicament who knows what ought to have been done in it, and would unquestionably have done it too—at last, I say, he began to think that the source and secret of this ghostly light might be in the adjoining room, from whence, on further tracing it, it seemed to shine. This idea taking full possession of his mind, he got up softly and shuffled in his slippers to the door.

The moment Scrooge's hand was on the lock, a strange voice called him by his name, and bade him enter. He obeyed.

It was his own room. There was no doubt about that. But it had undergone a surprising transformation. The walls and ceiling were so hung with living green, that it looked a perfect grove; from every part of which, bright gleaming berries glistened. The crisp leaves of holly, mistletoe, and ivy reflected back the light, as if so many little mirrors had been scattered there; and such a mighty blaze went roaring up the chimney as that dull petrifaction of a hearth had ever known in Scrooge's time, or Marley's, or for many and many a winter season gone. Heaped up on the floor, to form a kind of throne, were turkeys, geese, game, poultry, brawn, great joints of meat, sucking-pigs, long wreaths of sausages, mince-pies, plum-puddings, barrels of oysters, red-hot chestnuts, cherry-cheeked apples, juicy oranges, luscious pears, immense twelfth-cakes, and seething bowls of punch, that made the chamber dim with their delicious steam. In easy state upon this couch there sat a jolly Giant, glorious to see; who bore a glowing torch, in shape not unlike Plenty's horn, and held it up, high up, to shed its light on Scrooge, as he came peeping round the door.

"Come in!" exclaimed the Ghost. "Come in! and know me better, man!"

Scrooge entered timidly, and hung his head before this Spirit. He was not the dogged Scrooge he had been; and though the Spirit's eyes were clear and kind, he did not like to meet them.

"I am the Ghost of Christmas Present," said the Spirit. "Look upon me!"

Scrooge reverently did so. It was clothed in one simple deep green robe, or mantle, bordered with white fur. This garment hung so loosely on the figure, that its capacious breast was bare, as if disdaining to be warded or concealed by any artifice. Its feet, observable beneath the ample folds of the garment, were also bare; and on

. . . *there sat a jolly Giant, glorious to see; who bore a glowing torch, in shape not unlike Plenty's horn, and held it up, high up, to shed its light on Scrooge, as he came peeping round the door.*

its head it wore no other covering than a holly wreath, set here and there with shining icicles. Its dark brown curls were long and free; free as its genial face, its sparkling eye, its open hand, its cheery voice, its unconstrained demeanour, and its joyful air. Girded round its middle was an antique scabbard; but no sword was in it, and the ancient sheath was eaten up with rust.

"You have never seen the like of me before!" exclaimed the Spirit.

"Never," Scrooge made answer to it.

"Have never walked forth with the younger members of my family; meaning (for I am very young) my elder brothers born in these later years?" pursued the Phantom.

"I don't think I have," said Scrooge. "I am afraid I have not. Have you had many brothers, Spirit?"

"More than eighteen hundred," said the Ghost.

"A tremendous family to provide for," muttered Scrooge.

The Ghost of Christmas Present rose.

"Spirit," said Scrooge submissively, "conduct me where you will. I went forth last night on compulsion, and I learnt a lesson which is working now. To-night, if you have aught to teach me, let me profit by it."

"Touch my robe!"

Scrooge did as he was told, and held it fast.

Holly, mistletoe, red berries, ivy, turkeys, geese, game, poultry, brawn, meat, pigs, sausages, oysters, pies, puddings, fruit, and punch, all vanished instantly. So did the room, the fire, the ruddy glow, the hour of night, and they stood in the city streets on Christmas morning, where (for the weather was severe) the people made a rough, but brisk and not unpleasant kind of music, in scraping the snow from the pavement in front of their dwellings, and from the tops of their houses, whence it was mad delight to the boys to see it come plumping down into the road below, and splitting into artificial little snow-storms.

The house fronts looked black enough, and the windows blacker, contrasting with the smooth white sheet of snow upon the roofs, and with the dirtier snow upon the ground; which last deposit had been ploughed up in deep furrows by the heavy wheels of carts and wagons; furrows that crossed and recrossed each other hundreds of times where the great streets branched off; and made intricate channels, hard to trace, in the thick yellow mud and icy water. The sky was gloomy, and the shortest streets were choked up with a dingy mist, half thawed, half frozen, whose heavier particles descended in a shower of sooty atoms, as if all the chimneys in Great Britain had, by one consent, caught fire, and were blazing away to their dear hearts' content. There was nothing very cheerful in the climate or the town, and yet was there an air of cheerfulness abroad that the clearest summer air and brightest summer sun might have endeavoured to diffuse in vain.

For the people who were shovelling away on the housetops were jovial and full of glee; calling out to one another from the parapets, and now and then exchanging a facetious snowball,—better-natured missile far than many a wordy jest,—laughing heartily if it went right, and not less heartily if it went wrong. The poulterers' shops were still half open, and the fruiterers' were radiant in their glory. There were great, round, pot-bellied baskets of chestnuts, shaped like the waistcoats of jolly old gentlemen, lolling at the doors, and tumbling out into the street in their apoplectic opulence. There were ruddy, brown-faced, broad-girthed Spanish onions, shining in the fatness of their growth like Spanish Friars, and winking from their shelves in wanton slyness at the girls as they went by, and glanced demurely at the hung-up mistletoe. There were pears and apples, clustered high in blooming pyramids; there were bunches of grapes, made, in the shopkeepers' benevolence, to dangle from conspicuous hooks, that people's mouths might water gratis as they passed; there were piles of filberts, mossy and brown, recalling, in their fragrance, ancient walks among the woods, and pleasant shufflings ankle-deep through withered leaves; there were Norfolk Biffins, squab and swarthy, setting off the yellow of the oranges and lemons, and, in the great compactness of their juicy persons, urgently entreating and beseeching to be carried home in paper bags and eaten after dinner. The very gold and silver fish, set forth among these choice fruits in a bowl, though members of a dull and stagnant-blooded race, appeared to know that there was something going on; and, to a fish, went gasping round and round their little world in slow and passionless excitement.

The Grocers'! oh, the Grocers'! nearly closed, with perhaps two shutters down, or one; but through those gaps such glimpses! It was not alone that the scales descending on the counter made a merry sound, or that the twine and roller parted company so briskly, or that the canisters were rattled up and down like juggling tricks, or even that the blended scents of tea and coffee were so grateful to the nose, or even that the raisins were so plentiful and rare, the almonds so extremely white, the sticks of cinnamon so long and straight, the other spices so delicious, the candied fruits so caked and spotted with molten sugar as to make the coldest lookers-on feel faint and subsequently bilious. Nor was it that the figs were moist and pulpy, or that the French plums blushed in modest tartness from their highly decorated boxes, or that everything was good to eat and in its Christmas dress; but the customers were all so hurried and so eager in the hopeful promise of the day, that they tumbled up against each other at the door, crashing their wicker baskets wildly, and left their purchases upon the counter, and came running back to fetch them, and committed hundreds of the like mistakes, in the best humour possible; while the Grocer and his people were so frank and fresh that the polished hearts with which they fastened their aprons behind might have been their own, worn outside for general inspection, and for Christmas daws to peck at if they chose.

But soon the steeples called good people all to church and chapel, and away they came, flocking through the streets in their best clothes, and with their gayest faces. And at the same time there emerged from scores of by-streets, lanes, and nameless turnings, innumerable people, carrying their dinners to the bakers' shops. The sight of these poor revellers appeared to interest the Spirit very much, for he stood with Scrooge beside him in a baker's doorway, and, taking off the covers as their bearers passed, sprinkled incense on their dinners from his torch. And it was a very uncommon kind of torch, for once or twice when there were angry words between some dinner-carriers who had jostled each other, he shed a few drops of water on them from it, and their good-humour was restored directly. For they said, it was a shame to quarrel upon Christmas Day. And so it was! God love it, so it was!

In time the bells ceased, and the bakers were shut up; and yet there was a genial shadowing forth of all these dinners and the progress of their cooking, in the thawed blotch of wet above each baker's oven, where the pavement smoked as if its stones were cooking, too.

"Is there a peculiar flavour in what you sprinkle from your torch?" asked Scrooge.

"There is. My own."

"Would it apply to any kind of dinner on this day?" asked Scrooge.

"To any kindly given. To a poor one most."

"Why to a poor one most?" asked Scrooge.

"Because it needs it most."

"Spirit," said Scrooge, after a moment's thought, "I wonder you, of all the beings in the many worlds about us, should desire to cramp these people's opportunities of innocent enjoyment."

"I!" cried the Spirit.

"You would deprive them of their means of dining every seventh day, often the only day on which they can be said to dine at all," said Scrooge; "wouldn't you?"

"I!" cried the Spirit.

"You seek to close these places on the Seventh Day!" said Scrooge. "And it comes to the same thing."

"I seek!" exclaimed the Spirit.

"Forgive me if I am wrong. It has been done in your name, or at least in that of your family," said Scrooge.

"There are some upon this earth of yours," returned the Spirit, "who lay claim to know us, and who do their deeds of passion, pride, ill-will, hatred, envy, bigotry, and selfishness in our name, who are as strange to us and all our kith and kin as if they had never lived. Remember that, and charge their doings on themselves, not us."

Scrooge promised that he would; and they went on, invisible, as they had been before, into the suburbs of the town. It was a remarkable quality of the Ghost (which Scrooge had observed at the baker's) that, notwithstanding his gigantic size, he could accommodate himself to any place with ease, and that he stood beneath a low roof quite as gracefully and like a supernatural creature as it was possible he could have done in any lofty hall.

And perhaps it was the pleasure the good Spirit had in showing off this power of his, or else it was his own kind, generous, hearty nature, and his sympathy with all poor men, that led him straight to Scrooge's clerk's; for there he went, and took Scrooge with him, holding to his robe; and on the threshold of the door the Spirit smiled, and stopped to bless Bob Cratchit's dwelling with the sprinklings of his torch. Think of that! Bob had but fifteen "Bob" a week himself; he pocketed on Saturdays but fifteen copies of his Christian name; and yet the Ghost of Christmas Present blessed his four-roomed house!

Then up rose Mrs. Cratchit, Cratchit's wife, dressed out but poorly in a twice-turned gown, but brave in ribbons, which are cheap and make a goodly show for sixpence; and she laid the cloth, assisted by Belinda Cratchit, second of her daughters, also brave in ribbons; while Master Peter Cratchit plunged a fork into the saucepan of potatoes, and, getting the corners of his monstrous shirt-collar (Bob's private property, conferred upon his son and heir in honour of the day) into his mouth, rejoiced to find himself so gallantly attired, and yearned to show his linen in the fashionable Parks. And now two smaller Cratchits, boy and girl, came tearing in, screaming that outside the baker's they had smelt the goose, and known it for their own; and basking in luxurious thoughts of sage and onion, these young

Cratchits danced about the table, and exalted Master Peter Cratchit to the skies, while he (not proud, although his collars near choked him) blew the fire, until the slow potatoes, bubbling up, knocked loudly at the saucepan lid to be let out and peeled.

"What has ever got your precious father, then?" said Mrs. Cratchit. "And your brother Tiny Tim! And Martha warn't as late last Christmas Day by half an hour!"

"Here's Martha, mother!" said a girl, appearing as she spoke.

"Here's Martha, mother!" cried the two young Cratchits. "Hurrah! There's *such* a goose, Martha!"

"Why, bless your heart alive, my dear, how late you are!" said Mrs. Cratchit, kissing her a dozen times, and taking off her shawl and bonnet for her with officious zeal.

"We'd a deal of work to finish up last night," replied the girl, "and had to clear away this morning, mother!"

"Well! never mind so long as you are come," said Mrs. Cratchit. "Sit ye down before the fire, my dear, and have a warm, Lord bless ye!"

"No, no! There's father coming," cried the two young Cratchits, who were everywhere at once. "Hide, Martha, hide!"

So Martha hid herself, and in came little Bob, the father, with at least three feet of comforter exclusive of the fringe hanging down before him; and his threadbare clothes darned up and brushed, to look seasonable; and Tiny Tim upon his shoulder. Alas for Tiny Tim, he bore a little crutch, and had his limbs supported by an iron frame!

"Why, where's our Martha?" cried Bob Cratchit, looking round.

"Not coming," said Mrs. Cratchit.

"Not coming!" said Bob, with a sudden declension in his high spirits; for he had been Tim's blood horse all the way from church, and had come home rampant. "Not coming upon Christmas Day!"

Martha didn't like to see him disappointed, if it were only in joke; so she came out prematurely from behind the closet door, and ran into his arms, while the two young Cratchits hustled Tiny Tim, and

. . . in came little Bob, the father, with at least three feet of comforter exclusive of the fringe hanging down before him . . . and Tiny Tim upon his shoulder.

bore him off into the wash-house, that he might hear the pudding singing in the copper.

"And how did little Tim behave?" asked Mrs. Cratchit, when she had rallied Bob on his credulity, and Bob had hugged his daughter to his heart's content.

"As good as gold," said Bob, "and better. Somehow he gets thoughtful, sitting by himself so much, and thinks the strangest things you ever heard. He told me, coming home, that he hoped the people saw him in the church, because he was a cripple, and it might be pleasant to them to remember upon Christmas Day who made lame beggars walk and blind men see."

Bob's voice was tremulous when he told them this, and trembled more when he said that Tiny Tim was growing strong and hearty.

His active little crutch was heard upon the floor, and back came Tiny Tim before another word was spoken, escorted by his brother and sister to his stool beside the fire; and while Bob, turning up his cuffs,—as if, poor fellow, they were capable of being made more shabby,—compounded some hot mixture in a jug with gin and lemons, and stirred it round and round and put it on the hob to simmer, Master Peter and the two ubiquitous young Cratchits went to fetch the goose, with which they soon returned in high procession.

Such a bustle ensued that you might have thought a goose the rarest of all birds; a feathered phenomenon, to which a black swan was a matter of course—and in truth it was something very like it in that house. Mrs. Cratchit made the gravy (ready beforehand in a little saucepan) hissing hot; Master Peter mashed the potatoes with incredible vigour; Miss Belinda sweetened up the apple sauce; Martha dusted the hot plates; Bob took Tiny Tim beside him in a tiny corner at the table; the two young Cratchits set chairs for everybody, not forgetting themselves, and mounting guard upon their posts, crammed spoons into their mouths, lest they should shriek for goose before their turn came to be helped. At last the dishes were set on, and grace was said. It was succeeded by a breathless pause, as Mrs. Cratchit, looking slowly all along the carving-knife, prepared to plunge it in the breast; but when she did, and when the long-expected gush of stuffing issued forth, one murmur of delight arose all round the board, and even Tiny Tim, excited by the two young Cratchits, beat on the table with the handle of his knife, and feebly cried Hurrah!

There never was such a goose. Bob said he didn't believe there ever was such a goose cooked. Its tenderness and flavour, size and cheapness, were the themes of universal admiration. Eked out by apple sauce and mashed potatoes, it was a sufficient dinner for the whole family; indeed, as Mrs. Cratchit said with great delight (surveying one small atom of a bone upon the dish), they hadn't ate it all at last! Yet every one had had enough, and the youngest Cratchits in particular were steeped in sage and onion to the eyebrows! But now the plates being changed by Miss Belinda, Mrs. Cratchit left the room alone—too nervous to bear witnesses—to take the pudding up, and bring it in.

Suppose it should not be done enough! Suppose it should break in turning out! Suppose somebody should have got over the wall of the backyard, and stolen it, while they were merry with the goose—a supposition at which the two young Cratchits became livid! All sorts of horrors were supposed.

Hallo! A great deal of steam! The pudding was out of the copper. A smell like a washing-day! That was the cloth. A smell like an eating-house and a pastry-cook's next door to each other, with a laundress's next door to that! That was the pudding! In half a minute Mrs. Cratchit entered—flushed, but smiling proudly—with the pudding, like a speckled cannon ball, so hard and firm, blazing in half of half a quartern of ignited brandy, and bedight with Christmas holly stuck into the top.

Oh, a wonderful pudding! Bob Cratchit said, and calmly, too, that he regarded it as the greatest success achieved by Mrs. Cratchit since their marriage. Mrs. Cratchit said that, now the weight was off her mind, she would confess she had her doubts about the quantity of flour. Everybody had something to say about it, but nobody said or thought it was at all a small pudding for a large family. It would have

. . . *Mrs. Cratchit entered—flushed, but smiling proudly—with the pudding, like a speckled cannon ball, so hard and firm, blazing in half of half a quartern of ignited brandy, and bedight with Christmas holly stuck into the top.*

been flat heresy to do so. Any Cratchit would have blushed to hint at such a thing.

At last the dinner was all done, the cloth was cleared, the hearth swept, and the fire made up. The compound in the jug being tasted, and considered perfect, apples and oranges were put upon the table, and a shovelful of chestnuts on the fire. Then all the Cratchit family drew round the hearth, in what Bob Cratchit called a circle, meaning half a one; and at Bob Cratchit's elbow stood the family display of glass. Two tumblers and a custard-cup without a handle.

These held the hot stuff from the jug, however, as well as golden goblets would have done; and Bob served it out with beaming looks, while the chestnuts on the fire sputtered and cracked noisily. Then Bob proposed:—

"A Merry Christmas to us all, my dears. God bless us!" Which all the family re-echoed.

"God bless us every one!" said Tiny Tim, the last of all.

He sat very close to his father's side, upon his little stool. Bob held his withered little hand in his, as if he loved the child, and wished to keep him by his side, and dreaded that he might be taken from him.

"Spirit," said Scrooge, with an interest he had never felt before, "tell me if Tiny Tim will live."

"I see a vacant seat," replied the Ghost, "in the poor chimney corner, and a crutch without an owner, carefully preserved. If these shadows remain unaltered by the Future the child will die."

"No, no," said Scrooge. "Oh, no, kind Spirit! say he will be spared."

"If these shadows remain unaltered by the Future, none other of my race," returned the Ghost, "will find him here. What, then? If he be like to die, he had better do it, and decrease the surplus population."

Scrooge hung his head to hear his own words quoted by the Spirit, and was overcome with penitence and grief.

"Man," said the Ghost, "if man you be in heart, not adamant, forbear that wicked cant until you have discovered What the surplus is, and Where it is. Will you decide what men shall live, what men shall die? It may be that in the sight of Heaven you are more worthless and less fit to live than millions like this poor man's child. O God! to hear the Insect on the leaf pronouncing on the too much life among his hungry brothers in the dust!"

Scrooge bent before the Ghost's rebuke, and trembling cast his eyes upon the ground. But he raised them speedily, on hearing his own name.

"Mr. Scrooge!" said Bob; "I'll give you Mr. Scrooge, the Founder of the Feast!"

"The Founder of the Feast, indeed!" cried Mrs. Cratchit, reddening. "I wished I had him here. I'd give him a piece of my mind to feast upon, and I hope he'd have a good appetite for it."

"My dear," said Bob, "the children! Christmas Day."

"It should be Christmas Day, I am sure," said she, "on which one drinks the health of such an odious, stingy, hard, unfeeling man as Mr. Scrooge. You know he is, Robert! Nobody knows it better than you do, poor fellow!"

"My dear," was Bob's mild answer. "Christmas Day."

"I'll drink his health for your sake and the Day's," said Mrs. Cratchit, "not for his. Long life to him! A Merry Christmas and a Happy New Year! He'll be very merry and very happy, I have no doubt!"

The children drank the toast after her. It was the first of their proceedings which had no heartiness in it. Tiny Tim drank it last of all, but he didn't care twopence for it. Scrooge was the Ogre of the family. The mention of his name cast a dark shadow on the party, which was not dispelled for full five minutes.

After it had passed away, they were ten times merrier than before, from the mere relief of Scrooge the Baleful being done with. Bob Cratchit told them how he had a situation in his eye for Master Peter, which would bring in, if obtained, full five-and-sixpence weekly. The two young Cratchits laughed tremendously at the idea of Peter's being a man of business; and Peter himself looked thoughtfully at the fire from between his collars, as if he were deliberating what particular investment he should favour when he came into the receipt of that bewildering income. Martha, who was a poor apprentice at a milliner's, then told them what kind of work she had to do, and how many hours she worked at a stretch, and how she meant to lie abed to-morrow morning for a good long rest; to-morrow being a holiday she passed at home. Also how she had seen a countess and a lord some days before, and how the lord was much about as tall as Peter; at which Peter pulled up his collars so high that you couldn't have seen his head if you had been there. All this time the chestnuts and the jug went round and round; and by and by they had a song, about a lost child travelling in the snow, from Tiny Tim, who had a plaintive little voice, and sang it very well, indeed.

There was nothing of high mark in this. They were not a handsome family; they were not well dressed; their shoes were far from being waterproof; their clothes were scanty; and Peter might have known, and very likely did, the inside of a pawnbroker's. But they were happy, grateful, pleased with one another, and contented with the time; and when they faded, and looked happier yet in the bright sprinklings of the Spirit's torch at parting, Scrooge had his eye upon them, and especially on Tiny Tim, until the last.

By this time it was getting dark and snowing pretty heavily; and as Scrooge and the Spirit went along the streets, the brightness of the roaring fires in kitchens, parlours, and all sorts of rooms was wonderful. Here the flickering of the blaze showed preparations for a cosy dinner, with hot plates baking through and through before the fire, and deep red curtains, ready to be drawn to shut out cold and darkness. There all the children of the house were running out into the snow to meet their married sisters, brothers, cousins, uncles, aunts, and be the first to greet them. Here, again, were shadows on the windowblinds of guests assembling; and there a group of handsome girls, all hooded and fur-booted, and all chattering at once, tripped lightly off to some near neighbour's house; where woe upon the single man who saw them enter—artful witches, well they knew it—in a glow!

But if you had judged from the numbers of people on their way to friendly gatherings, you might have thought that no one was at home to give them welcome when they got there, instead of every house expecting company, and piling up its fires half-chimney high. Blessings on it, how the Ghost exulted! How it bared its breadth of breast, and opened its capacious palm, and floated on, outpouring with a generous hand its bright and harmless mirth on everything within its reach! The very lamplighter, who ran on before, dotting the dusky street with specks of light, and who was dressed to spend the evening somewhere, laughed out loudly as the Spirit passed, though little kenned the lamplighter that he had any company but Christmas!

And now, without a word of warning from the Ghost, they stood upon a bleak and desert moor, where monstrous masses of rude stone were cast about, as though it were the burial-place of giants; and water spread itself wheresoever it listed; or would have done so, but for the frost that held it prisoner; and nothing grew but moss and furze, and coarse, rank grass. Down in the west the setting sun had left a streak of fiery red, which glared upon the desolation for an instant, like a sullen eye, and, frowning lower, lower, lower yet, was lost in the thick gloom of darkest night.

"What place is this?" asked Scrooge.

"A place where Miners live, who labour in the bowels of the earth," returned the Spirit. "But they know me. See!"

A light shone from the window of a hut, and swiftly they advanced towards it. Passing through the wall of mud and stone, they found a cheerful company assembled round a glowing fire. An old, old man and woman, with their children and their children's children, and another generation beyond that, all decked out gaily in their holiday attire. The old man, in a voice that seldom rose above the howling of the wind upon the barren waste, was singing them a Christmas song,—it had been a very old song when he was a boy,—

and from time to time they all joined in the chorus. So surely as they raised their voices, the old man got quite blithe and loud; and so surely as they stopped, his vigour sank again.

The Spirit did not tarry here, but bade Scrooge hold his robe, and, passing on above the moor, sped whither? Not to sea? To sea. To Scrooge's horror, looking back, he saw the last of the land, a frightful range of rocks, behind them; and his ears were deafened by the thundering of water, as it rolled, and roared, and raged, among the dreadful caverns it had worn, and fiercely tried to undermine the earth.

Built upon a dismal reef of sunken rocks, some league or so from shore, on which the waters chafed and dashed, the wild year through, there stood a solitary lighthouse. Great heaps of sea-weed clung to its base, and storm-birds—born of the wind one might suppose, as sea-weed of the water—rose and fell about it, like the waves they skimmed.

But even here, two men who watched the light had made a fire, that through the loophole in the thick stone wall shed out a ray of brightness on the awful sea. Joining their horny hands over the rough table at which they sat, they wished each other Merry Christmas in their can of grog; and one of them—the elder, too, with his face all damaged and scarred with hard weather, as the figure-head of an old ship might be—struck up a sturdy song that was like a gale in itself.

Again the Ghost sped on, above the black and heaving sea—on, on—until, being far away, as he told Scrooge, from any shore, they lighted on a ship. They stood beside the helmsman at the wheel, the look-out in the bow, the officers who had the watch,—dark, ghostly figures in their several stations,—but every man among them hummed a Christmas tune, or had a Christmas thought, or spoke below his breath to his companion of some bygone Christmas Day, with homeward hopes belonging to it. And every man on board, waking or sleeping, good or bad, had had a kinder word for one another on that day than on any day in the year; and had shared to some extent in its festivities; and had remembered those he cared for at a distance, and had known that they delighted to remember him.

It was a great surprise to Scrooge, while listening to the moaning of the wind, and thinking what a solemn thing it was to move on through the lonely darkness over an unknown abyss, whose depths were secrets as profound as Death—it was a great surprise to Scrooge, while thus engaged, to hear a hearty laugh. It was a much greater surprise to Scrooge to recognise it as his own nephew's, and to find himself in a bright, dry, gleaming room, with the Spirit standing smiling by his side, and looking at that same nephew with approving affability!

"Ha, ha!" laughed Scrooge's nephew. "Ha, ha, ha!"

If you should happen, by any unlikely chance, to know a man more blest in a laugh than Scrooge's nephew, all I can say is I should like to know him, too. Introduce him to me, and I'll cultivate his acquaintance.

It is a fair, even-handed, noble adjustment of things that, while there is infection in disease and sorrow, there is nothing in the world so irresistibly contagious as laughter and good-humour. When Scrooge's nephew laughed in this way, holding his sides, rolling his head, and twisting his face into the most extravagant contortions, Scrooge's niece, by marriage, laughed as heartily as he. And their assembled friends, being not a bit behindhand, roared out lustily.

"Ha, ha! Ha, ha, ha, ha!"

"He said that Christmas was a humbug, as I live!" cried Scrooge's nephew. "He believed it, too!"

"More shame for him, Fred!" said Scrooge's niece indignantly. Bless those women! they never do anything by halves. They are always in earnest.

She was very pretty; exceedingly pretty. With a dimpled, sur-prised-looking, capital face; a ripe little mouth, that seemed made to be kissed—as no doubt it was; all kinds of good little dots about her chin, that melted into one another when she laughed; and the sunni-est pair of eyes you ever saw in any little creature's head. Altogether she was what you would have called provoking, you know; but satisfactory, too. Oh, perfectly satisfactory.

"He's a comical old fellow," said Scrooge's nephew, "that's the truth; and not so pleasant as he might be. However, his offences carry their own punishment, and I have nothing to say against him."

"I'm sure he is very rich, Fred," hinted Scrooge's niece. "At least, you always tell *me* so."

"What of that, my dear!" said Scrooge's nephew. "His wealth is of no use to him. He don't do any good with it. He don't make himself comfortable with it. He hasn't the satisfaction of thinking— ha, ha, ha!—that he is ever going to benefit Us with it."

"I have no patience with him," observed Scrooge's niece. Scrooge's niece's sisters, and all the other ladies, expressed the same opinion.

"Oh, I have!" said Scrooge's nephew. "I am sorry for him; I couldn't be angry with him if I tried. Who suffers by his ill whims! Himself, always. Here he takes it into his head to dislike us, and he won't come and dine with us. What's the consequence? He don't lose much of a dinner."

"Indeed, I think he loses a very good dinner," interrupted Scrooge's niece. Everybody else said the same, and they must be allowed to have been competent judges, because they had just had dinner; and with the dessert upon the table, were clustered round the fire, by lamplight.

"Well! I am very glad to hear it," said Scrooge's nephew, "because I haven't any great faith in these young housekeepers. What do *you* say, Topper?"

Topper had clearly got his eye upon one of Scrooge's niece's sisters, for he answered that a bachelor was a wretched outcast, who had no right to express an opinion on the subject. Whereat Scrooge's niece's sister—the plump one with the lace tucker, not the one with the roses—blushed.

"Do go on, Fred," said Scrooge's niece, clapping her hands. "He never finishes what he begins to say! He is such a ridiculous fellow!"

Scrooge's nephew revelled in another laugh, and as it was impossible to keep the infection off, though the plump sister tried hard to do it with aromatic vinegar, his example was unanimously followed.

"I was only going to say," said Scrooge's nephew, "that the consequence of his taking a dislike to us, and not making merry with us, is, as I think, that he loses some pleasant moments, which could do him no harm. I am sure he loses pleasanter companions than he can find in his own thoughts, either in his mouldy old office or his dusty chambers. I mean to give him the same chance every year, whether he likes it or not, for I pity him. He may rail at Christmas till he dies, but he can't help thinking better of it—I defy him—if he finds me going there, in good temper, year after year, and saying, 'Uncle Scrooge, how are you?' If it only puts him in the vein to leave his poor clerk fifty pounds, *that's* something; and I think I shook him yesterday."

It was their turn to laugh now, at the notion of his shaking Scrooge. But being thoroughly good-natured, and not much caring what they laughed at, so that they laughed at any rate, he encouraged them in their merriment, and passed the bottle joyously.

After tea, they had some music. For they were a musical family, and knew what they were about, when they sung a Glee or Catch, I can assure you; especially Topper, who could growl away in the bass like a good one, and never swell the large veins in his forehead, or get red in the face over it. Scrooge's niece played well upon the harp; and played among other tunes a simple little air (a mere nothing, you might learn to whistle it in two minutes), which had been familiar to the child who fetched Scrooge from the boarding-school, as he had been reminded by the Ghost of Christmas Past. When this strain of music sounded, all the things that Ghost had shown him came upon his mind; he softened more and more; and thought that if he could have listened to it often, years ago, he might have cultivated the kindnesses of life for his own happiness with his own hands, without resorting to the sexton's spade that buried Jacob Marley.

But they didn't devote the whole evening to music. After a while

The way he went after that plump sister in the lace tucker was an outrage on the credulity of human nature. Knocking down the fire-irons, tumbling over the chairs, bumping up against the piano, smothering himself amongst the curtains, wherever she went, there went he!

they played at forfeits; for it is good to be children sometimes, and never better than at Christmas, when its mighty Founder was a child himself. Stop! There was first a game at blindman's buff. Of course there was. And I no more believe Topper was really blind than I believe he had eyes in his boots. My opinion is that it was a done thing between him and Scrooge's nephew; and that the Ghost of Christmas Present knew it. The way he went after that plump sister in the lace tucker was an outrage on the credulity of human nature. Knocking down the fire-irons, tumbling over the chairs, bumping up against the piano, smothering himself amongst the curtains, wherever she went, there went he! He always knew where the plump sister was. He wouldn't catch anybody else. If you had fallen up against him (as some of them did) on purpose, he would have made a feint of endeavouring to seize you which would have been an affront to your understanding, and would instantly have sidled off in the direction of the plump sister. She often cried out that it wasn't fair; and it really was not. But when at last he caught her; when, in spite of all her silken rustlings, and her rapid flutterings past him, he got her into a corner whence there was no escape, then his conduct was the most execrable. For his pretending not to know her, his pretending that it was necessary to touch her head-dress, and further to assure himself of her identity by pressing a certain ring upon her finger, and a certain chain about her neck, was vile, monstrous! No doubt she told him her opinion of it, when, another blindman being in office, they were so very confidential together, behind the curtains.

Scrooge's niece was not one of the blindman's buff party, but was made comfortable with a large chair and a footstool, in a snug corner where the Ghost and Scrooge were close behind her. But she joined in the forfeits, and loved her love to admiration with all the letters of the alphabet. Likewise at the game of How, When, and Where, she was very great, and, to the secret joy of Scrooge's nephew, beat her sisters hollow, though they were sharp girls too, as Topper could have told you. There might have been twenty people there, young and old, but they all played, and so did Scrooge; for wholly forgetting, in the interest he had in what was going on, that his voice made no sound in their ears, he sometimes came out with his guess quite loud, and very often guessed right, too; for the sharpest needle, best Whitechapel, warranted not to cut in the eye, was not sharper than Scrooge, blunt as he took it in his head to be.

The Ghost was greatly pleased to find him in this mood, and looked upon him with such favour, that he begged like a boy to be allowed to stay until the guests departed. But this the Spirit said could not be done.

"Here is a new game," said Scrooge. "One half hour, Spirit, only one!"

It was a Game called Yes and No, where Scrooge's nephew had to think of something, and the rest must find out what; he only answering to their questions yes or no, as the case was. The brisk fire of questioning to which he was exposed elicited from him that he was thinking of an animal, a live animal, rather a disagreeable animal, a savage animal, an animal that growled and grunted sometimes, and talked sometimes, and lived in London, and walked about the streets, and wasn't made a show of, and wasn't led by anybody, and didn't live in a menagerie, and was never killed in a market, and was not a horse, or an ass, or a cow, or a bull, or a tiger, or a dog, or a pig, or a cat, or a bear. At every fresh question that was put to him this nephew burst into a fresh roar of laughter, and was so inexpressibly tickled, that he was obliged to get up off the sofa and stamp. At last the plump sister, falling into a similar state, cried out:—

"I have found it out! I know what it is, Fred! I know what it is!"

"What is it?" cried Fred.

"It's your uncle Scro-o-o-o-oge!"

Which it certainly was. Admiration was the universal sentiment, though some objected that the reply to "Is it a bear?" ought to have been "Yes;" inasmuch as an answer in the negative was sufficient to have diverted their thoughts from Mr. Scrooge, supposing they had ever had any tendency that way.

"He has given us plenty of merriment, I am sure," said Fred, "and it would be ungrateful not to drink his health. Here is a glass of mulled wine ready to our hand at the moment; and I say, 'Uncle Scrooge!' "

"Well! Uncle Scrooge!" they cried.

"A Merry Christmas and a Happy New Year to the old man, whatever he is!" said Scrooge's nephew. "He wouldn't take it from me, but may he have it, nevertheless. Uncle Scrooge!"

Uncle Scrooge had imperceptibly become so gay and light of heart, that he would have pledged the unconscious company in return, and thanked them in an inaudible speech if the Ghost had given him time. But the whole scene passed off in the breath of the last word spoken by his nephew; and he and the Spirit were again upon their travels.

Much they saw, and far they went, and many homes they visited, but always with a happy end. The Spirit stood beside sick beds, and they were cheerful; on foreign lands, and they were close at home; by struggling men, and they were patient in their greater hope; by poverty, and it was rich. In almshouse, hospital, and jail, in misery's every refuge, where vain man in his little brief authority had not made fast the door, and barred the Spirit out, he left his blessing, and taught Scrooge his precepts.

It was a long night, if it were only a night; but Scrooge had his doubts of this, because the Christmas Holidays appeared to be condensed into the space of time they passed together. It was strange, too, that while Scrooge remained unaltered in his outward form, the Ghost grew older, clearly older. Scrooge had observed this change, but never spoke of it, until they left a children's Twelfth Night party, when, looking at the Spirit as they stood together in an open place, he noticed that its hair was grey.

"Are spirits' lives so short?" asked Scrooge.

"My life upon this globe is very brief," replied the Ghost. "It ends to-night."

"To-night!" cried Scrooge.

From the foldings of its robe it brought two children; wretched, abject, frightful, hideous, miserable . . . "Oh, Man! look here. Look, look, down here!" *exclaimed the Ghost.*

"To-night at midnight. Hark! The time is drawing near."

The chimes were ringing the three quarters past eleven at that moment.

"Forgive me if I am not justified in what I ask," said Scrooge, looking intently at the Spirit's robe, "but I see something strange, and not belonging to yourself, protruding from your skirts. Is it a foot or a claw?"

"It might be a claw, for the flesh there is upon it," was the Spirit's sorrowful reply. "Look here."

From the foldings of its robe it brought two children; wretched, abject, frightful, hideous, miserable. They knelt down at its feet, and clung upon the outside of its garment.

"Oh, Man! look here. Look, look, down here!" exclaimed the Ghost.

They were a boy and a girl. Yellow, meagre, ragged, scowling, wolfish; but prostrate, too, in their humility. Where graceful youth should have filled their features out, and touched them with its freshest tints, a stale and shrivelled hand, like that of age, had pinched, and twisted them, and pulled them into shreds. Where angels might have sat enthroned, devils lurked, and glared out menacing. No change, no degradation, no perversion of humanity, in any grade, through all the mysteries of wonderful creation, has monsters half so horrible and dread.

Scrooge started back, appalled. Having them shown to him in this way, he tried to say they were fine children, but the words choked themselves, rather than be parties to a lie of such enormous magnitude.

"Spirit! are they yours?" Scrooge could say no more.

"They are Man's," said the Spirit, looking down upon them. "And they cling to me, appealing from their fathers. This boy is Ignorance. This girl is Want. Beware of them both, and all of their degree, but most of all beware this boy, for on his brow I see that written which is Doom, unless the writing be erased. Deny it!" cried the Spirit, stretching out its hand towards the city. "Slander those who tell it ye! Admit it for your factious purposes, and make it worse! And bide the end!"

"Have they no refuge or resource?" cried Scrooge.

"Are there no prisons!" said the Spirit, turning on him for the last time with his own words. "Are there no workhouses?"

The bell struck twelve.

Scrooge looked about him for the Ghost, and saw it not. As the last stroke ceased to vibrate, he remembered the prediction of old Jacob Marley, and, lifting up his eyes, beheld a solemn Phantom, draped and hooded, coming like a mist along the ground towards him.

STAVE IV

THE LAST OF THE SPIRITS

THE Phantom slowly, gravely, silently, approached. When it came near him, Scrooge bent down upon his knee; for in the very air through which this Spirit moved it seemed to scatter gloom and mystery.

It was shrouded in a deep black garment, which concealed its head, its face, its form, and left nothing of it visible, save one outstretched hand. But for this it would have been difficult to detach its figure from the night, and separate it from the darkness by which it was surrounded.

He felt that it was tall and stately when it came beside him, and that its mysterious presence filled him with a solemn dread. He knew no more, for the Spirit neither spoke nor moved.

"I am in the presence of the Ghost of Christmas Yet To Come?" said Scrooge.

The Spirit answered not, but pointed onward with its hand.

"You are about to show me shadows of the things that have not happened, but will happen in the time before us," Scrooge pursued. "Is that so, Spirit?"

The upper portion of the garment was contracted for an instant in its folds, as if the Spirit had inclined its head. That was the only answer he received.

Although well used to ghostly company by this time, Scrooge feared the silent shape so much that his legs trembled beneath him, and he found that he could hardly stand when he prepared to follow it. The Spirit paused a moment, as observing his condition, and giving him time to recover.

But Scrooge was all the worse for this. It thrilled him with a vague uncertain horror, to know that behind the dusky shroud there were ghostly eyes intently fixed upon him, while he, though he stretched his own to the utmost, could see nothing but a spectral hand and one great heap of black.

"Ghost of the Future!" he exclaimed, "I fear you more than any spectre I have seen. But as I know your purpose is to do me good, and as I hope to live to be another man from what I was, I am prepared to bear you company, and do it with a thankful heart. Will you not speak to me?"

It gave him no reply. The hand was pointed straight before them.

"Lead on!" said Scrooge. "Lead on! The night is waning fast, and it is precious time to me, I know. Lead on, Spirit!"

The Phantom moved away as it had come towards him. Scrooge followed in the shadow of its dress, which bore him up, he thought, and carried him along.

They scarcely seemed to enter the city; for the city rather seemed to spring up about them, and encompass them of its own act. But there they were in the heart of it; on 'Change, amongst the merchants; who hurried up and down, and chinked the money in their pockets, and conversed in groups, and looked at their watches, and trifled thoughtfully with their great gold seals, and so forth as Scrooge had seen them often.

"No," said a great fat man with a monstrous chin, "I don't know much about it either way. I only know he's dead."

The Spirit stopped beside one little knot of business men. Observing that the hand was pointed to them, Scrooge advanced to listen to their talk.

"No," said a great fat man with a monstrous chin, "I don't know much about it either way. I only know he's dead."

"When did he die?" inquired another.

"Last night, I believe."

"Why, what was the matter with him?" asked a third, taking a vast quantity of snuff out of a very large snuff-box. "I thought he'd never die."

"God knows," said the first, with a yawn.

"What has he done with his money?" asked a red-faced gentleman with a pendulous excrescence on the end of his nose, that shook like the gills of a turkey-cock.

"I haven't heard," said the man with the large chin, yawning again. "Left it to his company, perhaps. He hasn't left it to *me*. That's all I know."

This pleasantry was received with a general laugh.

"It's likely to be a very cheap funeral," said the same speaker; "for upon my life I don't know of anybody to go to it. Suppose we make up a party and volunteer?"

"I don't mind going if a lunch is provided," observed the gentleman with the excrescence on his nose. "But I must be fed if I make one."

Another laugh.

"Well, I am the most disinterested among you, after all," said the first speaker, "for I never wear black gloves, and I never eat lunch. But I'll offer to go, if anybody else will. When I come to think of it, I'm not at all sure that I wasn't his most particular friend; for we used to stop and speak whenever we met. Bye, bye!"

Speakers and listeners strolled away, and mixed with other groups. Scrooge knew the men, and looked towards the Spirit for an explanation.

The Phantom glided on into a street. Its finger pointed to two persons meeting. Scrooge listened again, thinking that the explanation might lie here.

He knew these men, also, perfectly. They were men of business, very wealthy and of great importance. He had made a point always of standing well in their esteem; in a business point of view, that is; strictly in a business point of view.

"How are you?" said one.

"How are you?" returned the other.

"Well!" said the first. "Old Scratch has got his own at last, hey?"

"So I am told," returned the second. "Cold, isn't it?"

"Seasonable for Christmas-time. You are not a skater, I suppose?"

"No. No. Something else to think of. Good morning!"

Not another word. That was their meeting, their conversation, and their parting.

Scrooge was at first inclined to be surprised that the Spirit should attach importance to conversations apparently so trivial; but feeling assured that they must have some hidden purpose, he set himself to consider what it was likely to be. They could scarcely be supposed to have any bearing on the death of Jacob, his old partner, for that was Past, and this Ghost's province was the Future. Nor could he think of any one immediately connected with himself to whom he could apply them. But nothing doubting that to whomsoever they applied they had some latent moral for his own improvement, he resolved to treasure up every word he heard, and everything he saw; and especially to observe the shadow of himself when it appeared. For he had an expectation that the conduct of his future self would give him the clue he missed, and would render the solution of these riddles easy.

He looked about in that very place for his own image; but another man stood in his accustomed corner, and though the clock pointed to his usual time of day for being there, he saw no likeness of himself among the multitudes that poured in through the Porch. It gave him little surprise, however; for he had been revolving in his mind a change of life, and thought and hoped he saw his new-born resolutions carried out in this.

Quiet and dark, beside him stood the Phantom, with its outstretched hand. When he roused himself from his thoughtful quest, he fancied from the turn of the hand, and its situation in reference to himself, that the Unseen Eyes were looking at him keenly. It made him shudder, and feel very cold.

They left the busy scene, and went into an obscure part of the town, where Scrooge had never penetrated before, although he recognised its situation and its bad repute. The ways were foul and narrow; the shops and houses wretched; the people half-naked, drunken, slipshod, ugly. Alleys and archways, like so many cesspools, disgorged their offences of smell, and dirt, and life, upon the straggling streets; and the whole quarter reeked with crime, with filth and misery.

Far in this den of infamous resort, there was a low-browed, beetling shop, below a pent-house roof, where iron, old rags, bottles, bones, and greasy offal were bought. Upon the floor within were piled up heaps of rusty keys, nails, chains, hinges, files, scales, weights, and refuse iron of all kinds. Secrets that few would like to scrutinise were bred and hidden in mountains of unseemly rags, masses of corrupted fat, and sepulchres of bones. Sitting in among the wares he dealt in, by a charcoal stove, made of old bricks, was a grey-haired rascal, nearly seventy years of age; who had screened himself from the cold air without by a frowzy curtaining of miscellaneous tatters hung upon a line, and smoked his pipe in all the luxury of calm retirement.

Scrooge and the Phantom came into the presence of this man, just as a woman with a heavy bundle slunk into the shop. But she had scarcely entered, when another woman, similarly laden, came in, too; and she was closely followed by a man in faded black, who was no less startled by the sight of them than they had been upon the recognition of each other. After a short period of blank astonishment, in which the old man with the pipe had joined them, they all three burst into a laugh.

"Let the charwoman alone to be the first!" cried she who had entered first. "Let the laundress alone to be the second; and let the undertaker's man alone to be the third. Look here, old Joe, here's a chance! If we haven't all three met here without meaning it!"

"You couldn't have met in a better place," said old Joe, removing his pipe from his mouth. "Come into the parlour. You were made free of it long ago, you know; and the other two ain't strangers. Stop till I shut the door of the shop. Ah! How it skreeks! There ain't such a rusty bit of metal in the place as its own hinges, I believe; and I'm sure there's no such old bones here as mine. Ha, ha! We're all suitable to our calling, we're well matched. Come into the parlour. Come into the parlour."

The parlour was the space behind the screen of rags. The old man raked the fire together with an old stair-rod, and, having trimmed his smoky lamp (for it was night) with the stem of his pipe, put it into his mouth again.

While he did this the woman who had already spoken threw her bundle on the floor and sat down in a flaunting manner on a stool; crossing her elbows on her knees, and looking with a bold defiance at the other two.

"What odds, then! What odds, Mrs. Dilber?" said the woman. "Every person has a right to take care of themselves. *He* always did!"

"That's true, indeed!" said the laundress. "No man more so."

"Why, then, don't stand staring as if you was afraid, woman; who's the wiser? We're not going to pick holes in each other's coats, I suppose?"

"No, indeed!" said Mrs. Dilber and the man together. "We should hope not."

"Very well, then!" cried the woman. "That's enough. Who's the worse for the loss of a few things like these? Not a dead man, I suppose?"

"No, indeed," said Mrs. Dilber, laughing.

"If he wanted to keep 'em after he was dead, a wicked old screw," pursued the woman, "why wasn't he natural in his lifetime? If he had been, he'd have had somebody to look after him when he was struck with Death, instead of lying gasping out his last there, alone by himself."

"It's the truest word that ever was spoke," said Mrs. Dilber. "It's a judgment on him."

"I wish it was a little heavier judgment," replied the woman; "and it should have been, you may depend upon it, if I could have laid my hands on anything else. Open that bundle, old Joe, and let me know the value of it. Speak out plain. I'm not afraid to be the first, nor afraid for them to see it. We knew pretty well that we were helping ourselves, before we met here, I believe. It's no sin. Open the bundle, Joe."

But the gallantry of her friends would not allow of this; and the man in faded black, mounting the breach first, produced *his* plunder. It was not extensive. A seal or two, a pencil-case, a pair of sleeve-buttons, and a brooch of no great value, were all. They were severally examined and appraised by old Joe, who chalked the sums he was disposed to give for each, upon the wall, and added them up into a total when he found that there was nothing more to come.

"That's your account," said Joe, "and I wouldn't give another sixpence, if I was to be boiled for not doing it. Who's next?"

Mrs. Dilber was next. Sheets and towels, a little wearing apparel, two old-fashioned silver teaspoons, a pair of sugar-tongs, and a few boots. Her account was stated on the wall in the same manner.

"I always give too much to ladies. It's a weakness of mine, and that's the way I ruin myself," said old Joe. "That's your account. If you asked me for another penny and made it an open question, I'd repent of being so liberal and knock off half a crown."

"And now undo *my* bundle, Joe," said the first woman.

Joe went down on his knees for the greater convenience of opening it, and having unfastened a great many knots, dragged out a large heavy roll of some dark stuff.

"What do you call this?" said Joe. "Bed-curtains!"

"Ah!" returned the woman, laughing, and leaning forward on her crossed arms. "Bed-curtains!"

"You don't mean to say you took 'em down rings and all, with him lying there?" said Joe.

"Yes, I do," replied the woman. "Why not?"

"You were born to make your fortune," said Joe, "and you'll certainly do it."

"I certainly shan't hold my hand, when I can get anything in it by reaching it out, for the sake of such a man as he was, I promise you, Joe," returned the woman coolly. "Don't drop that oil upon the blankets, now."

"His blankets?" asked Joe.

"Whose else's do you think?" replied the woman. "He isn't likely to take cold without 'em, I dare say."

"I hope he didn't die of anything catching? Eh?" said old Joe, stopping in his work, and looking up.

"Don't you be afraid of that," returned the woman. "I ain't so fond of his company that I'd loiter about him for such things, if he did. Ah! You may look through that shirt till your eyes ache, but you won't find a hole in it, nor a threadbare place. It's the best he had, and a fine one too. They'd have wasted it, if it hadn't been for me."

"What do you call wasting of it?" asked old Joe.

"Putting it on him to be buried in, to be sure," replied the woman, with a laugh. "Somebody was fool enough to do it, but I took it off again. If calico ain't good enough for such a purpose, it isn't good enough for anything. It's quite as becoming to the body. He can't look uglier than he did in that one."

Scrooge listened to this dialogue in horror. As they sat grouped about their spoil, in the scanty light afforded by the old man's lamp, he viewed them with a detestation and disgust, which could hardly have been greater, though they had been obscene demons, marketing the corpse itself.

"Ha, ha!" laughed the same woman, when old Joe, producing a

. . . *they sat grouped about their spoil, in the scanty light afforded by the old man's lamp . . . "This is the end of it, you see? He frightened every one away from him when he was alive, to profit us when he was dead! Ha, ha, ha!"*

flannel bag with money in it, told out their several gains upon the ground. "This is the end of it, you see? He frightened every one away from him when he was alive, to profit us when he was dead! Ha, ha, ha!"

"Spirit!" said Scrooge, shuddering from head to foot. "I see, I see. The case of this unhappy man might be my own. My life tends that way, now. Merciful Heaven, what is this!"

He recoiled in terror, for the scene had changed, and now he almost touched a bed—a bare, uncurtained bed, on which, beneath a ragged sheet, there lay a something covered up, which, though it was dumb, announced itself in awful language.

The room was very dark, too dark to be observed with any accuracy, though Scrooge glanced round it in obedience to a secret impulse, anxious to know what kind of room it was. A pale light rising in the outer air, fell straight upon the bed; and on it, plundered and bereft, unwatched, unwept, uncared for, was the body of this man.

Scrooge glanced towards the Phantom. Its steady hand was pointed to the head. The cover was so carelessly adjusted that the slightest raising of it, the motion of a finger upon Scrooge's part, would have disclosed the face. He thought of it, felt how easy it would be to do, and longed to do it; but had no more power to withdraw the veil than to dismiss the spectre at his side.

Oh, cold, cold, rigid, dreadful Death, set up thine altar here, and dress it with such terrors as thou hast at thy command, for this is thy dominion! But of the loved, revered, and honoured head, thou canst not turn one hair to thy dread purposes, or make one feature odious. It is not that the hand is heavy and will fall down when released; it is not that the heart and pulse are still; but that the hand WAS open, generous, and true; the heart brave, warm, and tender; and the pulse a man's. Strike, Shadow, strike! And see his good deeds springing from the wound, to sow the world with life immortal!

No voice pronounced these words in Scrooge's ears, and yet he heard them when he looked upon the bed. He thought, if this man could be raised up now, what would be his foremost thoughts? Avarice, hard-dealing, griping cares? They have brought him to a rich end, truly!

He lay, in the dark, empty house, with not a man, a woman, or a child, to say he was kind to me in this or that, and for the memory of one kind word I will be kind to him. A cat was tearing at the door, and there was a sound of gnawing rats beneath the hearthstone. What *they* wanted in the room of death, and why they were so restless and disturbed, Scrooge did not dare to think.

"Spirit!" he said, "this is a fearful place. In leaving it, I shall not leave its lesson, trust me. Let us go!"

Still the Ghost pointed with an unmoved finger to the head.

"I understand you," Scrooge returned, "and I would do it if I could. But I have not the power, Spirit. I have not the power."

Again it seemed to look upon him.

"If there is any person in the town who feels emotion caused by this man's death," said Scrooge, quite agonised, "show that person to me, Spirit, I beseech you!"

The Phantom spread its dark robe before him for a moment, like a wing; and withdrawing it, revealed a room by daylight, where a mother and her children were.

She was expecting some one, and with anxious eagerness; for she walked up and down the room; started at every sound; looked out from the window; glanced at the clock; tried, but in vain, to work with her needle; and could hardly bear the voices of her children in their play.

At length the long, expected knock was heard. She hurried to the door and met her husband; a man whose face was careworn and depressed, though he was young. There was a remarkable expression in it now; a kind of serious delight of which he felt ashamed, and which he struggled to repress.

He sat down to the dinner that had been hoarding for him by the fire, and when she asked him faintly what news (which was not until after a long silence), he appeared embarrassed how to answer.

"Is it good," she said, "or bad?"—to help him.

"Bad," he answered.

"We are quite ruined?"

"No. There is hope yet, Caroline."

"If *he* relents," she said, amazed, "there is! Nothing is past hope, if such a miracle has happened."

"He is past relenting," said her husband. "He is dead."

She was a mild and patient creature, if her face spoke truth; but she was thankful in her soul to hear it, and she said so, with clasped hands. She prayed forgiveness the next moment, and was sorry; but the first was the emotion of her heart.

"What the half-drunken woman, whom I told you of last night, said to me, when I tried to see him and obtain a week's delay, and what I thought was a mere excuse to avoid me, turns out to have been quite true. He was not only very ill, but dying, then."

"To whom will our debt be transferred?"

"I don't know. But before that time we shall be ready with the money; and even though we were not, it would be bad fortune indeed to find so merciless a creditor in his successor. We may sleep to-night with light hearts, Caroline!"

Yes. Soften it as they would, their hearts were lighter. The children's faces, hushed and clustered round to hear what they so little understood, were brighter; and it was a happier house for this man's death! The only emotion that the Ghost could show him, caused by the event, was one of pleasure.

"Let me see some tenderness connected with a death," said Scrooge; "or that dark chamber, Spirit, which we left just now, will be for ever present to me."

The Ghost conducted him through several streets familiar to his feet; and as they went along, Scrooge looked here and there to find himself, but nowhere was he to be seen. They entered poor Bob Cratchit's house, the dwelling he had visited before, and found the mother and the children seated round the fire.

Quiet. Very quiet. The noisy little Cratchits were as still as statues in one corner, and sat looking up at Peter, who had a book before him. The mother and her daughters were engaged in sewing. But surely they were very quiet!

" 'And he took a child, and set him in the midst of them.' "

Where had Scrooge heard those words? He had not dreamed them. The boy must have read them out, as he and the Spirit crossed the threshold. Why did he not go on?

The mother laid her work upon the table, and put her hand up to her face.

"The colour hurts my eyes," she said.

The colour? Ah, poor Tiny Tim!

"They're better now again," said Cratchit's wife. "It makes them weak by candle-light; and I wouldn't show weak eyes to your father when he comes home, for the world. It must be near his time."

"Past it rather," Peter answered, shutting up his book. "But I think he has walked a little slower than he used, these few last evenings, mother."

They were very quiet again. At last she said, and in a steady, cheerful voice, that only faltered once:—

"I have known him walk with—I have known him walk with Tiny Tim upon his shoulder, very fast indeed."

"And so have I," cried Peter. "Often."

"And so have I," exclaimed another. So had all.

"But he was very light to carry," she resumed, intent upon her work, "and his father loved him so, that it was no trouble; no trouble. And there is your father at the door!"

She hurried out to meet him; and little Bob in his comforter—he had need of it, poor fellow—came in. His tea was ready for him on the hob, and they all tried who should help him to it most. Then the two young Cratchits got upon his knees and laid, each child, a little cheek against his face, as if they said, "Don't mind it, father." "Don't be grieved!"

Bob was very cheerful with them, and spoke pleasantly to all the family. He looked at the work upon the table, and praised the indus-

" 'And he took a child, and set him in the midst of them.' "

try and speed of Mrs. Cratchit and the girls. They would be done long before Sunday, he said.

"Sunday! You went to-day, then, Robert?" said his wife.

"Yes, my dear," returned Bob. "I wish you could have gone. It would have done you good to see how green a place it is. But you'll see it often. I promised him that I would walk there on a Sunday. My little, little child!" cried Bob. "My little child!"

He broke down all at once. He couldn't help it. If he could have helped it, he and his child would have been farther apart perhaps than they were.

He left the room, and went up stairs into the room above, which was lighted cheerfully, and hung with Christmas. There was a chair set close beside the child, and there were signs of some one having been there, lately. Poor Bob sat down in it, and when he had thought a little and composed himself, he kissed the little face. He was reconciled to what had happened, and went down again quite happy.

They drew about the fire, and talked; the girls and mother working still. Bob told them of the extraordinary kindness of Mr. Scrooge's nephew, whom he had scarcely seen but once, and who, meeting him in the street that day, and seeing that he looked a little—"just a little down you know," said Bob, inquired what had happened to distress him. "On which," said Bob, "for he is the pleasantest-spoken gentleman you ever heard, I told him. 'I am heartily sorry for it, Mr. Cratchit,' he said, 'and heartily sorry for your good wife.' By the bye, how he ever knew *that* I don't know."

"Knew what, my dear?"

"Why, that you were a good wife," replied Bob.

"Everybody knows that!" said Peter.

"Very well observed, my boy!" cried Bob. "I hope they do. 'Heartily sorry,' he said, 'for your good wife. If I can be of service to you in any way,' he said, giving me his card, 'that's where I live. Pray come to me.' Now, it wasn't," cried Bob, "for the sake of anything he might be able to do for us, so much as for his kind way, that this was quite delightful. It really seemed as if he had known our Tiny Tim, and felt with us."

"I'm sure he's a good soul!" said Mrs. Cratchit.

"You would be sure of it, my dear," returned Bob, "if you saw and spoke to him. I shouldn't be at all surprised—mark what I say!—if he got Peter a better situation."

"Only hear that, Peter," said Mrs. Cratchit.

"And then," cried one of the girls, "Peter will be keeping company with some one, and setting up for himself."

"Get along with you!" retorted Peter, grinning.

"It's just as likely as not," said Bob, "one of these days; though there's plenty of time for that, my dear. But however and whenever we part from one another, I am sure we shall none of us forget poor Tiny Tim—shall we—or this first parting that there was among us?"

"Never, father!" cried they all.

"And I know," said Bob,—"I know, my dears, that when we recollect how patient and how mild he was, although he was a little, little child, we shall not quarrel easily among ourselves, and forget poor Tiny Tim in doing it."

"No, never, father!" they all cried again.

"I am very happy," said little Bob, "I am very happy!"

Mrs. Cratchit kissed him, his daughters kissed him, the two young Cratchits kissed him, and Peter and himself shook hands. Spirit of Tiny Tim, thy childish essence was from God!

"Spectre," said Scrooge, "something informs me that our parting moment is at hand. I know it, but I know not how. Tell me what man that was whom we saw lying dead?"

The Ghost of Christmas Yet To Come conveyed him, as before— though at a different time, he thought; indeed, there seemed no order in these latter visions, save that they were in the Future—into the resorts of business men, but showed him not himself. Indeed, the Spirit did not stay for anything, but went straight on, as to the end just now desired, until besought by Scrooge to tarry for a moment.

"This court," said Scrooge, "through which we hurry now, is where my place of occupation is, and has been for a length of time. I see the house. Let me behold what I shall be, in days to come."

The Spirit stopped; the hand was pointed elsewhere.

"The house is yonder," Scrooge exclaimed. "Why do you point away?"

The inexorable finger underwent no change.

Scrooge hastened to the window of his office, and looked in. It was an office still, but not his. The furniture was not the same, and the figure in the chair was not himself. The Phantom pointed as before.

He joined it once again, and wondering why and whither he had gone, accompanied it until they reached an iron gate. He paused to look round before entering.

A churchyard. Here, then, the wretched man whose name he had now to learn lay underneath the ground. It was a worthy place. Walled in by houses; overrun by grass and weeds, the growth of vegetations's death, not life; choked up with too much burying; fat with repleted appetite. A worthy place!

The Spirit stood among the graves, and pointed down to One. He advanced towards it trembling. The Phantom was exactly as it had been, but he dreaded that he saw new meaning in its solemn shape.

"Before I draw nearer to that stone to which you point," said Scrooge, "answer me one question. Are these the shadows of the things that Will be, or are they shadows of the things that May be, only?"

Still the Ghost pointed downward to the grave by which it stood.

"Men's courses will foreshadow certain ends, to which, if persevered in, they must lead," said Scrooge. "But if the courses be departed from, the ends will change. Say it is thus with what you show me!"

The Spirit was immovable as ever.

Scrooge crept towards it, trembling as he went; and following the finger, read upon the stone of the neglected grave his own name, EBENEZER SCROOGE.

"Am *I* that man who lay upon the bed?" he cried, upon his knees.

The finger pointed from the grave to him, and back again.

"No, Spirit! Oh, no, no!"

The finger still was there.

"Spirit!" he cried, tight clutching at its robe, "hear me! I am not the man I was. I will not be the man I must have been but for this intercourse. Why show me this, if I am past all hope!"

For the first time the hand appeared to shake.

"Good Spirit," he pursued, as down upon the ground he fell before it; "your nature intercedes for me, and pities me. Assure me that I yet may change these shadows you have shown me, by an altered life!"

The kind hand trembled.

"I will honour Christmas in my heart, and try to keep it all the year. I will live in the Past, the Present, and the Future. The Spirits of all Three shall strive within me. I will not shut out the lessons that they teach. Oh, tell me I may sponge away the writing on this stone!"

In his agony, he caught the spectral hand. It sought to free itself, but he was strong in his entreaty, and detained it. The Spirit, stronger yet, repulsed him.

Holding up his hands in a last prayer to have his fate reversed, he saw an alteration in the Phantom's hood and dress. It shrunk, collapsed, and dwindled down into a bedpost.

STAVE V

THE END OF IT

YES! and the bedpost was his own. The bed was his own, the room was his own. Best and happiest of all, the Time before him was his own, to make amends in!

"I will live in the Past, the Present, and the Future!" Scrooge repeated, as he scrambled out of bed. "The Spirits of all Three shall strive within me. O Jacob Marley! Heaven, and the Christmas-Time be praised for this! I say it on my knees, old Jacob; on my knees!"

He was so fluttered and so glowing with his good intentions that his broken voice would scarcely answer to his call. He had been sobbing violently in his conflict with the Spirit, and his face was wet with tears.

"They are not torn down," cried Scrooge, folding one of his bed-curtains in his arms, "they are not torn down, rings and all. They are here—I am here—the shadows of the things that would have been may be dispelled. They will be. I know they will!"

His hands were busy with his garments all this time; turning them inside out, putting them on upside down, tearing them, mislaying them, making them parties to every kind of extravagance.

"I don't know what to do!" cried Scrooge, laughing and crying in the same breath; and making a perfect Laocoön of himself with his stockings. "I am as light as a feather, I am as happy as an angel, I am as merry as a school-boy. I am as giddy as a drunken man. A merry Christmas to everybody! A happy New Year to all the world! Hallo here! Whoop! Hallo!"

He had frisked into the sitting-room, and was now standing there, perfectly winded.

"There's the saucepan that the gruel was in!" cried Scrooge, starting off again, and going round the fireplace. "There's the door by which the Ghost of Jacob Marley entered! There's the corner where the Ghost of a Christmas Present sat! There's the window where I saw the wandering Spirits! It's all right, it's all true, it all happened. Ha, ha, ha!"

Really, for a man who had been out of practice for so many years, it was a splendid laugh, a most illustrious laugh. The father of a long, long line of brilliant laughs!

"I don't know what day of the month it is," said Scrooge. "I don't know how long I have been among the Spirits. I don't know anything. I'm quite a baby. Never mind; I don't care. I'd rather be a baby. Hallo! Whoop! Hallo here!"

He was checked in his transports by the churches ringing out the lustiest peals he had ever heard. Clash, clash, hammer; ding, dong, bell. Bell, dong, ding; hammer, clang, clash! Oh, glorious, glorious!

Running to the window, he opened it, and put out his head. No fog, no mist; clear, bright, jovial, stirring, cold; cold, piping for the blood to dance to; golden sunlight; Heavenly sky; sweet fresh air; merry bells. Oh, glorious, glorious!

"What's to-day?" cried Scrooge, calling downward to a boy in Sunday clothes, who perhaps had loitered in to look about him.

"Eh?" returned the boy, with all his might of wonder.

"What's to-day, my fine fellow?" said Scrooge.

"To-day!" replied the boy. "Why, CHRISTMAS DAY."

"It's Christmas Day!" said Scrooge to himself. "I haven't missed it. The Spirits have done it all in one night. They can do anything they like. Of course they can. Of course they can. Hallo, my fine fellow!"

"Hallo!" returned the boy.

"Do you know the Poulterer's, in the next street but one, at the corner?" Scrooge inquired.

"I should hope I did," replied the lad.

"An intelligent boy!" said Scrooge. "A remarkable boy! Do you know whether they've sold the prize Turkey that was hanging up there?—not the little prize Turkey; the big one?"

"What, the one as big as me?" returned the boy.

"What a delightful boy!" said Scrooge. "It's a pleasure to talk to him. Yes, my buck!"

"It's hanging there now," replied the boy.

"Is it?" said Scrooge. "Go and buy it."

"Walk-er!" exclaimed the boy.

"No, no," said Scrooge, "I am in earnest. Go and buy it, and tell 'em to bring it here, that I may give them the directions where to take it. Come back with the man, and I'll give you a shilling. Come back with him in less than five minutes, and I'll give you half a crown!"

The boy was off like a shot. He must have had a steady hand at a trigger who could have got a shot off half so fast.

"I'll send it to Bob Cratchit's," whispered Scrooge, rubbing his hands, and splitting with a laugh. "He shan't know who sends it. It's twice the size of Tiny Tim. Joe Miller never made such a joke as sending it to Bob's will be!"

The hand in which he wrote the address was not a steady one; but write it he did, somehow, and went down stairs to open the street door, ready for the coming of the poulterer's man. As he stood there, waiting his arrival, the knocker caught his eye.

"I shall love it as long as I live!" cried Scrooge, patting it with his hand. "I scarcely ever looked at it before. What an honest expression it has in its face! It's a wonderful knocker!—Here's the Turkey. Hallo! Whoop! How are you! Merry Christmas!"

It *was* a Turkey! He never could have stood upon his legs, that bird. He would have snapped 'em short off in a minute, like sticks of sealing-wax.

"Why, it's impossible to carry that to Camden Town," said Scrooge. "You must have a cab."

The chuckle with which he said this, and the chuckle with which he paid for the Turkey, and the chuckle with which he paid for the

"Here's the Turkey. Hallo! Whoop! How are you! Merry Christmas!"

cab, and the chuckle with which he recompensed the boy were only to be exceeded by the chuckle with which he sat down breathless in his chair again, and chuckled till he cried.

Shaving was not an easy task, for his hand continued to shake very much; and shaving requires attention, even when you don't dance while you are at it. But if he had cut the end of his nose off, he would have put a piece of sticking plaster over it, and been quite satisfied.

He dressed himself "all in his best," and at last got out into the streets. The people were by this time pouring forth, as he had seen them with the Ghost of Christmas Present; and walking with his hands behind him, Scrooge regarded every one with a delighted smile. He looked so irresistibly pleasant, in a word, that three or four good-humoured fellows said, "Good morning, sir! A merry Christmas to you!" And Scrooge said often afterwards that, of all the blithe sounds he had ever heard, those were the blithest in his ears.

He had not gone far, when coming on towards him he beheld the portly gentleman who had walked into his counting-house the day before, and said "Scrooge and Marley's, I believe?" It sent a pang across his heart to think how this old gentleman would look upon him when they met; but he knew what path lay straight before him, and he took it.

"My dear sir," said Scrooge, quickening his pace, and taking the old gentleman by both his hands. "How do you do? I hope you succeeded yesterday. It was very kind of you. A merry Christmas to you, sir!"

"Mr. Scrooge?"

"Yes," said Scrooge. "That is my name, and I fear it may not be pleasant to you. Allow me to ask your pardon. And will you have the goodness"—here Scrooge whispered in his ear.

"Lord bless me!" cried the gentleman, as if his breath were taken away. "My dear Mr. Scrooge, are you serious?"

"If you please," said Scrooge. "Not a farthing less. A great many back-payments are included in it, I assure you. Will you do me that favour?"

"My dear sir," said the other, shaking hands with him, "I don't know what to say to such munifi—"

"Don't say anything, please," retorted Scrooge. "Come and see me. Will you come and see me?"

"I will!" cried the old gentleman. And it was clear he meant to do it.

"Thankee," said Scrooge. "I am much obliged to you. I thank you fifty times. Bless you!"

He went to church, and walked about the streets, and watched the people hurrying to and fro, and patted the children on the head, and questioned beggars, and looked down into the kitchens of houses, and up to the windows; and found that everything could yield him pleasure. He had never dreamed that any walk—that any thing— could give him so much happiness. In the afternoon he turned his steps towards his nephew's house.

He passed the door a dozen times, before he had the courage to go up and knock. But he made a dash, and did it.

"Is your master at home, my dear?" said Scrooge to the girl. Nice girl! Very.

"Yes, sir."

"Where is he, my love?" said Scrooge.

"He's in the dining-room, sir, along with mistress. I'll show you up stairs, if you please."

"Thankee. He knows me," said Scrooge, with his hand already on the dining-room lock. "I'll go in here, my dear."

He turned it gently, and sidled his face in, round the door. They were looking at the table (which was spread out in great array); for these young housekeepers are always nervous on such points, and like to see that everything is right.

"Fred!" said Scrooge.

Dear heart alive, how his niece by marriage started! Scrooge had forgotten, for the moment, about her sitting in the corner with the footstool, or he wouldn't have done it, on any account.

"Why, bless my soul!" cried Fred, "who's that?"

"It's I. Your uncle Scrooge. I have come to dinner. Will you let me in, Fred?"

Let him in! It is a mercy he didn't shake his arm off. He was at home in five minutes. Nothing could be heartier. His niece looked just the same. So did Topper when *he* came. So did the plump sister, when *she* came. So did every one when *they* came. Wonderful party, wonderful games, wonderful unanimity, won-der-ful happiness!

But he was early at the office next morning. Oh, he was early there. If he could only be there first, and catch Bob Cratchit coming late! That was the thing he had set his heart upon.

And he did it; yes, he did! The clock struck nine. No Bob. A quarter past. No Bob. He was full eighteen minutes and a half behind his time. Scrooge sat with his door wide open, that he might see him come into the tank.

His hat was off, before he opened the door; his comforter too. He was on his stool in a jiffy; driving away with his pen as if he were trying to overtake nine o'clock.

"Hallo!" growled Scrooge, in his accustomed voice as near as he could feign it. "What do you mean by coming here at this time of day?"

"I am very sorry, sir," said Bob. "I *am* behind my time."

"You are!" repeated Scrooge. "Yes. I think you are. Step this way, sir, if you please."

"It's only once a year, sir," pleaded Bob, appearing from the tank. "It shall not be repeated. I was making rather merry yesterday, sir."

"Now, I'll tell you what, my friend," said Scrooge. "I am not going to stand this sort of thing any longer. And therefore," he continued, leaping from his stool, and giving Bob such a dig in the waistcoat that he staggered back into the tank again; "and therefore I am about to raise your salary!"

"And therefore," he continued, leaping from his stool, and giving Bob such a dig in the waistcoat that he staggered back into the tank again; "and therefore I am about to raise your salary!"

Bob trembled, and got a little nearer to the ruler. He had a momentary idea of knocking Scrooge down with it, holding him, and calling to the people in the court for help and a straight-waistcoat.

"A merry Christmas, Bob!" said Scrooge, with an earnestness that could not be mistaken, as he clapped him on the back. "A merrier Christmas, Bob, my good fellow, than I have given you for many a year! I'll raise your salary, and endeavour to assist your struggling family, and we will discuss your affairs this very afternoon, over a Christmas bowl of smoking bishop, Bob! Make up the fires, and buy another coal-scuttle before you dot another i, Bob Cratchit!"

Scrooge was better than his word. He did it all, and infinitely more; and to Tiny Tim, who did NOT die, he was a second father. He became as good a friend, as good a master, and as good a man, as the good old city knew, or any other good old city, town, or borough, in the good old world. Some people laughed to see the alteration in him, but he let them laugh, and little heeded them; for he was wise enough to know that nothing ever happened on this globe, for good, at which some people did not have their fill of laughter in the outset; and knowing that such as these would be blind anyway, he thought it quite as well that they should wrinkle up their eyes in grins, as have the malady in less attractive forms. His own heart laughed; and that was quite enough for him.

He had no further intercourse with Spirits, but lived upon the Total Abstinence Principle, ever afterwards; and it was always said of him that he knew how to keep Christmas well, if any man alive possessed the knowledge. May that be truly said of us, and all of us! And so, as Tiny Tim observed, God bless Us, Every One!

Gad's Hill Place,
Higham by Rochester, Kent.

Friday Fourth October 1851.

"And so, as Tiny Tim observed, God bless us every one!" —

Charles Dickens

The closing line of A Christmas Carol, *written out by Charles Dickens.*

SUGGESTIONS FOR
FURTHER READING

BY CHARLES DICKENS

Charles Dickens, 1812–1870: An Anthology from the Berg Collection. Compiled by Lola L. Szladits; Foreward (1990) by Francis O. Mattson. New York: The New York Public Library, 1990. A leisurely stroll through the rich trove of Dickensiana in the Henry W. and Albert A. Berg Collection of English and American Literature, one of the jewels of The New York Public Library. Many of the treasures reproduced in the Collector's Edition of *A Christmas Carol and Other Haunting Tales* are housed in the Berg Collection.

DICKENS, CHARLES. *A Christmas Carol. The Public Reading Version. A Facsimile of the Author's Prompt-Copy.* Introduction and notes by Philip Collins. New York: The New York Public Library, 1971. A handsomely produced facsimile edition of the prompt-copy (now held by the Berg Collection) from which Dickens gave his public readings of this most loved tale. Two pages from the original (the sole surviving prompt-copy of the *Carol)* are reproduced in the present volume.

———. *Dickens on America & the Americans.* Austin: University of Texas Press, 1978. A nicely illustrated gathering of Dickens's ruminations on the United States and its brash and colorful (and Dickens-idolizing) citizenry, with an enjoyable introduction by Michael Slater.

———. *The Letters of Charles Dickens.* The Pilgrim Edition. Oxford, Eng.: Clarendon Press; New York: Oxford University Press, 1965– (in progress). Volumes 1–8 (1829–58), edited by Madeline House et al. The lavishly praised scholarly edition of the collected correspondence of the man who must be—hands down—one of the liveliest and funniest letter writers to have applied pen to paper in the history of the English language.

————. *The Public Readings*. Edited by Philip Collins. Oxford, Eng.: Clarendon Press, 1975. A scholarly edition of the twenty-one texts prepared by Dickens for his readings (only sixteen were actually performed), with a comprehensive and illuminating introduction. Head notes to each reading are packed with interesting information (including eyewitness accounts and contemporary reviews). Reprinted in 1983 as an Oxford University Press "World's Classics" paperback, with a condensed introduction (as *Charles Dickens: "Sikes and Nancy" and Other Public Readings*).

BIOGRAPHY

ACKROYD, PETER. *Dickens*. New York: HarperCollins Publishers, 1990. An absolutely superb biography, deeply felt and marvelously textured, written with both nuance and great style.

Dickens: Interviews and Recollections. Edited by Philip Collins. London: Macmillan Press, 1981. 2 volumes. A fascinating collection of memoirs—by family and friends, colleagues and strangers, the famous and the forgotten—of the man who was "so far beyond the ordinary run of mortals," with informative introduction and notes.

KAPLAN, FRED. *Dickens: A Biography*. New York: William Morrow, 1988. A vivid portrait by the author of, among other works, *Dickens and Mesmerism: The Hidden Springs of Fiction* (Princeton, N.J.: Princeton University Press, 1975).

TOMALIN, CLAIRE. *The Invisible Woman: The Story of Nelly Ternan and Charles Dickens*. New York: Alfred A. Knopf, 1991. Splendid biography of the woman who, following Dickens's death in 1870, was all but erased from the public record of his life. Compassionate and beautifully written, this is an enthralling work of literary sleuthing.

CRITICISM

BUTT, JOHN. "Dickens's Christmas Books," in *Pope, Dickens, and Others*. Edinburgh: Edinburgh University Press, 1969. An influential study that has been described as "the first important assessment of the Christmas Books."

Charles Dickens: A Critical Anthology. Edited by Stephen Wall. Harmondsworth, Eng.: Penguin, 1970. An engrossing and wide-ranging collection of critical responses to Dickens, which also helpfully includes excerpts of a number of the novelist's letters, speeches, and prefaces. There are many important figures here: Ruskin, Trollope, Arnold, James, Shaw, Eliot, Woolf, Forster, Huxley, Greene, Auden; and there are substantial chunks of the Gissing and Orwell works recommended below.

CHESTERTON, G. K. *Charles Dickens: The Last of the Great Men.* New York: Readers Club, 1942. First published in 1906 as *Charles Dickens: A Critical Study* and still perfectly wonderful. To Peter Ackroyd, as to many who have read him, Chesterton may well be Dickens's best critic. Sometimes cranky but always a pleasure to read, Chesterton is also, as W. H. Auden put it, "without any doubt one of the finest aphorists in English literature." This classic study is included in volume 15 of *The Collected Works of G. K. Chesterton* (San Francisco: Ignatius Press, 1986–), a volume that also reprints Chesterton's *Appreciations and Criticisms of the Works of Charles Dickens* (1911) and his *The Victorian Age in Literature* (1913), as well as the splendid biography of Dickens he prepared for the 14th edition of the *Encyclopaedia Britannica* (1929).

Dickens: The Critical Heritage. Edited by Philip Collins. London: Routledge & Kegan Paul, 1971. This excellent anthology of reviews and essays published during Dickens's lifetime also includes a few less formal items, such as an excerpt from Queen Victoria's diaries.

GISSING, GEORGE. *Charles Dickens.* London: 1898. Writing in 1941, Edmund Wilson described this study as "the best thing on Dickens in English" and "one of the few really first-rate pieces of literary criticism produced by an Englishman of the end of the century."

ORWELL, GEORGE. "Charles Dickens," in volume 1 of *The Collected Essays, Journalism and Letters of George Orwell.* Edited by Sonia Orwell and Ian Angus. Harmondsworth, Eng.: Penguin, 1970. First published in his *Inside the Whale* (1940), this landmark study opens with a bang.

"Dickens," Orwell informs us, "is one of those writers who are well worth stealing." Since his death in 1870, Dickens had been ignored, for the most part, by serious literary critics. But then, as Harry Levin has written, "in the year of stress 1940 . . . the staunch and far-sighted George Orwell published his pioneering essay in revaluation."

STONE, HARRY. *Dickens and the Invisible World: Fairy Tales, Fantasy, and Novel-Making*. Bloomington, Ind.: Indiana University Press, 1979. A richly detailed study of Dickens's early reading and imagining, both of which profoundly shaped his writings—a shaping, Stone believes, "that has the fairy tale as its matrix."

WILSON, ANGUS. *The World of Charles Dickens*. New York: Viking, 1970. Evocative and imaginatively illustrated study by the distinguished English novelist and short story writer.

WILSON, EDMUND. "Dickens: The Two Scrooges," in *The Wound and the Bow*. Boston: Houghton Mifflin, 1941. Penetrating and very influential study by one of America's greatest men of letters.

CHECKLIST OF ILLUSTRATIONS

All of the illustrations in this edition are from the collections of The New York Public Library's Center for the Humanities.

Page xxiv: The revised conclusion of "Sikes and Nancy," one of three manuscript pages written out by Dickens on blank pages at the end of the prompt-copy from which he gave his public readings. Entitled *"Sikes and Nancy:" A Reading from* Oliver Twist (London: Printed by William Clowes & Sons, ca. September 1868), this volume is heavily marked with Dickens's manuscript revisions, additions, stage-directions, etc. Bound in three-quarter red morocco, with marbled-paper front and back covers. With Dickens's bookplate and the label from the sale of his library at Gad's Hill Place in June 1870. Cortlandt F. Bishop bookplate.
Berg Collection

Page xxv: "Mr. Charles Dickens's Last Reading." Wood-engraved portrait of Dickens at his reading desk (which accompanied an article on his farewell to the stage), clipped from the *Illustrated London News*, March 19, 1870.
Miriam and Ira D. Wallach Division of Art, Prints and Photographs

Page xxviii: "Bob Cratchit and Tiny Tim." Wood engraving by A. V. S. Anthony, after the drawing by Sol Eytinge, Jr. Published as one of the special portfolio of "Christmas Pictures" featured in the December 31, 1870, issue of *Every Saturday: An Illustrated Journal of Choice Reading* (New Series, volume 1, number 53).
Wallach Division

Pages xxxiv–xxxv: Autograph letter from Charles Dickens to Cornelius Felton, Devonshire Terrace, London, January 2, 1844.
Berg Collection

Pages xxxviii–xxxix: Two pages from Charles Dickens's prompt-copy of *A Christmas Carol*, from which he gave his public readings. The volume was assembled by cutting pages from a trade printing (12th edition; London: Bradbury & Evans, 1849), which were inlaid into large octavo pages, and the whole then bound in three-quarter red morocco, with marbled-paper front and back covers. With Dickens's copious deletions, additions, condensations, clarifications, directions for vocal expression, etc.—in ink and

some few in pencil—throughout. With Dickens's bookplate and the label from the sale of his library at Gad's Hill Place in June 1870.
Berg Collection

Page 24: "The Haunted Man." Steel engraving by R. Hinshelwood, after the drawing by Felix Octavius Carr Darley, ca. 1861.
Wallach Division

Pages 34, 55, 71: Three wood-engraved illustrations by Edward Austin Abbey for *The Haunted Man*. From the Household Edition of *Christmas Stories*. With original illustrations by E. A. Abbey. New York: Harper & Brothers, 1876.
Berg Collection

Page 132: A wood-engraved illustration by Charles Stanley Reinhart for "Nurse's Stories." From the Household Edition of *The Uncommercial Traveller, Hard Times, and The Mystery of Edwin Drood*. New York: Harper & Brothers, 1876 (Reinhart provided thirty-three illustrations, engraved on wood by J. T. Howland and others, for the first two works; those for *The Mystery of Edwin Drood* were by Fred Barnard, and were copied from the Chapman & Hall edition.)
Berg Collection

Page 165: An original pen-and-ink drawing by Thomas Sibson for "The Story of the Bagman's Uncle." From an album of ten (unpublished) drawings, with quotations from the story written out by the artist beneath his designs, ca. early 1840s.
Berg Collection

Page 181: An illustration for "To Be Taken with a Grain of Salt." Wood engraving (proof) by Dalziel Brothers, after a design by Edward Gurden Dalziel, for the illustration in the Household Edition of *Christmas Stories from "Household Words" and "All the Year Round."* London: Chapman & Hall, ca. 1870s.
Wallach Division

Page 197: The front cover of "Dickens' Christmas Story of Goblins Who Stole a Sexton." Illustrated by Thomas Nast. New York: McLoughlin Bros, 1867.
Rare Book Division

Page 206: "Sairey Gamp and Betsey Prig" (under title: "Drink fair, Betsey, wotever you do!"). Wood engraving by A. V. S. Anthony, after the drawing by Sol Eytinge, Jr. Published as the "Supplement" to the May 7, 1870, issue of *Every Saturday: An Illustrated Journal of Choice Reading* (New Series, volume 1, number 19), the first of the designs commissioned from Eytinge by *Every Saturday* for its "Dickens Gallery."
Wallach Division

Page 232: An original pencil-and-watercolor drawing by F. W. Pailthorpe, captioned "A foul deed," illustrating the murder of Nancy by Sikes in *Oliver Twist*. This is the model for one of the twenty-one etchings, after drawings by Pailthorpe, published as a set of extra illustrations to *Oliver Twist*, in a limited edition of two hundred copies, by Robson & Kerslake in 1886; and is bound into the M. C. D. Borden extra-illustrated copy of the first edition of *Oliver Twist* (London: Richard Bentley, 1838). The Borden copy includes original pencil tracings for all the George Cruikshank illustrations for the first edition, except the "Fireside" plate, but including one for its cancel; Cruikshank's original drawing for volume 3, page 30, of the first edition ("Fagin and his pupil recovering Nancy"); twenty-one original watercolor drawings by F. W. Pailthorpe for the set of etchings published by Robson & Kerslake, London, 1886; twenty-seven original pen-and-ink drawings by James Mahoney, executed for the Household Edition of the novel (London: Chapman & Hall, ca. 1870s); and several original pen-and-ink drawings by Sol Eytinge, Jr., executed for the Diamond Edition of the novel (Boston: Ticknor & Fields, 1867).
Berg Collection

Page 245: Portrait of Mrs. Martha Bardell and her son, Master Tommy. From an album of mounted wood-engraved portraits (each with four lines of humorous verse) that were originally published as a large broadside

(51 cm × 75 cm) under the title *Sam Weller's Scrap Sheet, Containing all the Pickwick Portraits, with the Poetical Effusions of Augustus Snodgrass, Esq., M.P.C.* London: Printed by Jones, City Road; Sold at Cleave's "Penny Gazette" Office, Shoe Lane, Fleet Street, ca. 1837.
Berg Collection

Pages 258, 264, 266, 276, 283, 294, 296, 304, 311, 314, 323, 327, 331, 338, 343, 351, 355: Seventeen illustrations from the Holiday Edition of *A Christmas Carol,* published by Fields, Osgood, & Co. in 1868. Wood engravings (proofs) by A. V. S. Anthony after the drawings by Sol Eytinge, Jr.
Wallach Division

Page 357: The closing line of *A Christmas Carol,* written out by Charles Dickens on a sheet of blue notepaper with Gad's Hill Place letterhead, signed with a flourish, and dated "Friday Fourth October 1861." Folded in two, this autograph manuscript is tipped into the front of a copy of *A Christmas Carol. In Prose. Being a Ghost Story of Christmas.* With illustrations by John Leech. 2nd edition. London: Chapman & Hall, 1843.
Berg Collection

Endpapers: Two color plates (lithographs) by Alfred Crowquill [pseudonym of Alfred Henry Forrester], with character studies of some of the *dramatis personae* of "The Trial from *Pickwick*" and "The Story of the Bagman's Uncle." These are two of the forty plates published as *Pictures Picked from the Pickwick Papers.* London: Ackermann & Co., 1837. In original parts as issued May 1–November 9, 1837. Forty colored lithographs by Standidge & Co. Lithography from the drawings of Alfred Crowquill.
Berg Collection

Mr. Skimpin   Mr. Phunkey.

Seargeant Buzfuz.

Mrs Cluppins' Examination.